Raymond L

The Forgotte

Banishment

A Forgotten Empire Novel

(The Forgotten Empire: Banishment, Book 1)

By

Raymond L. Weil

USA Today Best Selling Author

The Forgotten Empire: Banishment

Books in the Forgotten Empire Series

The Forgotten Empire: Banishment (Book 1)
The Forgotten Empire: Earth Ascendant (Book 2) (April 2020)

Website: http://raymondlweil.com/

Copyright © February 2020 by Raymond L. Weil
All Rights Reserved
Cover Design by Humblenations.com
ISBN: 9798618173056
Imprint: Independently published

Raymond L. Weil

This book is a work of fiction. Names, characters, places, and incidents are either products of the author's imagination or used fictitiously. Any resemblance to actual events, locales, or persons, living or dead, is purely coincidental. All rights reserved. No part of this publication can be reproduced or transmitted in any form or by any means without permission in writing from the author.

DEDICATION

To my wife Debra for all of her patience while I sat in front of my computer typing. It has always been my dream to become an author. I also want to thank my children for their support.

I also want to thank everyone who has stood by me during my bout with kidney disease. With a little luck I'll be having a transplant sometime in the near future.

Raymond L. Weil

The Forgotten Empire: Banishment

Raymond L. Weil

The Forgotten Empire: Banishment
Book One

Chapter One

The Eighth Fleet of the Human Empire was on patrol in the Shoran Expanse, an area containing just a few stars and several large dust clouds. The fleet was on watch for pirates, who had been raiding the space lanes between several heavily populated Human worlds. So far, the patrol had been uneventful, with no signs of any pirates. Of more concern was the growing tension between the Confederation and the Empire. There was a distinct possibility war could break out any day. High Prince Aiden Starguard didn't want to bring his fleet out here with the current tensions, but his father had insisted. The High King felt that, by Aiden putting in an appearance away from the capital, it would help calm the population. Aiden's father and sister both believed war with the Confederation was far-fetched. Aiden was not so certain.

The tension between the Confederation and the Empire was growing steadily, with demands from the Confederation for the Empire to cease its expansion and to allow Confederation warships into all systems controlled by the Empire for inspections. Aiden's father had sent a firm no and had reminded the Confederation how they had no say in what the Empire did. Every day the reports near the borders of the Empire confirmed increased Confederation fleet activity, which greatly concerned Aiden. Today it looked as if the situation between the Empire and the Confederation had taken a sudden turn for the worse.

Aiden gazed with deep concern at the tactical display. He was on board the Empire Class Dreadnought *Vindicator*, the flagship of the Eighth Fleet, also the Empire's largest force of military ships. During the last two hours confirmed reports of Confederation ships entering Empire space had grown.

"We've lost contact with the Hadrian Star Cluster, the Vortex Worlds, and the Lamina Stars," reported Admiral Malden Cross, his eyes narrowing sharply. "All three reported large fleets of Confederation warships in their vicinity before we lost contact."

"We cannot contact the Third, Fourth, Ninth, and Twelfth Fleets," added Lieutenant Breams from Communications. "There were some vague references about encroaching Confederation warships and then silence."

"We are receiving reports of Confederation fleets and ships in numerous systems of the Empire," added Admiral Cross, as he stepped away from Communications. "Star Command has just issued a warning of possible conflict with the Confederation. They are still trying to determine exactly what's happening. Admiral Vexx believes we are now possibly in armed conflict with the Confederation and has ordered us to act accordingly."

"So they finally made their move," said Aiden, a deep frown covering his face. He could feel his heart pounding at the implications. This was exactly what he had warned his family about. The Empire's fleets were scattered and could easily be picked off, one by one, by the Confederation.

"The Confederation has always feared us," replied Admiral Cross. "For years they have been displeased with our rapid colonization of worlds. We pushed them too far, and now we'll pay the price."

The High Prince let out a deep breath. "I warned the Royal Court that we were treading a dangerous line. The Confederation has ruled the galaxy for nearly thirty thousand years and would never allow us to become a major threat. I'm surprised they waited this long."

"But our fleets," said Captain Brunson, his eyes narrowing. "We have hundreds of warships!"

The High Prince shook his head. "We have hundreds, and they have thousands. The seven major races of the Confederation control hundreds of thousands of inhabited worlds. For decades they have been limiting our trade with other civilizations. They have placed taxes on our trading vessels and even severely limited the items we can trade for."

"We are receiving reports of large Confederation fleets in the Mall Star Cluster," reported the communications officer. "We have unconfirmed reports of several cities being bombed."

"The Mall Star Cluster," said Captain Brunson, raising his eyebrows sharply. "Surely the Confederation isn't considering attacking our homeworld?"

The High Prince nodded his head. "They would if they want to end our threat completely."

This was something else Aiden had warned his father and the other members of the Royal Family about. The Confederation, while they often moved slowly, would eventually move against the Empire. Now it seemed as if Aiden's warnings were coming true with dire consequences. He just hoped the reports of bombed cities were nothing more than wild rumors. Hundreds of billions of people were in the Empire.

"Set a course for home and recall all fleet units," ordered Aiden, making a quick decision. "If we can show a united front, perhaps the Confederation will pull back."

Aiden knew the odds of that were remote. While the Confederation moved very slowly in making decisions, once one was made, it was never reversed. "See if we can contact my father. We need to know exactly what's going on."

A few minutes later the 112 ships of the Eighth Fleet were in hyperspace, speeding toward the Mall Star Cluster, hoping they were not too late.

For thirty thousand years the seven major civilizations of the Confederation had ruled the galaxy. Most of the seven races had possessed interstellar spaceflight for thousands of years before joining together. None of the seven races were humanoid, though they controlled vast regions of the galaxy. The controlled races in those regions, while not treated terribly, were not awarded full citizenship in the Confederation. They were considered second-class citizens with some basic rights. The seven major Confederation races tended to look down upon them, almost as if they were lower life-forms. These second-class races served the Confederation in whatever way the Confederation races saw fit. While, to many, this seemed cruel, to the Confederation races, it was simply the way life was.

On Golan Four in the Imperial Palace, High King Bramdon Starguard the Ninth leaned back in his chair in shock. "What's the latest reports?" he asked, looking at his military advisor.

"Large Confederation fleets are reported throughout the Empire," Kalen Lamply answered. "We have confirmed reports of antimatter weapons being used on Vidon Seven and Helgoth."

"Aiden warned us," said High Princess Layla, her eyes filled with worry. "He said the Confederation would be coming, and we didn't believe him."

Numerous voices spoke, as many members of the Royal Court were in attendance. Some were in disbelief and others fearful of what might soon happen.

High King Starguard blinked his eyes. "What is the status of our fleets?" He knew they didn't have the ships to stop the Confederation. The fleets were only there for a deterrent. One that was failing miserably, if the early reports were correct.

"The Third, Fourth, Ninth, and Twelfth Fleets are confirmed destroyed," answered Lamply in a strained voice. "Everywhere we've tried to fight back, the Confederation has used overwhelming force and technology to crush all resistance. We have reports of Druin ground troops landing on numerous worlds." The Druins were the most populous of the Confederation races and were a cold-blooded species. They were also ruthless killers.

"Druins!" called out a member of the Royal Court, sounding fearful. "They have no emotions. They will show no mercy!"

Others echoed the same belief. More people were talking, trying to understand what was happening.

High Princess Layla shifted her frightened gaze to Lamply. "What of Aiden and the home fleet?"

"They are on their way back here, as well as the Second, Sixth, and Tenth Fleets. No others have responded."

"This is the end," said High King Starguard, deciding not to hide the truth from his people. He had made a serious miscalculation, and now it would cost all of them.

"Can we not contact the Confederation and beg for mercy?" pleaded Layla, her expression revealing her deep concern for the people of the Empire.

High King Starguard shook his head. "No, we are being made an example of. The Confederation will destroy our Empire to ensure nothing like this ever arises again to oppose them. It is their way of keeping the galaxy under their firm control."

"And we can do nothing?" Layla couldn't believe this was the end of everything she knew and loved. "Over one thousand worlds are in the Empire!"

High King Starguard drew in a deep breath. "I fear those of us who survive will soon be serving the Confederation. Our days of freedom are about to end." The High King knew he should have listened more closely to Aiden. His son had repeatedly asked for the defensive fleets to be increased in size. Bramdon had refused, feeling the lack of warships would keep the Confederation from fearing the Empire. Bramdon had been wrong, and that error was about to cost them everything. The High King turned to face Lamply. "When the High Prince arrives, the defense of Golan Four will be left up to him. If he loses, then we shall surrender unconditionally to the Empire."

High Princess Layla folded her hands in her lap. She leaned back in her chair and closed her eyes. Very slowly, she opened them and looked at her father. "What will happen to us?"

High King Starguard shook his head with a sad look on his face. "That is out of our hands now." Bramdon looked around the Royal Court. Nearly 140 men and women were in the large ornate chamber. Most were related to the Royal Family in some way, either through birth or marriage. "I suggest everyone go home and spend this time with your families. There is no way to know what will happen after today."

Starguard watched in silence as everyone filed out. He looked at Layla, seeing the uncertainty in her gaze. "Don't be afraid. We will find some way to survive this." In his heart, he knew his words to be lies. Many of those who had left the chamber, or were leaving, would probably be dead in the next day or two. The Confederation would not allow any of the Empire's leadership to survive. Bramdon just hoped their deaths were quick.

"Coming up on the Golan Four System," reported Admiral Cross.

"The Second, Sixth, and Tenth Fleets are in the system," added Captain Brunson. "They are deployed around Golan Four. Also some survivors from our other fleets appear to be here as well."

Aiden drew in a deep breath. He gazed at the tactical display, showing the nearer star systems. In many of the systems around Golan Four, large clusters of red threat icons were visible. The Confederation had numerous large warfleets nearby. It was evident they were allowing the Empire to gather its forces for one final titanic battle. They would wipe out all resistance and end the Empire as it now was.

"What does Star Command have to report?"

"Heavy fighting throughout the Empire," reported Admiral Cross. "Most of it is on the ground, as the Confederation is moving to capture all government buildings. Our ground troops are resisting, but the Confederation has landed millions of Druin troops. They are encased in battle armor and are crushing our defenses. Our own troop losses are already in the tens of millions. We have confirmed reports of the use of antimatter weapons on various Imperial planets."

Aiden frowned deeply. Antimatter was not allowed on any ships of the Empire. It was just too dangerous. While the Empire knew how to make antimatter weapons, they had been forbidden, so as not to anger the Confederation. Aiden knew, if antimatter had been used by the Druins, the civilian casualty rate could easily be in the hundreds of millions, if not billions.

"Drop out in the Golan Four System in seventeen minutes," reported Captain Brunson. "We have contact with Star Command, and our priority is to defend Golan Four until some peace deal can be worked out with the Confederation."

"They don't want peace," muttered Admiral Cross. "They want our destruction."

"We now have reports coming in from across the Empire," reported the communications officer. "All government buildings are being destroyed, and military and civilian casualties are heavy. For the most part the rural areas are being left alone."

Admiral Cross let out a deep sigh. "At least they don't appear to be exterminating us."

"Destroying one thousand worlds would shake the stability of the galaxy," Aiden replied. "Even the Confederation would hesitate risking that."

"I have your father on the comm," reported the communications officer. "He wishes to speak to you."

Aiden nodded and sat in his command chair, activating the communications unit. "Father, it appears the Confederation has launched a full-scale assault against the Empire. What are your orders?"

"You were right in your warnings, Aiden," the High King replied in a solemn voice. "I fear I have led the Empire to its ruin. I should have listened to you."

Aiden remained silent. There was little he could say.

"When your fleet gets here, you need to buy us some time. We are trying to contact the Confederation to reach some acceptable terms of surrender."

"What about Operation Exodus?"

This time his father remained silent for several long moments. "Underway. As soon as the first reports came in of Confederation attacks, the plan was implemented."

Aiden nodded to himself. Exodus was a last-ditch effort to give hope for the future. "We'll buy you the time you need. I won't let you down."

"I know you won't," the High King replied. "Good luck, Aiden."

On board the Druin battleship *Expanse*, Admiral Kalar nodded in satisfaction at the reports coming in from around the Human Empire. Kalar stood eight feet tall and came from a high-gravity world. His form was slightly humanoid but squat, with his head sitting directly atop his torso on a short neck. His arms were massive and could easily snap a Human in two. He was also cold-blooded with limited emotions.

"All Human forces are in retreat," reported his second in command. "Our soldiers are reporting nearly four hundred of their planets are now under our control."

"They are an inferior species," replied Kalar, his large cold eyes narrowing. "The Humans are barbaric, and we should never have allowed them to expand from their homeworld. It was an error on our part, and we must be careful not to make such a mistake again."

"They lack the logic to become civilized," added the science officer. "It is necessary we take them under our guidance. We have many uses for Humans in the Confederation."

"Their High King is still trying to contact us," reported the communications officer.

"No doubt seeking surrender terms," said Kalar. "I will not speak to him until after we have completed the destruction of their warships and have conquered all their worlds. Then we will speak of surrender terms."

Kalar's second in command turned toward him. "The last of their known warships will be in their home system shortly. We may have missed a few, but they will not be a threat, as they will have no support bases to use for resupply."

"Move the fleets into position," ordered Kalar. "It is time we end this."

Aiden felt the flagship drop from hyperspace near Golan Four. His gaze was instantly drawn to the large viewscreens spread across the front wall of the Command Center. They flickered with static and then cleared. On the centermost screen a blue-white planet appeared. This was Golan Four, the birthplace of the Human race. The planet had four large oceans and three huge continents. Nearly 62 percent of the planet was covered in water. It was a garden world with a population of three point four billion. For centuries the population on the planet had been carefully controlled to prevent overcrowding. It was also Aiden's home.

"How many warships do we have?" Glancing at the tactical display, he could tell there weren't near as many as he would like.

"We have the Second, Sixth, and Tenth Fleets," reported Captain Brunson. "Also a few stragglers from other fleets."

"Counting our fleet, that gives us 374 ships," Admiral Cross informed Aiden. "Less than one-third of our original fleet strength."

"Druin fleets have entered hyperspace," reported the sensor officer. "Twenty-eight minutes before the first of them will arrive."

Aiden leaned back in his command chair. He was about to fight a battle he knew he could not win. However, the battle had to be fought in order to get the Druins to listen to his father's offer to surrender. Aiden wondered how they had allowed events to lead to this. Even in his wildest nightmares, he had never believed the Confederation would attack with such force and ferocity.

On the planet, Princess Layla was in her quarters, pacing back and forth. She knew her brother had arrived with his fleet and would soon be facing impossible odds in battle. She also knew it was very unlikely he would survive.

"What will become of us?" asked Krista, her cousin. Krista and Layla were very close and often confided in one another. Krista was a few years younger than Layla.

Layla sat down, trying not to fidget. She felt as if the world were tumbling down around her. "I don't know." Her voice felt tight in her throat, and her heart pounded. Outside in the corridor she could hear the armored feet of her security detail, as they prepared to defend her, if the Druins came into the palace.

Layla had never seen a Druin in person, though she knew what they looked like. They were horrid creatures to look upon. She could not imagine what it would be like to see one in person. Looking upward, she wondered what Aiden was thinking and if she would ever see him again.

"All fleets are in formation," reported Admiral Cross, as he stood in front of the large holographic tactical display.

"Druin ships are dropping from hyperspace," reported Captain Brunson.

Aiden drew in a deep breath. "How many?"

Captain Brunson turned to face the prince with a grim look on his face. "Over two thousand so far, with more still exiting hyperspace."

Aiden felt a cold chill spread over him. This was overkill by the Druins. Not only were their ships larger but they were also more advanced. "Stand by for combat." Aiden looked at one of the viewscreens, showing the planet he defended. His entire family was on that planet. He knew the odds of him ever seeing any of them again were very small.

The Human fleet gathered into a globe formation, with the *Vindicator* in the center. Energy screens were up, and weapons were ready to fire. Around the planet, cargo ships and passenger liners were entering hyperspace to escape the fighting, though there was really no place for them to go.

"Druins are in a large cone formation," reported Admiral Cross. "They are advancing toward us. Combat range in seven minutes."

Aiden stood and walked to the tactical display, examining the red threat icons, seeing how heavily outnumbered his fleet was. He clasped his hands behind his back, considering his options in the coming battle. "Has there been any Druin response to my father's requests for communications?"

"No," answered the communications officer. "So far the Druins are refusing any contact."

"All the orbiting stations, including the shipyards, are being evacuated," added Captain Brunson. On the tactical display, numerous small green icons, representing shuttles and small ships, were visible, heading toward the planet.

Aiden returned to his command chair and pressed an icon on his control console, which put him in contact with all the ships of the fleet. "This is High Prince Aiden Starguard. In a few minutes we will be engaged against the Druin fleet, which is advancing toward Golan Four. We are trying to buy time for my father to establish contact with the commander of the Druin forces to offer our surrender." Aiden paused, taking a deep breath. "Most of us will not survive this battle, but we will make sure the Druins and the Confederation long remember this day. It has been an honor to serve as your commanding officer."

Looking at the main viewscreen, now showing the Druin fleet up close, Aiden felt his breath catch in his throat. The Druin battleships were nearly twice the size of the *Vindicator* and very deadly.

On board the Druin flagship, Admiral Kalar stood with his thick arms folded across his chest. Shortly this threat to the Confederation would be crushed, and the Humans would become vassals to the seven major Confederation races. The Humans could serve in thousands of ways.

"The Human fleet has formed into a defensive globe," reported his second in command. "We should easily destroy it."

"Engagement range," reported the tactical officer in a cold voice.

Admiral Kalar drew in a deep breath. "Fire, destroy the Humans." Once the Human fleet was destroyed, he would make his demands of their King. Nothing short of a complete and unconditional surrender would be accepted.

Aiden felt the *Vindicator* shake violently from the opening salvos of the battle. On the main viewscreens, several ships in his fleet were blown apart in huge explosions of raw energy. Aiden looked over meaningfully at Admiral Cross. "How long can we survive?" He wanted to buy his father as much time as possible.

"Not long," replied Cross, as several more Human ships vanished from the tactical display.

Aiden's face grew stormy. He had never thought his life would end this way. For several heart-stopping minutes he issued orders, as he tried to keep his fleet alive for as long as possible.

In the Human fleet, intense rays of raw energy from the Druin battleships slammed into energy shields, in many cases overloading them. The bow section of a cruiser exploded, and debris drifted away from the ship as it lost power and then blew apart. Another Druin energy beam penetrated the weakened shield of a small support ship, blowing an energy beam turret to shreds and blasting out a massive hole in the hull. It was the same throughout the fleet, as the overwhelming power of the Druin vessels threatened to make this a short and costly battle for the Humans.

The *Vindicator* shuddered when two sublight missiles hit her energy shield, severely jarring the ship. The screen seemed to flicker, and then the flickering vanished as the screen returned to full power.

Aiden looked quickly around the Command Center to see if everyone was okay. Everyone was still at their consoles, issuing orders and keeping the ship functioning.

"We're losing ships too rapidly," reported Admiral Cross, a pained look in his eyes. "We've already lost sixty-eight vessels, and we've only managed to destroy seven Druin ships."

"Close the formation," ordered Aiden. "We must give my father more time to get through to the Druins."

Just then the deck heaved under High Prince Starguard, and he found himself flying through the air. He crashed to the deck, coming up hard against the navigation console. He heard alarms sounding and people shouting commands.

"Prince Starguard, are you okay?" asked Captain Brunson, rushing to the fallen prince.

"Barely," Aiden answered. Struggling to stand, he stumbled back to his command chair. Looking around, he saw smoke and sparks everywhere. Alarms screamed from the damage control console, as red lights rapidly blinked on. "What happened?" He knew the *Vindicator* was heavily damaged.

"Four energy beams penetrated our energy screen," reported Admiral Cross, stepping close to Aiden. The admiral's left arm hung limply at his side. "Our energy shield is down, and we're streaming atmosphere."

"Your arm?" asked Aiden, his eyes widening.

"Broken," replied Admiral Cross with a grimace. "I took a painkiller. I'll be fine."

Aiden looked at Captain Brunson, speaking with the damage control officer. The captain looked back at Aiden, shaking his head.

Taking a deep breath, Aiden prepared to die with his ship. From the look on the face of Captain Brunson, Aiden knew his ship could not withstand another energy beam or missile strike. He wished he could have seen and spoken to his parents and his sister one last time.

On board the Druin flagship, *Expanse*, Admiral Kalar nodded in satisfaction as the Human fleet was methodically destroyed.

"Their flagship has been heavily damaged," reported the second officer.

Admiral Kalar paused for a moment, as if in thought. "Capture it intact. Its commanding officer might be useful."

"What about the rest of its crew?"

"Exterminate all but the command crew," ordered Kalar. "Those will be the only ones of value."

Over the next few minutes all the Human ships except the flagship were obliterated. Space near the planet was filled with the glowing wreckage of its once-proud fleets. When the fighting finally stopped, only the flagship survived. It was heavily damaged, with most of its weapons destroyed, as well as its drive systems. The ship could not escape as Druin shuttles docked to the vessel, blasting open the hatches, allowing heavily armored Druin soldiers to board.

Aiden was in his command chair, listening to the reports coming in from across his ship of Druin soldiers working their way toward the Command Center. Heavy fighting sounded throughout the ship.

"They're killing everyone," said Captain Brunson, his face pale as a ghost. "They are sparing no one. Even unarmed crewmembers are dying."

Aiden stepped to the arms locker near the tactical station, taking a small energy pistol from it. Most of the command crew was now armed and prepared to make the final sacrifice for the Empire.

Taking a deep breath, Aiden heard the sound of energy weapons firing in the corridor beyond the sealed hatch. Then, with a loud roar, the thick hatch was flung off its hinges, and several round objects were tossed into the Command Center.

"Grenades!" yelled Captain Brunson, stepping over to shield the prince with his body.

The grenades went off, and Aiden felt his consciousness fade away. The battle for him was over.

Chapter Two

Layla was in her quarters when Admiral Vexx came in. "Princess, it's time for us to go."

"My brother?"

Admiral Vexx shook his head. "Unknown. His fleet and the others were destroyed in orbit. We know the Druins boarded the *Vindicator*, but no word has been received."

Layla nodded her head in acceptance and turned toward Krista. "Is everything packed?"

"Yes, Princess," Krista replied. "Everything has been sent ahead."

Layla turned toward the admiral. "What about my father and mother?"

"Your parents are remaining here. The King feels it's his duty to negotiate with the Druins for the sake of the Empire."

Layla's face turned pale. "They will kill him!"

Admiral Vexx blinked his eyes and did not reply.

"Come, Princess. We must go," urged Krista, as she took the Princess's hand. "We don't have a lot of time."

Princess Layla drew in a deep breath. Her world was coming to an end. Her brother was most likely dead, and her parents would soon be also. It was her duty to preserve the Royal Line. She looked at Admiral Vexx. "Where are we at on Operation Exodus?"

"Ahead of schedule. Most of the ships assigned have already left. Your own ship is ready and is only waiting for your arrival."

"Can we make it off the planet?"

Admiral Vexx nodded. "It's a small stealth cruiser, and the Druins cannot detect it, but we need to hurry. They will begin landing troops at any moment."

Layla hesitated as she looked around her quarters. This had been her home her entire life. She knew that, once she left, she could never come back. "Let's go," she said, as she turned and stepped through the door.

As they made their way through the Imperial Palace, Layla couldn't help but notice the absence of people. Even most of the palace guards seemed to be missing.

"Where is everybody?" she asked.

"Many have fled to the countryside," replied Admiral Vexx, as he ushered them down a side corridor. "They fear reprisals from the Druins when they arrive. We are already hearing horror stories from other Imperial worlds. The Druins are executing the governors and ruling families on many of our more prosperous planets. Many have gone into hiding. Also some antimatter weapons have been used, though we're not certain how many. Casualties will be in the millions, if not more."

Layla felt faint. The Empire was coming to an end. "What will they do here?" This greatly concerned her, since Golan Four was the homeworld of the Human race, as well as the seat of Imperial power.

"They will set an example," replied Admiral Vexx as they neared a door, where two guards waited. "The Druins will most likely destroy the palace, as well as execute anyone who remains."

Going through the door, Layla saw an aircar waiting for them. As soon as they were inside, the aircar took off and flew rapidly toward a small private spaceport on the edge of the city. Looking out the windows, Layla could see the roads and airways were full of vehicles, all fleeing the city.

It didn't take them long to arrive at the spaceport. The aircar sat down next to a small spacecraft, and Admiral Vexx quickly got the two women on board. Once that was done, he turned to leave.

"Aren't you staying with us?" asked Princess Layla. She had known the admiral for years; he was almost like an uncle.

Admiral Vexx shook his head. "No, my duty is to your father, and I must remain. People at your destination will take care of you. Remember, Princess. You represent the future of the Empire. It is our great hope that someday you will return and will free us from the clutches of the Confederation. Long live the Empire!" With that, the admiral left, the Princess and Krista stood watching as he got back into the aircar and headed toward the palace.

"Come with me, Princess," said a young man in a captain's uniform. "We must leave shortly. Reports indicate the Druins are beginning their landing operations."

The hatch shut, and Layla and Krista followed the captain down a short corridor to another hatch. He opened it and indicated for them to go inside.

"These will be your quarters until we reach Sanctuary. If you need anything, let one of the other officers know."

Layla stepped inside and was surprised at how spacious the quarters were. She turned back to the captain. "How many others are coming with us?"

"Just you and Krista," replied the captain. "Everyone else has already lifted off. This ship was specifically designed to get at least one member of the Royal Family to safety."

Layla nodded. "You better get to your duties, Captain. I'm sure Krista and I will be fine."

The captain nodded. "Two acceleration couches are in your room. Buckle yourselves in, and later I'll announce the all clear when it's okay for you to move around again. While I don't expect any problems, we don't know for certain how well this ship's stealth systems will hold up against the sensors on Druin ships." With that, the captain shut the door, leaving the two women alone.

Layla looked at Krista. She could see the nervous look on her cousin's face. "Don't worry. We'll be fine. Now let's go find those two acceleration chairs and buckle in. Afterward we can check out our new quarters as well as the ship."

Captain Derrick Masters made his way quickly to the Command Center in the small stealth cruiser. The ship had been designed to protect the Royal Family and to get them safely away from harm's way. He was about to find out just how well his fancy ship was built.

Taking his seat, he took in a deep breath. "Are we ready?"

"Yes, sir," replied Lieutenant Commander Audrey Banora. "All systems are powered up, and we're ready to leave."

"I would recommend we do it quickly," added Lieutenant Keela Nower from the sensor console. "I'm detecting large numbers of Druin assault shuttles heading toward the surface. Many toward the palace."

"Lieutenant Viktor, get us out of here," ordered Derrick, looking at the navigation and helm officer.

"Activating thrusters," replied Viktor, as his hands grasped the controls in front of him.

The *Destiny* rose up on its thrusters and then darted away from the palace, staying low until they were over the countryside. Then the ship arrowed up toward orbit.

Derrick looked at one of the viewscreens, which was focused on the capitol. The airways and roads were full of vehicles fleeing the city. Already thick smoke rose from numerous accidents, and even a few buildings were burning. Derrick still had several cousins on the surface. He hoped they would be okay.

"Picking up a lot of wreckage in orbit," reported Lieutenant Nower. "Most of it fleet ships with wreckage mixed in from a few Druin vessels."

"At least we got some of them," said Lieutenant Commander Banora, as the view on the screens shifted to the wreckage.

Derrick felt stunned and sickened at seeing the ruins of the fleet. It had been shattered. Every vessel on the viewscreens had been blown apart. He doubted if anyone could have survived. Even if they did, no one was here to rescue them.

"Sir, I have located the *Vindicator*."

The flagship appeared on the main viewscreen. It was heavily damaged but still intact. Druin assault shuttles were docked to it.

"What will the Prince do?" asked Lieutenant Cleo Ashen from Communications. "Will he surrender?" She had a lot of respect for the Prince.

Derrick shook his head. "No, I know Prince Starguard very well. We went to the academy together. He won't be captured alive, if he can help it." Derrick felt great sadness, knowing his friend would most likely die in the fighting on board the flagship, if he hadn't already. "Are any other ships intact?" Derrick didn't want to believe the entire fleet had been destroyed.

"No, sir," replied Lieutenant Nower, shaking her head. "Only the *Vindicator* is left."

Lieutenant Commander Banora looked at Derrick. "Ships may still be in other systems."

Derrick shook his head. "No, the Druins are attempting to send a message. This galaxy belongs to the Confederation races now, and the rest of us must stay in line. The citizens of our Empire will now become second-class citizens in the Confederation, with nothing more than a few basic rights."

"Our people won't like that," said Audrey, pursing her lips. "They'll fight back."

"They will either have to accept it or die," replied Derrick. "The Druins will accept no excuses and won't hesitate to execute anyone who does not obey the rules of the Confederation."

"Then all hope is lost," said Audrey, her gaze looking longingly at one of the smaller viewscreens showing their home planet.

"No," replied Derrick. "Prince Starguard and others made a plan, in case this day ever came about. Someday the Human race will rise again. It won't be anytime soon, but we Humans are not done with the Confederation. And though it may take a thousand years or longer, our Empire will still be here to take back. The

Druins and the Confederation have now made the Human race their enemy. And we will remember for a very long time what they have done to our worlds and to our people."

"We're in orbit and have not been detected," reported Lieutenant Nower.

Derrick nodded. He had hoped their stealth systems would keep them hidden from the Druin sensors. The Druins had no reason to believe the Empire had such advanced stealth technology. "Lieutenant Viktor, set a course for the Haven Nebula. From there, we will go to our destination."

Viktor entered the course and then activated the ship's hyperdrive, sending the stealthed light cruiser into safety. No vessel could be attacked while a ship was in hyperspace.

Derrick leaned back in his command chair. He had a set of coordinates to deliver the Princess too. Once there, his ship and crew would remain. There was no returning from this mission. For the Human race and the Confederation, the Princess and Krista will have vanished. Great pains had been taken in the capital city by trusted members of the Imperial Guard to make it appear the Princess had been killed in an aircar accident as she fled the palace. Even a body had been cloned to make it appear the Princess had, indeed, died.

Derrick looked at the viewscreens, showing the stars in front of the vessel. He knew a computer program generated the view, taking into account the ship's rapid movement through hyperspace. They had a long voyage ahead of them. It would take them more than three weeks to reach their destination. That included several changes of direction to ensure they were not tracked or followed, though Derrick knew of no technology that could trace a ship once it made the transition into hyperspace. Derrick let out a deep sigh. He just hoped the Princess was ready for what was in front of her. The life she was about to lead was nothing like what she had experienced at the Imperial Palace.

Princess Layla was relieved when a voice came over the ship's comm, saying she and Krista could get out of their acceleration couches. The couches were comfortable, but Layla hated lying here with the safety harness holding her down.

"Let me get you some water, Princess," said Krista, as she unbuckled herself and headed to the small refrigeration unit she had spotted earlier. Opening it, she found bottles of flavored water from several worlds.

"I think it's best if you drop the *Princess*," said Layla, as she accepted the water and took a deep drink. "We're cousins, and there's no reason we can't use our first names."

Krista sat back down and grinned. "Force of habit. It's how all of us were raised in the palace."

Layla didn't reply for several long moments, and then she spoke. "We'll never see home again. Even if we do, it won't be the same. The Druins and the Confederation have ruined everything my father and brother were trying to build."

"We moved too fast," replied Krista. "My father was afraid the Confederation would take action, due to our continued expansion."

Layla nodded. "It was argued in the Royal Court. Some felt, as your father did, that, if we continued to expand the Empire, it would draw the attention of the Confederation. Others felt, if the Empire became large enough, the Confederation would not intervene. No one except Aiden expected a war. I guess we were wrong, and he was right."

Layla walked over and sat down on a comfortable couch, gesturing for Krista to join her. "I wonder what happened to Aiden?" Layla and her brother were very close. She knew he had taken great pride in commanding the flagship of the fleet, the *Vindicator*.

"Maybe Captain Masters will know something. I'm sure they were running sensor scans as the ship made orbit and then jumped into hyperspace."

A tear rolled down Layla's face. "What about our parents? My father and mother are still at the palace, and so are yours."

28

Krista nodded. Her eyes clouded. "Our parents know their duty. They will stay in the palace to confront the Druins. I can hear your father now, demanding they leave, with my father standing at his side. They're brothers, and, while they may have disagreements, they will not abandon one another."

On board the *Vindicator*, Aiden struggled back to consciousness. He opened his eyes to find himself in one of the lower holds of the ship. Looking around, he saw most of the command crew, as well as a few others. Most were lying down, still unconscious, with a few sitting up. Aiden noticed his hands were bound behind his back. Shifting around, he managed to sit up and lean against the cold metal wall.

"How do you feel?" asked Admiral Cross, who was close to him. The admiral's arms were bound as well, even though one was broken.

Aiden shook his head. "I've got a terrible headache. What happened?" Aiden noticed a half-dozen heavily armed Druins near the entry hatch, keeping an eye on the Humans.

"They tossed some stun grenades into the Command Center, knocking everyone out. When I came to, we were all in here."

Doing a quick count, Aiden realized only twenty of his crew were present. Twenty out of more than one thousand. With a deep sigh, Aiden knew the others were probably dead. Everyone in the hold seemed to be ranking officers. "What do you think they want?"

"We're prisoners," replied Cross. "I imagine we'll be taken to the planet to participate in whatever the Druins have planned. They don't usually take prisoners, but I suspect they wanted you alive, since you're a member of the Royal Family and are next in line to become the High King."

Aiden switched to a quieter voice. "I wonder if Layla got away."

"Most likely," replied Cross. "Captain Masters should have been standing by with his stealth cruiser. By now they should be long gone."

Aiden felt a chill run down his back, knowing he would never see his sister again. At least Layla and Krista should have gotten away, as well as the rest of the people involved in Operation Exodus. If everything worked out, the Druins would never learn about the plan. Nearly all who did know had left on the ships assigned to the project.

In the Imperial Palace, High King Bramdon Starguard sat in his chair in the ornate chambers of the Royal Court. Heavily armed Imperial Guards were present, as well as his brother Dom Starguard. A few of his closest advisors were present as well. Only a few minutes ago he had heard the sound of Druin assault shuttles landing. The quiet was broken periodically by the sound of blaster and laser fire, as some of the few remaining guards put up a futile resistance.

"They're coming," said Dom, as the sound of heavy footsteps approached the large double doors of the Royal Court.

"Hold your fire," Bramdon ordered the guards, who had moved to shield him from the Druins. "No point in anyone else dying in a hopeless cause."

"It is our duty to defend you," replied Maldric Pinal, a captain in the Imperial Guard, responsible for the guards currently in the Royal Court.

"And you have done a fine job," replied Bramdon, standing up and stepping to Maldric. "Have your men lay down their arms. No point in them dying."

Maldric hesitated and then gave the order. "Disarm!"

The fourteen Imperial Guards laid down their laser rifles and pistols. The war for them was over.

The doors to the chamber suddenly swung open, and numerous heavily armed Druins entered. Bramdon stepped in front of the guards and gazed unafraid as the Druins advanced. His brother Dom was at his side.

"I am High King Starguard," he said, showing no fear in his stance or voice. "Why have you attacked the Empire? You have killed millions for no civilized reason. We have kept our treaties and have not interfered with any of the worlds of the Confederation."

The Druins did not reply. Several marched forward and gathered all the weapons the Imperial Guards had placed on the floor. After that, they formed a half arc in front of High King Starguard and his brother, and then stood still, as if waiting for something important to happen.

Another group of Druins marched in, followed by an officer dressed in a uniform adorned with numerous campaign decorations.

The officer gazed at the Humans for several moments and then spoke. "I am Admiral Kalar of the Druin fleet and the Confederation. Your race has been found guilty of violating the Articles of Confederation, as established by the founding races."

"We are not a member of the Confederation," protested Bramdon, frowning. "None of our ships have trespassed into Confederation space other than to trade, according to our trade agreements."

"That is debatable," replied Admiral Kalar, his voice turning cold. "Your exploration ships and colony ships have been spotted in regions adjoining the Confederation that we have a future interest in. This cannot be allowed."

"The Confederation should have made their claims to that territory clear to us," replied Bramdon. "We would have pulled our ships back."

"It is irrelevant," replied Admiral Kalar coldly. "The Confederation has voted to annex all Human space as part of the Confederation. As such, your people will be subject to Confederation rules and citizenship."

"But as second-class citizens," objected Bramdon. "Our people will not have the same rights as yours do."

"We are one of the founding races," replied Admiral Kalar by way of explanation. "Perhaps in another ten or twenty thousand years you Humans may take your place as a true member of the Confederation."

"You've killed millions of us!" protested Bramdon in anger. "We were not a threat to you. Our worlds are burning because of you!"

Admiral Kalar's eyes narrowed. "Maybe not now, but in a few thousand years you may have been a threat. Your worlds are now ours. Your people will now serve us. You are not allowed to possess any armed spacecraft, though your worlds will be allowed to do some trading of items not on the banned lists."

"What of my family and the other members of the Royal Court?"

Admiral Kalar looked directly into Bramdon's eyes. "All of you will be executed of course. We cannot allow your continued existence to serve as a rallying point for your people. It is what is best for the Confederation."

Bramdon had been expecting this. It was one of the reasons for Operation Exodus. "What about banishment? Allow my family and the other members of the Royal Court to be taken to another world."

Admiral Kalar seemed to consider this. "It cannot be done. No other world will take you."

"A primitive world then," pleaded Bramdon. "One that has no technology. Let my people live out their lives in peace."

"It would have to be a primitive Human world," replied Admiral Kalar. "I have no knowledge of such a place."

"We found one years ago," replied Bramdon carefully. "One of our exploration vessels found it deep in unexplored space in the Bacchus Region."

"The Bacchus Region?" replied Kalar, his gaze showing a hint of disbelief. "That is an area of dead space. No habitable worlds have ever been found there."

"There is one," replied Bramdon. "It has a very primitive Human society. They have no technology at all."

"Where is this world? We must inspect it. If it is as you say, I will agree to sending the surviving members of the Royal Court there. However, your life must be forfeit. It will serve as an example to the Humans of your Empire."

Bramdon felt a cold chill spread over him. He had expected this demand. However, if he could save the other members of the Royal Court it would be worth the sacrifice.

"I agree."

"No!" several voices behind Bramdon called out.

Bramdon turned to face those who had cried out. "It is what must be done."

Four days later the fighting in the Empire was over. All the Human forces had surrendered and had turned in their weapons. The final death toll from across the Empire was well over two billion dead.

"Father, are you sure about this?" asked Aiden. "Let them take me instead of you."

Bramdon smiled. "No, it is me who they want. I am a symbol, the rest of you are not. It is the only reason they're even allowing banishment."

"How did you know they would agree to accept banishing the rest of us?"

"I've studied the different races of the Confederation. They consider banishment a fate worse than death. We're sending our people to an uncivilized planet. The only thing they're allowed to take with them are some food, medical supplies, camping gear, and a few other basic necessities."

Aiden frowned. "Don't forget that I'm part of those people."

Bramdon reached out and put his hand on Aiden's shoulder, squeezing gently. "You'll get to live out your life. That's all that I can ask for. Keep in mind, where you're going, they're a very primitive people. Yet they have great potential and someday will be a power to be reckoned with. It is up to you and the others to sow the seeds of that future greatness."

Aiden took in a deep breath. His mother had elected to stay with her husband. Aiden struggled with the fact he was leaving both of his parents behind to die. "I'll do as you say."

Bramdon looked at the Druins, who were watching them. "I guess this is goodbye. Our friends over there seem to be getting restless. Now go aboard the ship. Your mother and I are pleased with the knowledge that both you and your sister will be safe and away from this." Giving Aiden's shoulder another squeeze, Bramdon turned and walked toward the awaiting Druins. His execution was scheduled for the following day. It would be broadcast across the Empire to quell any hope for the future and to remind all the Humans who their new overlords were.

Aiden watched as the Druins surrounded the High King, escorting him away, until Aiden could no longer see his father.

"It's time to go," said Dom, in a soft and solemn voice. "We shall do as your father commanded."

Turning, Aiden and Dom went up the ramp into the large passenger liner. Two liners and one small cargo ship would take them to their destination. Also numerous Confederation ships would serve as an escort and then would scan the planet to determine if it was, indeed, primitive. Once that was confirmed, the landings would begin.

With a deep sigh, Aiden knew he would never see his father, his mother, his sister, or the Empire again.

Chapter Three

Aiden stepped out of the shuttle onto their new world. The air was clean and fresh with a light breeze. Other shuttles were also landing, depositing their loads of Humans and cargo.

"Well, I guess we're here," commented Admiral Cross. His arm was in a sling, after being set by one of the Human medical personnel.

"Fourteen hundred of us," replied Aiden, as he saw people standing around, unsure of what they should be doing. Some of the women were still dressed in their fancy court dresses. Aiden hoped they had brought other more practical clothing.

Captain Brunson came over, a deep frown on his face. "I've checked the supplies. We have sufficient food and water for about six months and enough medical supplies for a few years. So we need to find water and to assess our possibilities for hunting food here. Those larger crates have some military tents, which we can set up to provide protection for our people. We have no electronic equipment of any kind or even power tools. We'll have to do everything by hand. This will not be easy for many of the people who came with us."

Aiden looked at several members of the Royal Court, who were standing around, looking confused. No doubt they were used to being waited on and given nearly everything they wanted. Very few, if any, would know any of the basics of surviving off the land. Fortunately about eighty military personnel were here, and all of them had gone through survival training.

"Let's get the tents set up and start some of the others gathering firewood. Even though it's warm now, it might be much cooler tonight, and we'll want the fires. The fires will also help to keep any large predators away. We need to get the people doing things to take their minds off what's happened to us."

"I'll get some teams organized," replied Captain Brunson. "It looks as if it's midday here, so we still have quite a few hours of daylight left." Captain Brunson left to gather some of the other officers and to organize the camp.

Aiden looked up into the afternoon sky. A few white clouds were visible, and he knew several Druin ships were still in orbit. No doubt they would remain there, observing and watching for an unknown number of days. In the distance, he could see a towering volcano. Fortunately it was far enough off not to be among their more pressing problems.

"I wonder what Layla is doing?" Aiden missed his family. He knew by now that his father and mother would have been executed, and his sister was at the Operation Exodus complex, or Sanctuary as they had nicknamed it. He felt great sadness and anger at what had been done to his parents.

"She's probably just as concerned about you as you are about her," replied Admiral Cross. "Everyone here is devastated by what's happened. Our old way of life is gone, and now we're faced with a new one that'll be much harder and extremely trying for some."

"It bothers me knowing she's so close, and yet I have no way to speak to her."

Admiral Cross nodded. "It has to be that way. We have no idea how long the Druins will keep monitoring us. It would not surprise me if they set up some permanent monitoring system, just to make sure we stay primitive."

"Other Humans are on this planet," said Aiden. "In time we will need to contact them and to see about bringing them out of barbarism."

"It will have to be gradual. We don't want to bring to the Druins' attention that we're manipulating this planet's Humans."

Aiden looked toward Captain Brunson and his officers, who were gathering different groups of people to work on the projects they must complete in order to survive on this world. Most people seemed receptive, though a few looked at Captain Brunson in shock and disdain at what he was saying.

Aiden sighed. "We need to find a way to preserve our knowledge and our technology. We have to pass it down to future generations."

"We shall," promised Admiral Cross. "We have a few of our more renown scientists in the Royal Court with us. We also managed to sneak a few books as well as some primitive weapons into our supplies. Some of those crates have false bottoms. The Druins scanned for power sources and metals. They didn't scan for books and wooden crossbows. We'll wait a few weeks, or even months, before we remove them. There are a few other items we managed to sneak through as well."

"They did allow us to bring some axes and other basic tools," said Aiden. "At least we can build a decent settlement."

"It will take time." Admiral Cross looked where several doctors and nurses were inventorying their medical supplies. "Our normal lifespan with the life-extension drugs we have all taken is well over two hundred years. In future generations our children will be lucky to live to see one hundred. It could be even less."

Aiden sat down on a small crate that contained food rations. "I wish I could live long enough to see the Confederation and the Druins get what's coming to them." He still felt extreme anger at what had been done to the Empire and to his family. He wanted revenge, but the Druins and the Confederation were permanently out of his reach.

Admiral Cross looked around. "This world could do just that someday. It's up to us to sow the seeds for that future. True, we won't live to see it, but our distant ancestors will."

Aiden looked at the admiral. "Where's the nearest Human settlement?"

"None are close," replied Cross. "We chose this location for its isolation. We're on a very large island with massive continents north and south of us. We need to give our people time to acclimate to their new surroundings. Once we're ready, we can send out teams to help the locals."

"We'll need to be careful," Aiden replied. "Any sudden advances could bring the Druins back."

Admiral Cross nodded. "Once we get our settlement built, we can gather some of the more knowledgeable among us to decide upon the best ways to advance the Humans of this world, without drawing the attention of the Druins. We can teach the locals many things to make their lives better and more productive."

Aiden looked to where Lieutenant Maya Breams was organizing a team of able-bodied men and women to set up some of the large military tents. For the first time Aiden noticed the lieutenant was a very pretty woman. Aiden let out a deep sigh; fortunately over 30 percent of the people marooned on this planet were young women. It wouldn't be long before their population began to grow.

Standing back up, Aiden decided to go lend a hand. They had a lot of work to do, and, for all of them, the war against the Confederation was over. At least for now.

Princess Layla stood in the massive ship-construction bay of Project Exodus. Four new large dreadnoughts were in the process of construction. Most of the work was being done by robots and automatic construction machinery.

"What good is this fleet if we can't use it?" She was confused by what she was seeing.

"We have four construction bays, such as this one," answered Captain Masters. "All are highly automated and require little Human supervision. Humans man the Control Centers for each bay, but they're the only ones involved in the construction here."

Krista looked around in awe. She couldn't believe all that had been done here. "How did all this get built?"

Captain Masters smiled. "It was all part of Prince Starguard's and High King Starguard's contingency plan, in case the Confederation ever attacked the Empire. They realized the

Empire's continued expansion could some day illicit a response from the Confederation, though your father thought the possibility of an actual Confederation attack was very low. This place has been under construction for years. It's still not quite done, but enough of the installation is finished to allow us to use it."

"How many people are here?" asked Layla.

Captain Masters frowned. "The Confederation moved faster than we thought possible. The base is designed to hold a working population of nearly two hundred thousand. We only have 68,000 here."

Layla watched as robotic arms put in place a large sheet of battle armor on one of the ships. "So what will we do?"

Captain Masters took in a deep breath. "This base has numerous cryochambers. Most of the personnel will be put to sleep, with just enough awake to finish the base and to keep an eye on the ship-construction bays. When a ship is finished, a stasis field will be placed around it."

"What's a stasis field?" asked Krista.

"It's a new development," explained Captain Masters. "Anything inside a stasis field will stay unchanged, as long as the field is active."

Krista felt a cold chill pass over her. "How long can these fields be used?"

Captain Masters looked directly at Krista. "Hundreds even thousands of years, if necessary. If we put a stasis field around my cruiser and came back to it one thousand years from now, it would look the same as it does today."

Krista felt overwhelmed by everything. So much had happened in the last few weeks. She was thankful that Layla was here with her.

"Why are we going into cryosleep?" asked Layla. She had read about it and had even seen a few experiments done at the Imperial University.

"We know of one planet in this system with primitive Humans. They have not developed any measurable technology. We'll stay in cryo until such a time as they've advanced to the point where they can provide the crews for our ships. Then we will return to the Confederation and free the Empire."

"But that could be hundreds or even thousands of years away," protested Princess Layla, her face turning pale.

Captain Masters nodded. "However long it takes for the primitive planet in this system to become civilized. We anticipate one thousand years at the earliest, to avoid added interest from the Druins. With the Druins and the Confederation in charge of the Empire, there will be little change in its technology or civilization. The Confederation will not allow any more technological advances. The Empire will stay static and unchanged, as long as it's controlled by the Confederation."

Layla realized that everyone she knew would be gone when she was reawakened. "What about my family? Do we know what happened to them?"

"I'm sorry to say the High King, your mother, and a few others, including Admiral Vexx, were executed to set an example. The executions were broadcast across the Empire. I can also assure you, it was quick and painless."

Layla felt faint. With her father, her mother, and her brother gone, it made her the highest-ranking member of the Royal Family. She was now the High Queen of the Empire. However, her Empire technically no longer existed. Layla felt Krista's hand on her arm, steadying her.

"Your father wanted us to get you away to safety. We have a future ahead of us, though it might be some years before we fully realize just what that future is."

"What about my brother? Was he killed on the *Vindicator*?" In some ways Layla was relieved that her brother had not lived to see what had happened to the Empire and to their parents.

"What about my parents?" asked Krista.

Captain Masters seemed to hesitate. "Prince Starguard is still alive, as are your parents, Krista. They're all on the primitive planet in this system. The High King managed to work out a deal, allowing most of the members of the Royal Court to be banished to this system, with the caveat that they could not take any technology or power tools."

"They'll die!" cried out Krista. "We must rescue them!"

Captain Masters shook his head. "We can't. The Druins have ships in orbit around the planet, looking for such a rescue attempt. Even my stealth cruiser might be detected. If that were to happen, then everything we've worked for here could be put in jeopardy. Aiden and your parents would not want that."

Layla squared her shoulders. Technically, with Aiden still alive, that made him the High King of the Empire. However, with him marooned on the planet, it left her and Krista as the only free members of the Royal Family. For all intents and purposes that made her the High Queen. It was up to her to set an example for her people. "Captain Masters is right. We can't risk a rescue, which might expose our secret plan to attack the Confederation in the future. We must allow our families to live out their lives on the primitive planet, no matter how much we love them. As they no doubt must let us live out ours in Sanctuary, mostly in cryo. It's what must be done, if we want to free the Empire from the Confederation some day." It was painful for Layla to say that. Her heart felt the loss of her parents, as well as knowing her brother was so near but out of reach.

Krista looked at Layla and nodded. Her eyes were wet. "You're right. I must remember who we are and why we are here."

Layla took in a deep steadying breath. "Captain Masters, I believe there is more to this installation you wanted to show us."

Captain Masters continued with the tour, taking the girls through much of the base, except the uncompleted sections. Work was ongoing, as the robots built tunnels and added workstations. It would still be another two years before all the work was complete.

"How soon do we need to go into cryosleep?" asked Krista. "Does it have to be soon?"

"No," replied Captain Masters. "We can wait a few weeks, or even months, if you want. We still have a lot of work that needs to be finished before many of our people can be put into cryo."

"You said earlier that some people would stay awake," said Layla. "How many?"

"About four hundred," replied Captain Masters. "That's the minimum number our psychologists recommended. Each group will work for five years, and then a second group will be awakened to take their places. In case of an emergency, more can be brought out of cryo if needed."

"I believe we're ready to return to our quarters," said Layla. "Krista and I have a lot to talk about."

"As you wish, my ladies," replied Captain Masters. "If you need anything, you can use the comm unit in your quarters to summon me. Someone will find me, and I'll the there as soon as I can."

"Thank you," replied Layla. "You have been very helpful."

On the planet, Prince Starguard was hard at work. They had cut down some trees and were now sawing the trunks into manageable pieces for some permanent structures. Several of the Imperial Guards had indicated they had built such structures in the past for hunting cabins. Captain Pinal had taken over supervising them.

"Everything's going pretty well," reported Captain Brunson, a satisfied look on his face. "There was some grumbling at first from a few people, but, when I told them, if they didn't work, they wouldn't be allowed to eat, they fell into line. They're not happy, but they're pulling their share of the work."

"We've also removed a few of the crossbows," Captain Pinal explained, "from the hidden compartments in a few of the crates. Due to their construction, I'm pretty certain, if the Druins detect them, they'll just assume we made them ourselves out of local materials."

"We've given them to members of the Imperial Guard, as they're responsible for our security," added Admiral Cross. "The nearest Human settlement is about eighty kilometers from here, so we don't expect any problems from that source. Our hunting parties have spotted a few medium-size cats and some smaller animals, but nothing considered extremely dangerous. A lot of birds are here, as well as some other animals that should be good sources of protein."

"What about fishing?" asked Aiden. "We're not that far from the ocean."

Captain Brunson nodded. "Once we have the settlement finished, we'll see about building some small boats. We have no idea what might be in that ocean. I will feel better if we have some decent-size boats for us to use before we get out on the water."

"We have found some edible fruits and berries," added Admiral Cross. "We also have seeds we brought from home. Some of those should be compatible with this environment. It might be a good idea to get some people busy working on some gardens."

"Rabbits are here as well," said Captain Brunson. "It seems as if those small animals are found on nearly every Human world."

Aiden watched several men place a log in place on a stone foundation. They had already experienced several rainstorms since their arrival on the planet, and they had been quick to set up a rustic rain-barrel collection system. Now it was essential they get the cabins built to provide better protection. "We'll need some underground storage rooms to store some of our provisions."

"Already thought of that," replied Captain Brunson. "As soon as we get enough cabins built, we'll start on that as well.

We'll need a smokehouse for meat, and there are some local animals we can capture and place in pens. We could breed them and have a steady supply of protein."

Aiden was satisfied with the progress they were making. He was anxious to get the settlement done and to begin the process of helping this world advance its civilization.

Later Aiden stood outside his tent, looking up at the stars. Not near as many as back home on Golan Four. Still there were enough to form some star patterns, though none were recognizable. With a deep sigh, he wondered what Layla and Krista were doing. He knew they were in Sanctuary, which was built as part of Operation Exodus. He also knew they were here in this system nearby. Aiden took a deep breath as he thought over the plans for Sanctuary. It wasn't quite finished, but it was far enough along to serve its purpose.

Someday the people of this planet would find Sanctuary and would realize their future destiny. It would be up to them to free the Empire from the clutches of the Confederation. Aiden wished he could be a part of that, but it was not in his future. His future was ensuring the people with him survived and that future generations worked toward the goal of advancing the Humans on this world. "I love you, Layla," he whispered quietly. Turning he went inside his tent to get some sleep. Still a lot of work needed to be done here, and a good night's rest was calling. He had also been spending some time with Lieutenant Breams. He was surprised at how much they had in common.

Several days later Princess Layla stood in front of a cryotube, along with Krista and Captain Masters. "I don't know if I'm ready for this."

Captain Masters smiled in understanding. "It's perfectly safe and will be just like falling asleep. We've already put several thousand families into cryo."

"It's not that," replied Layla, a sad look on her face. "It's just knowing that Aiden and many others will be long dead when I wake up."

"I'll be here," said Krista, taking Layla's hand.

"So will I," added Captain Masters. "I'll be going into cryo in a few more months."

Layla nodded and turned to the medical personnel, who were standing near them. "I guess we're ready."

Dr. Sharma stepped closer. "We will give both of you several injections to help your bodies handle the cryosleep. Let me assure you that it's perfectly safe. We've kept people in cryo for nearly one hundred years with no measurable side affects."

"But this might be much longer," said Krista worriedly.

"Won't be a problem," assured Dr. Sharma. "We'll wake people up periodically to study the effects of long-term cryosleep. We're not expecting any problems. There will always be few medical personnel awake, just in case a problem does occur."

Layla and Krista climbed into the two cryotubes set aside for them and the only two tubes in the room.

"I'll see you when we wake up," Krista said, as she closed her eyes, and the tube slid shut.

Layla felt her eyelids grow heavy, and she soon found herself drifting off to sleep.

Captain Masters watched as the tubes were activated and the lids frosted over.

"It's done," said Dr. Sharma, as he checked some readings on the control panels on the end of each cryotube. "Everything's working properly. Computers will monitor all the cryotubes in the facility. If any problems arise, the medical personnel on duty will be notified immediately."

"Nearly all of us will be in cryo soon," replied Captain Masters. "I wonder what we'll find when we all wake up."

"A new world," replied Dr. Sharma.

Captain Masters nodded. He knew, when they woke up, it would be time for war. War against the Druins and the

Confederation. He wondered what the people of the world Aiden Starguard had gone to would think about that.

"What do the primitive people of the planet call their world?" asked Dr. Sharma.

"Earth," replied Captain Masters. "They call it Earth."

Chapter Four

Admiral Kalar of the Druins stared down at the ruins of the Human world below his fleet. The world of Dorman Three was on fire. The world was in the Haven Nebula and had refused to accept the rule of the Confederation. As a result, antimatter missiles had been dropped on all cities with a population greater than 250,000. Huge mushroom clouds rose into the air, marking the destruction of the huge metroplexes.

On the viewscreens, the planet's atmosphere turned darker in color, as ash and other contaminants rose to pollute the air. A short nuclear winter would occur, where, most likely, more of the planet's frail Human inhabitants would die. This mattered little to Admiral Kalar. The Human worlds had large populations, and the loss of a few billion here and there would only be a minor inconvenience.

"Human ships are attempting to leave the planet," reported the Druin sensor officer.

"How many?" Admiral Kalar did not want anyone to escape. Those attempting to escape were probably heavily involved in the revolt and needed to be dealt with.

"Twelve passenger liners and four cargo ships. Two of the passenger liners are lightly armed with weak energy shields."

"Bring them up on the viewscreens." The Humans had been told that no ships were allowed weapons or energy shields. This was a clear violation of one of the Confederation's edicts.

On the viewscreens sixteen large ships appeared. All were heading upward toward orbit. No doubt to jump into hyperspace to escape the Druin fleet.

Admiral Kalar did not hesitate. "Shoot them down. Let no one escape. We will send this world back into barbarism, as an example to the other Human worlds. We will not tolerate dissent from our rule."

"Locking on targets," reported the tactical officer. "Firing fusion energy beams."

From the *Expanse*, bright beams of light flashed down toward the lumbering ships, attempting to clear the planet's atmosphere. Most of the ships had no defenses or energy shields to protect them. The beams cut easily through the hulls, tearing apart the vessels. In bright explosions, the ships blew up, raining flaming debris down upon the planet, adding to the devastation below. The two lightly armed ships returned fire, but their weak beams failed to penetrate the powerful Druin energy screens. However, the Druin fusion beams had little trouble penetrating the weak screens protecting the passenger liners. In massive fireballs, the two passenger liners blew up.

"All ships have been destroyed," confirmed the sensor officer. "No other ships are detected."

"Some asteroid mining operations are nearby, as well as some small Human colonies on several of the other planets and moons in this system," said Kalar in a cold and nearly emotionless voice. "We will proceed there and destroy them as well. After we are finished in this system, we will make sure the rest of the Human worlds know what we have done. They won't dare to challenge our rule again, for fear of what we may do to them."

The fleet of Druin warships proceeded throughout the system, stopping periodically to destroy any signs of Human activity. City domes on the moons and on two of the planets were blasted open. Antimatter weapons were used upon functioning mining sites. When the Druins were done, the only surviving Humans in the system were those on Dorman Three in the smaller cities.

Admiral Kalar studied the reports from his ships. He was satisfied that he had accomplished the goal the Confederation had given him. He seriously doubted any Human world would dare challenge Confederation rule again. If they did, his fleet would be ready to delve out punishment. "Set a course for the Confederation. I must deliver my report on this action to the Council."

Moments later Admiral Kalar felt the *Expanse* transition into hyperspace for its long journey to one of the main worlds of the Confederation. Behind him, he left a devastated star system and nearly two and a half billion dead Humans.

As soon as the Druins left, other Human ships from nearby worlds arrived to help the survivors and to comb through the wreckage. The formerly inhabited moons and the other planets were searched for survivors, with few found. Ships were sent to the asteroid mining sites to search through the devastation. Calls were sent out to other worlds to help with repairing the planet's biosphere.

Already word was spreading as to what the Druins had done, fueling much anger and frustration throughout the Empire. For the present, further thoughts of rebellion had been quelled. They had no surviving military personnel or ships to resist the Confederation, and, even if they did, the Confederation was too powerful. The Humans had no choice but to comply and to obey the rules of the older races.

As the years passed, the Human Empire went into stasis. New discoveries and research were discouraged by the Confederation. Worlds were allowed to continue at their current level of advancement, but the implementation of new technologies had been harshly curtailed. Trade between worlds was allowed and even encouraged, so there would be no drain of resources on the Confederation. However, possession of armed vessels was strictly prohibited.

At least twice every year Druin warships would go into orbit around each world of the Empire for an inspection. Any world found in violation of any of the Confederation rules was severely punished. The Druins had no problem dropping an antimatter weapon here and there to remind the Humans who was in charge. Millions of Humans were drafted to serve in dangerous jobs throughout the Confederation. Each year Confederation ships would come to the worlds of the Empire and remove tens of thousands of young adults from each world to serve the Confederation planets. Failure to comply always resulted in stiff punishments.

Every child was still taught the history of the Empire, and many believed that someday the Empire would be reborn. Rumors continued of a secret base hidden somewhere in the galaxy, but there was no evidence to prove those rumors were true. Parents told their children stories of the Empire, and the children, when they became adults, passed the stories on to their children. While the Confederation might be in control, the Humans still held a powerful desire for freedom and for a return to the glory days of the Empire.

On the Human planets, considerable unrest grew over what was not allowed, as far as research and advancement. Even so, a few secret research centers were established deep underground, and some research progressed. Great care was taken to ensure none of these centers were ever discovered by the Druins, for fear of what would be done to the Human populations of those worlds.

A secret Imperial agency was established to monitor the research and to keep it secret from the Confederation. A few distant surviving members of the Royal Family were chosen to head the agency, in the hopes of someday freeing the Empire and restoring the constitutional monarchy. The plan was a long-range one and might take centuries to implement. At least they had a plan, and, with that plan, a little hope for the future. They were based on Lydol Four, since it was far away from the core worlds.

Several centuries passed and, in the Bacchus Region, all Druin warships were withdrawn. The original Human castaways were long dead, and their children showed no indications of ever becoming a danger. By now, much of their knowledge of any advanced Human technology should be long gone. However, due to the planet being inhabited by Humans, a quarantine system was set up by the Druins to prohibit the Human inhabitants of the system from ever leaving it or contacting other civilizations. The quarantine system was self-repairing and only required a Druin or other Confederation ship to check on it every century or two. The Confederation felt certain they had ensured the Humans of Earth would never become a threat.

On Earth, civilization entered the Renaissance Period. Unknown to the Humans of the time, the marooned citizens of the Empire and their descendants were encouraging the sudden advancements—such as those made rapidly in art, architecture, politics, science, mathematics, and literature. Most of the new advances started in Italy and then spread across Europe, which highly encouraged individuals to use observation and inductive reasoning to advance science and other fields of study.

Across Europe, small groups of Humans spread out, suggesting new ways of doing things. They met with some of the most intelligent people of those times, helping to explain various types of phenomena and even diseases. In some regions, advancement was rapid; while, in others, it was much slower. But one thing was certain. Earth's civilization had set itself upon a path toward a future technological civilization.

These advances were noted and reported to the Druins. The Druins took note of the advancements but considered them to be a natural development of the Humans of this world.

On the large island where the people from the Empire had been marooned, great pains were taken to preserve their knowledge. Much of their science and technology were recorded in written books and hidden away for the future. Even so, only a small core of the original descendants of the Empire knew of their past and what their destiny was. This core group worked hard at advancing the world around them.

The Forgotten Empire: Banishment

As time passed, and the centuries rolled by, this core group became smaller and smaller. They still went out occasionally and dropped hints that resulted in rapid advancement in some areas. They spoke to such people as Galileo, Sir Isaac Newton, Michael Faraday, Thomas Edison, Marie Curie, Louis Pasteur, Albert Einstein, and Nikola Tesla, among others. A few simple hints dropped here and there helped to encourage these people to make advancements and to promote theories that would be far-reaching and that would quicken the path toward the future civilization needed to fight the Druins and the Confederation.

Years rolled by. Satellites were launched into orbit, and the first spacecraft was sent to the Moon and then eventually to Mars. Spacecraft spread through the Solar System, exploring the asteroids and the other planets. The first permanent Moon base was established, and then the first colony was placed on Mars. Space travel became more common and more economical. The Druin observation system took note of this but did not consider the current level of Earth's technology to be a threat.

Several years later, in orbit of Earth, the spacecraft *Endeavor* was built. It was designed to answer the question of whether other intelligent life was out in the galaxy. The highly advanced spacecraft would journey past the Kuiper Belt and then would use its sensitive communications array to listen to the space between the stars. Some of the more talented scientists on the team believed that, by getting away from the sun and from the tremendous amount of communication signals generated from Earth, this silent area would allow the detection of other civilizations, if they were, indeed, out there.

Others were not so certain. Conflicting theories existed as to why no other civilizations had been detected. The mission of the *Endeavor* was to determine which of the many theories was correct.

Andrew Wilcox stepped aboard the *Endeavor* and marveled at what a special day this was. The *Endeavor* was the most advanced spacecraft ever built by Earth and would set out on the longest journey into space to date for a manned craft. The ship had artificial gravity and an ion drive powered by fusion energy. It could accelerate as high as four gravities for an extended period of time, if necessary. The journey out past the Kuiper Belt was expected to take a little over three months, counting some stops along the way, where the *Endeavor* would take some readings on a few asteroids, as well as make a flyby of Neptune.

Andrew was of average height and build with dark hair. He was very dedicated in his work with a touch of genius. People found him easy to be around and he had a good sense of humor.

"Welcome aboard Mr. Wilcox," greeted Captain Mira Greer. "We'll be departing early tomorrow." Captain Greer was an older woman in her late forties, and the first female commander of a long-range exploration mission.

"Is all my equipment on board?"

"Yes, and it's been stowed away."

Andrew spent a few minutes looking around. The *Endeavor* was the largest spacecraft ever built. It was nearly two hundred meters in length and thirty meters at its widest. Much of that space was taken up by the ion drive and the fusion power plant. For the last six months Andrew and most of the crew had spent their time on a full-scale mock-up of the ship down on Earth.

"The rest of the crew?"

"A few are already on board, and the rest should be arriving shortly. We'll spend twenty-four hours getting the ship ready to leave orbit, and then we'll set out for the Kuiper Belt."

"This looks just like the mock-up."

Captain Greer smiled. "In every detail. We felt it was easier to train on Earth rather than here in space. That way, if something went wrong, we wouldn't cause billions in damages to the ship or the station."

The huge orbital station was at the LaGrange Point between the Earth and the Moon. Most expeditions to the other planets left from that station, which was capable of doing repairs and building about anything the ships might need. Routine trips were now occurring between Earth, the Moon, the station, and Mars. A few prospecting ships were even venturing out to the asteroid region to search for minerals to sell back on Earth. Space travel was expanding rapidly, and already discussions were ongoing about enlarging the station.

Andrew made his way through the ship to the central section, where the crew's quarters were. He passed a few others on the way before reaching the hatch with his name on it. Opening the hatch, he went inside, finding a bunk, work desk, and several comfortable chairs. The restroom and showers were at the end of the corridor and would be shared by the entire crew. Separate restrooms had been established for the men and the women.

Looking around, Andrew saw his bags on the bed, so he got busy unpacking. He had brought one bag on board with him, and this one he carefully stowed away. Andrew was a communications specialist, and part of the communications array on the hull of the ship had been designed by him. It was more advanced than it should be, as part of it was based on Imperial technology.

It had taken a lot of work to get Andrew assigned to the *Endeavor* project. Fortunately the Imperials had amassed a large fortune over the centuries and had used that to partially fund the *Endeavor*, under the conditions it would carry some specialized communications equipment and Andrew to operate it.

One thing greatly concerned Andrew. If his group was correct as to why no communication signals from other interstellar civilizations were being received, this could be a dangerous mission. There was a good chance Andrew would not be coming back. Even so, he had volunteered for this trip out beyond the Kuiper Belt. It had always been a dream of his to travel into space. This mission was a culmination of his childhood fantasies and the hard work he had put in at Cal Tech in Pasadena, California, demonstrating his knowledge in natural science and particularly engineering, involving advanced communications technology.

The classes at Cal Tech had been a breeze, considering his knowledge of Imperial science. It had also allowed him to build the communications equipment that had been emplaced on the *Endeavor* without drawing undo attention to the massive breakthrough in communication technology it represented.

Finished with his unpacking, Andrew left his quarters and headed for the Command Center of the ship, located at the front of the vessel with several large viewports. Stepping inside, Andrew noted that several of the consoles were already manned by some of the crew. The ship had a mixed crew of civilian specialists and military.

"Mr. Wilcox, I'm glad to see you're here," said Lieutenant Commander Ganlon Meadows. "If you would take your spot at the communications console, it would be helpful. We have a lot of work to do before we're ready to depart."

"Yes, sir," replied Andrew, as he walked to the comm console and sat down. Reaching forward, he activated the console, and several computer screens came to life. Almost instantly a list of messages came up on one of the screens. Beside each message was an indicator, listing who the message was for. Most of the messages could be sent to the computer stations in the private quarters of the crew. Several were meant for Captain Greer and the Executive Officer, Lieutenant Commander Meadows.

"I have several messages for you and the captain," reported Andrew.

"Send the messages to the command console, and I'll inform the captain."

Looking out the large viewports, Andrew could see hundreds of unblinking stars, also a large section of the space station the *Endeavor* was docked to. Andrew wished the *Endeavor* was armed, but it was designed as a peaceful vessel. Not even any handguns were on board. The total crew of the ship consisted of twenty-seven people. Eighteen military and nine civilians. The civilians were all scientists of some type.

"I studied some of the papers you wrote on your new communications array while you were at Cal Tech," said Rachael Newberry. "I found some of your concepts quite intriguing. Where did you come up with your ideas?"

Rachael was the science officer for the *Endeavor* and had advanced degrees in six fields of study. She was a petite blonde with a charming attitude and was rather nicely endowed.

Andrew smiled. He wasn't surprised by this question, as his array was quite revolutionary. He suspected no one on board knew just how revolutionary it was. "You won't believe this, but I'm an avid reader of science fiction. I read the idea in a book called *From Earth to Mars*, written back in the nineties. The more I thought about it, the more I realized the technology mentioned might be possible. So, when I went to Cal Tech, I set out to invent a new and better communication method. We'll know how well it works when we get out past the Kuiper Belt and begin scanning for messages from other worlds."

"From a science fiction novel," mused Rachael, grinning. "I used to read them as well. You know that many science fiction authors spend considerable time doing research to make their stories sound more plausible. So it's not surprising to find some good ideas in some of those stories."

Andrew nodded. "I thought about writing one myself, but I don't know where I would find the time."

"So what do you think about this mission of ours? Do you think, by going out past the Kuiper Belt, we'll pick up signals from aliens?"

Andrew grinned at the alien remark. Little did Rachael know of the hundreds of inhabited Human worlds out in the galaxy. "Maybe. A professor at Cal Tech claims our system has been quarantined by the advanced races of the galaxy because we're so primitive. Thus all communication signals are blocked so we can't receive them."

"That's ridiculous," interrupted Professor Alan Tower. "That would indicate the entire Solar System is enclosed in some protective bubble, preventing signals from getting in. I don't see how that's possible. The thought of alien life is too incredible to believe."

Rachael shook her head. "I'm in the crowd that believes, while there is intelligent alien life out there, it's so distant that any communication signals are so weak that, by the time they get here, we can't detect them. They also may be using methods of communication we haven't even considered."

"It's possible," Andrew answered deftly. "This mission should spill some light on some of those theories."

"Your communications array," Rachael continued. "What do you think the odds are of it detecting such signals?"

"If the signals are out there, my array will pick them up."

Rachael nodded. "When we have the time, I have some questions about the array. There are parts of it I don't understand."

"Sure," replied Andrew. "I would be glad to explain how it functions." At least part of it. Other parts of the array no one could be told about. He also wouldn't mind spending more time with Rachael.

Over the next few hours the rest of the crew arrived and got settled in. Equipment was checked, and final preparations were made to get underway.

The ship was divided into five primary sections. The forward section was the small Command Center, which controlled all the ship's functions. The next section was a common area, where the crew could eat their meals as well as exercise. The third area housed the crew's individual quarters. The fourth area was a small research section, containing various scientific instruments. The final and largest area was Engineering, which contained the ion drive, the fusion power plant, as well as other ship systems. Everything could be accessed through a large central corridor that ran from the front of the ship to the back.

Large metal hatches, in case of an emergency, could seal off each section.

"All systems check out," reported Lieutenant Commander Meadows.

"Excellent," replied Captain Greer. "Let's all go to the station and get something to eat, as well as a good night's rest. We'll return to the ship in the morning and go through our final checklists. Then, if everything goes as expected, we'll activate the ion drive at 14:00 hours tomorrow."

The captain turned to Andrew. "Mr. Wilcox, please inform Station Flight Control that the crew of the *Endeavor* will be coming back on board the station shortly. All tests look good, and we should be ready to begin our mission tomorrow."

"Yes, Captain," replied Andrew, as he quickly sent the message.

"Why don't you join me in the station's cafeteria?" suggested Rachael. "I would like to speak to you about the new communications array."

Andrew nodded. "Sure, just let me get a few things from my quarters."

"See you in about an hour then?" asked Rachael.

Andrew nodded and smiled.

A few minutes later Andrew had packed a small overnight bag and was on his way to the station. He had quarters on the station where he would be staying tonight, and then he would spend the next six months or more on the *Endeavor*. He was also pleased to be eating with Rachael. This would be their last night before becoming cooped up in the limited space on the ship, and he wanted to make the most of it.

An hour later Andrew made his way to the large cafeteria on the station. The station had a normal crew of nearly three hundred and was quite busy with ships stopping at the station before continuing to the Moon or Mars. Stepping into the cafeteria, he saw Rachael and another woman sitting at a table. Rachael saw Andrew and motioned for him to come over.

Andrew recognized the other woman as Kala Wright, who was an astrophysicist and would also be traveling on the *Endeavor*. He had met her before and had spoken with her a few times during their training in the mock-up on Earth. She was quite bright and also something of a flirt.

"I hope you don't mind me joining you," said Kala, smiling up at Andrew.

"No, not at all," replied Andrew, as he sat down. He knew he would have to be a little guarded in what he told the two women. Both were extremely intelligent, or they wouldn't be going on this mission.

"What do you think of the ship?" asked Kala.

Andrew looked at the two women. "It's exactly like the mock-up on Earth. Just walking through it today, I couldn't believe the details that had gone into the mock-up."

"Only everything on this ship works," said Rachael, as she sipped her glass of tea. "I do wish more civilians were going on this mission. Most of the crew is made up of military personnel."

"I agree," said Kala. "But most of the military are highly trained, and some even have advanced science degrees. I've met most of them, and they seem very qualified."

"Let's go get our food, and we can talk while we eat," suggested Rachael, standing. "I'm starving!"

After the three went through the serving line and sat back down, Rachael turned toward Andrew. "Your array seems to have some technology I'm not familiar with to help boost the signals it picks up. How did you go about designing the technology?"

Andrew considered his answer. While the array seemed pretty straightforward, it was capable of far more than what anyone could imagine. With the array, he could intercept hyperlight signals as well as send hyperlight messages, if he wanted. It was also capable of detecting Druin warships and installations, if any were within range. "I worked on it while at Cal

Tech, along with a few other engineers. I had theories on what I wanted the array to do, and some of the other engineers constructed the equipment to make it work. It's quite complicated, and even parts of the equipment I'm not completely familiar with."

"So it was a group project," mused Rachael. "It must have been fun seeing something you had written and designed on paper come into reality."

Andrew nodded. "We designed it just for this mission. We were pleased when our design was accepted." Andrew couldn't mention that most of those who worked on the design with him were Imperials too.

The three continued to talk for well over an hour. Afterward they went to one of the large observation lounges on the station, where they could see the Moon as well as Earth.

"The Moon looks so large here," said Rachael, as she stared through one of the large viewports.

Kala nodded. "It should be. We're much closer to it than we are to Earth."

Andrew looked around. Numerous comfortable chairs and even a few tables were here, where people could sit and relax or play a friendly game of cards. Currently about a dozen people were in the observation room.

"Look. You can see the lights from the Moon base," said Kala, pointing them out.

Andrew looked, and, sure enough, the lights from the sprawling Moon base were visible. Andrew took a deep breath. A few Imperials worked on the Moon, as well as several here on the space station. As the civilization on Earth had become more technologically advanced, the Imperials had been taking a more active role in helping to advance science and technology. The new fusion ion drive on the *Endeavor* was a good example. An Imperial scientist had helped make the breakthrough on functional fusion power plants that could be used on spacecraft.

However, great pains had been taken to prevent Earth from discovering hyperspace travel. Such travel would immediately draw the attention of the Druins and the Confederation, and Earth was not ready for that confrontation yet.

The three stayed in the observation lounge for nearly two hours, talking about Earth, the Moon, and Mars. Finally they went their separate ways back to their quarters. They had to be up bright and early the next day to board the *Endeavor* and go through all the preflight checklists before leaving early that afternoon.

Andrew was in his quarters, reading, when a knock came on his door. "Enter," he said.

The door opened, and Major Loren Henderson stepped in. He was second in command of the station, as well as an Imperial.

"Major Henderson, I wasn't expecting a visit from you."

Major Henderson took a seat and looked at Andrew. "I wanted to talk to you about this mission. The Council spent a lot of time debating whether to have one of our people on the ship. If the Druins have emplaced a quarantine system around this star system, there's a good chance you won't be coming back. The odds are very high, almost 90 percent."

"I understand the risk, sir. But we must know if that system is there. We can't allow this world to make numerous advances if the Druins are monitoring us."

Major Henderson let out a deep sigh. "Andrew, less than two hundred of us know our past and have kept up with the knowledge of Imperial technology. Over the years we have been very careful and selective as to where we've elected to interfere with the development of this world. We've done everything we can to make it look like the advances in science have come about naturally, so as not to draw the Druins' suspicion."

"We need to find Sanctuary," said Andrew. "It was rumored to be somewhere in this system. My comms may allow us to confirm that."

Major Henderson shook his head. "There's been no sign of it. It's been nearly one thousand years, and not once have we been contacted by an Imperial from Sanctuary. I'm starting to believe that Sanctuary is not in this system or that it was destroyed by the Druins early on."

Andrew blinked his eyes and answered. "I disagree. I think it's here, and we need to find it. Earth's science is developing rapidly, and it's only a matter of time before they stumble on the hyperdrive themselves. Once that happens, it will bring the Druins and the Confederation down upon us."

"I wish I could share your optimism about Sanctuary." Major Henderson folded his arms across his chest. "I know both of your parents. They must be very unhappy about your decision to go on this mission."

Andrew took in a deep breath. Neither of his parents had said too much when he had told them about his decision to go on the *Endeavor* mission. He strongly suspected they disapproved. Both of them wanted him to settle down and to have a large family. However, Andrew had other ideas.

"There's still a 10 percent chance you won't find anything."

"No, we both know that's not true. If something wasn't blocking the hyperspace communication frequencies, Earth would be picking up hundreds, if not thousands, of signals with the big arrays on the surface and in orbit."

"Okay," Major Henderson said. "The bigger question is, what will the system that's in place—quarantining our system—do when it detects the *Endeavor*?"

Andrew knew this was a legitimate question. "I guess the only way we'll know is when I get out there. I have a communicator in my quarters which I can hook up to the communications array to get a message back to the station."

"I know. I have a receiver to pick up such a message. It's already hooked up to the station's communication equipment, though no one suspects what it does. I had it installed last month."

Major Henderson stood and offered Andrew his hand. "Good luck. I hope I'm wrong, and you make it back. I'll await your signal."

"Thank you, Major," Andrew said, shaking the major's hand.

After the major left, Andrew prepared to go to sleep. As he lay in bed, he couldn't help wondering if he had volunteered for a one-way mission. He knew the odds were not in his favor, but, one way or another, he would be coming back.

Chapter Five

Andrew was back on board the *Endeavor*, waiting for launch. The crew had been on board the ship since 0700, prepping the ship to activate the ion drive.

"Cutting station power," reported Lieutenant Williams from the engineering console. "We are now on internal power, with the fusion power plant operating at 20 percent."

"Systems check!" called out Captain Greer.

Each department head checked in, reporting all systems were in the green.

"Inform Flight Control we're ready to disconnect from the station."

"Permission granted," replied Andrew, after speaking to Flight Control.

"Helm, activate maneuvering thrusters, and move us one thousand meters from the station."

"Disconnecting from station," confirmed Lieutenant Suarez. "Activating thrusters at 10 percent power."

Tension in the Command Center was high, as the ship moved away from the station. Through the viewports, more of the massive space station became visible. Two small ships bound for the Moon and a larger one going to Mars were still docked.

"Four hundred meters from station," reported Lieutenant Morrison at the sensor console.

"Everything is still in the green," added Lieutenant Commander Meadows.

The ship continued to move away from the station, and, when it reached one thousand meters, the vessel came to a halt.

"We're at station-keeping, holding steady," announced Lieutenant Suarez, as she shut down the thrusters. "Ship is oriented for initial ion drive burn."

Andrew looked at one of the small viewscreens showing Earth. He knew their launch was being viewed by the entire planet. For several days now the media stations had been full of videos of the *Endeavor*, its crew, and the goals of the mission. Everyone was excited at the thought of finally finding out if other intelligent life was in their galaxy.

"Stand by for initial ion drive burn in thirty seconds," ordered Captain Greer.

"Fusion power plant is at 70 percent," reported Lieutenant Williams. "Ready for ion drive activation."

Andrew took in a deep breath. Fortunately the ship had artificial gravity, and the system could counter the thrust from the ion drive, though initially they would only be accelerating at one gravity.

"Activate," ordered Captain Greer.

"Ion drive activated." A dull and barely perceptible rumble could be heard inside the ship.

Andrew saw the space station suddenly grow smaller. He knew anyone watching from the station's observation lounges would see a bright blue glow behind the ship from the ions being released at high speed.

"Ship is operating as expected," reported Lieutenant Commander Meadows.

"We're on our way," said Captain Greer with a grin. "Next stop is the asteroid Juno."

Andrew knew the ship would do a close flyby of Juno and take numerous scientific readings before proceeding on. They were on their way, and he would soon know if a Druin presence lurked on the outskirts of the Solar System, monitoring the Humans. He hoped the Druins weren't there, but, due to the absence of communication signals from the rest of the galaxy, Andrew was almost certain some presence was there. If so, it would pose a major problem for future advancements by the Humans. It would also make finding Sanctuary that much harder.

For days the ship continued to accelerate as it flew farther and farther from Earth. The crew got into a routine of doing regular ship maintenance and making scientific observations. The scientists in the crew had set an ambitious schedule for making observations and analyzing the data they collected.

During times when the crew had little to do, they congregated in the common area to talk, to play games, and to have their meals. Also some computers were in several alcoves, where the crew could send private messages back to Earth. Sometimes the scientists would get into heated discussions over their observations or what they hoped to accomplish on the mission.

The *Endeavor* passed the orbit of Mars, but the red planet was on the far side of the sun, so they couldn't see it or take any observations. A few days later the ship reached the outskirts of the asteroid field and continued toward Juno.

Andrew was at his communications console, scanning all the nearer asteroids with his array. If anyone asked, he would just tell them that he was running routine communication scans. He was convinced that Sanctuary had to be somewhere in the asteroid zone and probably inside one of the larger ones. Slightly more than 140 main-belt asteroids had a diameter greater than one hundred kilometers. Any one of those could be the home to Sanctuary. Andrew couldn't see Sanctuary being in any of the smaller asteroids because of the resources the base would need. It just made sense for it to be inside one of the larger ones. On this mission, Andrew planned to scan all the major asteroids on this side of the system.

"What are you doing?" asked Rachael, coming over from her science station.

Andrew looked up and replied, "Just scanning various communication frequencies. I'm creating a baseline to search when we get far enough out from the sun."

"Do you really think it's possible the solar radiation from the sun or its magnetic field is blocking us from receiving transmissions from other civilizations?"

Andrew shook his head. "It's doubtful. I think it must be something else."

"We have several probes out there, and they're still transmitting," said Rachael.

"Some frequencies might be immune to whatever is jamming communications," replied Andrew.

Rachael looked stunned as she thought about Andrew's comment. "You think it's something artificial!"

"Maybe, we'll just have to see when we get out there."

Rachael looked around at the rest of the crew, who were busy at their stations. "Have you mentioned your suspicions to anyone else?"

"No, not until I have more evidence."

Rachael nodded. "That's probably wise. A few of the scientists would think you're nuts for having such ideas."

Andrew grinned. "What about you?"

"I definitely don't think you're nuts. After graduating from Cal Tech and knowing a few of the people you worked with there, I won't question your sanity. Just promise to tell me if you pick up anything out of the ordinary with your array."

"I will," promised Andrew. "You'll be the first to know."

"We'll be arriving at Juno tomorrow," added Rachael. "Maybe we'll find a trace of your aliens there." She turned and went back to her console with the hint of a smile on her face.

The next day the *Endeavor* arrived at Juno, encountering few problems in their passage through the asteroid zone. Some systems had to be fine-tuned, but it wasn't anything the crew couldn't handle, particularly since they could contact the space station for technical advice if needed. They had to deal with a slight communications lag time, due to the distance. The lag time would get worse the farther out they traveled.

"We're coming up on Juno," reported Lieutenant Morrison.

"We've slowed the ship some to give us more time on the flyby," added Lieutenant Commander Meadows.

On one of the ship's small viewscreens, the asteroid became visible. Juno was irregularly shaped with a huge impact crater. The crater was at least one hundred kilometers across.

"I wouldn't have wanted to be there when that happened," commented Kala Wright. "It would have thrown out a massive debris cloud."

"A couple ships looking into asteroid mining are heading out this way soon," said Captain Greer, as she studied the image. "It's one of the reasons we want to collect all the data we can on Juno and send it back. Of particular interest is that big asteroid crater."

"What do you think, Andrew?" asked Rachael. "Do you think asteroid mining will ever be practical?" Rachael was busy at her console, aiming some of the scientific equipment on board the *Endeavor* at the asteroid.

Andrew was surprised by the question. He had been spending a lot of his free time with Rachael and Kala, discussing the mission. "Maybe. I guess it depends on what type of mining they want to do."

Andrew studied the image of Juno closely. He wondered if it was possible that Sanctuary was located inside the asteroid. Some of the Imperials on Earth believed it might have been placed on one of the moons of Jupiter or Saturn. However, the lack of contact was a growing concern. The Imperials had had some secret discussions about financing several expeditions to find out just what had happened to the secret base.

Also apprehension grew that, with the rapid pace of development on Earth, the Druins might intervene rather than let the planet develop its own space navy. The Imperials' general consensus was that time was rapidly running out.

"All instruments are focused on Juno," reported Rachael.

"As soon as we're finished with our observations, we'll send all the data to the station to be analyzed," said Captain Greer. "The scientists on board will be quite interested in our readings. I believe a group of investors on Earth are discussing sending a mining ship to see just how easy working on an asteroid would be."

Andrew wondered if it was part of his group of Imperials. He had become a little out of touch since he had joined the *Endeavor* project. Coming out as part of an asteroid mining project would be excellent cover to search for Sanctuary.

Kala peered into a scope at the asteroid. Occasionally she made some adjustments and seemed very intent on what she was doing. "I'm getting some great views of the asteroid, particularly the impact crater. I wish we had time to land and take some samples."

"Unfortunately this ship is not designed to land anywhere," said Captain Greer. "I do agree it would be nice if we had a couple of landers on board. It's a recommendation I'll make when we get back. I suspect, once we return, the *Endeavor* will be assigned some new missions. This ship was designed to be used for quite some time. Once we return to the station, it will take only about four weeks to check the ship from bow to stern and have it prepared to leave again."

"I can see a number of impact craters," said Kala excitedly. "Most are probably millions or billions of years old."

"That's not surprising," commented Rachael. "Most of the larger asteroids show multiple impacts."

"How often does that happen?" asked Captain Greer. "Is it something we need to be concerned about?"

Lieutenant Suarez shook her head. "No, our course has been plotted to keep us away from all the known asteroids. Even though we're in the asteroid region, they are still widely spaced. It's not like there's an asteroid every few kilometers. They're hundreds of kilometers apart, and that includes many the size of a marble. All the asteroids combined have less mass than the Moon."

"Our sensors are designed to detect any that might be a danger," added Lieutenant Commander Meadows. "We can easily use our thrusters to adjust our course, if need be, so we're not in any real danger."

"We're at our nearest approach," Lieutenant Suarez informed everyone.

Andrew looked at the irregularly shaped asteroid on the viewscreen. The impact crater was plainly visible. He shuddered thinking what an impact like that would do if Sanctuary was, indeed, located inside one of the asteroids. "How often are there impacts between asteroids?"

Kala smiled. "Rarely. Most asteroids have their own orbits and stay in them, unless something, such as a comet, disturbs them. In the early days, when the asteroid field first came into being, there were probably a considerable number of impacts, but now everything is pretty stable."

"Professor Crayton requests we rotate the *Endeavor* by eight degrees along our axis to give them better views for their instruments," said Lieutenant Commander Meadows. "He sounded pretty demanding."

Andrew grinned. Professor Crayton was an older scientist, and the actual head of the science team on the ship. It was also his firm belief that something prevented messages from other civilizations reaching Earth. He was also a little impatient when talking to others.

"We're collecting an enormous amount of data," said Rachael, smiling hugely. "All of our instruments seem to be working perfectly."

Andrew continued to watch the viewscreen as the ship pulled away from Juno. Unnoticed by the crew in the Command Center, Andrew manipulated his communications array to search the nearby asteroids for any strange signals or emissions. To the casual observer, the information scrawling across his screen would make little sense.

To Andrew each line represented a possible communication frequency, both in real time as well as in hyperlight speed. He had been taking these readings on a regular basis as they neared the asteroids. So far his search had revealed nothing. His communications array also served as a highly sensitive sensor system. It could detect objects far more efficiently than the regular sensors the ship was equipped with.

"What are all those lines on your screen?" asked Lieutenant Commander Meadows. "I've noticed them several times in the last few hours."

"Just routine scans of known communication frequencies," replied Andrew, showing no concern. "As we travel farther out in the Solar System, I'm using the array to search for any strange signals. I'm not expecting to detect anything until we're out past Pluto and, more likely, past the Kuiper Belt."

"We still have a long way to go," commented Captain Greer. "Our journey is only beginning."

Everyone knew the captain was right. The jaunt out to the asteroid belt was a short one compared to their eventual goal just out past the Kuiper Belt.

Later most of the scientists and part of the crew were in the common area, discussing the flyby of Juno. A few were eating, and some were sitting in front of computer consoles, sending messages back home to family and other scientists interested in the mission.

"We should have slowed down more and spent more time at Juno," huffed Professor Crayton.

"No," replied Professor Alan Tower in disagreement. "It would have added several weeks to our mission to slow down to the point you wanted. We have more data on Juno than ever recorded. We have a list of potential mineral sites, as well as locations where it should be safe for a mining expedition to land on the surface. Our mission at Juno was to do the preliminary survey, and that's exactly what we did."

Professor Crayton frowned and slowly shook his head. "We're a research expedition. Time should have been set aside for a slower flyby. When we return, I will complain to the program director."

Professor Tower did not reply; instead he stood and walked over to one of the small freezer compartments on the wall and removed a frozen meal. Rather than argue with Professor Crayton, he would eat instead.

"Is Professor Crayton always like that?" asked Andrew. A number of them sat at one of the larger tables.

Rachael grinned. "No, today was a good day. I think he always seems to be a little grumpy. The man's a genius and doesn't hesitate to let everyone around him know he's the smartest person on this mission. We've learned to just tolerate him and to not get into arguments."

Kala nodded in agreement. "Just the other day he was explaining my own research to me, pointing out areas where he thought I was making mistakes."

"You think that's bad? I'm responsible for the well-being of everyone on this ship," said Dr. B. J. Summers. "He refuses to come in for regular checkups. Every time it's his scheduled appointment time, I literally have to find him and drag the professor to my office."

"Why do we do the routine checkups?" asked Lieutenant Edward Thomas, the chief engineer on the ship.

"As a safety precaution," replied Dr. Summers. "Fortunately we have artificial gravity on the ship, so we don't have to worry about long-term exposure to weightlessness. However, we are exposed to cosmic rays and other radiation that's normally found away from the protective magnetic field of Earth. The checkups are just a routine precaution to make sure everyone is doing okay. I don't expect to see any problems. The ship is pretty well shielded."

"How are your arrays functioning?" asked Rachael, looking at Andrew. "Have you picked up anything interesting?"

"No," replied Andrew. He dared not mention what he was searching for. "I've been running routine checks and have been scanning Earth's communication bands. Everything's coming in crystal clear. I suppose everyone has noticed we can watch Earth media stations while on board the *Endeavor*, and they come in almost perfectly."

"I wondered about that," commented Dr. Summers, nodding her head. "I was watching a news channel last night and was marveling at how clear it came in. So you're the one responsible for that. I've been on other expeditions, and I've never seen reception as clear as what we have on the *Endeavor*."

Andrew was very careful in how he answered, so as not to raise suspicions about the array. "It took some fine-tuning, and, yes, the array is what we're using to bring in the media channels as well as to communicate with Earth. I'm hoping, by making some more minor adjustments, they will be even more sensitive to receiving signals from other civilizations."

"Do you believe they're out there?" asked Kala, her focus on Andrew.

"I do," said Rachael, interrupting. "The universe is just too big for us to be the only ones. There should be hundreds or possibly thousands of other civilizations out there."

"I believe that as well," replied Andrew. "I fully expect, if we can get out far enough past the Kuiper Belt, we should pick up one or two."

Andrew didn't want to mention that his equipment and the array would pick up thousands of transmissions from other worlds. The people of this Solar System had no clue as to what was out there. In some ways they were fortunate to live in the Bacchus Region, with no neighboring interstellar civilizations.

"Can you imagine what the effects would be at home if we made the announcement that we've detected transmissions from another civilization?" asked Lieutenant Thomas. "Of course those transmission would be decades or possibly centuries old.

Traveling at the speed of light, it would take that long for them to reach us."

"Unless they have a method of sending messages faster than the speed of light," suggested Rachael.

Thomas shook his head. "Not possible. If you're talking about hyperspace or warp speed, all of that is very theoretical."

"What about an Alcubierre Drive?" asked Kala. "I understand an experimental model is being built at the space station."

"What's an Alcubierre Drive?" asked Dr. Summers, frowning.

"To put it simply, it contracts space in front of a ship and expands space behind the vessel," explained Kala.

"Won't work," replied Thomas. "To power an Alcubierre Drive, you need exotic matter. To the best of my knowledge we have none."

Kala looked at Andrew. "What do you think?"

Andrew was surprised by the question. "We're still learning a lot every day. If other civilizations are out in the galaxy, I believe it's safe to presume they've perfected some method to travel quickly and safely between star systems."

"I would have to see it with my own eyes," said Thomas doubtfully. "If we ever go to the stars, it will be in generation ships with massive crews, and the trips will be one-way."

Kala reached out and touched Andrew on the hand, lingering longer than necessary. "Would you ever consider going on a generation ship?"

Andrew was startled by Kala's touch. "No, I don't think I would want to live out my entire life on board a spacecraft. It would be too restrictive, no matter what the size." Andrew caught Rachael frowning at Kala. He felt his face flush, realizing Rachael had noticed how Kala had touched his hand. Surely Rachael wasn't jealous. Besides, it was only a friendly touch.

"I think I'll turn in," said Rachael, standing and stretching. "It's been a long day, and I want to go over some of the readings we took of Juno tomorrow."

"So do I," said Kala. "Professor Marcus wants to see the data, so she can compare it to some of the Kuiper Belt objects she's studied." Professor Adrian Marcus was an expert on Kuiper Belt objects, and she also had a very pleasant personality.

Andrew watched as the two women left the common area.

"You better watch those two," commented Lieutenant Thomas, grinning widely.

"We're all just friends," replied Andrew a little uncomfortably. He didn't have a lot of experience with women, as he had focused very intensively on his career.

"Nevertheless, we're on a long voyage, and things tend to happen when people are cooped up in such close proximity to one another. If I were you, I would definitely take advantage of it. Both of those women are good-looking."

"Thanks for the advice, but, for now, I'll just keep them as friends. Now I'm going to go get some rest. I want to run some diagnostics on the arrays in the morning."

Lieutenant Thomas looked curious. "If you need any help, let me know. I'm interested in just how your arrays work. I looked at some of the schematics, and I have to admit that they're way beyond anything I've seen before."

"I'll let you know when I start," replied Andrew. "Keep in mind that the arrays were designed by a team at Cal Tech, so they're very advanced."

Later Andrew lay in bed, reading. He enjoyed reading to pass the time and had downloaded hundreds of books on his personal reader. Some of the books were technical and science manuals, while others were works of fiction.

Placing his reader on the small stand by his bed, he closed his eyes and thought about what some of his readings from the sensors had revealed today. He had been unobtrusively searching for any traces of Sanctuary in the nearby asteroids. Unfortunately the arrays had detected nothing on any communication frequencies or with their highly developed sensors.

"Where are you?" Andrew said softly to himself. "I know you're out here somewhere."

Andrew recalled a recent meeting he had had with several other Imperials while he was still on Earth. They had growing concerns that, with Earth's current developments in technology and now space travel, it was only a matter of time before the Confederation reacted. If Sanctuary still existed, they needed to step in and help Earth prepare for what might be coming.

"There's a good chance Sanctuary did not survive," Brett Newcomb said, who was part of Earth's Imperial Council. "The attack of the Druins was so sudden and unexpected that many of the personnel who were supposed to go to Sanctuary never made it."

"But some did," pointed out Professor Mallory Stark, who taught at Cal Tech. "Enough that they could have finished construction before going into cryo."

Andrew had listened to the two argue for quite some time before he interrupted them. "What if Sanctuary is remaining silent for fear of the Druins detecting them?"

Professor Stark frowned and then replied, "It's possible. But, at some point, they must reveal themselves. The primary purpose of having the Druins maroon us in this system was so we could someday bring Earth to the point where we could return to the Empire and free it from the clutches of the Druins and the Confederation."

"Will they even remember us?" asked Andrew. "After all, it's been over one thousand years."

Brett leaned back in his chair before responding. "It all depends on the Druins and the Confederation. They may have made a concentrated effort to remove all information from Human history books about the Empire. What the people may remember would be determined from what was handed down by word of mouth or in hidden books."

Andrew looked concerned. "So the average person in the Empire may have forgotten about us? We're from a forgotten Empire?"

"Not completely forgotten," replied Professor Stark. "Other plans were supposed to preserve the memory of the Empire. Of course we have no idea what may have happened to those who were supposed to implement those plans on some of the worlds of the Empire. There's no doubt in my mind that, on some worlds, yes, the Empire probably has been forgotten, while, on others, its memory may still live. We won't know until we return."

"And, in order to return, we must find Sanctuary."

Professor Stark nodded, looking at Andrew. "That's where you come in. We've made the necessary arrangements to get you on the *Endeavor*, as well as the new sensor and communications array. This will be our first actual attempt to find any traces of Sanctuary. If you fail, we will launch other missions to different regions of the Solar System to search."

Andrew stood, looking at the two Imperials. "Let's hope I don't fail. I greatly fear the Druins won't give us much more time. Not only that but it's just a matter of time before the Humans of Earth develop their own faster-than-light drive. Once they do, the Druins will come for us."

Shortly after that meeting, the *Endeavor* had launched, and now it was up to Andrew to find Sanctuary. The fate of the Humans in this star system depended on Sanctuary still existing.

Chapter Six

The days passed by uneventfully as the *Endeavor* continued its journey through the Solar System. In two more days the spacecraft would make its nearest approach to the planet Neptune.

"We set a new record yesterday for traveling the farthest of any manned mission," announced Captain Greer. Everyone was in the Command Center, except Lieutenant Commander Meadows and Lieutenant Suarez, who were in the common area.

"Only a couple billion more miles to go," quipped Lieutenant Thomas, causing everyone to laugh. "Then we can take our readings, see if we can hear any aliens, and then go back home."

"Are we slowing down for Neptune?" asked Professor Crayton with narrowed eyes. "We could take more detailed readings if we reduce our speed and increase the amount of time we'll be near the planet. It's hard telling when another manned mission will be out this far."

Captain Greer turned her attention to the professor. "We are slowing down some. However, once we're past Neptune, we'll be accelerating at two gravities to make up for the time lost."

"Two gravities?" said Linda Snow, the ship's nurse as well as biologist. "Will we have to stay in our acceleration seats the entire time?"

"Don't worry. Our artificial gravity field will counteract the increased acceleration. As long as it functions properly, you won't notice the increase."

Linda looked relieved. "This is my first long-distance space mission, and I was concerned about the acceleration. I'm glad to hear it won't be a problem."

"What about your fancy array?" asked Professor Alan Tower, looking at Andrew. "What if we get to where we're going and hear nothing? Will that prove once and for all there is no other intelligent life besides what's on Earth?"

Andrew allowed himself to grin. "I think we'll detect something. The universe is too vast for us to be the only intelligent life."

Professor Tower shook his head. "I've spent years in the large orbital arrays above Earth, scanning the stars for signs of intelligent life. Not once have we detected a signal. I no longer believe anything's out there. We're alone in this universe."

"Perhaps," replied Andrew guardedly. "We'll know in a few more weeks, once we turn the array toward the stars."

"I'll be there, watching," replied Tower. He looked around the Command Center and then continued. "Mark my words, we will hear nothing but silence."

Professor Marcus cleared her throat and then spoke, ignoring Professor Tower. "What if we need to go out farther into the Oort Cloud?"

Captain Greer folded her arms across her chest and then answered. "We have sufficient supplies to allow us to extend our mission by several months, if necessary. However, before we even attempt to venture into the Oort Cloud, I would want to hear everyone's opinion. We're going out about fifty AUs from Earth to make our initial search for extraterrestrial signals. The Oort Cloud extends out to over two hundred thousand AUs. It would require us operating the ion drive at three gravities for us to reach it and to extend our mission to the maximum."

"We can't do that!" objected Professor Tower. "Going out farther will make no difference. Nothing's out there!"

"Then why did you come on this mission?" demanded Professor Crayton. "Why didn't you stay on Earth?"

Tower was silent for a moment and then answered. "I want to be there when you all fail. For years I have claimed there were no other intelligent races in the universe, and we on Earth were created by an accident of nature. An accident that has not been repeated anywhere else."

"How can you be so shortsighted?" asked Kala, shaking her head in disbelief. "The universe is just too big for there to be only us. Other civilizations must be out there."

"Then where are they?" Professor Tower's face took on a look of anger. "We spent billions building this spacecraft and then sent it on a useless mission. It could have been used for far better purposes."

Captain Greer realized the discussion was getting out of hand. "This mission has been assigned to us. When we get to our destination, we'll see who's right. Until then, there's no point arguing about it."

"I agree with the captain," said Professor Marcus. "We should be focusing on the Neptune flyby. It may be years before another expedition comes out this far, so we need to take advantage of this opportunity to study the planet."

Professor Tower stood and headed toward his quarters, without saying another word.

Rachael watched as the professor vanished down the corridor. "What if he's right? Is there any possibility we're wrong, and we're alone in the universe?"

Andrew reached out and took Rachael's hand, squeezing it. "He's not right. My communications array will prove that to everyone's satisfaction."

"You seem so certain," said Kala, looking intently at Andrew. "How do you know?"

Andrew grinned. "Well, me and my colleagues wouldn't have built the array if we felt it would serve no purpose, now would we?"

Rachael laughed. "You people from Cal Tech have some of the strangest ideas."

Andrew didn't reply. He wondered what everyone would think when his array didn't just pick up one or two signals but tens of thousands. Of course the problem with the Druins still remained. If this solar system was quarantined, as the Imperials on Earth suspected, was there a defensive system as well to prevent a ship from leaving? Those questions wouldn't be answered until the ship reached the Kuiper Belt.

Time passed, and the *Endeavor* neared Neptune. Andrew was in the Command Center, using his array to scan the gas giant. Andrew knew the planet's atmosphere was composed primarily of hydrogen, helium, and methane gas. The methane gas absorbed the red light from the sun, making the planet look blue in color. A magnified view of the planet was currently on the main viewscreen.

However, what interested Andrew were the fourteen moons, which orbited the planet, including Triton, one of the largest moons in the Solar System. While the others were busy with their scientific scans of the planet and its moons, Andrew continued his search for any signs of Sanctuary. He was scanning for any communication signals, as well as signs of advanced technology.

For over two hours he sat at his console, scanning each individual moon with the same disheartening result. He found nothing to indicate an Imperial base had ever been in the Neptunian System.

"Detecting any radio signals?" asked Kala, who had just finished her observations. "You have a very intent look on your face." She came over and placed her hands possessively on Andrew's shoulders. "You also seem very tense."

Andrew shook his head. "No, nothing. I wasn't expecting to detect anything until we're farther out. However, I like to check, just in case I'm wrong. We don't want to miss anything."

"You're very thorough," said Kala, smiling approvingly. "I can definitely tell you've had scientific training."

Andrew didn't explain to Kala how that, with his Imperial training, he had the knowledge of at least six Earth degrees in various fields of study. He was still considering how he would explain all the signals the array would soon be picking up, without giving away too many of his secrets. The array was designed to penetrate any energy field the Druins might be using to block incoming signals to the Solar System. All Andrew knew for certain was that, when the signals started coming in, a lot of questions would be raised.

The *Endeavor* was past Neptune and on its way to the Kuiper Belt just outside the orbit of Neptune. The main part of the belt was composed of millions of small icy objects but also hundreds of thousands that were larger than one hundred kilometers. In addition to rocks and water ice, the objects in the belt contained other frozen compounds, like methane and ammonia. The destination of the ship was the edge of the main belt region, which was about fifty AUs from the Sun.

Andrew was in the common area, speaking to Lieutenant Thomas, when Kala came and sat down next to him.
"You're a very mysterious person," she said, blinking her eyes. "You don't speak much about your life before Cal Tech."
Andrew was surprised and looked at Kala. She sat so close to him that their legs touched. He wondered if she had done that on purpose. "Not much to talk about. I lived a pretty boring life."
Kala stared into Andrew's eyes. "I don't believe it could be that boring. Where were you raised?"
"I was born in Michigan and attended school in Grand Rapids."
"Have you ever been out of the country?"
Andrew wondered where this questioning was leading. "I've been to Europe."
"What about Cyprus?"
Now Andrew grew concerned. Cyprus was the island the Imperials had originally been marooned on. Why would Kala be asking about that? "Once my parents took me there right after I graduated from high school for our vacation. Why do you ask?"
Kala looked thoughtful. "My father is an archeologist and is working at a site on Cyprus. He claims he's working on a discovery that will change what we know of Human history."

Andrew felt a cold chill run over him. The Imperials had taken great pains to ensure no visible traces of them remained on the island. However, a cache of old books and artifacts were hidden deep inside a cave. The cave's entrance had been sealed up and hadn't been opened in years. Andrew wondered if there was any chance this could be what Kala's father was looking for. "Did he say what it is he's hoping to find?"

Kala shook her head. "No, just that it's so fantastic that no one will believe him until he's done with the excavation. My father's always been very secretive about his research."

Andrew wondered if he should send a message to Brett about Kala's father. After a moment he decided not to risk it, as Brett should already be aware if someone was digging around any of the ancient Imperial sites on Cyprus.

"Maybe he'll dig up a skeleton of a giant," suggested Thomas, the chief engineer, grinning widely. "Some say that back in our past a race of Humans stood over ten feet tall."

Kala frowned. "That's rubbish. All those stories have been disproved as hoaxes."

"Still it would be interesting to find something like that," continued Thomas unabashed. "Can you imagine what a race that tall would be like?"

"Clumsy and short-lived," said Kala, trying not to bite her lower lip.

"Just because someone's tall doesn't make them clumsy," protested Thomas.

"That's not what I meant," replied Kala. "In the distant past, being tall like that would make it more difficult to hide from predators."

"Like a saber-toothed tiger!" said Thomas, his eyes lighting up. "I wish we still had those."

Andrew was glad Thomas had changed the conversation. "Animals go extinct for a number of different reasons. Who knows what might have existed in the past. There are things about Earth we will probably never know."

Thomas looked thoughtful. "If we succeed in receiving messages from other civilizations, what do you think those worlds will be like? How different from us will aliens be? I mean, they won't be Human."

Kala looked at Andrew, waiting to hear his answer. She had a curious look on her face.

"It's hard to say," replied Andrew. How could he tell Thomas that over one thousand worlds in the galaxy were inhabited by Humans? There were also numerous races similar to Humans, while others were so alien that communication was nearly impossible. "We won't know until we get to meet them someday."

"So you think interstellar travel is possible?" asked Kala, raising her eyebrows.

Andrew leaned back. He had to be careful what he said. Kala was too sharp, and he didn't want to get her suspicious. "I'm sure if any civilizations are out there that some have surely solved the problem of traveling between the stars. As to what method they use, who knows? Perhaps, if we can communicate with them, we can find out."

"How would we communicate with them?" asked Kala, her eyes narrowing. "It would take years or possibly centuries for a message from us to reach them."

Andrew knew he had nearly slipped up. His own communications array on the *Endeavor* had a hyperlight receiver as well as a transmitter. Pausing, Andrew thought of his answer. "It might be far easier to build a hyperlight transmitter then a hyperlight space drive."

"Maybe," replied Kala doubtfully. "I still think breaking the speed of light will be a problem."

"Not if you go around it," answered Andrew. "Just like the Alcubierre Drive is supposed to."

Kala was silent as she thought that over. "I'll have to see the Alcubierre Drive work first before I believe in faster-than-light communications."

This didn't surprise Andrew. While technology on Earth had developed considerably in the last 150 years, they were still far behind what the technology in the Empire was or had been. He wondered what Kala would say if she knew an actual hyperlight transmitter and receiver were on the *Endeavor*. Of course Andrew would make sure that never happened.

On Earth, Professor Charles Wright worked on an excavation on the island of Cyprus on the side of a small mountain. The work was hot and tiring, but he felt he was very close to reaching his goal. In the valley below he had found signs of a very advanced civilization. The stonework and foundations of buildings uncovered were too far advanced for the time period they were built in. He found several clues in the valley excavation site that had led him to this mountainside, searching for a cave that supposedly led deep into the mountain.

"We've detected a possible cavity behind that rock wall where we're digging," reported Alan Foster, who was in charge of the small excavation team. "The only way we'll get inside is either to drill or to blast."

"How thick is the rock?" Professor Wright asked.

"Nearly four meters," replied Foster, wiping the sweat from his brow.

Charles stood gazing at the rock wall that separated him from proving his theory of what had once existed in this valley. "We have a permit to do some minor blasting to remove obstacles. Let's see if we can blast a hole through that wall of rock."

Foster nodded. "It will save us days of drilling, considering how difficult it would be to get the drilling equipment up here. Let me get Jose. He's responsible for setting demolition charges."

Charles watched as Foster went back down the mountain to get Jose Gutierrez, who had worked in the military as a demolitions expert and was very good at handling explosives.

While he waited, Charles reviewed some of the discoveries he had recently made. He had long suspected there had to be a reason for the sudden advances made in the Renaissance Period as well as in more recent Human history. Some of the advances seemed to have come out of the blue, with no sound reason for their discoveries. It was as if someone had stepped up to certain people and had helped them solve some of the dilemmas in their research or had helped them navigate through some of the more difficult parts. If a person knew what he was looking for, it was very evident that someone or some group for the last seven or eight hundred years had been guiding the Human race toward a technologically advanced civilization.

All the clues pointed to an advanced civilization of Humans living on Cyprus in the distant past. Where those Humans had gone to, Charles had no idea, though he strongly suspected some of them were still around, working in the background of many of the world's major universities and research centers. He had voiced his opinion to several colleagues to only be laughed at and then told how ridiculous he sounded. He had lost his teaching job at the university because of it. It had taken him nearly two years to raise the money to allow him to fly to Cyprus to see if his theories were correct. Now his vindication waited just beyond the stone wall in what he firmly believed was a cave. The artifacts he assumed were in that cave were what he was interested in.

Taking a drink of water, he waited for Foster and Jose to arrive. Looking upward, he wondered what his daughter was doing on the *Endeavor*. Since arriving at Cyprus, he had been out of touch with her, and he was becoming anxious to hear from her again.

–

After a few minutes Foster and Jose arrived with Jose carrying a small backpack. "Where's this wall I'm supposed to blast open?"

Charles pointed at the rock wall, where a few workers with picks and shovels stood. They had cleared a small area around the wall of rocks and other debris.

Jose walked up to the wall and spent a few moments examining it. "Are you sure it's only four meters thick?" He hit the wall a few times with a small rock hammer, knocking a chip off. He took a moment to examine the rock chip, determining what type of stone it was.

Foster nodded. "We took some readings to make sure. A large void space is behind it."

Jose ran his hands over the wall and then turned toward Charles. "It will take several sets of charges to knock a hole in this wall. The material is very strong. I'll blast out a hole in the center to begin with and then set the main directional charge inside the hole. That should allow the explosive to crack open the rock wall."

Charles nodded. "Let's do it. I'm anxious to see what's inside."

Jose, along with the two workers, drilled small holes in the rock wall to set the first charges.

"We better get back down the mountainside," suggested Foster. "We don't know what blasting here might do. There could be a rockslide."

Looking one last time at the rock wall, Charles headed down the mountain. The path was a little treacherous, with small boulders and areas of loose gravel. After about fifteen minutes they were down where the tents of their base camp were set up.

"They're ready for the first blasts," Foster reported to Charles, having spoken with Jose over the handheld radio.

"Do it," ordered Charles, who looked expectantly back up the mountain.

Suddenly a loud explosion echoed through the valley, and dust and smoke could be seen on the mountainside. After a few minutes the smoke cleared.

"Jose is setting the next series of charges. He says the rock is split pretty well, and this set should penetrate to the cave."

Charles nodded. Every minute he came closer to his goal. He could hardly wait to get inside the cave. Looking around, he studied the excavation site in the valley. At one time a large settlement had been here. A very advanced settlement for its time. Carbon dating the site had indicated that those people had lived in this valley for nearly five hundred years before the settlement was abandoned. Charles suspected it was due to the eruptions and the earthquakes caused by nearby Mount Etna.

Another set of explosions on the mountain drew his attention. Looking up to where he knew the cave was, he spotted another cloud of smoke and dust rising.

"Jose reports the entrance is open," Foster informed Charles. "He says to be careful coming back up, as the explosions caused more gravel and small rocks to slide down."

"Get some men together and lights. I want to see what's inside that cave."

It took a while to get everything together, but finally Charles started back up the slope of the mountain, heading toward the cave. It was tiring going up the steep slope, but eventually he made it. Coming to a stop, he saw a narrow entrance in the stone wall.

"Get some men clearing out this rubble," ordered Charles. "I don't want anything falling on us." Charles waited impatiently as men worked, clearing the rubble, and making sure the cave entrance was safe to enter.

Finally Foster turned toward Charles. "It's safe now. I'll get some lights and we can go in."

Charles waited as Foster dug some handheld lights from a backpack. He handed one to Charles and kept one for himself, gesturing toward the cave entrance. "This is your discovery. I'll follow you."

Stepping up to the cave entrance, Charles wiggled his way inside until he stood in a narrow tunnel. Looking around with his light, he could see this was not a natural cave. Someone had dug it through the hard rock into the side of the mountain. Charles waited until Foster and several other men joined him. "Let's go. What we want is deeper inside."

Walking down the tunnel, Charles studied the cave walls. The walls looked as if they had been chiseled smooth as well as the floor. There was no sand or loose rock. They walked about forty yards when the tunnel suddenly widened into a large chamber.

"Let me get some brighter lights set up so we can see better," said Foster, as he gestured toward several of the men to open the packs they carried. After a few minutes the portable lights were set up, and the chamber was lit up.

Charles felt the breath catch in his throat. This was much more than he had imagined. The walls of the chamber were covered in writings and paintings. He stepped over to one wall in disbelief. It was covered in complicated mathematical equations. Walking along the wall, he recognized chemical formulas, physics equations, mathematical formulas, and numerous other scientific descriptions of various processes. He finally came to a stop at a series of paintings on the wall. He couldn't believe his eyes. The first picture showed a massive spacecraft with people descending a ramp, carrying crates of supplies. The next showed the spacecraft gone, and a large camp of tents set up.

Moving along the wall, he found another group of paintings. This showed aliens shooting Humans with some type of energy weapon. Other paintings showed spacecraft battling one another in space.

"What does all this mean?" asked Foster, as his eyes roamed over the walls and the paintings.

Charles took a deep breath. "We'll have to call in some other scientists, as well as the government. This is far more than what I expected."

Walking along the wall, Charles was surprised to find a large stone sarcophagus. "Help me open this."

"What if this is someone's tomb?" asked Alan Foster.

"It's not. I'm certain of that. Let's get it open!"

Foster gestured to several of the men, and between them they shoved off the heavy lid. A hissing noise was heard as the lid came off.

"The damn thing was in a partial vacuum!" exclaimed Foster in amazement.

Charles shone his light inside, and he stopped breathing. The sarcophagus was full of books! Extremely old books from the look of them. "I don't want anyone to touch these until we get some experts in here. Let's put the lid back on this sarcophagus, and then let's leave this cave. I need to make some phone calls. We've just made the greatest discovery of the century, if not of the ages. I want two armed guards placed at the entrance. No one is to enter without my permission."

Charles could hardly wait to call Kala on the *Endeavor* and tell her what he had found. He had been vindicated, and soon the entire world would know of his discovery.

—

Foster followed Charles outside of the cave. The entire team went back down the mountain to base camp, where Charles could make his calls with his satellite phone. Foster sent two of his most trusted men up to the cave entrance to stand guard. He watched as Charles hurried to his tent to retrieve his phone. While Charles was busy doing that, Foster made his way to his own tent and retrieved a small communication device.

"Brett, this is Alan. Professor Wright found the cave. He's already been inside, and he's seen the writings and the paintings on the wall. He found the books as well. It won't take him long to figure out some of us are still around if he doesn't suspect already."

"Don't reveal yourself to him," ordered Brett. "Continue to play along, as you have. I'll meet with the Imperial Council to discuss our next move. We don't want to do anything until we hear from Andrew."

"As you wish," replied Alan. "I'll stay here and keep an eye on things."

Alan ended the call and took in a deep breath. Things on Earth were about to get extremely interesting, and he would be right in the middle of it.

Chapter Seven

The *Endeavor* continued to the outskirts of the Solar System, reaching the beginning of the Kuiper Belt. Tensions were high in the ship, as they were far beyond any hope of possible rescue if anything went wrong. Andrew continued to use the array to scan the region of space around the *Endeavor* for signs of Sanctuary. He knew it had to be somewhere; he just couldn't find it. It was possibly on the far side of the Solar System, and that was why his instruments were failing to locate it.

Kala sat at her console, watching Andrew. She was curious as to why he spent so much time at his console, monitoring his computer screens.

She had recently received a message from her father, and if what he said was true, much of Human history would have to be rewritten. It had also raised some serious questions about Andrew and his unusually advanced communications array. Several times when she had spoken to Andrew, she had the distinct feeling he was hiding something. She wondered if her father's discovery had something to do with what Andrew was keeping secret.

"Still no luck in your search?" asked Kala.

Andrew looked startled and slowly turned to face Kala. "No, I believe we need to go out another few AUs and then we should pick up some signals."

"Signals from other civilizations?" mused Kala, looking at Rachael. "What do you think?"

"It's what we came out here for. We still have several days of travel time ahead of us before we reach the region of space the scientists back on Earth felt we should be able to receive signals."

"When we hear nothing, we can go home," grumbled Professor Tower. He was in the Command Center, using one of the ship's scanners to take some readings on some of the objects in the Kuiper Belt. "I'll recommend the *Endeavor* be reconfigured to go to Jupiter. The moons of Jupiter offer a vast opportunity for new resources, plus the four larger moons can be colonized."

"What if we pick up signals?" asked Kala. She knew for some reason Andrew avoided getting into arguments on this subject, as if he knew something everyone else didn't. The mystery that surrounded Andrew was a magnet that drew Kala to him.

Professor Tower laughed. "It won't happen. We've wasted our time coming out this far. I've already sent a message back to Earth, requesting that the *Endeavor* make a slow flyby of Jupiter on our way back."

Captain Greer looked at the professor with a frown. "Any suggestions in changing the parameters of our mission should be run by me first, Professor Tower."

The professor didn't reply but left the Command Center, as if insulted.

"How did he ever get on board this ship?" asked Kala with a deep frown.

"Politics," replied Captain Greer. "Numerous people in our government want to see us fail. If we detect any signals, it will have massive ramifications for our world. Many don't want to see the changes it would cause."

Kala didn't reply. If what her father had told her was true, things would change anyway. Her eyes returned to Andrew, wondering if he knew what was in the excavation her father had found.

Andrew sat in his quarters, reading, when a hesitant knock came on his door. "Enter."

The door opened, and Kala stood there. She wore standard ship clothing, but her blouse seemed a little tighter than normal, and one of the top buttons was undone, showing a little cleavage. Andrew let out a deep sigh. Kala had been coming on to him for weeks, and he found it harder every day to resist her charms. She was a good-looking woman, and she knew it.

"Hello, Andrew," said Kala, coming in and shutting the door behind her. "Can we talk?"

"Sure, have a seat." Andrew gestured to one of the two chairs in his quarters. He sat down in one and Kala in the other. "What can I do for you?"

Kala hesitated. Andrew could tell she was uncertain about what to say.

"I received a message from my father yesterday," she began, looking strangely at Andrew.

Andrew felt a cold chill sweep over him. "Is this about his excavations on Cyprus?"

"Yes, he found a cave, and what's inside is more than he had dreamed of. He says it will change Human history."

Andrew forced out the words. "What did he find?"

Kala's eyes narrowed. "Evidence of Humans from another world who came to Cyprus around one thousand years ago. He believes they have been manipulating Human history."

Andrew remained silent. He needed to get a message off to Brett and let him know of this development, if he didn't already. If word of such a discovery were to get out, it might cause an immediate response from the Druins. A response the Earth was not prepared for. "What do you believe?"

"I don't know. My father sounds pretty certain."

"If what your father says is true, what happened to those people?"

Kala looked directly at Andrew. "He believes they're still among us. He also thinks there is a good chance one of them is on this mission."

Andrew felt his breath catch in his throat. "Is that why you came to see me? Do you believe I'm one of these mysterious space people?"

"I don't know," admitted Kala, her gaze focused on Andrew. "Your array is far more advanced than it should be. I haven't mentioned that to anyone else. I've watched you for weeks working with it. It's as if you're searching for something. Something you haven't found, and it's not messages from space."

"What if I were one of these space people?" asked Andrew carefully. "What would you do?" Andrew suspected Kala had already guessed the truth about him and was only here to confirm it.

Kala closed her eyes and slowly opened them. "I don't know. I suppose I would have to tell Captain Greer."

"What if my mission involved the fate of the entire Solar System?"

Kala shivered. Was this an admission of who Andrew was? "If you had a reason for being on this ship, and if it was important, I would be willing to listen." Kala could feel her heart pounding in her chest. She had developed feelings for Andrew since she had first met him on Earth during training. She had tried to keep those feelings to herself, but she still found herself strangely drawn to the man.

Andrew stood and stepped closer to Kala. "Give me two more days and then we'll talk again. I'm not saying that you're right, but at that time my array will prove other civilizations are out there. Once I've done that then I'll tell you everything."

Kala stood. She knew she would give Andrew those two days. "Very well, two days. And, if I'm not satisfied with your explanations, I'll talk to the captain." They stood very close together. Kala was extremely aware of his presence.

"We'll talk to her together," said Andrew, stepping forward and pulling Kala into his arms. His lips met hers in a gentle kiss.

Kala knew, at that moment, she would do anything she could to help Andrew. She pulled free and looked up into his eyes. "I better go before this gets out of hand." Kala opened the door and fled down the corridor. She couldn't believe she had let Andrew kiss her.

Andrew watched the door shut. He wondered if he had made a mistake. He had allowed Kala's charms to get the best of him. Going to his locker, he removed what looked like a simple laptop.

In actuality it was a hyperlight communicator, which he could use to contact Brett, who was on the Imperial Council on Earth. Brett needed to know about these latest developments involving Kala's father.

Rachael saw Kala emerge from Andrew's quarters and hurry down the corridor to vanish into her own room. Rachael wondered what was going on. She knew Kala was highly interested in Andrew, but Rachael was also certain that Andrew would not take advantage of the situation. She hoped she was right.

Two days later the *Endeavor* reached its planned destination in the Kuiper Belt. Everyone who could was in the Command Center, waiting for Andrew to turn on his communications array and to scan for alien communication signals. The ship had come to a stop and held its position a few thousand kilometers from a small field of icy remnants.

"We're ready," said Captain Greer, looking expectantly at Andrew.

Andrew took a deep breath. They were far enough out that, even if a Druin field prevented hyperlight communications from getting through to Earth, his array would now penetrate it. "Activating the array."

Professor Tower laughed. "What a waste of time and money. Let's get this over with so we can go home and do some real research."

"Quiet, Professor," said Kala, glaring at the older man. "Let's see what happens."

Almost instantly the communications screens lit up with tens of thousands of communication intercepts. "Confirmed communications from outside the Solar System," said Andrew, watching the faces of the others.

"What! Impossible!" uttered Professor Tower, his face turning pale. "You must be reading something wrong. Your array must be picking up communication signals from Earth!"

The Forgotten Empire: Banishment

Andrew reached forward and pressed an icon on one of the screens. Instantly the screen changed to show a view of an alien speaking. The alien looked like a cross between a praying mantis and a lizard.

"What trickery is this!" screamed Tower. "You've set this all up. That's not real. It's some video you've loaded on your computer!"

"No, he hasn't," said Rachael in a calm voice. "My instruments are showing the same thing. What the array is picking up is coming from outside the Solar System."

Captain Greer took a deep breath. "Can you tell how many different civilizations we're dealing with?"

This was a momentous event. They now knew they were not alone in the universe. The captain also knew it was her duty to gather as much information as possible about these communications. As soon as she was satisfied with what they were receiving, she would send a message back to the space station near the Moon. She could feel her heart racing as she realized the magnitude of this discovery.

Andrew nodded. "Just a moment. I'll have to make some adjustments to the array. The computer system it's connected to will analyze and give us a number as to how many different languages it's detecting."

The crew grew silent as they waited. Everyone knew this was a massive discovery and one that would drastically change how people thought of the Solar System but also how they thought about a lot of other related matters.

Andrew waited as the system analyzed the different messages. He also watched another screen for any signs of Druin interference. There was no doubt in his mind now. If a Druin presence was in the Kuiper Belt, they were now aware of the *Endeavor*'s presence. The computer finished its analysis, and a number appeared on the screen. "The computer confirmed 22,716 different languages."

Professor Tower glared at the computer and then turned around and left the Command Center.

"So, what now?" asked Professor Adrian Marcus. "We've just proven the galaxy is full of life, most of it probably much more advanced than we are."

Professor Crayton smiled. "We stay here and record as much of this as possible. We try to determine where some of these messages are coming from. Once we return to Earth, the linguists can try to decipher these messages and see what languages are the most common. We have a lot of work ahead of us for the next few days or even weeks. The number of messages we're receiving is far more than anyone expected. It appears our galaxy is heavily populated with intelligent species, and many of them are talking to one another."

"Something I don't understand," said Lieutenant Commander Meadows. "Why couldn't we detect any of these messages on Earth? With so many? A few should have gotten through."

"There has to be some type of interference," suggested Professor Marcus. She looked around at the others in the Command Center. "There must be some interference field that's preventing the messages from reaching Earth. That's why we came out this far. Many of the scientists I'm associated with believe it's some field generated by the sun."

"What if it's something artificial?" asked Lieutenant Mindy Suarez from her navigation console. "If it is, who put it in place?"

Captain Greer frowned and then she spoke. "We don't know if it's artificial, but I think it would be wise if we keep a careful watch on our sensors to see if we can pick up anything else. For all we know, this could be some field generated by our sun, like Professor Marcus has suggested. This field prevents the messages from reaching us, and by traveling out this far, we have passed through it."

"I don't think the sun is doing this," commented Rachael. "If it was, we would have detected the field years ago. No, I believe it must be something artificial. Perhaps put here by an advanced race to keep our system isolated, until we are ready for contact with other advanced civilizations."

"I don't believe that," said Professor Crayton. "I tend to believe it's a field generated by our sun. That's the most logical explanation."

Captain Greer looked at Lieutenant Morrison. "Keep a close watch on those sensors. If you so much as see anything that might be out of the ordinary, I want to know immediately."

Morrison nodded and returned his attention to his sensor console. "Everything's quiet so far. All we have on sensors are some hunks of rock and ice, plus a few small comets."

Kala looked at Andrew. She had noticed that he was not in the least bit surprised about the number of messages the ship had detected. It was as if he had suspected or already knew what the array would find. She wondered if she should say something. Watching Andrew, she saw him slowly shake his head.

This only confirmed to Kala that he did know something. She wondered now if he was one of these mysterious people her father believed were manipulating the Human race on Earth. Once she had an opportunity to get him alone, she was determined to find out the truth.

A few million kilometers away a small Druin observation station had recorded the approach of the *Endeavor* and transmitted the contact information to one of the eight larger stations in orbit around this star system. Once the message had been sent, the observation station continued to track the small spacecraft. The larger station would determine what response needed to be taken. This system was under quarantine, and no ship must leave it or enter it.

The AI on the larger station analyzed the message from the observation station and then searched its command imperatives to see how the situation should be handled. It found the necessary instructions and then set about complying with its orders. A large hatch on the station opened, and a small attack drone was launched. It would take the drone about six hours to reach its target and destroy it. Satisfied it had taken care of the potential problem, the AI went back to monitoring the rest of the observation stations in its section of space. The AI also decided that, for now, it was not necessary to send a hyperlight message to the Druins, informing them of the situation. The scans from the observation station indicated the spacecraft was quite primitive by galactic standards.

On board the *Endeavor* Andrew watched one of his screens, which was a highly developed Imperial sensor. It was currently set to long-range, searching for any signs of Druin activity. It only took a few moments after he activated the sensor before alarms went off.

"What's that?" asked Captain Greer, seeing the flashing red light on the console and hearing the alarm that sounded.

"We've been detected by the beings who set up the interference field around the Solar System," replied Andrew. No point keeping anything secret now. The *Endeavor* had no chance of surviving the encounter with the attack drone the Druin station had just launched. Andrew looked at Kala. "The beings are called Druins and are one of seven older races who control most of the galaxy. The *Endeavor* has been detected by their surveillance system, and an attack drone has been launched to deal with our ship. It will arrive in approximately six hours. We have no defense against it."

Dead silence met Andrew's words. Everyone except Kala looked at him like he had gone nuts.

"How do you know this?" demanded Captain Greer, her gaze focused sharply on Andrew.

"It's complicated. My people have known about the Druins and the possible existence of this surveillance system for many years."

"Are these the same aliens who marooned your people on Earth over a thousand years ago?" asked Kala.

Andrew hesitated and then nodded. "Yes, and they are quite ruthless. They will show no mercy and won't hesitate to kill everyone on this ship."

"I'm confused," said Captain Greer. She looked at Kala. "Are you saying that what Mr. Wilcox just said is all true and that his family comes from another world?"

Kala nodded. "Yes, my father is excavating a site on Cyprus and what he has found confirms everything Andrew just said. It wasn't just Andrew's family who was marooned there but many more."

Captain Greer looked at Andrew. "Why did you not speak up before? Now the ship is in danger if your statement from earlier is true."

"Would you have believed me?"

Greer slowly shook her head. "I'm still not certain that I do. However, all those alien messages we're picking up tells me to at least consider your story."

"Captain, I'm detecting a small artificial structure just over two million kilometers from us," reported Lieutenant Morrison. "It's definitely not anything I'm familiar with."

"Andrew is telling the truth," said Kala, a pleading look in her eyes. "If we want to survive, we need to ask him what to do."

Captain Greer looked from Kala and then back to Andrew. "I have no idea what's going on. What I am concerned about is the safety of this ship." Greer spent several long moments thinking about her options. "Mr. Wilcox, do you have any suggestions?"

Andrew took a deep breath. The *Endeavor* couldn't evade a Druin attack drone. The best they could hope to do was put some distance between it and the *Endeavor* to delay the inevitable for as long as possible. "Run," replied Andrew. "Turn the ship around and accelerate as hard as possible. We can't outrun the drone, but there is a very small possibility I can call for help."

"Call who?" asked Lieutenant Commander Meadows. "None of our ships are anywhere close to us. We're out farther than anyone else has been before."

Andrew looked at Meadows. "The people I'll try to call are not from Earth."

Andrew turned back to his console and set it to broadcast a hyperlight message. He used the array to broadcast the message toward a major portion of the asteroid field on this side of the sun. If Sanctuary was hidden inside one of those asteroids, just maybe they would receive his message. If not, then they were all doomed. He also made sure the signal wasn't too strong to avoid any Druin stations possibly detecting it. The signal would fade out after it passed through the asteroid zone.

The *Endeavor* turned and accelerated back into the Solar System. The ship quickly reached its top acceleration of four Gs and fled from the Kuiper Belt. Behind it, the Druin attack drone took note of the changing position of its target. It would do no good. The drone increased its own speed, accelerating to ten Gs. It wouldn't take long to run down its quarry and then a fusion energy beam would make short work of it.

On board the *Endeavor*, the crew waited tensely as the ship fled through space. Lieutenant Morrison had finally detected the Druin attack drone on his sensors.

"The damn thing is coming fast. We can't escape it."

"Well, that confirms Andrew is telling the truth," said Kala. "What do we do now?"

"What weapons will this drone have?" asked Captain Greer. She was still having a hard time accepting what was happening.

"The drone will be equipped with a fusion energy beam which will tear right through the hull of this ship. It may also be equipped with antimatter missiles. If one of those explodes anywhere near the ship, it will vaporize the entire vessel."

"Andrew, is there anything we can do?" asked Rachael.

Andrew knew the odds of any of them surviving was growing smaller with every passing moment. "The only thing I can recommend is to evacuate the ship. Use the escape pods and leave the vessel before the drone reaches us. Once the pods are clear of the ship, they should cut power and wait. After a few hours it should be safe to restore power."

"We can't survive in the pods for long," pointed out Lieutenant Williams. "They're designed for short-term survival. At the most we can expect to survive for seventy-two hours before the power runs out."

"If we stay on board the ship, we'll all be dead long before that," replied Andrew.

Captain Greer drew in a deep breath. "Mr. Wilcox, these people you attempted to contact. Has there been any response?"

Andrew shook his head. "No, I wouldn't expect there to be any. They don't want the Druins to learn of their presence."

"So we have a choice," said Lieutenant Commander Meadows, looking at the sensor screen, showing the rapidly approaching Druin attack drone. "We evacuate the ship, giving us a very remote chance of rescue, or we stay on the ship and die. I say we evacuate and take our chances on being rescued by Mr. Wilcox's friends."

"They may not exist," warned Andrew. "It's just a slim possibility someone may still be out here."

"A slight chance is better than none," replied Meadows, looking at the captain.

"This is sheer madness," said Professor Tower who had returned to the Command Center. "I say we stay on the ship. Surely the vessel approaching us can be reasoned with."

Andrew shook his head. "The Druins cannot be reasoned with. Besides, no biological entities are on the attack drone. It is controlled by computers and will not deviate from its orders."

The captain knew Meadows was right in suggesting they evacuate. "I'll stay on the ship, and anyone who wants to use the escape pods can do so. If I can talk this drone out of attacking, I'll come back and pick up all of you. If I don't return then you will know the *Endeavor* has been destroyed. If anyone wants to stay on the ship, I'll leave that decision up to you."

"I'll stay," said Lieutenant Suarez. "You'll need someone to fly the ship."

A few others volunteered to stay on board as well. Overall sixteen members of the ship's complement decided to take their chances in the escape pods. Some of the crew, including a few of the scientists, decided to stay on board. Professor Tower was one of the scientists who was staying on the *Endeavor*.

"You're fools for leaving the ship. I'm sure we can negotiate with this drone if it is even real."

"It's real," said Lieutenant Morrison. "I'm tracking it on the ship's sensors."

Professor Tower shook his head. "I'll believe it when I see it on the ship's viewscreens. For all we know, this is some fancy trick Mr. Wilcox has dreamed up."

"I assure you it is not," replied Andrew. This entire encounter was rapidly spinning out of control.

"Stand by to evacuate the ship," ordered Captain Greer. "Considering how quickly the attack drone is closing on the *Endeavor*, we need to launch the escape pods within the next hour. During that time I want to load the pods with extra batteries, food, air, and water. If we do that, we can double the amount of time the pods will remain functional. It will also give me more time to recover them if we find the evacuation was unnecessary."

Everyone rushed to load the necessary supplies in the escape pods. At least one ship's officer was assigned to each one.

Andrew found himself assigned to pod number three along with Kala, Rachael, and Professor Adrian Marcus.

"We have twenty minutes until we're ejected from the *Endeavor*," said Rachael, as she stowed the last of the supplies.

"We'll be in tight quarters, but it can't be helped. These pods were designed in case something drastic happened to the *Endeavor*. They have a small ion drive and a few thrusters but little else."

Time passed as they finished stowing everything securely in the pod, and then the comm system activated.

"Attention all escape pods," announced Captain Greer. "The attack drone is still on an intercept course. We will make contact as soon as the pods are ejected. I would recommend that all pods move away from the *Endeavor*'s current course for ten minutes and then shut down. Everyone will wear spacesuits. Those suits are good to keep you alive for nearly twelve hours. Allow at least six hours to pass and then reactivate the pod's power systems. Hopefully by then I'll either be coming back to pick you up or the attack drone will be out of range. Good luck and I hope to see all of you soon."

Rachael shut the hatch, sealing them all in. Four acceleration couches were in each pod, with just enough room to move around to operate the pod's controls. Most of their time in the pod would be spent in the acceleration couches.

"Stand by for ejection!" said Captain Greer over the comm. "Ten seconds."

"Hold tight," ordered Rachael, as she checked her safety harness.

The lights in the small cabin suddenly flashed red and a loud popping noise came. All four of the people in the pod felt a sudden burst of acceleration, which pushed them back into the acceleration couches. After a few moments the acceleration came to an end.

"Stand by for ion drive activation," said Rachael, as she pressed several icons on her computer screen. "We will do a ten-minute burn and then shut down all our systems."

Andrew felt the ion drive kick in. The acceleration was slight, as it pushed them away from the *Endeavor* at one quarter of normal Earth gravity in acceleration. For ten minutes the drive moved them away from the ship, and then it shut down.

"What now?" asked Kala, concern in her voice. "This isn't exactly how I planned on spending today."

"We wait," said Andrew. "The attack drone has been programmed to attack and to destroy the *Endeavor*. There's a good chance it will ignore all of the pods."

Professor Marcus looked at Andrew. "What are the chances of your friends rescuing us?"

Andrew had been thinking about the same thing. If Sanctuary was on this side of the sun, there was a reasonable chance they had received his message. If they were on the far side of the sun then Andrew and the rest in the pods were on their own. "About one in ten. All we can do is wait."

Professor Marcus nodded. "We all knew this could be a dangerous mission. We just didn't expect to encounter aliens."

"I hate spacesuits," muttered Kala. She looked through her helmet at the others. "Did anyone bring a deck of cards?"

Andrew grinned. At least Kala still had her sense of humor. Now their survival depended on Sanctuary existing and if they were willing to risk sending a rescue ship.

Chapter Eight

Captain Greer sat in her command chair, staring at the sensor screen now showing a red icon rapidly approaching the *Endeavor*. It moved far faster than the *Endeavor* could at its top speed.

"Seven minutes until contact," reported Lieutenant Morrison uneasily.

"Sending first contact message," added Lieutenant Commander Meadows, who had taken over the communications console. The first contact message had been designed just in case the *Endeavor* found aliens on their mission, though that possibility had been deemed extremely low to nonexistent.

"Putting the alien vessel on the viewscreen," said Lieutenant Williams from his engineering console. "This is at our highest magnification."

On the ship's main viewscreen, a bulbous vessel appeared, with several weapon turrets and numerous small hatches.

"The alien drone is twenty meters in length and is not slowing down," said Lieutenant Morrison.

Captain Greer looked at Lieutenant Commander Meadows. "Any response to the first contact message?"

Meadows shook his head.

"Five minutes to contact," reported Lieutenant Morrison. "Several hatches have opened on the drone."

An hour earlier Captain Greer had sent a brief report back to the space station on their discoveries and the possible attack on the *Endeavor* by an alien drone. Due to the time lag, the drone would reach them before any reply was possible.

Inside the Druin drone, the ship's main computer analyzed the incoming message and chose to ignore it. Its mission was very simple. Destroy the intruding vessel. It had opened two hatches containing antimatter missiles. The drone was also powering up one of its fusion projectors. From the current range to the intruding vessel, it was evident the vessel was not protected by any energy shield. The drone's sensors also could not detect any weapons on the vessel. This would be an easy kill and then the drone would return to its base and report a successful mission.

The drone had detected several smaller vessels exiting the ship earlier. Analysis had indicated these were most likely escape pods of some type. Sensor scans had shown they did not have sufficient power or life support to save the few crewmembers they contained, so the computer had decided annihilating the small escape pods didn't warrant the energy expenditure to destroy them. In a few days any surviving crewmembers inside the escape crafts would be dead.

Studying the enemy craft in front of it, the drone decided to simply use one of its fusion beams. The beam should easily cut through the thin hull of the ship, and it would take only a few shots to destroy the vessel.

"I'm getting an energy spike from the alien drone," warned Lieutenant Morrison. "I think it's getting ready to fire."

"Close all hatches," ordered Captain Greer. "Lieutenant Commander Meadows, send a message saying that we surrender."

Meadows looked at the captain in surprise and then did as ordered. "No reply, Captain."

Captain Greer leaned back in her command chair. There was nothing else she could do. She couldn't believe their mission would end like this.

"All hatches are shut," confirmed Lieutenant Williams.

"What's happening!" demanded Professor Tower. "Why won't they respond? They're obviously intelligent. Captain Greer, you must do something!"

"They have come to destroy us just as Mr. Wilcox said," replied Captain Greer, wishing she could do something more. "We can't outrun them, and we're unarmed. We're at their mercy."

"They won't fire on us," proclaimed Professor Tower. "I still believe this is all some alien simulation rigged by Wilcox. That ship is not really there."

"Massive energy buildup," reported Lieutenant Morrison, trying to sound calm. "They're firing."

On the screen, a blue beam of energy shot out from one of the drone's turrets, striking the *Endeavor* near the crew's quarters. The ship shook violently, and alarms sounded.

"Still think it's all fake?" demanded Lieutenant Commander Meadows.

Tower did not reply. His face had turned as white as a ghost.

"Major damage to the ship," reported Lieutenant Williams, as he checked his engineering console. "We have six compartments open to space, and we're bleeding atmosphere. Power is failing."

"They're firing again!"

The *Endeavor* shook violently. Several secondary explosions rattled the ship, and the lights dimmed. Several consoles stopped functioning.

"We just lost propulsion," reported Williams. "I can't detect anything in the back half of the ship. I don't believe it's there anymore."

"We're going to die!" screamed Professor Tower. "Do something!"

Captain Greer closed her eyes and then slowly opened them. "There is nothing we can do. They came here to kill us, and that's exactly what they're going to do."

"They're firing again," reported Morrison, as he closed his eyes.

Greer took a deep breath. This was it. The ship shook violently, and the Command Center seemed to erupt in fire.

—

The *Endeavor* was shaken by more explosions, and then blew apart in one final blast, hurling flaming wreckage in all directions.

—

The computer in the drone scanned the wreckage, determining there were no survivors, and the ship was no longer functional. It had been blown into thousands of small pieces. Reversing on its axis, the drone headed back toward its base to make its report. The threat had been eliminated, and now the AI at the base would decide if any more steps were necessary.

Andrew was in his acceleration couch, thinking. The escape pod was still powered down, and they were surviving on the life support from their spacesuits.

"Do you think the *Endeavor* managed to escape?" asked Rachael.

Andrew shook his head. "No, once the drone has a target, the drone must then destroy its target. Nothing prevents it from carrying out its orders. Unfortunately the *Endeavor* had no weapons, and even if it did, it couldn't destroy the drone. The drone is protected by an energy shield, and none of the weapons so far developed on Earth would be a threat to it."

Kala looked long and hard at Andrew. She knew that Andrew must be part of the group of advanced Humans who were manipulating the technological development on Earth. "Andrew, I know from what my father has told me who you are and what your people have been doing on Earth. Perhaps it's time to enlighten Rachael and Professor Marcus."

Andrew let out a deep sigh. "I guess it doesn't matter that much anymore. If we're rescued, you'll know the truth anyway. And, if we're not, then what I'm about to tell you will die with us."

For the next several hours Andrew told the other three the complete story about the Human Empire and the Royals and their close friends and family stranded on Earth. Andrew explained how a core group had kept intact the knowledge from the Empire and had passed it down from generation to generation. When he was nearly finished, he told them about Sanctuary.

Professor Marcus slowly shook her head. "Andrew, this all sounds so fantastic. If not for the *Endeavor* detecting the Druin drone, I don't know if I would have believed it. It's hard to imagine that over one thousand Human worlds are out in the galaxy."

"There are," replied Andrew. "And they are all much more advanced than Earth, though, at the present time, they are under the rule of the Confederation. Personal freedom on those worlds will have been limited, and research into many fields banned."

"My dad found the ruins of Andrew's people on Cyprus," explained Kala. "All Andrew just told us is revealed in paintings on a cave wall. There are advanced mathematical equations and scientific proofs there too. Also paintings of advanced spacecraft battling each other and eventually ships coming to Earth. Father found a treasure trove of books in a stone sarcophagus."

Rachael looked at Andrew. "Do you believe this Sanctuary is out here?"

Andrew hesitated for a long moment. "Maybe. If it's not, then everything we've tried to do on Earth will be a waste. At some point in Earth's development, the scientists will discover a faster-than-light drive. Once the Druin stations monitoring the Solar System detect a ship leaving the system, the AI in charge will notify the Druins for instructions. It's very likely the Druins will instruct the stations to launch their attack drones and use antimatter weapons to drastically reduce Earth's population."

Professor Marcus looked stunned. "But why?"

"It's how the seven races controlling the majority of our galaxy operate. No other race can be allowed to become a threat. That's what the Human Empire did, and the Druins were sent to put us in our place. They wiped out our fleet, destroyed many of our cities, and executed all the leaders in our government, as well as part of the Royal Family."

Kala asked the next question. "Why is this Sanctuary so important?"

"My people believe it's inside a major asteroid or even a moon around one of the outer planets. Our people managed to build a secret base there, in case one of the seven races attacked the Empire. The base is capable of building spacecraft. Or I should say, advanced warships. They've had over one thousand years to build a fleet. Someday we'll retake our Empire and free the hundreds of Human worlds under control of the Confederation."

"You want Earth to be a part of that, don't you?" asked Kala accusingly. "You want us to become a part of your war."

Andrew nodded. "Yes, we'll need people. You must understand, the Confederation considers all Humans to be under their control, including Earth. As long as Earth remained primitive, it was not a threat, but that's changing rapidly now. Even if my people had not interfered, the Druins would have come eventually."

"So what do we do now?" asked Rachael. She hated being confined inside the spacesuit. She wasn't claustrophobic, but being cooped up in one for six hours or more in a small escape pod wasn't exactly her idea of how to spend a pleasant stress-free day.

Andrew let out a deep sigh. "We wait and hope my message reached Sanctuary. Even if it did, there's a chance they might not respond for fear of revealing themselves."

"Then we may die in this pod?" asked Kala. It meant she would never see her father again.

"Let's hope not," replied Andrew. "I suggest we all get some rest. It's better to sleep in these pods, as it will conserve energy and life support."

Time passed with all four of them trying to sleep. It was difficult, and sleep came in short naps only. Finally, six hours had passed since the escape pod had been ejected from the *Endeavor*. Rachael reached forward and turned the power back on in the pod. It would take a few minutes for the now functioning life support system to bring the temperature back up and to raise the air pressure in the small cabin.

Finally a green light came on, and Rachael tentatively removed her helmet and then smiled. "It's safe."

The other three quickly took off their helmets, and they all sat here, looking at one another.

"What now?" asked Kala. She looked at Andrew. "I don't suppose you have some futuristic communication device with you?"

Andrew laughed. He pulled out his laptop from a small case he had brought with him. "How did you know?"

Everyone looked at Andrew in astonishment as he activated his laptop.

"Even if you can send a message, it will take hours to reach Earth from here," said Rachael.

Andrew shook his head. "No, this uses hyperlight technology. Communication between here and Earth will be instantaneous."

Professor Marcus's eyes widened. "That means all those messages we were receiving on the *Endeavor* were real time?"

"Close," replied Andrew. "Some of the messages, due to the distance involved, were probably delayed by a few minutes or maybe a little more."

Andrew pressed the Transmit icon on his laptop and waited patiently for an acknowledgment. For nearly ten minutes the little icon continued to blink, and then it changed to Connection Verified. Andrew activated the small speaker on the laptop, so everyone could hear what he said and could also hear the response.

"Major Henderson, this is Andrew. Can you hear me?"

"Loud and clear," replied the voice over the laptop. "Is there a problem?"

Andrew took a deep breath. "I can confirm a Druin interdiction system surrounds the entire Solar System. The *Endeavor* was attacked and destroyed by a Druin attack drone.

When we became of aware of the drone, I informed Captain Greer of the situation. Part of the crew elected to stay on the ship and attempted to outrun the drone. The rest of the crew were ejected into space in four of the ship's escape pods. I'm currently in one of the pods with Rachael Newberry, Kala Wright, and Professor Adrian Marcus."

"Damn!" uttered Major Henderson. "Andrew, we have nothing that can come out and rescue you. I don't know what to say. We knew there was a remote chance something like this might happen. We were hoping that it wouldn't."

"I sent a directed emergency message toward a number of asteroids, hoping one of them contains Sanctuary. Our only hope is that they received the message and will send a rescue ship."

"That's a long shot," replied Major Henderson. "Even if they receive the message, they may not respond."

"I know. Something else you need to be informed about. Kala's father, Professor Charles Wright, has found the cave on Cyprus. He's about to reveal our existence to the world. I've already informed Brett."

"We're already taking steps to handle that situation. Our secret for the time being will remain safe."

"You won't harm my father?" asked Kala, worry in her voice.

"No, we won't," replied Major Henderson. "Your father will be taken aside and the situation explained to him. If he refuses to listen, no one will believe him. We already have people in place, removing the artifacts from the cave. When your father returns, all he will find are some primitive drawings on the walls, and a few shattered pieces of old pottery."

"It will ruin my father's reputation," gasped Kala.

"We'll see that your father is taken care of," promised Major Henderson. "He'll be just fine."

"Major, will you talk to my parents?" asked Andrew. The possibility of not seeing them again bothered him.

There was a short silence, and then Major Henderson responded. "I will speak to them. Andrew, you must know that, even if Sanctuary sends a ship, they might not return any of you to Earth."

"I know," replied Andrew. "We're willing to take that risk."

"We can't risk too much communication. We don't want the Druin interdiction system to detect it. Our best protection is that they don't know about us."

"I'll contact you once every three or four hours. We'll hold our communications to a minimum."

"Very well," replied Major Henderson. "Good luck, Andrew. I wish there was something I could do."

"I knew the risk when I volunteered for the mission. Talk to you later." With that, Andrew turned the power off on his laptop.

Rachael looked at Andrew. "What did he mean that, even if we're rescued, we might not be returned to Earth?"

Andrew took a deep breath. This was hard for him as well. "Sanctuary is our best hope for a future and to eventually free the worlds of the Human Empire. Nothing can risk endangering that secret. If Sanctuary does send a ship, we might be required to live out the rest of our lives there."

Everyone was silent. No matter what happened, their lives would never be the same. They might never see their friends and families again.

The hours passed by slowly. Three more times Andrew contacted Major Henderson and informed him of their situation. As time passed, Andrew wondered if Sanctuary would respond. What really concerned Andrew was that, if Sanctuary were on the other side of the sun, then his message would never have reached it. Andrew might be waiting for a rescue that would never come.

With a deep sigh, Andrew saw it was time to contact Major Henderson again. Talking in the escape pod had grown less and less over the hours as each of them became lost in their own private thoughts. Pressing the Connection icon, Andrew was surprised when nothing happened. He checked his laptop but could find nothing wrong.

"What is it?" asked Kala, seeing the aggravated look on Andrew's face.

"My communicator has stopped functioning."

Suddenly a strange voice came over the laptop. "This is Lieutenant Cleo Ashen of the Sanctuary cruiser *Destiny*. We will be docking with your escape pod shortly. Make sure your helmets are on in case something goes wrong. The pod will barely fit into our cargo hold."

Andrew felt a flood of relief. "This is Andrew Wilcox to the *Destiny*. We're putting on our helmets. Thanks for coming to get us."

"We'll talk more about that when you're on board."

Kala looked at Andrew with an excited look on her face. "We made it! They came."

"It appears that way," replied Andrew. "Now let's put our helmets back on. I'm sure all of you will have a million questions to ask once we're on board the *Destiny*." Andrew had a lot of questions to ask as well.

The minutes passed slowly by and then they felt a slight jarring. Several times they heard scraping noises, and Andrew winced, realizing just how tight a fit the pod must be to get inside the ship's cargo hold. After another minute or two, the communicator on Andrew's laptop activated.

"It's safe to come out now."

Rachael unfastened her safety harness and then very carefully reached for the hatch. She pressed several buttons and pushed a large lever, which slowly moved. With a loud hissing noise, the hatch sprang open with bright lights shining in. Several people in spacesuits waited to assist them from the escape pod.

"Come with us," said one of them. "We'll take you to some temporary quarters, where you can clean up. Captain Masters will speak to you as soon as you're ready."

The four followed the two crewmembers out of the cargo hold and down a short corridor. Andrew was shown one hatch to enter and the women another. "You will find a shower and the necessary toiletry items you need to make yourselves presentable. You've spent a lot of time in those spacesuits, and I'm sure you're ready to get out of them."

"A shower sounds fantastic," said Kala, with a smile. "Thank you."

Andrew stepped into the cabin indicated, seeing a bed, a couch, and a desk. A small door to one side indicated where the shower and other facilities were located. Andrew quickly stripped out of his spacesuit and used the facilities and then took a long relaxing shower. He knew the water in the ship would be recycled, so he was not concerned about using too much. Opening a small cabinet, he found shaving supplies and everything else he would need to make himself presentable.

When he was satisfied with how he looked, he opened the door and stepped back into the cabin, finding a ship's uniform laying on the bed. His spacesuit was missing. He quickly put on the uniform, finding it was very close to his size. He also found a pair of shoes and socks as well. When he was finally dressed, he sat down on the couch allowing himself to relax. His desperate plan to contact Sanctuary had worked. Sanctuary had responded and had sent out a rescue ship. He now knew Sanctuary did, indeed, exist.

He also suspected that Major Henderson would realize the same thing, since all contact with Andrew had come to a sudden stop. With a smile, Andrew knew he had succeeded in his mission. He had located the Druin observation system, as well as Sanctuary, though not quite as he had planned. Andrew felt extremely sad that Captain Greer and the others on board the *Endeavor* had died. He wished things had turned out differently, but there had been no way to predict how the Druin interdiction system would react to the *Endeavor*'s approach.

Trying to relax, he wondered what the meeting with Captain Masters would be like. There was a good chance the captain was an actual Imperial from over one thousand years ago. Andrew knew thousands were supposed to have gone to Sanctuary and into cryosleep. It only made sense for them to awaken an experienced captain and crew to send on this rescue mission. Andrew also wondered how long it would take to rescue the other escape pods.

Time passed, and finally the door to his cabin opened, and a young woman stood there. "I'm Lieutenant Commander Audrey Banora. If you will come with me, I'll take you to the captain."

Andrew stepped out into the corridor, finding the three women waiting for him. All three were dressed in ship uniforms.

Lieutenant Commander Banora started down the short corridor and stopped next to a closed hatch, opened it, and gestured for the others to enter. "I must return to the Command Center. We're on our way back to Sanctuary and should be arriving there in a few hours."

Rachael looked at the lieutenant commander with concern. "What about the rest of the escape pods?"

"Captain Masters will explain the reasons for not rescuing them. I'm sorry." With that, Lieutenant Commander Banora turned and went down the corridor to another hatch. After opening it, she passed through and then shut it.

"Let's go in and find out what's going on," suggested Andrew, as he gestured for the three women to go in first.

The women went through the hatch, and Andrew followed. They were in a small conference room. An officer in an Imperial captain's uniform sat at the head of the table. Seeing the four of them, the captain stood. "I'm Captain Masters of the stealth light cruiser *Destiny*. If all of you will sit down, I will try to explain what's going on."

Andrew took a seat, and the three women sat down as well. All turned and looked expectantly at the captain.

"I'm sure all of you are wondering why we're not rescuing the other three escape pods."

"Yes," said Rachael, the aggravation showing in her voice. "We have friends and fellow shipmates on board those pods. Very shortly they will run out of life support."

Captain Masters let out a deep sigh. "It was a very difficult decision. There was a serious debate about whether we should even risk rescuing your pod. The only reason we did is because of Mr. Wilcox's presence and the fact he had in his possession a hyperlight transmitter. This is the only stealth ship Sanctuary possesses, and it's over one thousand years old."

"So, you'll just let them die?" Rachael could not believe what she was hearing.

"We have little choice," replied Captain Masters. "Just rescuing the four of you carried significant risk. The Druin interdiction system monitors the entire Solar System for signs of any suspicious activity. We dare not lead them back to Sanctuary. Too much is at stake. Even now we are monitoring the Druin system. If there are any signs we've been detected, we can't return."

"You said you rescued us because Andrew was on board. Why?"

Captain Masters looked at Andrew. "We've been monitoring Earth for centuries. We were well aware that some of the advancements made on the planet were coming about too quickly. It was obvious some group was manipulating various scientific discoveries on the planet. We suspected it was descendents of the Imperial survivors who were banished there over one thousand years ago. When we detected the hyperlight message from Andrew, it pretty-well confirmed that. Our leaderships wants to speak to Andrew to get a better understanding of what is happening on Earth and what Andrew's people are planning. It is far too early for Earth to draw the attention of the Druins. The planet needs to continue to advance until it has a unified government and its technology reaches the level of the Empire when we left it. That part will be difficult, as Earth must not develop hyperlight travel. That would bring an immediate response from the Druins."

"The Alcubierre Drive we're working on," said Rachael, her eyes widening. "We're only a few years away from testing it."

"That must not happen," said Captain Masters. "Faster-than-light travel needs to be delayed for at least another one hundred years."

Andrew decided to speak up. He had been listening carefully to everything Captain Masters had said. "It won't work as expected. My own people are involved in the project. The Alcubierre Drive needs some exotic matter to function properly. What will be used only allows a top speed of just below that of light. It will make more of the Solar System accessible but still keep Earth away from the nearer stars. We don't believe the Druins will react to the new drive system as long as it stays below light speed."

"Perhaps," replied Captain Masters, his gaze focused on Andrew. "Our leadership will be interested in hearing from you. As I said before, it was the primary reason we decided to risk rescuing your escape pod."

"I still wish we could do something for the others," said Rachael, feeling guilty about being rescued while the others would be left to die.

"It was a difficult decision," said Captain Masters. "You must realize, as far as we're concerned, we're still at war with the Confederation. Sometimes in war, sacrifices must be made, even very unpleasant ones. I promise you, if I could safely rescue the other pods I would do so."

Andrew understood the reasoning. They had experienced some of the same things on Earth in the past. "How soon before we reach Sanctuary?"

"Six hours," replied Captain Masters. "There is food available in the galley, if you are hungry. As far as answering more of your questions, that will have to wait until we reach Sanctuary. I'm sure you have many more, but I've told you all that I'm allowed to."

Captain Masters pressed a button on a small screen in front of him, and moments later an ensign appeared.

"Please escort Mr. Wilcox and these ladies to the galley and show them how to operate the food preparation systems. I'll be returning to the Command Center."

The ensign nodded. "I'm Ensign Brenda Allert. "If you will follow me, I'll take all of you to the galley."

As the group left, Captain Masters stood, a look of worry on his face. He hadn't told them that none of them would ever be allowed to leave Sanctuary. He also still felt badly about not being able to rescue the other pods.

Chapter Nine

Major Henderson was in his quarters at the space station, gazing worriedly at the blank screen of his hyperlight communicator. Andrew had missed his last two check-ins.

"Still nothing?" asked Brett over the communicator.

"No," replied Henderson. "I can come up with only two explanations. Something happened that destroyed the escape pod, or they were rescued by a ship from Sanctuary."

"Have you received a message from the *Endeavor*? I'm certain Captain Greer would have sent one, explaining the situation."

"I arranged for that message to be intercepted and routed to my quarters. For the time being, it will appear the ship has vanished."

Brett was silent for a moment. "I'll use our connections with the space program and the government to make an announcement that the *Endeavor* was lost to an unknown hazard and that we're currently investigating to discover what happened to the ship."

"I guess all we can do is wait and see if we hear from Andrew. Which brings up another subject. What will we do about Kala Wright's father?"

"That's being taken care of. I have him meeting with a government official and several of our own scientists. While he's doing that, I have a crew under Alan Foster, clearing out the cave. When Professor Wright returns, all he will find is an empty cave and a few pieces of broken pottery. The paintings and writings on the wall are being removed and replaced with primitive drawings."

"He won't be pleased with that," said Henderson. "I sort of feel sorry for the man."

"Don't worry about it. Foster will be there when he returns, and after he sees the cave, Foster will take him to the side and explain what has happened and the reason why."

"What will we tell him about his daughter?"

"Nothing yet, not until we know more."

Henderson understood the reasons for all the caution. "Let's just hope we hear from Andrew soon."

"We're all hoping that," replied Brett. "I'll go see his parents later today and explain what we think may have happened. Let's just hope, if he is at Sanctuary, they allow him to communicate with us."

Andrew was in his quarters, talking to Kala, when Ensign Allert came in. "We will be docking at Sanctuary in twenty minutes. Mr. Wilcox, Captain Masters has requested your presence in the Command Center."

Andrew was both surprised and pleased by this request.

"I guess I'll talk to you later," said Kala, as she stood to go to her quarters.

Andrew followed Ensign Allert through the ship to the Command Center. Upon entering, Andrew looked around, stunned at all the modern equipment. It made the Command Center of the *Endeavor* look archaic. Large viewscreens covered the walls, and numerous manned consoles were strategically placed about the room. Captain Masters sat on a slightly raised platform in the center, where he could easily see everything.

"How has your stay been so far, Mr. Wilcox?" asked Captain Masters.

"Wonderful," replied Andrew. "I never expected to be on an Imperial warship."

Captain Masters smiled. "We're not much of a warship. We're a stealth vessel, and our best offensive weapon is not to be seen."

Andrew nodded. "Where are we going?"

Captain Masters gestured to one of the viewscreens, showing a magnified view of an asteroid.

"Pallas," gasped Andrew, recognizing the asteroid. "I scanned Pallas and could not detect anything."

"That's because everything is buried deep beneath the ground. We only have a few sensors and communication devices on the surface, and they're camouflaged."

Andrew watched as Pallas grew larger on the viewscreen. When they were close to the asteroid, a large hatch disguised as a crater slid open, revealing a dimly lit interior. The *Destiny* moved slowly inside and then lowered itself onto a waiting spacedock.

"This spacedock was built specifically for the *Destiny*," explained Captain Masters. "It was believed there might be occasions where we had to take the ship out. As I said before, it's the only ship we have that's fully stealth capable."

On one of the viewscreens, the hatch slid shut, and a green light flared up on one of the consoles. Instantly the lights outside the ship brightened to full intensity.

"Atmosphere and temperature are normal," reported Lieutenant Keela Nower from her sensor console.

"What now?" asked Andrew. On the viewscreens, he could see numerous uniformed people moving around outside the ship.

"Ensign Allert will show the four of you to your quarters. Then someone will come to take you to a meeting with our Imperial Council. I'm sure you have a number of questions you would like to have answered, and the Council will have some they would like you to answer."

"Are we held as prisoners?" asked Andrew.

Captain Masters let out a deep sigh. "No, but I don't know if you will be allowed to return home because of the added security risk. It probably would not be a problem with you, but for the other three it may well be."

Andrew didn't know if he would feel comfortable going home and leaving the others here. It was something he would have to think about.

Ensign Allert led Andrew and the three women to their new quarters. Stepping inside, Andrew looked around in amazement. The room was quite comfortable and even had a small kitchen in one end.

"The bedroom is through that door," said Brenda, "and through the other door is the restroom. You should find everything you need. I'll have someone come by and measure you for a proper uniform and civilian clothes for the three women."

"Thank you," replied Andrew. He looked at Brenda and asked a question that he was curious about. "Were you born in the Empire?"

Brenda hesitated and then nodded. "Yes, I was born on the capital world of Golan Four, which is the birthplace of the Human race. I was fortunate to be included in Project Exodus and placed on board the *Destiny*. Captain Masters is one of our best commanding officers."

"Are any Royals here?"

"I can't answer that," Brenda replied uneasily. "You must ask the Council that question."

Andrew nodded. From her answer, he was certain there were. He wondered who it was. "Do you know how soon I will be summoned to come in front of the Council?"

"Tomorrow," answered Brenda. "It will be best for the four of you to have a good meal and then a night of rest. Tomorrow may be a long day for all of you. I know the Council is particularly interested in hearing from you. They will have a lot of questions about what your people have been doing on Earth and what their future plans are."

"I'll answer as best as I can," promised Andrew. He hoped they would answer his questions as well.

"I know you will. I need to contact the store's clerk and have him send someone to come by and measure you for your uniform. He will also check with the women to see what they would like to wear. If you want, I can be present to give them some suggestions so they won't feel out of place. Not everyone on Pallas is military. We have a quite large civilian population as well."

"That would be great," replied Andrew. "I'm sure they will appreciate that." He wanted the women to feel as comfortable as possible. He knew what was going on had to be difficult for all three of them. Particularly after losing the rest of the crew.

Brenda nodded and left Andrew, closing the door behind her. Andrew noticed it was not a metal hatch but a regular door. He explored his quarters, finding nearly everything was recognizable. Even a computer station but he couldn't access it as it asked for a password. He found a video screen on the wall in the bedroom with a remote control. Turning it on, he found several entertainment channels and one news channel. He sat on the bed, listening to the news channel as it reported the destruction of the *Endeavor* and the rescue of part of its crew.

"The question was raised with the Council as to why they risked the revelation of Sanctuary in order to rescue one of the escape pods from the destroyed ship. Supposedly a descendent of the Imperials was on board, from those stranded on Earth over one thousand years ago. Even more important, this Imperial knows about the Empire and is fully aware of the war with the Confederation. He and those with him were rescued so he could be questioned about the current progress of Earth and if more Imperials are on the planet."

The newscaster paused. *"In order to rescue the escape pod without revealing Sanctuary's presence, the crew of the* Destiny *were awakened. For those of you who don't know, the* Destiny *is an Imperial light cruiser with full stealth capabilities. It rescued the pod and its four occupants without exposing its presence."*

"Everyone is curious to hear what this Earth Imperial has to say. We're all hoping more Imperials are on Earth, as it would be a great help in what we here on Pallas are trying to accomplish."

Andrew lay back on the bed and spent the next several hours watching further newscasts. It was a good way to learn more about the Imperials living inside the asteroid.

A knock came at his door, and a young man wearing an ensign's uniform came in.

"I was sent to measure you for your uniform," the ensign informed Andrew.

"Go ahead," replied Andrew.

"Just stand straight, sir."

The ensign took out a small scanner and played it over Andrew's body. "That does it. I'll have several uniforms made up and delivered in a few hours."

"Are you going to the women's quarters next?"

The ensign nodded. "Yes, Ensign Allert is already with them and waiting on me."

"Then you better get going."

The ensign started to leave and then paused. "Ensign Allert asked me to invite you to the evening meal. The other three women will be coming as well."

"Sounds fine to me."

"I'll tell them." With that, the ensign left.

Andrew returned to the bedroom to watch more of the news. He wanted to know as much as possible about Pallas before he met with their Imperial Council.

—

Several hours later the ensign returned with the uniforms as well as other clothing, including a formal dinner jacket as well.

"Wear the jacket with your uniform when you meet the Council," suggested the ensign. "It will make an impression on them and show respect."

"Thank you," replied Andrew.

"If you want to go ahead and change, I'll wait and take you to the dining hall for the evening meal."

"Give me a few minutes," said Andrew, as he picked up one of the uniforms and a few other articles. He headed off to the bedroom to change clothes.

A few minutes later Andrew returned, cleaned up and wearing his new uniform. It had no insignia other than a patch on each shoulder, identifying him as an Imperial. It was also extremely comfortable. Andrew wondered what type fabric it was made out of. "Let's go."

The ensign nodded and led Andrew out the door and down the corridor. They walked for a considerable distance and took several turbolifts, until they reached the level where the dining hall was located.

Going inside, Andrew was surprised to see its size and immediately noted several hundred people were present, eating their evening meal. The ensign led him to a table where the three women sat, as well as Ensign Allert.

"Andrew," said Kala, standing and smiling. "You look absolutely stunning in that uniform. Here. Sit down next to me."

Andrew noticed that all three women wore simple blouses and colorful skirts. He sat down. Rachael frowned slightly.

A steward came over and stood at the table, looking at the group. "What would you like for tonight?"

Andrew looked at Brenda. "We have no idea what food you have available here. Why don't you order for all of us?"

Brenda nodded. "No problem. Later I'll have one of the stewards bring a menu over, and I'll explain what all the food items are." Brenda quickly placed the food order for all and then leaned back, relaxing. "This will be my first real meal in over one thousand years."

"What!" exclaimed Rachael, her eyes widening. "I don't understand."

"I've been in cryosleep since shortly after the *Destiny* came to Sanctuary. I fully expect to return to cryosleep sometime in the next few weeks."

"Why?" asked Kala. "I would think you would want to stay awake."

Brenda let out a deep breath. "I want to see my world freed from the Confederation and the Druins taught a lesson. I can't do that unless I'm awake when we're finally ready to fight back."

Andrew was not surprised to hear this. "How soon will that be?"

"Soon," answered Brenda, as one of the stewards brought over five glasses filled with a rose-colored liquid. He also placed five glasses of ice water in front of them as well.

Brenda picked up her glass with the rose-colored drink. "This is called Carlish. It's a weak alcoholic beverage that I believe all of you will like."

Kala picked up her glass and took a cautious sip. Her eyes lit up with recognition. "It tastes like strawberries!"

Andrew tasted his and nodded in agreement. "Yes, it does." He looked at Brenda. "I presume somewhere you have some large hydroponic farms."

Brenda nodded. "Yes, we grow a large assortment of vegetables and other crops. We even have some food animals as well."

The steward soon returned with a tray which held five salads. He placed one in front of each of the five, as well as several cups of different dressings.

Rachael tasted each one and then decided on one that tasted remarkably like Ranch dressing.

"Your people seem well-adjusted to living underground," said Professor Adrian Marcus, as she took a small bite of her salad.

Brenda smiled. "We have some large parks and open areas we can go to for relaxation during our free time. When we have time, I'll show them to you."

Captain Masters come in through the large double door. He spotted them and came over to their table. "Mind if I join you?"

"Of course not," replied Rachael, indicating for the captain to sit down next to her.

Masters sat down, and a steward hurried over and took his order. As soon as the steward left, Masters turned toward Andrew. "The Council will meet with you early tomorrow afternoon. Be prepared to spend several hours or more answering questions."

"What about us?" asked Kala.

"Much less. They have a few questions for you, but not as they will for Mr. Wilcox."

A steward returned with several large plates of steaming food. The plates contained various cuts of meats and some vegetables.

"I thought a variety would be best," explained Brenda. "Hopefully you will find something you like."

Andrew took his fork and selected several different slices of meat. He cut off a small slice and tasted it. "Not bad." He tried the other meat and laughed. "Tastes like chicken."

The girls sampled the food and found several they liked.

"What's life like here on Pallas?" asked Adrian, as she tried a vegetable that resembled a small potato.

"We're preparing for war daily. We've adopted Earth's twenty-four-hour time period and calendar to make everything easier when we finally reveal ourselves," answered Brenda. "The majority of our population is in cryosleep, though many more are awake now than in the beginning. Our population has been steadily expanding, and the base is now functioning as it was first envisioned."

Andrew put down his fork and took a deep drink of the Carlish. "How much longer do you think your people will stay in cryosleep?"

Captain Masters looked thoughtful. "I hope not too much longer. Earth is progressing very fast, and it won't be too long before the Druins take notice. We have to be ready before that day."

Andrew tried one of the vegetables, finding it very tasty. "How many attack drones do the Druins have in the interdiction stations?"

"We're not sure. Several of our military people, who are familiar with the stations the Druins use, estimate between twenty to forty in each of the primary stations. Unfortunately we don't know how many primary stations there are. There could be anywhere from four to twelve."

"What will cause them to attack?" asked Adrian.

"Earth's scientific advancement. If any of the AIs on the primary stations decide Earth has reached a point where it could be a danger to the Confederation, it will signal all the primary stations to attack. They will attack without warning and will use antimatter missiles to eliminate all of Earth's largest cities."

"You said the primary stations are controlled by AIs," said Rachael. "Has there been any discussion about using a computer virus to take control of the interdiction system?"

Captain Masters looked at Rachael in surprise. "Computer viruses are outlawed in the Empire, as well as in the Confederation. They could do tremendous harm on every world, as computers control nearly everything."

"Well, they are not outlawed on Earth, and we have some programmers who are experts at designing viruses to get into computer systems. What would happen if we use a virus to gain control of the entire interdiction system and cause it to continue to report Earth is still harmless to the Druins?"

Captain Masters looked stunned. "Are your programmers that good?"

Rachael nodded. "We would need to study your computer systems and run some tests on what would work. I presume your systems would be somewhat like the Druins' systems?"

"They would be," replied Captain Masters. "Only theirs will be more advanced, but the principal software will be the same."

Andrew decided he needed to ask a question. "It's obvious the Druins are depending on their AIs in the interdiction stations to report any abnormalities that might be a danger. How often do Druin warships come and check on our development?"

"Not often," replied Captain Masters. "From what I understand the last check was over fifty years ago, and they probably won't be back for another one hundred."

"So, if we could take over the interdiction stations, could your people send back the proper messages to make the Druins think everything is still okay?"

Captain Masters slowly nodded his head. "Yes, I'm certain of that."

"That means," Andrew noted, "if we can take over the system, we would have around one hundred years to get Earth ready for war."

Captain Masters stood, leaving the rest of his food untouched. "I need to speak to several of our computer people about this, as well as several Council members. Rachael, you may be summoned along with Mr. Wilcox instead of separately. You may have just solved our biggest worry."

Andrew watched as Captain Masters hurried off, his expression revealing his excitement about Rachael's suggestion.

"Well, I've never seen that before," said Brenda, as she took a drink of her Carlish. "The captain is normally quite calm about everything."

Later Andrew was in his quarters when a knock came on his door. Opening it, he expected to see Kala, but it was Rachael instead.

"May I come in?"

"Sure," replied Andrew.

Rachael entered and sat down on the sofa. "One thing I will say, these quarters are very comfortable."

Andrew sat down next to her, curious as to what was on Rachael's mind.

"Are we doing the right thing? If we design a virus to use against the interdiction system, are we putting Earth in danger?"

Andrew shook his head. "No more than it would be if we left everything as it is. At some point Earth will build an FTL-capable ship of some type. When the interdiction system detects it leaving the Solar System, the AIs will send in all their drones to attack and will probably notify the Druins at the same time. At Earth's current rate of advancement, that's most likely to happen in the next ten to fifteen years. If the drones attack in that time frame, we won't have anything capable of stopping them."

"And in another hundred years?"

"My people are working on bringing all of Earth's governments together—or at least the major ones. By that time we'll have ships with weapons and energy shields which can take on the Druins. We're in a section of space with few habitable worlds. It will take a while for the Druins to respond to us after their warship discovers the truth. This base here should also have a large fleet to contribute to Earth's defense. We may just be able to make Earth and the Solar System too hard of a nut for the Druins to crack."

Rachael nodded. "That helps." She paused and looked at Andrew. "May I ask you a personal question?"

"Sure."

"What do you think of Kala?"

Andrew hadn't been expecting this. "She's nice and very smart. I enjoy talking to her. Why do you ask?"

Rachael's face flushed slightly. "Oh, I was just curious. The two of you seem to be spending a lot of time together. I saw her leave your quarters on the *Endeavor* recently."

"Nothing happened," stammered Andrew. "We were just talking." He was certain she was referring to the night he had kissed Kala.

Rachael stood. "We're all adults here. If you want to sleep with Kala, it's okay with me. I better be going. It sounds as if we'll have a long day tomorrow."

Andrew was left speechless, not sure how to respond. He watched as Rachael left his quarters, knowing he should say something but not sure what it needed to be. "Women! Why are they so hard to understand?"

Letting out a deep sigh, Andrew decided to turn in for the night. He would worry about Kala and Rachael later. First he had to deal with his meeting with the Imperial Council. He suspected it would be a very interesting day for all concerned, as well as for the future of Earth and the Imperials on Pallas.

Chapter Ten

Andrew and Rachael were summoned to the Imperial Council chambers in the early afternoon. Ensign Allert came and escorted them to the meeting, explaining what would happen.

"They'll ask you about Earth and what your Imperial Council is planning," she explained to Andrew. "They may want to know quite a few details."

"What about me?" asked Rachael. She felt extremely nervous about appearing before the Council.

"You caused quite a stir with Captain Masters, when you told him about Earth programmers creating computer viruses. I'm sure the Council will have numerous questions for you about that. I haven't heard from Captain Masters today, though I expect him to be in the meeting."

Rachael nodded. She wasn't sure what the Council would be asking her, but she was determined to answer as best as she could.

It took them nearly twenty minutes to reach the Council chambers, after walking though several long corridors and taking several turbolifts, which took them deeper beneath the surface of Pallas.

They finally reached a pair of large decorated double doors with the insignia of the Human Empire on them. The insignia was a large starburst on a background of stars. Two armed guards stood on each side of the doors.

"I will leave you now," explained Brenda, as she came to a stop. "I don't have the security clearance for what you will be discussing inside. When the meeting is over, someone will summon me, and I'll show you how to get back to your quarters."

"Thanks for helping us," said Andrew. Looking at Rachael, he smiled. "Guess we better go in."

The guards opened the doors, and the two stepped through. Inside they found a large conference table with ten Imperials seated. Five men and five women. A small viewing section was close by, where twenty spectators sat, including Captain Masters. He nodded and smiled at seeing them.

The woman at the head of the table stood. "I'm Lena Prest, the current head of this Council. If the two of you will take a seat, we'll get this meeting underway. I'm sure both of you have a lot of questions, as do we." Lena gestured toward two vacant seats at the conference table. A glass of ice water sat in front of each councilor.

Andrew and Rachael sat down and waited expectantly.

"We'll start off by introducing the rest of the Council members. We each serve five-year terms, at which point we may elect to go back into cryosleep."

Each member of the Council introduced themselves, as well as what their responsibilities were on Pallas. Andrew was surprised that an admiral was a member of the Council. His name was Admiral Terrell Bract, and he was responsible for all the fleet units currently based inside Pallas.

After the introductions, Lena asked the first question. "We would ask that you answer our questions as truthfully as possible, and we will do the same. How many Imperials are there currently on Earth?"

Andrew considered his answer. "Tens of thousands are direct descendants of the Imperials who were stranded on Earth over one thousand years ago. However, only a little over two hundred are aware of our heritage and have been educated with a major understanding of Imperial science and technology."

"Only two hundred," replied Lena, a slight look of disappointment. "I would have expected more."

"Over the years many of our people married Earth Humans. It was decided that the regular citizens of Earth could not be allowed to know of our presence. For that reason, for those of us who married outside of our Imperial group, their children were not educated as an Imperial. Over the years our group has steadily been getting smaller. Discussions recently were concerned with substantially enlarging our circle, as Earth is expanding out into the Solar System."

Councilor Mila Rosen asked the next question. "What is your group's goal on Earth? We know from the way Earth has developed some of its science that Imperials must have been involved."

"We've always known that, at some point, the Druins would return and take over Earth. We have been working at bringing Earth's level of technology up to Imperial standards, yet not so much as to bring the Druins' attention on us, as well as working toward a more unified government. The current space program is a good example, as over thirty nations on Earth are currently involved, and that includes all the major ones."

Admiral Bract looked thoughtful. "How soon before Earth develops its own FTL drive?"

"Soon," answered Andrew. This was a major concern of the Imperials back on Earth. "They are already working on an Alcubierre Drive and will have an experimental model ready for testing in two or three more years. Fortunately we have several of our own people embedded in the program, and, when they test the drive, they'll find it is only capable of sublight speeds. However, we believe, sometime in the next few years after that, they will realize the mistake made and will correct the drive to allow for FTL speeds. So we're probably looking at five to seven years before they have an effective drive system."

This caused a stirring in the Council, as well as in those observing.

"That's not good," said Councilor Jalad Wiste. "We will not be ready by then. If the Druins detect a functioning FTL drive, they will send their drones in to attack Earth."

"We need to delay that drive development for at least another fifty to seventy-five Earth years," said Councilor Arianna Bliss. "Is there anything your people on Earth can do to accomplish that?"

Andrew shook his head. "Can't be done. Too many good scientists are already working on the project. Earth's space program wants a more economical way to travel between the planets and the moons of this system. At some point someone will perfect the Alcubierre Drive or stumble across the method to build a hyperspace drive instead."

"What can we do?" asked Councilor Rosen.

Lena stood and looked around the Council chambers. "Last night Captain Masters came to me with a daring plan. One that could keep the Druins from finding out about Earth's technological level for another seventy to one hundred years or even more."

"How?" asked Councilor Wiste. "Is he suggesting we intervene ourselves? It is true we could probably stop the drone attack with our warships, but what happens when a Druin fleet appears?"

Lena smiled. "We can't face a Druin fleet at this time. However, it seems Earth is very astute at designing viruses to gain access to other computer systems."

"Viruses!" sputtered Councilor Bliss, her face showing shock. "Those have long been outlawed in both the Empire and the Confederation because of the serious impact they could have on our economies."

"We're at war," pointed out Andrew. "How many Imperial citizens died in the attacks when they took over our Empire? I believe the number was in the billions."

Everyone nodded their heads, even Councilor Bliss. "That may be true, but the use of computer viruses could be extremely dangerous. What did you have in mind?"

Lena gestured toward Rachael. "Would you like to explain your idea?"

Rachael nodded. She had been expecting this. "I only recently became aware of you Imperials when Andrew told me. We've had a few discussions, and I don't want to see Earth destroyed by the Druins. I can't imagine what it must have been like for your worlds." Rachael paused and took a deep breath. "On Earth we have long had a problem with industrial espionage. We have much less today, as many of the larger countries are beginning to work together. However, all our computer systems are protected with various firewalls to prevent access by computer viruses. Over the years some very sophisticated viruses were developed that seriously compromised millions of computers."

"The exact reason why the Empire and the Confederation banned them," pointed out Councilor Bliss. "They were too dangerous."

"Probably a wise decision," replied Rachael. "As the years passed on Earth, the viruses became more highly sophisticated, as did virus protection software. Both were developed by companies, militaries, and even governments."

"What is your suggestion?" asked Admiral Bract. "That we neutralize the Druin interdiction system by infecting it with a virus? As soon as that happens, one of the AIs will report the presence of a virus to the Druins, and they will descend on us in force."

Rachael shook her head. "No, my plan is more complicated and safer. We use a virus to take over the interdiction system. Once it is under our control, we can continue to send reports back to the Druins that Earth is not a threat and that no FTL drive system has been detected."

The room was suddenly very quiet. Everyone looked at each other in shock at what Rachael had proposed.

"It might buy us the extra time we need to bring Earth up to Imperial standards in technology and to prepare it to take on the Druins," added Andrew. "From what I know of Earth programmers and hackers, they could very easily design a virus to take over the Druin interdiction system."

"Can Earth design software to protect our own computer systems?" asked one of the Imperials in the audience.

Andrew nodded. "I'm sure they can."

Captain Masters stood and spoke. "This could be a turning point for us. Imagine our ships protected by Earth firewalls? We could send viruses to Druin ships, commanding their systems to shut down. They would be helpless before our fleets."

"That may be so," said Admiral Bract, as he considered the possibilities. "But, at some point in time, they will develop their own viruses and use them against us."

"We can have a group of special programmers on guard against that," suggested Rachael. "We can constantly update our firewalls to protect us from the Druins and the rest of the Confederation."

This caused more heated discussions to break out in the Council chamber.

Lena called the meeting back to order. "I believe this is something we need to seriously consider. If we can't stop Earth from developing its own FTL drive then we are faced with a Druin attack sometime in the next ten years. We all know we're not yet prepared for that. I suggest we put together a team to study the practicality of what Rachael has suggested."

More discussions were had, with everyone eventually agreeing to form a team to look into the feasibility of Rachael's proposal. Admiral Bract would lead the team, along with several other Council members and a few Imperial computer programmers.

For the next several hours, different Imperials asked questions about Earth and particularly at what stage much of its technology was at compared to the Empire. Andrew and Rachael answered to the best of their ability. Some of the questions and answers were very detailed.

When the meeting finally wound down, Rachael asked one final question. "Will we be allowed to go home?"

Lena leaned back in her chair and placed her hands on the conference table. "I don't know. If we decide to implement your virus idea, someone must return to Earth and will probably speak to some of the Earth governments. We would also want the

Imperials on Earth to become involved. If we do that, there is a chance all of you could return to Earth."

Admiral Bract nodded. "It would make good sense and strategy, particularly if we gain control of the interdiction system. We could come out more in the open and help prepare Earth for the future conflict. There is a tremendous amount we could accomplish in the next seventy to one hundred years by working together."

Rachael immediately felt relieved. Just maybe she would get to go home after all.

Early the next morning Captain Masters took Andrew and Rachael on a tour of Pallas.

"How many people are currently awake?" asked Rachael. She had noticed a lot of Imperials around.

"Nearly twelve thousand," answered Captain Masters. "Our population has really grown over the last one thousand years. As time passed, more and more people were staying awake and having children. We have nearly 120,000 in cryosleep."

They walked down a long corridor and then through a heavily guarded hatch. Inside was a large observation room that overlooked a massive spacedock.

"We've been building dreadnoughts and support craft ever since we came to Pallas."

Andrew and Rachael stepped to the large glass windows. Rachael gasped at what was revealed. Dozens of large spaceships were in their docks. "Are those ships in stasis?"

Captain Masters nodded. "Yes, when a ship is finished, we run it though all its tests. Once it passes, we place a stasis field around it. We have hundreds of dreadnoughts and battlecruisers ready to deploy, once the proper crews have been trained."

"How many crews do you have if the Druins suddenly showed up?" asked Andrew.

Captain Masters let out a deep sigh. "Not as many as I would like. We have some trained crews from the original

Imperials who came here, and others we have trained over the years, but who have no actual experience in war. In an emergency we could activate about a dozen dreadnoughts and sixty battlecruisers."

Andrew's eyes widened. "How many ships do you have here inside Pallas?"

"We have a larger fleet here now than what the Empire did when it fell. We're covertly mining several nearby asteroids for raw materials, particularly heavy metals. We've done everything we can to hide our mining operations from the Druins. We use very primitive cargo ships so the Druin interdiction system will not detect them, and even if they did, they would only consider them to be harmless."

Rachael stared at the spacecraft in awe. Even the smallest was larger than what the *Endeavor* had been. "Have you heard anything about whether we'll be allowed to go home?"

Captain Masters shook his head. "No, we may have to wake up a few of our more esteemed scientists and computer people to discuss your virus proposal. At a minimum you'll be here for a couple weeks."

"Any chance I can contact my people?" asked Andrew. "I promise you they won't reveal to anyone where I'm at." Andrew wanted his parents to know he was still alive.

"I'll ask," said Captain Masters. "I can't promise anything, but, if the Council agrees to Rachael's request, it will be necessary for you to contact your people and to make some arrangements."

They continued the tour, with Captain Masters taking them to one of the large hydroponic farms. Once again they were in a large observation room, staring out at long rows of tanks filled with growing vegetables. The room was full of vegetation that nearly reached to the ceiling twenty feet above.

"We try to make use of every available space," Masters informed them.

"Do you grow enough food for all your people?" asked Rachael. "What would happen if you had to awaken more people from cryosleep?"

"We're currently growing a surplus, and all the extra goes into our food reserve. Over the years we've stockpiled a pretty large supply of reserve food if it were needed. I prefer the fresh vegetables myself."

"You said there were some large open areas."

Masters nodded. "Yes, there are several. I'll take the two of you to the nearest."

It took a while, as they took several long turbolift rides down to the lower levels. It didn't surprise Andrew that the open areas would be the deepest beneath Pallas. Finally the turbolift they were in came to a stop, and they stepped out. They went down a short corridor and then through a hatch. Andrew stopped and stared around in amazement. In front of him were trees, flowers, grass, and even a small flowing stream. He could hear the low hum of insects and even a few bird cries. Looking up he saw a series of bright lights in the ceiling far above. It was obvious they simulated sunlight.

"We tried to make this like home," explained Captain Masters, as he looked around with a trace of sadness in his eyes. "Golan Four was a garden world without pollution and a controlled population."

"How did you build all this?" asked Rachael as she tried to take it all in.

"The seeds and plants we brought with us," explained Captain Masters. "Same for the trees. Even the small fish in the stream were bred from some brought here one millennium ago. We have four of these small habitats inside Pallas."

Looking around, Andrew saw numerous people sitting on benches or just strolling along the paths that wound through the trees and near the stream.

A strange look came across Captain Masters' face. "I'm being summoned back to the Council chambers to answer some questions. I'll have Ensign Allert come to finish the tour and to return you to your quarters."

Andrew noted the small communication device in the captain's right ear. "We'll just enjoy the view until she gets here."

Captain Masters left through the hatch, leaving them standing in the habitat.

"Let's sit down," suggested Rachael, pointing to a bench close by that was empty.

Going to the bench, they sat down and gazed around.

"I can't imagine living underground all my life," said Rachael, as she examined some flowers near the bench. They were of a species she had never seen before. "It must be hard."

Andrew nodded. "At least they have some areas to go to, such as this, and I'm sure they have other recreational facilities as well."

Rachael watched a couple with two small children who were kicking a ball back and forth. "They seem so normal."

Andrew laughed. "They're not aliens. They're just as Human as you or me."

Rachael blushed slightly. "I didn't mean it that way. I mean, here we are, halfway across the Solar System, and two children are playing ball, just as they would on Earth."

The two sat talking for nearly an hour before Ensign Allert came hurrying through the hatch. "I'm sorry it took so long," she said, nearly out of breath. "I was working out in one of the gyms."

"It's all right," said Rachael, smiling. "We were just sitting here, admiring the view and talking."

"If you're ready, I'm supposed to take you to one of the construction docks to see how we build our warships."

Standing, they followed Brenda out of the habitat. Andrew was curious as to how the ships he had seen earlier were built. He suspected it was far different than how they were built on Earth.

Later Andrew was back in his quarters, preparing to go out for their evening meal. Ensign Allert would come by and get everyone shortly. Andrew fastened a button on his sleeve when a knock came on his door. Going to it, he opened it, expecting to see Ensign Allert. Instead Kala stood there. She wore a nice blouse and a colorful skirt.

"One thing about how they dress here is that everyone seems to prefer bright colors," she said, grinning. She stepped inside Andrew's quarters and sat down on the couch. "You've been spending a lot of time with Rachael the last few days."

Andrew sat down next to Kala. "Most of it's been on Imperial business. We both were questioned by the Imperial Council, and Captain Masters took us on a tour of Pallas."

Kala's eyes widened. "It's amazing what they've built here. I know much of it was done with automation and robots, but it's still astounding. I wonder what their homeworlds were like?"

"Similar to Earth but much more advanced. Pollution was a thing of the distant past, and most worlds had stringent population controls. It was one of the reasons the Empire was expanding so fast."

Kala moved a little closer to Andrew, with her leg touching his. "Do you have feelings for Rachael?"

Andrew wasn't sure where this was going. "I enjoy her company, if that's what you mean."

Kala crossed her legs, and Andrew saw her skirt riding up pretty high. "Maybe I should come by later?"

Before Andrew could reply, another knock was heard at his door. "That must be Ensign Allert," said Andrew, relieved at hearing the knock.

A disappointed look spread across Kala's face. "We'll talk more later."

Standing, the two went to the door, where Brenda waited. She already had the other two women with her. "Are we ready?" she said, grinning. "I have a special meal planned for tonight."

"Sure," answered Andrew, stepping out into the corridor, followed by Kala. Andrew saw the cold look Rachael gave Kala.

He wondered what mess he was getting himself into with these two women.

After a surprisingly good meal, they all returned to their quarters. Andrew lay on his bed, watching the Pallas news, trying to learn more about what went on daily in the massive Imperial base. He heard his door open and hesitant footsteps coming toward the bedroom. He wasn't surprised when Kala came in and stood beside his bed.

"I've decided to take matters into my own hand—or should I say, body." She reached up and unfastened the buttons on her blouse, letting it slide off her shoulders and to the floor. She wore nothing beneath it. Kala then slid the zipper down on her skirt and stepped out of it, standing completely nude in front of Andrew. "Well? Do I put my clothes back on, or should I join you in bed?"

Andrew laughed. "I think we both know the answer to that." Andrew stood and took Kala into his arms, feeling the softness of her body meld to his. He kissed her deeply. Moments later they were on the bed in a heated embrace, oblivious to their surroundings.

Rachael stood outside the door to Andrew's quarters. She had seen Kala go in. Rachael was half tempted to go in to interrupt whatever Kala had planned. With a deep sigh, Rachael turned around and headed back toward her quarters. Some time soon she and Andrew needed to have a long talk.

Chapter Eleven

Deep in the heart of the former Human Empire, unrest steadily grew. The Druins had clamped down on free speech and were even limiting what could be taught in the local schools. The leaders of three of the Imperial worlds were meeting in secret to discuss their options.

"We can't continue like this," proclaimed Governor Rastell of Bratol Three. "They take many of our young people every year and are making more and more demands."

"On Lydol Four they're demanding a major share of our heavy metals," said Governor Swen. "They'll cripple our economy." Lydol four had the largest of the secret bases established long ago.

"It's the same on my world," said Governor Alliton. "I've heard rumors they'll double the number of young people they'll take this year."

"We can't go on like this," said Rastell. "We must do something. We're an Empire."

"A forgotten empire," replied Swen, shaking his head. "All references to the Human Empire have been erased from our history books. No mention of the Empire can even be made in our schools. All that our children know of the former Empire is what is handed down by word of mouth from their parents."

"We have a small fleet we've built in secret," said Alliton. "We also have some defensive platforms we can place in orbit. We could decree our independence from the Confederation and request we be listed as free worlds."

"They won't agree," replied Rastell, his eyes narrowing. "The only worlds they allow to be free are very primitive with limited space travel."

"What if we agree to only allow space travel between our three star systems?"

Alliton shook her head. "I don't know. We must do something. The people are close to revolting as it is."

Governor Swen made a suggestion. "What if we combine our three fleets and all our orbital defenses and put them around just one world? Perhaps the Druins will agree to our demands rather than risk an armed confrontation."

Governor Alliton looked doubtful. "The last world to try that was nearly destroyed."

"That was centuries ago," pointed out Swen. "And they didn't have any heavily armed ships or a defensive system. I suggest we let one world negotiate for the others. That way we risk only one planet, if something goes wrong."

"And billions of people," said Governor Alliton. "This could be extremely dangerous."

"It may be, but we have to do something," said Governor Swen. "If all three systems go into open revolt, we would be risking so much more. At least this way, with only one planet stepping up, if the Druins do attack, the other two systems can come with aid to rebuild, if necessary."

"Then we're in agreement," said Governor Alliton. "The only question is, which system defies the Druins?"

"Mine," said Governor Swen. "My people seem to be the most worked up, so they should applaud my actions here. Plus we have the smallest population and will be the easiest to defend, as we have no major colonies on any of our moons, except a few mining operations."

Everyone nodded in agreement. "When do you want to proclaim your independence?" asked Governor Rastell.

"In one week," replied Governor Swen. "That will give us time to get our fleets in position, as well as the defensive grid."

"This is a huge risk," said Alliton, "but I agree we are out of options."

Governor Swen leaned back in his chair and let out a deep sigh. "Let's hope we're not making a huge mistake, but the Druins have driven us to this point."

"We're in this together," said Governor Alliton. "If the Druins attack your world, we'll furnish all the assistance we can to aid in the recovery."

"Let's hope it doesn't come to that," said Governor Rastell. "This will be dangerous. Let's just hope it works."

On Pallas several days had passed, and Andrew had been called back to meet with the Council. As Brenda led him through the complex to the Council chambers, Andrew couldn't help but wonder about the last few days. He knew he had gotten carried away with Kala, but what was a guy to do when a beautiful willing woman stood nude next to his bed? He didn't regret going to bed with Kala, but he had noticed that Rachael had been keeping her distance.

Reaching the Council chambers, Andrew went in, noting the full Council was present and the viewing stands were full as well.

"Welcome, Mr. Wilcox," greeted Lena Prest. "Have a seat, and we'll get this meeting underway."

Andrew sat down in the lone empty chair and turned his attention toward Lena.

"After much debate and after speaking with several of our scientists who are well versed in computers, we have decided to accept Rachael's idea of putting a virus in the Druin interdiction system to take it over. In order to make this happen, we will allow the following to occur. First, you will be allowed to contact your people and inform them you are still alive. You may not tell them exactly where you are. You may also tell them who the other survivors of the *Endeavor* are. What we need for you to do is set up a meeting with your Imperial leaders, as well as some of Earth's government officials on the space station near Earth's Moon. We will return you and your three crewmates to Earth on the *Destiny*, which Captain Masters will command. Several of our

Council members will go, as well as a few of our scientists to explain what our needs are. We are also recommending that a general revelation of our base not be made at this time."

Andrew nodded. He was relieved to hear they would all be allowed to go home. "I believe all that can be done. My people have connections with most of the major governments, so we should get the right people to the meeting."

"Excellent," replied Lena with a smile. She stood and looked at the other Council members, as well as those in the viewing stands. "Today is an important day, as it marks the beginning of us actively engaging in war against the Druins and the policies of the Confederation. For over one thousand years we have prepared this base and have built up our fleet. If we are successful in taking over the software running the Druin interdiction system then we stand a very good chance of someday returning to our homeworlds and freeing them from the clutches of terror they have been forced to endure."

"Will the Empire even be remembered?" asked one of the spectators. "We don't know what the Druins have done back home."

"No, we don't," admitted Lena. "But sometime very soon, we'll send a mission back to the Empire to determine exactly what remains and what we'll need to do to free it. However, we must contact Earth first and get the software engineers working on this project."

"So what do you want me to do?" asked Andrew, wanting a little clarification.

"Go with Captain Masters. He will take you to our communications center, where there is hyperlight communication equipment. Contact your people and inform them of what's going on. Just remember. For the time being, don't reveal our exact location."

Andrew nodded. "I won't."

Captain Masters stood and indicated for Andrew to follow him. Once they were out of the Council chambers, the captain paused and turned toward Andrew. "This is a big step we're taking. There's a big difference in preparing for war and participating in war. It was very difficult for the Council to come to this decision, but it is the right one."

Captain Masters then led Andrew through the complex and into the communications center. Stepping inside, Andrew was surprised at what was here. Dozens of viewscreens on the walls revealed current media programming from Earth.

"We monitor Earth's communications constantly," explained Masters. "Reports are given to the Council on a weekly basis on current advancements and political movements."

Masters led Andrew to a large communications console. "This is our hyperlight transmitter and receiver. Put in the coordinates of where you want the message to go and press Transmit."

Andrew sat down. He had brought his laptop with him. "Can I link this to the console?"

One of the technicians standing nearby stepped over and, after a few moments, had the laptop connected.

Taking a deep breath, Andrew pressed the Send button, which should put him in contact with Major Henderson on Earth's space station.

On board the space station, Major Henderson was startled when a red light on a nearby console started blinking.

"What's that?" asked Colonel Gleeson, the station's commanding officer.

Major Henderson walked over and turned off the blinking light. "Defective warning light. I'll have it replaced." Henderson returned to his command chair and then, after a few minutes, informed the colonel he was going to go inspect one of the small landing bays in the station.

A few minutes later Henderson was in his quarters and had retrieved a laptop, like the one Andrew had. "Andrew?"

"I'm here," replied Andrew. "I've found Sanctuary and have made some new friends. They want to bring a ship to the station, but they have a few requests to make first." For the next twenty minutes Andrew explained what the Imperials on Pallas wanted.

"Wow! That's a big list," said Henderson, impressed. "I'll have to get in contact with Brett and see what can be arranged. I also understand why your friends don't want to reveal their location, even though I can guess pretty close to where it must be. How soon do we need to plan this meeting?"

"As you probably have guessed, their ships are quite a bit faster than ours. I'll be traveling in a stealth light cruiser and one the Druin interdiction system should not be able to detect. Travel time from here to the station will only be a few hours."

Henderson thought over what he would need to do. First thing would be contacting Brett. "Contact me again in forty-eight hours. I should know something by then."

"Sounds good," replied Andrew. "One more thing. Would you tell my parents I'm still alive?"

"Definitely. That will be one job I'll thoroughly enjoy."

On Lydol Four, Governor Swen met with the admiral in command of the small fleet they were preparing to launch. "If this erupts into a battle between us and the Druins, it will not end well for us. We hope by showing a fleet and a defensive grid above the planet, the Druins will realize we're serious about this independence declaration. We're making some promises in the declaration that we hope the Druins will accept."

"Such as?" asked Admiral Cleemorl.

"Our fleet will not venture out of our system. It will only deal with pirates. None of our ships will venture into Confederation space. We will only trade with nearby Imperial worlds, and we will limit technological advancements."

Admiral Cleemorl let out a deep sigh. "I don't think the Druins will see it our way."

"What do you think their response will be?"

Admiral Cleemorl stood and walked over to the window, looking up at the stars. "They'll hit us with one of their fleets and then level all the cities on the planet. We'll lose, at a conservative estimate, 60 percent of our population. Maybe more."

Governor Swen shook his head. "I don't know what else to do. If we do nothing, our people will revolt. If they do, the Druins may destroy the entire planet."

"A rock and a hard place," uttered Admiral Cleemorl. "Our combined fleet consists of eight battlecruisers and twelve support ships. That's not a lot to oppose a Druin battle fleet."

"Let's hope it doesn't come to that."

"When will you make the announcement?"

"Tomorrow. We're putting up the defensive platforms tonight, and the last of the fleet units will be here in the morning."

Admiral Cleemorl returned to the governor's desk and sat down. "It will take the Druins a few days to respond. Maybe a week before the nearest fleet can get to us. I would suggest we evacuate all the larger cities and get as many people underground as possible."

Governor Swen nodded. "What do you expect will happen?"

Admiral Cleemorl looked directly at the governor. "If the Druins attack, I expect to die. I will do my duty to the Empire, but I don't see this ending well."

Governor Swen watched as the admiral left his office. Swen decided to call his wife. It might be a good idea if she took the kids and went to visit her aunt out in the country.

Andrew was in the Council chambers, making the final arrangements before they left for Earth. Brett, Professor Mallory Stark, and a few other Earth Imperials would be on the LaGrange Point station, as well as government representatives of five of the most major countries involved in the space program. The representatives didn't know for sure what was going on, other than it involved the *Endeavor* and what happened to it.

"Once we arrive," Andrew stated, "we'll board the station, and I'll introduce you to two members of Earth's Imperial Council. They, in turn, will introduce you to the government representatives who will be there. Once everyone's been introduced, Brett Newcomb will give a brief history of the Imperials on Earth to the representatives. Once that's done, he will have one of you explain exactly what the Human Empire is, the Confederation, and what happened with the Druins."

"Will they believe us?" asked Admiral Bract. "We'll be giving them a lot of information they will find hard to believe."

Andrew smiled. "We will have the *Destiny* to back up our claims. I have spoken to Captain Masters, and he has proposed making a short trip to Mars and back. That demonstration of advanced technology should easily convince the Earth representatives what they're hearing is the truth."

Lena nodded, as if satisfied with what she heard. "We will need to open up an embassy on Earth, where we can begin to work on rapidly advancing Earth's sciences, particularly its space program. If we can successfully implant a virus to control the Druin interdiction system then I see no reason why we can't drastically improve Earth's spacecraft, putting the entire Solar System within their reach. We have the science to completely terraform Mars within a twenty-year period, particularly after the discovery of so much liquid water beneath its surface. Venus can be terraformed as well, though its living conditions will never be like Earth or Mars due to its proximity to the sun."

Andrew nodded. "All you suggest will be strong reasons for the Earth governments to agree to our requests. While it's not necessary at this time that the entire planet be united, its space services need to be united under one agency."

They spent another hour discussing some of the finer details and then Andrew returned to his quarters. He was surprised to find both Rachael and Kala there, waiting for him. Rachael had finally started speaking to him again and had told him she knew about Kala spending the night. The two women had evidently worked everything out between them with no animosity. He led them both inside his quarters, pointing them to the two matching chairs.

"So, we're going home," said Kala, smiling. "It will be good to get back to Earth."

"We will all be glad to be back," said Rachael. "I just wonder how much will change with the revelations about the Imperials and the Druins?"

"Not a lot at first," replied Andrew, sitting down across from the two women. "At first this knowledge will be limited. It will be a strictly need-to-know basis, except for the higher levels of people in the space program. As more and more Imperial technology is introduced, we'll expand that group until we reach the proper time to reveal the existence of Pallas and what is here."

"Professor Marcus is staying here for now," said Rachael. "Adrian says she has so much to learn here that she's thinking about staying for a year or two. She doesn't have any close family back on Earth, and she enjoys being on Pallas."

Andrew nodded. "That won't be a problem. I suspect ships will regularly travel back and forth between Pallas and Earth once we gain control of the interdiction system."

"I might come back myself," said Kala. "I expect an influx of scientists and technicians from Earth coming to learn Imperial technology and science. I want to be a part of that group."

"Life will change," replied Andrew. He knew his would. "We will be leaving late tomorrow."

Rachael stood to leave. "I better go check on Adrian. She was going to one of the habitats, and there's a good chance she's gotten herself lost again. I'll probably have to get Brenda to help me find her." Rachael left Andrew's quarters, leaving him alone with Kala.

Kala gestured for Andrew to come sit down beside her. When he did, she leaned into his arms. "This is our last night together on Pallas. Let's make the most of it."

Andrew bent down and kissed her. He had no problem with what Kala suggested.

Above Lydol Four, Admiral Cleemorl was in his flagship, watching the approaching Druin fleet.

"It's not as big as I was expecting," said Captain Fulmar.

"Two hundred of their battleships is still far larger than what we have," replied Cleemorl. "Governor Swen will try to contact the Druin admiral and see if he can arrange a meeting to discuss the current situation. Even if they don't agree to our demands, they may be willing to reduce some of the restrictions they've placed on us to avoid an armed confrontation."

Captain Fulmar nodded. "The odds against us are not good. The Druins still have their fusion cannons and their antimatter weapons. If they attack our fleet, I'm afraid the battle will be very brief."

"The governor is trying to contact the Druin admiral," reported the communications officer. "So far there has been no response."

Several more minutes passed as the Druin fleet drew nearer.

"Governor Swen is now sending the list of our demands for peace."

Admiral Cleemorl's gaze was glued to the tactical display, hoping to see the Druin fleet come to a stop. It did not and continued to advance.

"No response," reported the communications officer.

Admiral Cleemorl drew in a sharp breath. "I was afraid of this. Take the fleet to Condition One and pull us back closer to the defensive grid. We'll add its firepower to ours and hope for the best. Maybe it will be enough to cause the Druins to pause and to consider our offer."

"I doubt that," said Captain Fulmar. "These are Druins, and they are cold-blooded. I don't believe they will talk. They have come here to destroy us and our world, and I'm afraid that's just what they'll do."

The small Human fleet moved closer to the defensive grid of Lydol Four. The grid consisted of seventy energy beam platforms and twenty missile platforms. All were protected by weak energy shields.

Beneath the surface of the planet, near the capital city, Governor Swen was in a deep underground bunker. It had been built as a secret Command Center, in case the Druins ever attacked the planet. It was also connected to the massive secret underground base.

"No response to our messages," reported the communications officer.

"They are still advancing on the planet," added the colonel, sitting in front of the sensor console. "They will be in attack range of our fleet and the defensive grid in another seven minutes."

General Creel stepped closer to the governor. "What do you want to do?"

Governor Swen let out a deep sigh. "What can we do? We've evacuated all the major cities, and many of our people are hiding in the mountains and in what underground shelters we have. The Druins and their policies forced us to this point."

"Admiral Cleemorl wants to know if he is cleared to fire on the Druins if they fire first?"

Swen leaned back in his chair. The chance of this working had been very small to begin with. "Keep attempting to contact the Druins. Tell them we're willing to stand down if they are willing to negotiate with us. No one needs to die today."

The communications officer spent several long minutes attempting to contact the approaching Druin spacecraft. "No response, sir. I'm positive they're receiving. They're refusing to acknowledge our communications."

Swen looked at the general. "Contact Admiral Cleemorl. He has permission to defend himself. If the Druins fire, the defensive grid will be activated immediately. Also order all bunkers and underground facilities to seal themselves in and to prepare for surface bombardment up to and including antimatter missiles."

Messages were quickly sent out as the people in the Command Center watched the tactical display and viewscreens with growing apprehension. All the media stations were now reporting that a Druin fleet was in the system, and there was a good chance the planet would be attacked. Everyone was told to take cover.

Governor Swen felt ill over what was about to happen. A little over two billion people lived on Lydol Four. He wondered how many would be alive in the following days.

"Engagement range," reported the tactical officer.

Admiral Cleemorl gazed tensely at the tactical display, hoping the Druins would not fire.

"Detecting missile launches and energy beam fire!" called out the sensor officer in a panicked voice.

The *Themis* shook slightly as an energy beam brushed its energy shield. On the viewscreens, massive explosions filled space, as antimatter missiles slammed into the energy shields of the small fleet of defenders.

"Return fire!" ordered Admiral Cleemorl, gripping the armrests of his command chair.

"Defense grid is firing," reported Lieutenant Bedell from Tactical. "Launching missiles."

Admiral Cleemorl felt the *Themis* shake slightly as missiles left the tubes. On the viewscreens, he saw two of his support craft vanish in antimatter explosions, which turned them into molten wreckage.

The *Themis* shook violently, and red lights appeared on the damage control console.

"Energy beam strike near the stern, close to Engineering," reported Captain Fulmar. "Emergency bulkheads have closed, sealing off the damaged compartments."

The defensive grid was now firing. Missiles and energy beams struck the incoming Druin battleships. The shields on the enemy ships glowed but did not go down.

"We can't bring down their shields!" cried out Lieutenant Bedell. "We've hit them with multiple fusion missiles to no effect. The same with our energy weapons."

On the viewscreens, another Human battlecruiser blew apart as its energy shield collapsed. The defense grid was also being blasted apart from heavy Druin fusion beam fire.

"Message from Governor Swen," reported Communications. "We're to withdraw and implement something called Last Resort."

Captain Fulmar looked at the admiral in confusion. "What the hell is this Last Resort?" It sounded ominous.

"I'll explain later," replied Cleemorl. "Communications, contact all our ships and inform them to transition into hyperspace and to meet at the Delius System." The Delius System was a red giant located twelve light-years from Lydol Four.

"Message sent," replied the communications officer. "However, I don't have very many ships responding."

Admiral Cleemorl nodded. "They're gone. Helm, get us out of here."

Moments later Admiral Cleemorl felt the *Themis* transition into hyperspace. "How many ships are with us?" He knew it wouldn't be many.

"One other battlecruiser and three support ships," replied the sensor officer.

"Better than I excepted," said Cleemorl. He had expected his entire command to be wiped out.

The admiral leaned back in his command chair. He greatly feared what the Druins were about to do to Lydol Four. Cleemorl also knew that he and his ships could never return to their homeworlds. To do so would invite even more destruction from the Druins.

Back at Lydol Four, the Druin fleet had completed the destruction of the planet's meager defense grid and had now gone into orbit. The sky of the planet was full of flaming debris from the destruction that had occurred in space.

On board the Druin flagship, Admiral Kreen gazed at the blue-white world on the ship's viewscreens. This planet had violated several of the major edicts of the Confederation. They had built warships and had tried to declare their independence. "I want all cities destroyed with a population larger than one hundred thousand. The use of antimatter missiles against the planet is approved. Also I want all the orbiting satellites destroyed, as well as the space station. Leave nothing in orbit."

On Lydol Four in the underground Command Center, Governor Swen watched helplessly as the Druins launched a rain of deadly antimatter missiles toward the planet. "Is there anything we can do?"

General Creel shook his head. "We have a few defensive missiles, but they will do little good. The Druins will continue to launch their missiles, until all their targets have been destroyed."

Governor Swen sank down into his chair, his head bowed. He had led his world to catastrophe. He had never dreamed the Druins would react like this. He had thought, at the worst, if they didn't agree to his terms, they might take out a few of the major cities, including the capital. That was why he had evacuated them. But now, on the tactical display, hundreds of Druin antimatter missiles plummeted toward the planet's surface.

Swen forced himself to look at the viewscreens. Several of the planet's larger cities were displayed. Suddenly a brilliant light formed above one of them, as an antimatter fireball formed. Buildings blew apart, while others burst into flame. Superheated air rushed to the center of the blast, forming a massive mushroom cloud that rose above the helpless city. The blast moved outward, destroying more buildings and setting more fires. Soon a firestorm enveloped the city, destroying everything.

"It's gone," said Swen, barely able to speak.

"At least there's no radiation," said the general. "We will rebuild, once the Druins leave."

"If they leave any of us alive," replied Swen, his gaze now glued to the viewscreens, showing the destruction ravishing his world.

In orbit, Admiral Kreen watched coldly as his missiles destroyed the cities on the planet. After nearly an hour he was satisfied that everything of importance on the planet had been annihilated. The survivors would be allowed to rebuild, but they had been taught a lesson they would not soon forget. The rules of the Confederation were not to be violated.

"Take the fleet out of orbit, and we will resume our patrol. This minor problem has been dealt with."

On the ship's main viewscreen, smoke, ash, and other debris darkened the atmosphere of the planet. It was no longer the pristine blue-white world it had been just a few hours earlier.

Admiral Cleemorl's flagship dropped out of hyperspace in the Delius System, along with the other surviving ships of his fleet.

"What do we do now?" asked Captain Fulmar.

"We're going to the Bacchus Region."

Captain Fulmar's eyes widened. "Why the Bacchus Region? Nothing's there. It's a dead area of space with no inhabited worlds."

Admiral Cleemorl leaned back in his chair with a deep sigh. "One of my remote ancestors was a distant relative of the Royal Family of the Empire. Immediately after the Druins attacked and conquered our worlds some thousand years ago, they gathered up most of the remaining Royal Family and members of the Royal

Court and took them to a system in the Bacchus Region. They were banished from ever returning to the Empire."

Captain Fulmar still didn't fully understand. "Why go there? By now they are probably long dead."

"Maybe not," answered Cleemorl. "Supposedly a primitive Human world was in the system."

Captain Fulmar slowly nodded his head. "You're hoping that, by now, they've developed a higher level of civilization, due to our people being marooned there?"

"Yes, it's the only real hope we have and the only place we can go to escape the Druins."

"What is the name of this world?"

"Earth," replied Admiral Cleemorl. "We're going to Earth."

Chapter Twelve

Andrew was in his quarters on the *Destiny*, speaking with Kala and Rachael. "We'll be at the station in another few hours. Have the two of you decided what you'll say?"

"I suppose we should describe the attack on the *Endeavor*," replied Kala. "The government people need to understand how dangerous the Druin interdiction system is."

"We also need to make certain they realize that Captain Greer tried everything she could to prevent her ship from being attacked and destroyed," added Rachael.

Andrew nodded. "The *Endeavor* did send a report on the drone approaching the ship. They were broadcasting sensor readings right up to the very end, so there is a full record on the station, as well as video of what happened." Major Henderson had that record, and Andrew didn't know if the major had made it available yet. Andrew would find out when they got to the station.

Rachael let out a deep sigh. "It's still hard to believe everyone else from the *Endeavor* is all gone. How can the Druins be so heartless?"

"They're a cold-blooded methodical race," replied Andrew. "They also make plans covering a long period of time. All the Confederation races do. Many of them have lifespans which measure anywhere from five hundred to nearly seven hundred years. So, to them, a plan that takes a century or two to come to fruition is normal."

Kala's eyes widened. "How long do Imperials live?"

Andrew hesitated and then replied. "With the proper life-extending medications, an Imperial can expect to live a productive life of nearly two hundred years, maybe a little longer."

"Have you taken those medications?"

"Yes, Earth's science reached the point only in the last fifty years where the compounds we needed for the life-extension drugs became available."

Kala looked at Andrew with an inquisitive look on her face. "What do you plan on doing when we get back?"

"I'm not sure. I'll have to speak to Earth's Imperial Council and see what they have planned."

"I need to speak to my father," said Kala, a concerned note in her voice. "His credibility with his colleagues is at an all-time low. He took many of them to see his discovery on Cyprus, and, as you know, everything had been removed. All that was replaced with a few broken shards of pottery and some primitive cave drawings of animals."

"After the other archeologists left, Alan Foster took your father aside and explained to him what had happened," said Andrew. "From what I understand, he was extremely upset, but the Imperial Council paid him a considerable sum to finance some other dig sites."

Kala nodded. "I'll speak to him when I get back and try to explain everything better. I'm sure he will understand."

Andrew looked seriously at the two women. "Remember. Once we return to Earth, we can't mention Pallas to anybody. Only the Imperials on Earth, some scientists, and a few government and military officials will know the truth of what happened to the *Endeavor*. In a few more years, everything will be more broadly known, but it's imperative we keep it a secret for now."

"At least until we can infect the Druin interdiction system with a virus," said Rachael. "I know several computer programmers who would be excellent at making such a virus or just over writing the code, allowing us control over the system. We even have a few on the space station."

A knock came on the door, and Ensign Allert came in. "Do any of you need anything before we arrive at the space station?"

"We're fine," replied Rachael. "What are your plans when we get there?"

Brenda came in and sat down. "I would love to see Earth. Captain Masters is thinking about letting the entire crew go down for a few days. Some of Earth's Imperials would be responsible for showing us around. I haven't been on a planet since we left the Empire. I miss the wide-open spaces. I would really like to visit one of Earth's oceans and go swimming. I used to swim all the time back home."

"Maybe we can arrange that," said Rachael.

In the Command Center of the *Destiny*, Captain Masters sat in his command chair, keeping a watchful eye on the tactical display as well as on the main viewscreen. The tactical display revealed a few green icons, which were Earth spacecraft on their way to Mars or the Moon. A large green icon pinpointed their destination, the Earth-Moon LaGrange Point, where the space station was located.

"Someday soon that space station will have to be armed," said Lieutenant Commander Banora. She had been watching the sensors as well, making sure there were no indications of the Druin interdiction system detecting the *Destiny*. With the *Destiny*'s stealth capabilities, that was unlikely this deep into the Solar System.

"There will be a lot of changes soon," replied Captain Masters. "As soon as we gain control over the interdiction system, I imagine some of our warships will be stationed near Earth on permanent patrols."

"We're really doing this, aren't we?" said Audrey. "This is our first step into going to war against the Confederation."

Derrick leaned back in his command chair and slowly nodded his head. "Yes, if this works, within one hundred years, we may be launching our first attacks to free our worlds."

"Are we going back into cryo? I would like to see our homeworlds freed."

"Eventually we may return to cryo," answered Derrick. "We may stay awake for a few years, until I'm satisfied everything's going as planned."

Lieutenant Commander Banora was pleased with this answer. "When will we awaken the Princess?"

"She'll be needed for the war. Once the people back in the Empire find out a member of the Royal Family survived, they will rally to our cause."

"If they still remember us?" Audrey reminded Derrick. "We don't know what changes there has been in the Empire under Confederation rule."

Derrick frowned at this reminder. However, plans had been made for a hidden resistance in the Empire. While some of the people might not remember the Empire, no doubt others still did. "If they've forgotten, we'll remind them."

"I hope it's as simple as that," said Admiral Bract, standing in front of the viewscreen, now showing a highly magnified view of Earth. "I'm afraid that, for a number of years, Earth will have to bear the responsibility of protecting the Empire and itself. The Confederation controls a major part of our galaxy and all the heavily populated regions. We'll eventually need the entire Empire behind us if we want to be successful in freeing our worlds from the Druins and the Confederation."

Lieutenant Commander Banora's gaze shifted to the admiral. "How long a war are we talking about? I always thought we would just free the Empire, and that would be it."

Admiral Bract shook his head. "No, it's a lot more complicated than that. This could become a very long war that might last for generations. In the end, either we'll survive and make major changes in the Confederation or we will fail. If we fail, then the Human race will be doomed to be under Confederation control for perhaps thousands of years."

Audrey shuddered at that thought. She knew how overbearing and demanding the Confederation could be.

On board the space station, Colonel Gleeson looked at his second in command. Orders from his superiors on Earth had temporarily placed Major Henderson in charge of the station. "I don't understand what's going on."

"Things are about to change," replied Henderson. "What if I told you a race of very advanced Humans in the Solar System and one of their ships was about to pay us a visit?"

Gleeson shook his head. "I would think you've been drinking or using drugs. There is no such race."

Major Henderson smiled. "But there is. I am a member of that race. Lieutenant Jenkins, focus your viewscreen on the following location." Henderson gave Jenkins a series of coordinates.

Jenkins adjusted the main viewscreen, and suddenly a black object appeared in the center of the screen. "That is the Imperial vessel *Destiny*. It is a stealth light cruiser of the ancient Human Empire."

"I'm not picking up anything on our sensors," reported Ensign Bryant. "It's as if nothing's there."

Colonel Gleeson stood and approached the viewscreen. "How fast is that ship moving?"

"Not sure," replied Jenkins. "But I'm having trouble keeping the viewscreen focused on it. It's moving far faster than any spacecraft we have."

Colonel Gleeson turned to face Major Henderson, waiting for an explanation.

"That ship will have the survivors from the *Endeavor*, as well as several emissaries from the Imperial Council," explained Major Henderson. Henderson had managed to intercept all the communications from the *Endeavor* describing the attack. All anyone in the station's Command Center knew was that the ship had disappeared.

"Survivors!" uttered Gleeson in disbelief.

"Yes, the Imperials rescued part of the crew."

Colonel Gleeson came back and sat down in his chair. His face was slightly pale. "Is there anything else you're not telling me?"

"Some," admitted Henderson. "Part of it is on a strict need-to-know basis. Eventually a superior officer will brief you. I can tell you that things in this station and around the Solar System are about to change and change drastically. How does flying from here to Mars in less than a few hours sound?"

"Impossible," replied Gleeson, his eyes growing wide.

Henderson gestured toward the ship on the viewscreen. "That ship can do it. If you want, I can arrange for the captain of that vessel to take you and a few others on a trip to Mars, just to prove what I said."

Realizing what Major Henderson had just offered, Colonel Gleeson suddenly grasped how important this first contact was going to be. Less than a day from Earth to Mars would revolutionize space travel. It would make all the rest of the planets and moons in the Solar System easily accessible. "Very well then. I'll withhold my judgment until later. If what you say is true, this could indeed be a historic meeting."

"Major Henderson, the ship will be here in another twenty minutes, as near as I can tell," reported Ensign Bryant.

Henderson had to smile. He would be pleased to see Andrew and the other survivors. Andrew had succeeded in his mission and was returning safely. He had found Sanctuary, and, more than that, they had a plan to deal with the Druin interdiction system.

—

The *Destiny* approached the space station and docked to an external docking port. Andrew, Kala, Rachael, Admiral Bract, and Councilor Arianna Bliss waited for the hatch to open. Captain Masters was staying on board so he could communicate with Pallas if necessary. Several scientists who had come with them would be staying on board as well until they were needed.

"This should be interesting," said Andrew, as he waited patiently. There were two hatches. The one on the outer airlock of the *Destiny* and the one on the end of the docking port.

The sound of the interconnecting corridor being pressurized signaled that the two hatches were about to open. With a slight hiss, the *Destiny*'s hatch slid back, and the adjoining hatch opened inward.

"Follow me," instructed Andrew. "We'll go through that second hatch and then through a short decontamination procedure. It won't take more than a minute or two."

The five went down the short docking corridor and opened the hatch at the end, stepping into a small room, just large enough to hold all of them. A series of lights came on, and after two minutes a light turned green, indicating decontamination was complete.

"That's it," said Andrew, as he opened the next hatch and gestured for everyone to follow him. Stepping into the station, he saw both Major Henderson and Brett Newcomb waiting for them.

"Hello," said Brett. "I'm Brett Newcomb and a member of Earth's Imperial Council."

Andrew quickly introduced the two Imperials with him.

Brett nodded. "If all of you will come with me, we have a briefing room set up with refreshments and sandwiches. Professor Mallory Stark and some government officials are waiting for us there. We have a lot to talk about."

—

For nearly six hours the group met behind closed doors, discussing the Druin interdiction system, the destruction of the *Endeavor*, and a myriad of other issues. To help the Earth officials to better understand the danger, the last messages transmitted from the *Endeavor* before it was destroyed were played, as well as some video that was received. Afterward, Brett put up a visual of a Druin attack drone and then one of an actual Druin, which brought gasps from the watching representatives.

"This is astonishing," said Vice President Hicks of the North American Union. "I'm very sad and horrified to find out the truth of what happened to the *Endeavor*. However, before I commit to any agreement, I would like to know more about the Human Empire. Was it a democracy, a republic, a dictatorship, or what? I mean, we have been told there was a Royal Family, as well as a King."

"It was what you would call a constitutional monarchy," answered Councilor Bliss. "Each world had a governor, elected by the people. Each world also elected a representative to attend government meetings on Golan Four in the House of Worlds. The representatives would make our laws, which the King would then carry out. The King did have considerable authority, but any order he gave could be rescinded by a meeting of the planetary representatives."

"If we agree to this, what's in it for us?" asked the Western European representative.

Imperial Admiral Bract stood and smiled. "We will provide you with a sublight space drive capable of reaching Mars in less than a day. We can terraform Mars to make it fully habitable in less than twenty years. We can do the same thing for Venus, though it won't be quite as hospitable as Earth or Mars. We also have considerable advancements in medical treatments that will cure many of your diseases. We can also add a few decades to the average Human lifespan. There are other things as well, but those will have to be worked out in more detail later. Of prime importance now is creating a computer virus to give us control of the Druin interdiction system before it attacks and kills off much of Earth's population."

"Why would they attack us?" asked the Chinese representative. "We've done nothing to them."

"It doesn't matter," answered Councilor Bliss. "Once you develop an FTL drive or your civilization reaches a certain point in technological development, the Druins will consider your world a threat to the Confederation. When that happens, they will either send their attack drones in to reduce your population or will send in one of their battlefleets to subdue your world. This is what they have done for tens of thousands of years. There is no negotiating with the Confederation. Look at what they did to the *Endeavor*, and it wasn't even armed."

"What do you recommend we do?" asked General Brier, who was the military representative from the North American Union.

Admiral Bract took a deep breath and then replied. "We need to delay the Druins from attacking Earth for as long as possible. In order to do that, we need to take control of their interdiction system by implanting a virus that will allow us to control it. We can send fake reports to the Druins for years, without them realizing what has happened. Eventually they will send a ship for a routine check of the system and to scan Earth. Once that happens, they will discover what we've done. That's how long we have to prepare. We estimate we're looking at between sixty to one hundred years before a Druin ships shows up."

"So, what are our options?"

Admiral Bract looked directly at General Brier. "We advance Earth as rapidly as possible to current Human Empire standards. We put up a massive defensive grid around Earth, the Moon, Mars, and possibly Venus. We train crews to operate our warships and to prepare for eventual war with the Confederation."

There was silence in the room as the representatives looked at one another. Then the silence was broken as all of them spoke at once.

"What you're asking is impossible," said the European Representative. You can't believe that Earth alone can take on the Confederation, which you say controls much of the galaxy. It would be suicide."

"If you do nothing, they will still come," pointed out Admiral Bract.

For the next several hours there was a heated debate. Finally a consensus was reached.

"We will agree to the following," said Vice President Hicks. "All of our space programs will be combined into one under a joint civilian and military command. We will work at creating a virus to allow the takeover of the Druin interdiction system. We will also furnish some military personnel to crew a limited number of your warships. For now, that's all we can offer, until we discuss this in far more detail with our governments. As far as a future war with the Confederation, that will have to be decided later as well."

Councilor Bliss nodded. "It is more than we had hoped for. We would like to assign some of our people to this station to help in its further development, and we would like to establish an embassy somewhere on Earth. It will be needed if we are to share some of our advanced technology."

This resulted in more debate, with each of the government representatives wanting the embassy in their region.

Finally Brett Newcomb interrupted. "May I make a suggestion? There is nowhere on Earth where everyone will agree to place an embassy. I suggest we place it instead on the Moon. The Moon is a neutral site, and Luna City is growing rapidly. It will have everything needed for the embassy."

After more discussion everyone agreed to Brett's suggestion.

"We have made a tentative agreement today," said Admiral Bract. "I suggest everyone contact their governments and confirm what we've decided. Then, in another day or two, we can meet and sign a formal agreement."

"What about going on a trip to Mars?" asked Colonel Gleeson. "It would help to prove everything you've told us."

Admiral Bract smiled. "I can arrange that. It won't take the *Destiny* more that a few hours to reach Mars and then a few hours to return. If you would like, I can set up the trip for early tomorrow."

Everyone nodded in agreement. None of the government representatives had ever been to Mars, and they were excited about the prospect. It would also give them an opportunity to see some of the Imperials' technology.

Several hours later, after everyone had eaten and retired to their quarters, Brett, Major Henderson, Mallory Stark, Andrew, and Admiral Bract were in a private meeting.

Admiral Bract had been given permission to reveal to the Earth's Imperial Council the location of Sanctuary.

"We were concerned the base might no longer exist," admitted Brett. "It's one of the reasons Andrew was placed on the *Endeavor*. We knew there was a chance the interdiction system, if it existed, might react violently to an Earth spacecraft venturing so far into the Kuiper Belt."

"We watched the *Endeavor* constantly from the time it was launched," said Admiral Bract. "We weren't sure ourselves how the interdiction system would respond."

Andrew took a drink of the tea in the glass he held. "It was frightening being on the *Endeavor* and knowing a Druin attack drone was on its way. Which brings up another question. What if we have problems inserting the virus in the Druin computer system on their primary interdiction stations? Is there a chance the stations might launch their drones if they realize what we're doing? These are AIs we're talking about."

Admiral Bract slowly nodded his head. "There's a chance there might be a response. For that reason I'll have part of our fleet crewed and ready to deploy if we see any sign of drones launching."

"Can you destroy them?" asked Brett.

Admiral Bract smiled. "Yes, we've had one thousand years to advance our weapons technology. We now have fusion energy beams and much more powerful energy shields. We can take out the drones."

"Let's hope so," said Major Henderson. "We can't afford to have Earth hit by the drones. Too much is at stake."

Later both Kala and Rachael stopped by Andrew's quarters.

"We're going home the day after tomorrow," said Kala, smiling. "I can't wait to see my father."

"Remember, there's not a lot you can tell him about what happened," cautioned Andrew.

"I know. I've already been debriefed by Major Henderson. "He's quite thorough."

Andrew looked at Rachael. "What about you?"

"I'll visit my mom and dad and spend a few weeks taking it easy. I've already spoken to Councilor Bliss about returning to Pallas. I want to study so much there."

"I'm sure they'll be glad to have you. I also suspect quite a few other scientists from Earth will be headed toward Pallas, as well as some military personnel."

Kala reached over and took Andrew's hand. "What about you? What will you do now?"

Andrew shook his head. "I'm not sure. I found Sanctuary, and now they're in contact with my people, as well as some of Earth's governments. I've thought about returning to Pallas and going into cryo. I would like to see what our actions today bring about in the future. I would also like to see our former homeworlds."

Kala pulled back her hand with a strange look on her face. "You would consider going into cryo for nearly one hundred years? Everyone you know would be dead!"

"I know. It's something I need to discuss with my parents. You could come with me."

"No, I don't think so. My life is here on Earth. I might go to Pallas for a while to do research, but I can't leave my parents or the rest of my family. I'm sorry, but going into cryo is something I can't do."

Andrew nodded in understanding. "I accept that. If I do decide to go into cryo, it won't be for another year or two."

Kala bit her lip. She was shaken by Andrew's admission about going into cryo. She had hoped they could build a life together, once they were safely back on Earth. "I guess this is it then. I'm looking for a long-term relationship. I was hoping you might feel the same."

Andrew smiled. "I do like you Kala, and in other circumstances what you're suggesting would sound really good. But for me, there is much more at stake since we found Sanctuary. I have to see how all of this ends."

Kala let out a deep breath. She had been falling in love with Andrew, and now all those dreams had just come crashing down. "If you change your mind, let me know." With that Kala stood and left Andrew's quarters, never looking back.

"I'm sorry, Andrew," said Rachael. "I think Kala wants a big family and has no interest in flying around the galaxy in an interstellar war. In many ways I can't blame her."

"Neither do I. Kala has a lot going for her, and I'm sure she'll find someone who will make her happy. I'm just not that person, it appears."

Rachael stood. "I better go check on her. She's probably not thinking very straight right now. Maybe I'll see you on Pallas."

Andrew nodded. "Maybe. I'll definitely be returning there as soon as I take care of some things down on Earth."

Andrew watched as Rachael left his quarters. With a deep sigh, he knew that this part of his life was over, and he was preparing to set out on a new one. He wondered what awaited him in the future.

The next morning Admiral Bract led the Earth government representatives and some others on board the *Destiny*. Captain Masters met them at the main airlock and took them on a brief tour of the light cruiser. The Imperial scientists on board had gone over to the space station for some meetings.

"This is amazing," said Colonel Gleeson, as he stared at the ship's sublight drive in Engineering. "That's far smaller than anything we've developed. How fast can it move this ship?"

Captain Masters smiled. "If we push it, we can get up to a speed of around one-quarter the speed of light. We could go faster, but we would need a better power source. Currently we use a very advanced fusion power core for our energy."

"Is this ship armed?" asked General Brier.

Captain Masters looked at Admiral Bract.

"Yes, it is," answered Bract. "It's been updated to our current Imperial standards. The ship is equipped with both fusion and antimatter missiles as well as fusion energy beam turrets. It also has a very powerful energy shield to use, if needed."

"And this is one of your smaller ships?"

Admiral Bract nodded. "Yes, our battlecruisers and dreadnoughts are far larger and capable of very long voyages, if necessary."

They continued through the ship with Captain Masters and Admiral Bract answering questions as they went through the different departments. Finally they arrived in the Command Center, where some seats had been added to accommodate the extra people.

"If everyone will take a seat, we'll be leaving the space station shortly," Derrick informed them. "The trip to Mars will take two hours and fourteen minutes."

A few minutes later Derrick gave the order to disconnect from the space station and to prepare to embark on their journey.

"Lieutenant Viktor, disconnect from the station and set a course for the planet Mars. We'll be traveling at one-fourth power, so our guests can experience what it's like to travel through space. I'm sure they will have a number of questions about how our Command Center functions."

The lieutenant quickly guided the *Destiny* away from the space station, as displayed on the main viewscreen. Then the station appeared to shrink and quickly vanish as the *Destiny* accelerated away.

"Remarkable," said Vice President Hicks. "I can't even tell we're moving. Is there any chance of the ship being struck by an asteroid?"

Derrick shook his head. "No, our sensors would detect it, and we have the energy shield up at low strength. It would either destroy or deflect such an object."

The rest of the trip to Mars was full of questions, with Captain Masters and Admiral Bract attempting to answer most of them. When the two hours were up, Mars appeared on the viewscreen.

"Take us into orbit," ordered Derrick. "We'll let our visitors get a good view of the planet."

For thirty minutes the *Destiny* slowly orbited Mars, before Derrick gave the order to return to Earth. He could tell the Earth representatives were impressed.

"I think this demonstration seals the deal," said General Brier. "If we can take over the Druin interdiction system, then I see great things ahead for Earth. We can colonize the Solar System and build up our own fleet."

The others nodded. They could all see the wisdom of accepting the current deal with the Imperials.

Admiral Bract had to smile to himself. This had gone far better than expected. Now if they could develop the virus to allow them to take control of the Druin interdiction system then Earth, along with the Imperials of both Earth and Pallas, would be ready to take their place as a galactic power. One that someday would fight to free the Human Empire. However, first they had to take everything one step at a time, and the interdiction system would be up first.

Chapter Thirteen

The *Themis* approached the Ridge Star Cluster, notorious for being the home to pirates and numerous other illegal activities. Most civilized races stayed far away from the cluster, as it was very dangerous to approach.

"Why here?" asked Captain Fulmar, gazing at the viewscreen showing the star cluster. He had heard many stories about the cluster. None of them were good. Too many ships had vanished in this region, most falling victim to pirates.

"Supplies," replied Admiral Cleemorl. "The trip to Earth is a long one, and we don't have its exact coordinates. I only know its general location." He did have some old maps in his quarters which he needed to go over. He was hoping the location might be on one of them.

—

The small fleet finally dropped out of hyperspace in a system filled with small and large asteroids. On several of the larger asteroids were huge domed cities, housing the races deemed refuse from Human space as well as thousands from other worlds. The asteroids were heavily armed with small patrol ships, scanning all the approaches. A massive black market operated in this system. If one had the credits, it was possible to buy anything one could imagine.

—

"Order the *Rhys* to remain here with our escorts. We'll take the *Themis* in and see if we can dock to take on supplies."

Captain Fulmar shook his head. "I don't like this. We're talking about pirates, who won't hesitate to betray us. What do we do if the Druins come here? They're bound to be looking for us."

"That's why we're not staying long," replied Cleemorl. "I have the names of a few contacts who might help us. While we're gone, the rest of the fleet will remain hidden behind one of the larger uninhabited asteroids."

Captain Fulmar watched on the tactical display, as the *Themis* separated from the fleet and moved toward the largest inhabited asteroid. The rest of the fleet moved behind another asteroid that should shield it from detection.

As the *Themis* approached the inhabited asteroid, Admiral Cleemorl stepped near the communications console. "When we get closer, we'll probably be contacted. Inform them we're here to do business with Cheryl Bannon."

"Cheryl Bannon!" exclaimed Captain Fulmar, his eyes opening wide in concern. "She's rumored to be one of the most dangerous pirates out here."

Admiral Cleemorl laughed. "I met this *dangerous* pirate a number of years back. I can promise you that she's nothing like you imagine."

"We're being contacted," reported the communications officer. "I told them we're here to see Cheryl Bannon. They want to know who we are."

"Tell them, Dylan Cleemorl. Don't mention my military rank."

The communications officer continued to speak over his comm and then turned toward the admiral. "We're to dock at bay fourteen. We'll be charged a fee of 15,000 credits per day for each day we're docked to Highland Station."

"Highland Station," mused Captain Fulmar. "Interesting name for a pirate base."

"You'll be surprised," replied Cleemorl. "Take us in to dock. I don't want any of the crew leaving the ship. You and I will make all the necessary arrangements for supplies."

"You've been here before," said Fulmar in realization. "When?"

"It was years ago, right after I finished my time at the academy. Even then Highland Station was a dangerous place to come to. I came out with some friends to party and to celebrate our graduation and to see somebody." A sad look came over the admiral's face. "Seven of us spent nearly a week drinking, partying, and chasing after women. At the end there was a fight, and two of my friends were killed. I've never been back since then."

"Sorry," replied Fulmar. "I assume we go armed?"

Cleemorl nodded. "Yes, you'll find that nearly everyone has a weapon, even the women."

Captain Fulmar turned to the navigation officer. "Take us into the bay. You have permission to communicate with Highland Station as needed."

On the main viewscreen, the asteroid rapidly grew larger. Hundreds of ships were in the area, ships of every type and size, some from Human worlds and others from non-Human worlds. Numerous shuttles moved back and forth between the ships and the large asteroid.

Many small warships here could be classified as destroyers. They cruised among the various ships, keeping order.

The station consisted of many domes on the surface of the asteroid. The asteroid itself was about 200 hundred kilometers in length and 170 wide. A series of large docking ports were located on the side of one of the domes. That was where the *Themis* headed.

"They've dug deep inside the asteroid," Admiral Cleemorl informed Captain Fulmar. "What you see on the surface is only about one-tenth of what's here. The last I heard, nearly three million sentients lived on the station. Nearly every civilized race is represented, except the Confederation races."

"How do they keep order? It must be a nightmare."

Cleemorl shook his head. "They have a police force, if you want to call it that. They ensure any arguments don't get too far out of hand. Even so, it's still easy to be robbed or even killed if you aren't on your guard."

They continued to watch as the *Themis* eased into the bay and was secured by docking clamps to keep the vessel in place.

"Time to go," said Cleemorl, standing. "This should be interesting. Lieutenant Bedell, you will be in charge while we're gone. Allow no one onto the ship, and allow no one to leave. We'll stay in contact with our comms."

Going to the arms locker, Admiral Cleemorl took out an energy pistol and strapped it to his waist. Captain Fulmar did the same.

"Good," said Cleemorl. "Now, let's go see if we can find Cheryl Bannon."

As they left the ship, Captain Fulmar was surprised to see how modern the docking facility was. They were met at the main hatch by a Human, who indicated they should report to the main docking terminal to pay their docking fees. Payment was demanded in advance, in case they had to leave in a hurry. Fulmar noticed the man wore two very large energy pistols.

Stepping through the hatch, Fulmar noted everything still looked clean and modern. Dock crews were busy servicing ships, and floaters filled with cargo were moving to and from the docked vessels.

"Not what you were expecting?" said Admiral Cleemorl, seeing the confused look on Fulmar's face.

Fulmar shook his head. "No, I was expecting everything to be run-down and falling apart."

Cleemorl laughed. "No, they make a lot of money with their docking facilities. They can repair most ship damage and replace older systems with new ones. Of course all that will cost, but, due to the people who come here, they find their docking services in high demand. They don't ask questions about any suspicious damage or why a ship captain wants certain equipment or weapons added to his vessel. They also don't tolerate any dangerous activity in the docking area."

They went down a well-lit corridor and passed through another hatch. They found themselves in a large dome with a three-story building directly in front of them.

"That's the docking terminal where we pay our fees."

Captain Fulmar looked nervous. "How will we do that? Neither of us is carrying 15,000 credits around with us."

"It's taken care of," replied Cleemorl.

They reached the terminal and found a half-dozen heavily armed guards at the entrance.

"State your business," demanded one of them. He was a large burly man with a half-grown beard.

"We're here to pay our docking fees," replied Cleemorl, his hand resting lightly on his energy pistol.

The guard nodded. "How long will you be staying?"

"A day or two," replied Cleemorl.

The guard eyed them for another few moments and then nodded. "Go on inside. The payment counter will be to your left."

Admiral Cleemorl nodded and passed through the door with Captain Fulmar.

"Those looked like some rough characters," muttered Fulmar, as they turned to their left and proceeded down a short corridor. An older woman sat behind a glass enclosure with a large sign that read Payment Window.

"You'll see a lot of those where we're going." Admiral Cleemorl stepped up to the window, where the woman waited.

The woman slid open the window and spoke. "I assume you're the owner of that battlecruiser that just docked?"

Cleemorl nodded. "Yes, I'm here to pay our docking fee."

The woman eyed him suspiciously and then spoke again. "We don't want any trouble while you're here. We don't see many warships as large as yours."

"We just need supplies," replied Cleemorl. "We're going on a long exploration trip."

The woman nodded. "Don't let the Confederation find out. They don't like anyone exploring anymore. How long will you be staying?"

"Two days," replied Cleemorl.

"And how will you be paying? We take Confederation credits and most civilized currencies, as well as heavy metals and other items used for trade."

Cleemorl took a small pouch from his pocket and dumped the contents on the counter in front of the woman. The pouch contained a fortune in rare jewels.

The woman's eyes widened. "I must have these appraised. One moment please." She reached forward and pressed a button on the comm unit on her desk. Almost instantly a man in a business suit came through one of the other doors into the woman's office.

"What is it?" he asked, sounding a little irritated.

"They want to pay with these," replied the woman, gesturing toward the jewels.

The man looked at the jewels, and his eyes widened. He took a small device from his pocket and passed it over the jewels. "They're genuine. I estimate their value at 2,873,000 credits."

"Make it 2,900,000," replied Cleemorl in a level voice.

The man looked surprised but then slowly nodded. "Very well, 2,900,000 credits. Would you like that in credits or a credit chip? The credit chip is accepted everywhere on the station."

"A credit chip," replied Cleemorl. "Take our docking fees out of that as well. Also give me ten thousand in cash, just in case."

The woman nodded and, after a moment, handed him a small metal computer chip and ten thousand credits. She then handed him a security code. "You will need this code to access the chip." She slid the jewels into one of her desk drawers and locked it.

"Let's go," said Cleemorl, as he turned toward the corridor, pocketing the chip and the cash.

"Admiral, those jewels were worth twice what you got for them."

"I know, but keep in mind where we're at. As it is, we got nearly two hundred thousand more than I was expecting. That will allow us to purchase all the supplies we'll need."

An hour later they were deep beneath the surface of the asteroid. Captain Fulmar looked around in amazement. They seemed to be in the entertainment section of a major city, with eating places, bars, strip joints, and nearly every kind of entertainment one might be interested in. Loud music could be heard in the streets, as well as laughter coming from some of the establishments. Everywhere he looked he saw weapons. Everyone seemed to be armed. He did notice the absence of children.

"Come with me," said Cleemorl, indicating one of the larger bars that seemed to be full of people.

Going inside, Fulmar saw sentients from probably a dozen different races. Most were like Humans but different in some way.

Cleemorl found an empty table and sat down, indicating for Captain Fulmar to do the same.

"What are we having today?" asked a scantily clad serving girl, who appeared quickly to take their order.

"Two comet raiders," replied Cleemorl. He knew a comet raider, while alcoholic, was a safe drink and wouldn't get them drunk.

"Two comet raiders coming up," replied the server. "Anything else?"

Cleemorl nodded. "Tell Cheryl that Dylan Cleemorl is here and would like to talk to her."

The girl frowned but nodded and left to get their order.

"Why here?" asked Fulmar.

Cleemorl gestured around. "Cheryl owns this place."

Cleemorl leaned back in his chair, looking around. The bar was packed full with loud music and a few girls dancing on a small stage. Voices were loud, and a lot of laughter filled the room. However, every person in the bar, except the servers and the dancing girls, was heavily armed.

"A lot of deals are made in these bars," explained Cleemorl. "Everything you can imagine is for sale, if you can find the right dealer."

The serving girl returned with their drinks, setting them down in front of the two men. "Cheryl will be out shortly," she said and left them.

"Why hasn't the Confederation done something about these outlaws and pirates?" Fulmar asked Cleemorl.

Cleemorl smiled. "It's easier to have all the riffraff in one spot than scattered on thousands of worlds. The Confederation does make punitive raids occasionally to keep the outcasts here under control."

The two sat, enjoying their drinks and watching the girls on the stage. After about twenty minutes had passed, a woman came to their table, eyeing Admiral Cleemorl. She was good-looking and modestly dressed.

"Last I heard, you were an admiral," she said, as she took a seat next to Cleemorl.

Cleemorl sighed and nodded. "Still am. In case you haven't heard, the Druins attacked Lydol Four and pretty well wasted it. I suspect they're hunting for what's left of my fleet."

Cheryl nodded. "I heard that one of the Human worlds had dared to defy the Confederation again. When will you learn that, every time that happens, people die? You can't defeat the Confederation. They're too large and powerful."

"Perhaps you're right," admitted Cleemorl.

Cheryl leaned forward, gazing at the admiral with a strange look in her eyes. "Why are you here?"

"What's left of my fleet is leaving this region of space. We're going very far away, where the Druins won't find us. We'll need a considerable amount of supplies."

Cheryl frowned and slowly shook her head. "I've known you long enough to know when you're not telling the truth. You'll seek out the old Imperials. The ones exiled when the Druins first conquered the Human Empire."

Admiral Cleemorl didn't reply. He wasn't surprised that Cheryl had figured out where he was going. She was a very intelligent woman.

Cheryl studied Cleemorl's face for a few moments, slowly nodding to herself. "How many credits do you have? What you seek won't be cheap."

"Two million nine hundred thousand," replied Cleemorl.

"How many ships in your fleet?"

"Two battlecruisers and three support vessels."

Cheryl shook her head. "How could you people dare to build warships, knowing what the Druins would do?"

"People want their freedom," replied the admiral defensively. "This would happen sooner or later, no matter what we did. We thought, or rather hoped, the Druins would negotiate with us."

"The Druins negotiate with no one," replied Cheryl harshly. "We are nothing to the Confederation races except cheap labor and a source of resources."

"Is that why you came out here?"

Cheryl was quiet for a long moment. "At least here I can choose how to live my life, and, for the most part, the Confederation leaves us alone. You know the other reason."

"Did the two of you know each other in the past?" asked Captain Fulmar, raising his eyebrow.

Cleemorl nodded his head. "We were engaged to be married at one time. Cheryl disagreed with my desire to be in the military."

"A secret military. It was foolhardy," replied Cheryl unabashed. "Look at what it's gotten you. You're running from the Druins, and you can never return home."

Admiral Cleemorl let out a deep sigh. "I did what I had to do."

Taking a deep breath, Cheryl asked her next question. "What will you do if you find the old Imperials? You have to know that, by now, they could have all died out."

"It's a chance I'm willing to take." Cleemorl couldn't help but notice how beautiful Cheryl was. Several times during his military career he had wondered if he had made a mistake in his decision to join the military. His life with Cheryl could have been very fulfilling.

Frowning, Cheryl slowly nodded her head. "You have always been stubborn. Give me your list of supplies, and I'll see what I can do."

Cleemorl did so. "Do you need my credit chip?"

"No, not yet. Let me get your supplies first, and then we'll discuss the price. Come back tomorrow at this time."

Cleemorl watched as Cheryl took the list and then left the table.

"She seems like an interesting woman," commented Fulmar impressed.

"She is. She's also the smartest one I've ever met."

A ruckus at one end of the bar drew their attention. Two Humans and a Devonian were involved in a loud argument. One of the Humans pushed the Devonian and drew his pistol threateningly. "Leave!" he demanded in a loud voice. "We don't have what you're seeking."

"Liar!" called out the Devonian, refusing to back down. "My sources confirm you have the artifact. Turn it over or risk the ire of my people."

Looking around, Cleemorl noticed that most of the people in the bar were ignoring the argument, an indication that this occurred quite regularly.

Several other Devonians moved to stand next to the other one. Both had their furry hands on their pistols.

The Humans stood face-to-face with the Devonians and then, as one, moved over to a large table and sat down. For the next few minutes they engaged in heated arguments. At the end, one of the Devonians handed over a credit chip, and one of the Humans slid a small package across the table.

"So that's how business is done here," said Captain Fulmar with a deep frown.

Cleemorl laughed. "Yes, and sometimes it can be very brutal. As I said earlier, everything you can possibly want is available here for the right price. However, a person must realize the people they're dealing with are very unscrupulous and potentially dangerous."

The two men finished their drinks, and Cleemorl left a few credits on the table to pay for them. "Let's get back to the *Themis*. The less time we spend out in the open, the better off we are."

The two men walked down the street toward the hatches that would lead them to the docking bays. They stopped at a restaurant and looked inside, where families were eating, as you would find anywhere in civilized space. They did notice several large guards at the entrance, who collected all weapons before allowing anyone to enter.

Fulmar stood, gazing at a family with three small children. "It's hard to imagine raising your family here."

Cleemorl nodded. "There are schools and everything else in the residential sectors, which are patrolled by hired guards to ensure they stay safe. Those areas have large parks, specialized stores, and are very spacious." Cleemorl gestured around them. "This is where all the action takes place and where all the credits change hands."

A few gunshots rang out down the street. Everyone ignored them and continued to go about their business.

"I don't think I could ever get used to this," muttered Captain Fulmar.

"I feel the same. That's one reason Cheryl and I could never get our relationship to work out after I joined the military and she came out here."

The two continued down the street and were soon back inside the safety of the *Themis*.

The next day they were back in the bar, waiting on Cheryl to put in an appearance. This time they ate a light meal, as the bar did have some food items.

They were nearly finished when Cheryl strolled into the bar and made her way directly toward their table. She came to a stop and placed her hands on her hips. "I have what you need and more. However, there are some conditions."

Admiral Cleemorl let out a deep sigh. With Cheryl, there were always conditions. He gestured for her to sit down. "What are they?"

Cheryl took a deep breath and then glanced directly at Cleemorl. "I'm coming with you."

"Now wait a minute," objected Cleemorl. "My ships are all military. They're not a place for a civilian, and where we're going is unknown territory."

"Not a problem," replied Cheryl. "I have my own ship."

Cleemorl leaned back in his chair and placed his arms over his chest, with a deep frown on his face. "Cheryl, where we're going will be very dangerous. Not only that, the Druins might be looking for us."

"I can confirm that," replied Cheryl. "A Druin battlecruiser came through earlier and scanned the system. Your ships are tucked away behind an asteroid, so I don't think they were detected. However, there's a good chance they'll be back. It won't take long for your presence to become known. Besides, if the Druins find out I helped you, I'm as good as dead."

Cleemorl looked at Captain Fulmar, hoping for some help.

"She's right," said Fulmar. "The Druins have shown to be completely without mercy. As much as I hate to say it, she needs to come with us."

Cleemorl let out a deep breath. He didn't like this, but what other choice did he have? "Very well, how soon can you have the supplies ready?"

"We can begin loading your battlecruiser within the hour. I did manage to scrounge up some fusion missiles for your missile tubes."

"Where did you find fusion missiles?" asked Fulmar, stunned.

Cheryl grinned. "In case Dylan didn't explain, if you have the right contacts and credits, you can find nearly everything here, including fusion missiles."

"What type of ship do you have?" asked Cleemorl. He finally accepted that Cheryl must come with them.

"There will be four. My yacht, two heavy corvettes, and a Class B supply ship.

Cleemorl's eyes widened. "Where did you get those?"

"I have my sources. My business has been very lucrative the past several years. I purchased the corvettes to help protect some of my assets in several nearby star systems."

"Will your ship captains accept my orders?"

Cheryl nodded. "Yes, that won't be a problem."

"Very well, we'll leave early in the morning. That should give you the necessary time to get ready."

"We will be." With a smile, Cheryl stood and left the bar.

Cleemorl noticed a couple heavily armed men following her. He had noticed the same the day before. It was obvious that Cheryl was taking no chances and never went anywhere without an armed escort.

"Well, it seems our fleet just got a little bit larger," said Captain Fulmar.

Cleemorl nodded. "I hope this doesn't cause any problems, but we need those supplies. Let's stop by a few stores on our way back to the ship. I want to pick up a few items."

Chapter Fourteen

Captain Derrick Masters sat in his quarters on board the *Destiny*, speaking with Andrew Wilcox. They had been discussing the history of the Empire and the last days before the Druins invaded.

"So Princess Layla Starguard is still in stasis?"

"Yes," replied Derrick, as he sipped a glass of tea. "She will stay in stasis until we are ready to free the Empire."

Andrew shook his head. "That's a massive undertaking. You're talking about defeating the Confederation. Has that ever been done before?"

"No, they've always been too powerful. However, we've had nearly one thousand years to rebuild our fleet. Not only that but we now have fusion energy beams and antimatter missiles. We didn't have either when the Druins attacked. This time it will be different."

Andrew took a deep breath. "All that may be true, but you still need crews for your warships, and, for that, you need Earth's help."

Derrick slowly nodded his head. "Yes, we do. That's one reason why we agreed to make contact. I just hope we can succeed in planting a virus in the Druin interdiction system, or all of this will have been for naught."

Andrew leaned back in his chair. "Let's assume we succeed in planting the virus and gain control over the system. What's next?"

"We bring Earth up to the same level of civilization as the Empire. We terraform Mars and Venus and begin colonization. We spread the Human race throughout the Solar System and bring about a new age of prosperity."

Andrew slowly nodded his head. "And how long will all that take?"

"Your civilization is already advanced enough that it can accept some of our technology immediately. The biggest change will be in your power systems and space program. With unlimited energy your world will be free to advance quickly into a modern Empire–like civilization."

"It sounds like a great future, as long as the Druins don't interfere and blow us up. What if one of their ships comes by to check on the interdiction system?"

Derrick smiled. "The Confederation is comprised of seven very old races. The don't normally do anything fast. They are very dependent on their AI systems to handle much of the day-to-day running of the Confederation. We don't expect to see a Druin ship for another sixty to one hundred years. By then we'll be ready for them."

"We have a meeting with NAU General Brier, Admiral Bract, our two station leaders—Colonel Gleeson and Major Loren Henderson—and Brett Newcomb tomorrow," said Andrew. "Maybe then we'll have a better idea of what will happen. From what I understand, the government representatives have returned to Earth to brief their respective countries. Hopefully some decisions have been made."

Derrick hoped so as well. He felt uncomfortable with the *Destiny* docked to the space station. While it still had its stealth field operating, there was always a small chance the Druin interdiction system might detect it. If that were to happen, then all bets would be off. The Druins would interpret the appearance of an Imperial ship as a Class One danger and would launch their attack drones almost immediately. If so, there was a good chance Earth would not survive.

Later that evening Andrew was in the observation lounge, speaking with Brett Newcomb. They watched as a ship from Earth slowly docked to the station. They could see the flashes from its thrusters as it maneuvered closer.

"You accomplished much more than we could have ever hoped for," said Brett. "I've spoken to the rest of the Council, and we've set a lot of projects into motion. Projects we've waited generations to initiate. We are fortunate to have some of our people in some government positions, as well as high up in many of the major companies. Once we have everything in place, advancement should move very rapidly."

Andrew was pleased to hear this. "First we have to take care of the Druin interdiction system." This worried him greatly, due to the threat it represented.

"Yes, that is a problem. We'll have some of our best programmers working on that shortly. I'm certain they will be successful. I understand you're thinking about returning to Pallas and possibly going into cryosleep?"

"I would like to see how this ends. I've spoken briefly to my parents, and they said they'll support whatever I decide to do. Captain Masters has also offered me a position on his crew as an engineer. I would just need some additional training on Pallas."

Brett nodded. "I guess I can't blame you. If I were younger, I might consider doing something similar."

Looking through the large observation ports, they saw the Earth ship had successfully docked to the station. It was now powering down.

"Even our own spacecraft are getting ready to change. With full access to Imperial technology, we'll have to redesign our vessels. Hell, we'll probably be enlarging this space station."

Andrew smiled. "It's progress and what we've worked for. We just didn't expect it to happen so quickly."

About then Andrew saw Kala come into the observation lounge.

Brett saw where Andrew's gaze had shifted. "I'll be going now. I believe the two of you have some unfinished business to discuss."

Andrew let out a deep sigh. "Yes, I'm not very good with relationships."

Brett laughed. "Most men aren't when it comes to women. We always seem to do or to say the wrong thing, no matter how hard we try." Brett stood and left the observation lounge.

Andrew was surprised when Kala came over and sat down next to him.

"Watching the ships coming and going?"

Andrew nodded. "Yes, Brett and I were discussing how much everything will change."

Pursing her lips, Kala nodded. "I'm sorry for being so emotional the last time we were together. I guess I was making plans without talking to you first."

"I understand," replied Andrew. He really did. If circumstances were different, a life with Kala would be fantastic.

Kala folded her arms across her chest and gazed questionably at Andrew. "So, where do we go from here? I would at least like to remain friends."

Taking a deep breath, Andrew spoke. "I'll be here on the station and on Earth for several weeks at least. A lot needs to be done, and the Council will need all of its Imperials. Once that's finished, I'll go to Pallas to get some training."

"Then into cryosleep," said Kala sadly. "When you wake, I'll be long gone and everyone else you know will be as well."

"You could join me," suggested Andrew. "We could see the future together."

Kala smiled weakly. "I thought about it. I really did, but I just can't. My world is here and now, not one hundred or two hundred years in the future."

Andrew let out a deep sigh. He would miss Kala. "It might be six months or a year before I go into cryo. We could be together during that time." Andrew made the offer, though he had no idea what Kala would make of it.

Kala closed her eyes and slowly shook her head. "As tempting as it sounds, I think it's best if we just remain friends. I have some good memories of our times together, and I'll always cherish them."

"So, what will you do now?"

"Go back to Earth for a few months and then maybe return to Pallas. I can learn a lot there. From my understanding, numerous Earth scientists and technicians will be traveling to Pallas eventually."

"And a number of Imperials from Pallas will come to Earth."

Kala stood and gazed out the viewports toward the stars. "Someday you'll get to travel to the stars. It's something I'll never do. I wish you the best of luck and hope everything works out for you. Maybe when I get to Pallas, we can go out to eat and see where our work is taking us."

"I'll look forward to that," replied Andrew, standing. He watched as Kala left the observation lounge, leaving him alone in the large room. With a deep sigh, Andrew decided to head to his quarters. He had a busy day coming tomorrow, and he still needed to work on a few things to be ready for his part. He did feel like a part of him had walked out of the room with Kala.

The next day Andrew took his seat at the large conference table. Around it, the other people who were needed for this project gazed at the folders placed in front of them.

"What you see is our proposal on how to infect the Druin interdiction system with a computer virus," General Brier informed them. "We're currently gathering some of the best programmers and hackers on the planet. In two weeks we will send them to Pallas, where they can work with the computer people on the Imperial asteroid in what will be the best way to neutralize the interdiction system."

"How long do you think it will take to design an effective virus?" asked Admiral Bract.

General Brier let out a deep sigh. "Possibly several months due to the complications involved in infecting the interdiction system which covers a vast amount of the space around the Solar System." General Brier looked at Admiral Bract. "It may be necessary to use more than one ship to deliver the virus. Some of our scientists suggest, in order to make the virus the most effective, it needs to be delivered to all eight of the larger interdiction stations at the same time, to ensure the virus spreads throughout the entire system." They had recently determined that the Druins had eight massive stations spaced equidistance around the Solar System.

"That might be a problem," said Admiral Bract with a deep frown. "Only the *Destiny* is fully stealthed. I would have to speak to our yard supervisor and see if we could convert some of our larger shuttles into stealthed craft. It wouldn't be practical to convert any of our larger warships to stealth. It would take too long."

"One thing I'm concerned about are the attack drones at the larger stations," said Andrew. He had experienced firsthand what being on the receiving end of one of those was like. "What if one or more of the stations manages to launch their drones toward Earth? What do we do?"

Everyone looked at one another, waiting for someone else to speak.

"Will our regular defenses handle them?" asked Colonel Gleeson. "We still have quite a few defensive missiles deployed across the planet."

Admiral Bract shook his head. "No, they would be ineffective. The drones would just stay out of range and hit Earth with their fusion energy beams and antimatter missiles. They could level the planet in less than an hour."

"Then what will we do?" asked General Brier. "We need some way to ensure Earth survives, in case one or more of the Druin stations launches against us."

"We can deploy some battlecruisers and a few dreadnoughts from Pallas," suggested Admiral Bract. "As soon as the virus is delivered, I can send them to Earth to ensure no Druin drones get within range to use their weapons."

"Can we arm this station?" asked Colonel Gleeson.

"It might be a wise idea," said Brett Newcomb. "The station will be a primary target."

Admiral Bract nodded. "We could install some advanced interceptor missiles. It would be relatively easy to attach several batteries to the outer hull. I would recommend against any overt presentation of energy weapons, as the interdiction system might detect them."

The meeting lasted for several more hours, as detailed plans were hammered out. In the end, they all felt they had a plan that could handle the Druin interdiction system, as well as protect Earth and the space station.

"I will be returning to Pallas on the *Destiny* tomorrow," announced Admiral Bract. "I still feel uncomfortable having the ship out in the open. It will be better to have the *Destiny* safely hidden on Pallas until we need her again. As soon as the programmers and hackers are ready to journey to Pallas, I'll order the ship to return to the station to pick them up. Of course, once the interdiction system is neutralized, we'll set up a regular schedule of ships coming and going between Pallas and Earth. We have a lot of work to do to prepare the Solar System for its future."

General Brier nodded in agreement. "Yes, we have a lot to do, and it needs to start now. I'll return to Earth in another few days, as I will be visiting a number of countries that we'll need in this effort. It'll be essential we make our space program into more of a planetary body and not just composed of a few countries. We'll also propose forming a planetary military force."

"How will you manage that?" asked Andrew. He had traveled around the planet and knew how divided some areas were.

General Brier smiled. "You will be surprised what can be done if we offer advanced technology as well as more advanced medical procedures. I'm certain most will come around."

Brett Newcomb looked at Andrew. "I understand you may be returning to Pallas in a few weeks as well?"

Andrew nodded. "Yes, I'm going to Earth to speak to my parents and then back to Pallas."

This seemed to please Brett. "In that case I want you involved with the programmers we're sending to Pallas. You've been out near the Druin interdiction system and witnessed an attack by one of its drones. Your input could be invaluable. You have a good scientific background as well."

Andrew blinked his eyes and nodded his head. "If you think that's best, I'll do it."

"Then it's decided," replied Brett. "Major Henderson, I want you working with Colonel Gleeson in getting this station armed with the interceptor missiles. I also want a better detection system, which I believe the Imperials from Pallas can provide. Once we have the Druin interdiction system under our control, I want to be able to detect anything that enters this system."

"Yes, sir," replied Henderson. "I'll need to work with some people from Pallas to get the necessary equipment."

"Just keep in mind we can't activate that equipment until we have control of the interdiction system," Admiral Bract reminded them. "We don't want to tip off the AIs in charge of the interdiction system as to what we're doing."

General Brier looked thoughtful and then spoke again. "From what I understand, you have a number of shipyards on Pallas. Is there any chance you could design and build some cargo and passenger ships for us? They wouldn't have to be too large. But, if we want to really start seriously colonizing Mars and other bodies in the Solar System, we'll need them."

Admiral Bract nodded. "We have some very large cargo and passenger ships in stasis on Pallas. They're the ones that brought most of our civilians there to begin with. I think we can reactivate a few of those and modify them for your use."

"Sounds like we have a plan," spoke General Brier, satisfied. "Once we get everyone organized, everything should move very rapidly."

Admiral Bract nodded. "Probably much faster than you think, with Pallas fully involved."

Two days later Andrew was on a shuttle heading back to Earth. He had to smile as the trip from the station to Earth took longer than the trip from Pallas to the space station.

Upon landing, he took a short flight to his parents' hometown, wondering exactly what he would say to them. He had already mentioned vaguely what he would like to do, but this time he would explain it in more detail. He let out a deep breath as he gazed out the plane's window at the clouds and the green and brown ground far below.

Closing his eyes, he leaned back in his seat, rehearsing in his mind how he would go about explaining to his parents that he wanted to go into cryosleep and someday journey to the Human Empire and help free it from the Confederation.

General Brier was back on Earth and at the Pentagon meeting with Vice President Hicks, as well as numerous other civilian and military leaders.

"This all sounds so amazing," commented Senator Crown, as he poured himself a cold glass of water. "Are we certain we're being told the truth?"

"It's been confirmed," answered Vice President Hicks. "We were all taken on a trip to Mars on board the *Destiny* and at a far greater speed than anything we're currently capable of."

"How soon before we meet some of these Imperials?" asked General Benson, in charge of the Marines in the North American Union.

"Soon," replied General Brier. "As soon as we've neutralized the Druin interdiction system then the people of Pallas will begin making regular trips to Earth to help advance our technology. They've also agreed to furnish us with some modern cargo and passenger ships."

Senator Cortez of Mexico stood with her hands on her hips. "This will kill our budget. It'll cost trillions to bring everything up to Imperial standards from what I've read and seen. It'll crash our economy."

"Hopefully the new technologies we'll be introducing will make that short-lived," replied the vice president. "What we want to do today is discuss our short-term strategy in dealing with what's about to occur. It's obvious we'll need to drastically expand the space station with the aid of the Imperials. We'll also need to expand our presence on the Moon."

"What about Mars?" asked Donovan Stewart, who was responsible for the space program that many countries were participating in.

"The Imperials say they can terraform the planet and make it completely habitable," answered General Brier. "If we're to survive, it'll be necessary to increase our population. I suspect, in just a few decades, we'll have thriving colonies on Mars as well as on other planets and moons in our Solar System."

Colonel Simpson, in charge of Pentagon security, frowned deeply. "Should we send some people to Pallas, just to confirm what we've been told? We're assuming they're telling the truth about everything. What if they're not?"

"We'll make sure everything they've told us is confirmed," replied General Brier. "In about two weeks the *Destiny* will be returning and taking some of our people to Pallas. As a matter of fact the ship will have to make several trips, considering all the people we want to send."

"I would like to go," volunteered Simpson. "I would feel much better about all this if I could see it firsthand and if I can verify what they've been telling us."

General Brier thought about it for a minute and then replied. "Why don't I assign you as a liaison officer to Andrew Wilcox? He will be overseeing the development of the virus, as well as its delivery. That should put you right in the middle of everything."

Colonel Simpson nodded. "That should work fine, sir."

"Excellent, you have two weeks to prepare."

The meeting lasted the rest of the afternoon with a long list of priorities made and a second list of wishful priorities. All of these would be discussed with Brett Newcomb and several other members of the Earth Imperial Council. For now they would be the go-to intermediaries between the Earth's governments and the Imperials on Pallas.

When the meeting was over, General Brier and Vice President Hicks remained behind.

"We need to be careful to keep all this off the airwaves," said Hicks. "From what the Imperials have told us, the Druin interdiction system monitors all of Earth's communications."

General Brier nodded. "We're taking precautions to ensure this doesn't get out. Only those with the need to know will be brought into the loop. General knowledge of the Imperials and the Confederation will not be released until after we have control of the interdiction system."

Vice President Hicks looked concerned. "What happens if our virus fails and then the Druin system launches its attack drones against Earth?"

"We have to hope the Imperials can stop the drones. The bigger worry will be what happens if one of the AIs in the interdiction system manages to get a message off to the Druins."

"We can't fight the Druins, can we?"

Brier shook his head. "No. In that case, I suspect the Imperials on Pallas would evacuate the Solar System and flee even farther into deep space. To stay here and fight the Druins would probably be a losing proposition, particularly since they don't have the people to crew all their warships they've been building."

Vice President Hicks leaned back and folded his arms over his chest. He couldn't believe how complicated everything had become in the last few weeks. "What do you think the chances are that we can take over the interdiction system and not be attacked?"

"I don't know. We've never done anything like this before. In the early years of this century, some of the more rogue countries launched successful virus attacks against electrical grids and other systems to make political points. We know it can be done. We just must hope we get it right. We only get one shot at this."

"Starting tomorrow I have to leave and begin briefing other world leaders. We need to get the ball rolling on some of these projects as soon as possible."

General Brier nodded. "The same here. I have meetings scheduled with numerous defense contractors and key military personnel. We need to start thinking about recruiting crews for some of the warships on Pallas. While not all of them will be activated anytime soon, enough will be to ensure the safety of the Solar System."

Vice President Hicks leaned forward. "You do realize we're discussing eventually entering into an interstellar war with a Confederation of ancient races that has never been defeated."

"Sounds frightening," replied Brier. "But what other choice do we have? Someday the Druins will realize we have neutralized their interdiction system, and, when they do, they'll be coming for us. It's a war we don't want, but a war we can't avoid."

On Earth, Andrew sat on the front porch of the family home, speaking with his father. He had already told his parents about his plans.

"Just promise me one thing," said the older Wilcox. "Before you go into cryosleep, come see your mother and me one last time. It'll be very hard on her when she realizes she will never see you again."

"I realize that," replied Andrew, feeling guilty for upsetting his mother. She had cried when Andrew had told them his plans in more detail.

Andrew's father took in a deep breath and continued to talk. "I understand you wanting to see the beginning of the war. It's what all of us have been working toward. Hell, if I were younger, I might consider doing the same thing."

"It was a difficult decision," admitted Andrew. Looking off in the distance, he could see the sun about to set. They were in the suburbs, and the view wasn't obstructed by any tall buildings. "There may be others who decide as I have."

"It wouldn't surprise me," replied Andrew's father. "Let's go back inside where your mother is, and let's not discuss you going into cryosleep any more tonight. We need to give her time to accept it."

Andrew nodded. "Why don't I order some pizza, and we can watch a movie together?"

Andrew's father nodded. "Yes, I think that would be good. We've had enough excitement for today."

They stood and went into the house. Behind them, the sun slowly set beneath the horizon.

Chapter Fifteen

Admiral Cleemorl gazed at one of the viewscreens focused on Cheryl's yacht and the three ships that accompanied it. The yacht was of moderate size, but he couldn't help but notice it was armed.

"Have them fall into formation, and we'll make our first jump into hyperspace," ordered Cleemorl.

The sooner they got away from this system, the better he would feel. Cheryl had made good on her promise. The *Themis* was fully loaded with supplies and spare parts. Supposedly the cargo ship had everything else they would need. Once they were safely away, they would drop out of hyperspace and transfer supplies to the other ships in the small fleet.

"Captain, I'm detecting Druin battlecruisers and several battleships dropping out of hyperspace on the far side of the system," reported Lieutenant Casella worriedly.

Captain Fulmar looked alarmed. "Can they detect us?"

"We're mixed in with a bunch of asteroids. I doubt if they can get a clear image."

"Inform all our ships we're making the transition into hyperspace. It's time for us to leave." Captain Fulmar stepped over to a console and called up a star map of the local region. "Set a course for Xenia Four. It's a red giant without any planets or asteroids. We'll get the fleet organized there and resupply our other vessels."

The navigation officer quickly imputed the hyperspace coordinates and transmitted them to the other ships.

"The Druins are headed toward Highland Station," reported Casella. "Numerous ships are jumping out."

Admiral Cleemorl nodded. No one wanted to be around when Druin battlecruisers showed up. "Excellent, it will help disguise our own exodus."

On the tactical display, dozens of ships vanished as they fled the system. No one wanted to stay around to see what the Druins wanted.

"Ready to jump," reported Captain Fulmar.

"Do so. We need to put some distance between us and the Druins."

Cleemorl felt the ship vibrate slightly and then a slight wrenching sensation as the ship made the transition into hyperspace. The Druins couldn't track them in hyperspace or attack them. From now until they arrived in the Xenia Four System, they would be safe.

"All other ships have made the transition," reported Casella. "No problems reported."

Cleemorl nodded. "Contact all our ships and inform them to avoid any unnecessary communications between vessels. We don't want to risk the Druins picking up any stray signals."

Captain Fulmar looked at the admiral. "What do you think the Druins will do to Highland Station?"

"They're Druins," replied Cleemorl. "If they discover we were there, I imagine they will launch a punitive assault against the station. Fortunately much of it is deep underground, so most of the civilians should be safe."

"If they're smart, they'll never admit we were there," commented Fulmar.

"Maybe," answered Cleemorl. "But it wouldn't surprise me if the Druins have a few spies inside the station. After all, it didn't take them long to arrive once we docked. I suspect someone tipped them off we were there."

Admiral Cleemorl leaned back in his command chair, not wanting to think about what might be happening soon to Highland Station. Someday he hoped it would be him teaching the Druins a lesson. However, for that to happen, he needed the old Imperials who were stranded on Earth to have thrived and to have built up a robust civilization. For, without it, all his hopes would be for naught.

Admiral Kreen gazed at the tactical display, showing a mass exodus of ships from the star system. This had been expected. He had ten ships with him, which would be sufficient to teach the refuse who lived in this system a lesson they would not soon forget.

"Are there any signs of the Human ships?"

"No," answered the sensor officer. "They may have left, or they could still be docked to the station."

Admiral Kreen was aggravated that this remnant of the Human fleet was taking up so much of his valuable time."

"The station is trying to contact us," reported the communications officer. "They say there will be no resistance and want to know why we have come here."

"Ask them where the Human ships are," ordered Kreen. Normally he wouldn't even respond to communications from inferior races, but, in this instance, he was curious as to what they would say.

The communications officer sent the demand and waited for a reply. Finally there was a response. "They left the station a few hours ago, and only one battlecruiser docked to the station."

Kreen's cold eyes narrowed. "Send a company of our soldiers to the station. I want to know if they're telling the truth. Have our other ships comb the system to ensure the Human ships are not hiding behind an asteroid."

Kreen's second in command nodded and went to carry out the order.

Inside Highland Station there was near panic as the civilians rushed to the safety of the civilian sectors buried deep beneath the surface. Along the main streets—where the stores, bars, and businesses were located—the doors and windows were hurriedly closed and locked. Inside, the owners waited nervously, not sure what to expect. The Druins were not known for being peaceful. Most knew, if the Druins did not find what they sought, there would be repercussions.

At the main docking terminal, the guards stood nervously watching as several large Druin shuttles descended to the station and docked. Out of each came heavily armed and armored Druins. The doors to the terminal remained open, as everyone inside knew, if they were locked, the Druins would simply blow them open and then execute everyone inside. They were hoping, if they answered the Druins' questions, that would be sufficient.

The Druins rapidly made their way to the terminal, where the guards and one of the terminal officials waited.

"Where are the Humans who came in the battlecruiser!" demanded the Druin officer in charge of the soldiers. "They are to be turned over to us immediately."

"They're no longer here," stammered the terminal official. "They were here for two days and left only a few hours ago."

"What did they want here?"

The terminal official looked frightened. He knew his life hung on his next words. "Supplies. They cashed in a large collection of jewels and then went into the city to seek supplies for their ship."

"Where are they going?"

The terminal official shook his head. "I don't know. They never said, and we didn't ask."

"A mistake on your part," said the Druin, as he pulled his energy pistol and shot the official in the chest. Before the guards could react, they too were gunned down by several of the Druin soldiers.

"Spread out and search the terminal for any indications of where the Humans went. Execute anyone who refuses to cooperate," the officer ordered his second in command. "The rest of us will go into the city and see what we can discover there."

Admiral Kreen waited patiently for the reports from his soldiers. He knew it wouldn't take long for them to discover any signs of the Humans who had dared to defy the Confederation. He had already sent some of his battlecruisers to search the asteroids in the system as well as several nearby star systems the Humans might have fled to. He was determined to find this pitiful fleet and destroy it. No one who defied the Confederation could be allowed to survive.

The *Themis* and the other ships in her small fleet dropped out of hyperspace in the Xenia Four System. A quick scan indicated no other ships present.

"Secure from Condition One and go to Condition Three," ordered Admiral Cleemorl, as he relaxed. Even if the Druins were pursuing them, it would take them hours to search all the systems between Highland Station and Xenia Four. That should give the fleet time to resupply before setting out for the Bacchus Region.

"All ships report being secure with normal operations," said Captain Fulmar. "The supply ship is moving closer to the *Rhys* for resupply. They will be using shuttles to transfer the supplies. As soon as the supplies have been transferred, the ship will send supplies to our three support ships."

Cleemorl nodded. "We need to get the supplies transferred as quickly as possible. We should have at least a few hours before any Druin ships show up."

"We'll get it done quickly," promised Fulmar.

Admiral Cleemorl leaned back in his command chair, wondering about what was ahead for his fleet. The journey to the Bacchus Region would take at least six weeks. He had no intention of going there directly. For the next week he would make a series of random jumps to throw off any Druins who might be searching for his fleet. Once satisfied no one followed them, Cleemorl would set off for the planet the old Imperials had been marooned on. He just hoped all this wasn't for nothing.

Admiral Kreen had just received the latest reports from his soldiers inside Highland Station. It was confirmed the Humans he sought had once more escaped. Not only that but a Human woman had assisted them and had added four ships to the Human fleet. One was a very large supply ship.

"Pull our soldiers back. They are to destroy the main docking terminal and then return to our ships. Once they have all returned, we will use our fusion weapons to destroy all the docking ports on the station. That will teach this refuse to deal with fugitives wanted by the Confederation."

An hour later Admiral Kreen watched coldly as fusion beams from his flagship tore apart the docking ports of Highland Station. Jagged pieces of wreckage were hurled away from the station, and several fires could be seen burning inside. A large explosion blew out a section of the docks where a ship waited to be loaded.

Admiral Kreen nodded. He knew the rabble that lived inside the asteroid would eventually rebuild everything. For now they had been taught a valuable lesson. "We will continue to search the nearby star systems for any trace of the Humans. They must not escape."

Moments later all the Druin battlecruisers and battleships entered hyperspace, traveling to different star systems. The search would continue.

Inside Highland Station, emergency crews sealed off parts of the dome as well as the underground sections. Fire-fighting crews battled the fires, while others examined the damage. Loss of life this time had been minimal. The docks could easily be rebuilt and should be back in full operation in a few months. Note was taken of the Human battlecruiser that had been the cause of the attack. It would not be allowed to dock again. Also Cheryl Bannon's assets were to be confiscated, and she would never be allowed to set foot back on the station.

In the Xenia Four System, Cheryl was in the Command Center of her yacht. The ship was lavishly furnished with a half-dozen guest quarters. Even the crew had better-than-normal living quarters.

"How soon before the resupply is finished?" she asked Captain Tucker. He had been with her for years and had been essential in completing many of her illegal transactions.

"Another thirty minutes," Tucker replied. "Are you sure we're doing the right thing? We have no idea where we're going."

Cheryl smiled. "Our time on Highland Station was about over anyway. We still have some hidden assets, if we ever decide to return."

Tucker nodded. "Well, I've always wanted to go exploring." He was quiet for a moment. "Does Admiral Cleemorl know I'm commanding the yacht?" He had met Cleemorl briefly in the past.

"Not yet," answered Cheryl. "I'll tell him next time we're together."

Cheryl wondered what her feelings were for Dylan. They had been so close once, and then she had fled to Highland Station when she had learned he was going into the military. For years she had wondered if that had been a colossal mistake.

With a deep sigh, she looked at a viewscreen focused on the *Themis*. The ship had a few burn marks on its hull from the battle with the Druins which the *Themis* and the other ships had escaped from. Cheryl hadn't asked Dylan too much about the battle and what had happened to the planet, though rumors indicted it had been heavily hit by the Druins. The Confederation had no remorse when it came to killing citizens of lessor races. Someday Cheryl hoped someone would teach them a lesson.

Admiral Cleemorl waited as reports came in from the support ships on the progress of the resupply. In another fifteen minutes it would be finished, and the fleet would be ready to depart.

"What course?" asked Captain Fulmar.

"Set a course for the Hagen Star Cluster. It will take us two days to get there, and it's a large-enough cluster that, even were the Druins to follow us there, they will have too many stars to search."

Captain Fulmar nodded. "A few inhabited systems are in the cluster. Are we stopping at any of them?"

Cleemorl shook his head. "No, if we do, the Druins might punish them. It's best we stay away from all civilized worlds for now." Dylan knew this would be hard on his crews. However, until they reached their destination, he didn't dare risk contact with anyone.

Captain Fulmar made his way to Navigation and spoke to the navigation officer about their new course.

On one of the viewscreens, Cheryl's yacht was visible. Dylan still felt uneasy about her accompanying him. He knew that, even after all these years, he still had feelings for her. Dylan let out a deep sigh. Once they were somewhere safe, he would have a long talk with Cheryl.

—

Finally the resupply was over, and the fleet was ready to enter hyperspace once more.

Leaning forward in his command chair, Cleemorl watched as the fleet made the transition into hyperspace. For two days they would be safe from the Druins. Hopefully they would lose them in the cluster, if they managed to trace the fleet there. It would take the Druins weeks to search every star system the fleet could be hiding in. By the time the Druins determined the Human fleet wasn't there, the fleet would be long gone.

—

Admiral Kreen was getting tired of this fruitless search. The Human fleet he pursued could be anywhere. There had been no traces of them since leaving Highland Station. "They've escaped us for now. In time they must return for supplies, and, when they do, we'll finish them. For now, we will return to our fleet and our patrol route."

"Should we leave a few ships in this region, just in case they return shortly?" asked the first officer.

"No, if the Humans return, we'll hear about it. There are not enough of them to be a threat. Let us return to our fleet. Send out messages to our other ships to join up with us. For now this search is over."

The *Themis* and the other ships of the fleet dropped out of hyperspace in the Hagen Star Cluster. For nearly a day they stayed put, watching their sensors for any signs of pursuit. Once Admiral Cleemorl felt certain they had lost the Druins, they made another short hyperspace jump to a white dwarf star with several planets as well as a substantial asteroid field. He intended to stay here, near the asteroids, for a good week, until he was satisfied they had truly lost the Druins. He also wanted to take the time to inspect all his ships, particularly those Cheryl had added to the fleet. The Themis still needed a little repair work from the battle with the Druins over Lydol Four.

Cheryl waited nervously for Dylan's shuttle to dock to her yacht. He was inspecting each ship of the fleet to better familiarize himself with the officers commanding the vessels. She stood in the small landing bay, along with Captain Tucker.

"I hope he finds the *Princess Haven* to his liking," commented Captain Tucker. He was dressed in his captain's uniform and had gone to great lengths to make sure it was wrinkle free and clean. He didn't want to make a bad impression on the admiral.

As they watched, the small shuttle entered the bay, and the docking hatch slid shut. An atmospheric force field ensured that, even with the hatch open, none of the air in the ship escaped. The door to the shuttle opened, and Admiral Cleemorl and two heavily armed Marines stepped out onto the deck of the ship.

Cheryl noted the armed guards as she stepped forward, followed by Captain Tucker. "Welcome aboard the *Princess Haven*."

"Cheryl," replied Dylan politely, then he frowned as he shifted his gaze to Captain Tucker. "Don't I know you?"

Tucker slowly nodded. "Yes, Admiral. We met on Lydol Four years ago. I was in the military school and dropped out when I realized I probably would not be getting command of a ship. I went ahead and got my captain's license through the regular channels after that."

Dylan nodded. "I remember you now. At least you have some military training. Can you follow orders?"

"Yes, sir," replied Tucker.

Cheryl looked distastefully at the two Marines. She had a few armed guards on the ship, but, for the most part, they stayed out of sight unless they were needed. "Why don't you have your Marines go to the galley? I believe my own guards are there eating."

Dylan found this request reasonable and ordered the Marines to head for the galley. Captain Tucker volunteered to show them where it was.

"I hope you have a lot of food in your galley," commented Dylan, as Tucker and the Marines vanished through a nearby hatch.

"It's well stocked," replied Cheryl with a smile. "Why don't I take you on a tour of the ship? I imagine Captain Tucker will meet up with us in the Command Center."

"What do you think about Tucker?" asked Dylan.

Dylan couldn't remember a lot about the man. On Lydol Four, joining the military was difficult as it was a secret organization. It took connections to get in or a special invite from one of the military officers. The Druins did not allow any of the Human worlds to have an armed military.

"He seems to be well qualified. I feel fully confident with him in command of my yacht."

For the next hour Cheryl took Dylan on a tour of her ship. They went through nearly every compartment, even the guest quarters. Dylan was amazed at how lavish everything was. Cheryl had all the most recent comforts, and he was surprised how large the crew's quarters were.

"What is the size of your crew?" asked Dylan, as they sat down on a comfortable couch in Cheryl's quarters.

"Forty-two," replied Cheryl. "That includes seven security personnel."

"I noticed it's a mixed crew of men and women."

Cheryl nodded. "I believe that works better. I have seventeen women on the ship."

Dylan looked around Cheryl's quarters. If one didn't know better you would think you were in a penthouse suite at a fancy hotel. "Cheryl, why did you decide to come with us? You could have simply gone to another star system." This was something Dylan had been extremely curious about. What game was Cheryl playing?

Cheryl looked over at Dylan. As much as she hated to admit it, she still had feelings for him. She didn't know how many times in the past she had seriously considered going to Lydol Four and seeking him out. Only her pride had prevented her from doing so.

"My time at Highland Station was coming to an end. Over the last few years it has steadily gotten more civilized, particularly in the residential civilian sectors. I was contemplating moving back to Lydol Four, when I heard what the Druins had done to it. I hate the Confederation as much as anyone. They've always made my ventures extremely difficult, even the legal ones. The thought of going off into the unknown was attractive to me. Who knows what might be out there? Perhaps we'll find a civilized world away from the Confederation."

Cheryl stood and walked to a unit on the wall and, opening it, took out two bottles of a nonalcoholic beverage she knew Dylan once liked. Going back to the sofa, she handed him one. "I have to admit the thought of going off into the unknown with you played a big part in it. I don't know if you still have any feelings for me, but I still do for you. I made a mistake all those years ago, when you chose to go into the military. I should have stayed."

Dylan looked surprised as he took a sip of his drink. He smiled and gazed at the bottle. "I haven't had one of these in years. I'd forgotten how good this tastes." He leaned back on the sofa and looked at Cheryl. "I have to admit my feelings for you are still there. They always have been. Several times I considered coming to Highland Station, to see if I could change your mind about leaving me."

"Why didn't you?" asked Cheryl. She wished he had come.

"The timing was always off. I did come out here once, but you were gone. After that, I never tried again."

Cheryl nodded. "My business ventures required a lot of traveling. That's another reason I chose to come with you. I would like to find someplace where I can settle down and not have to worry about a Druin or another Confederation battleship showing up."

Dylan took a deep breath. He knew it would take some effort on both of their parts to restore what they had lost. "Let's both agree to take this slow. I don't know what'll happen where we're going."

"Do you know where the old Imperials were marooned?"

Dylan nodded his head. "I have a general location. It's been handed down for years by some distant relatives of the Royal Family who managed to escape capture by the Druins. When we get there, I expect we'll have to search several star systems to find the one we're seeking. That area of space is rather desolate, with stars distantly spaced. We may have to spend several weeks searching before we find the world we're seeking."

"Do you think it will be civilized?"

"I hope so," replied Dylan. "If not, we'll have done all this for nothing, and all hope of establishing a future Human Empire will be lost."

Chapter Sixteen

Andrew was headed back to Pallas on board the *Destiny*. This time he was spending considerable time in the Command Center as well as Engineering. The ship was full of people from Earth. Computer programmers, scientists, and even a few military personnel. Several air force and naval officers on board would be shown the warships stored in stasis inside the huge docks of Pallas. Very soon personnel from Earth would be needed to help crew some of the massive vessels.

During his spare time, Andrew spent it talking to his new aide, Colonel Simpson. Andrew had to smile to himself. He was certain Simpson had been assigned to Pallas just to confirm all the information the Imperials had told everyone on the space station. Andrew had mentioned his suspicion to Captain Masters, who had only nodded.

"I would do the same thing," Derrick had replied. "A lot is at stake in this, and we all have to develop some trust. It's a sound strategy to verify everything your people have been told."

Andrew was currently in Engineering, speaking to the engineering officer, Alban Corrant. "Everything is fusion powered?"

Corrant nodded. They stood in front of a large control console that showed the current status of the ship's power systems as well as the hyperdrive and the subspace drive. "Fusion power has been around for a very long time. There are rumors that some of the Confederation worlds use antimatter as a power source, but we've never verified that."

"Antimatter would be on a completely different level when compared to fusion," commented Andrew.

"It would, but we have very efficient fusion power plants."

"Fusion will make a big difference on Earth. It will give us nearly unlimited and cheap power." Earth already had a few fusion power plants, but they were not near as efficient as the ones Pallas offered. The *Endeavor* had been equipped with a fusion power plant.

"The Human Empire at its highest was very dependent on fusion energy. It powered their cities, their vehicles, and their spacecraft."

Andrew spent a moment studying the control panel. He pretty much understood what everything was for. Once he reached Pallas, he would be trained in how to maintain ship systems, when he wasn't busy with the virus research. "Is Pallas doing research on antimatter?" Andrew asked Corrant.

"Some. We have antimatter warheads now that we didn't during the war. We've been working on developing antimatter as a power source, but, so far, we've been unsuccessful."

Checking the time, Andrew noted he should go to the Command Center. The ship would be making its approach to Pallas shortly, and Captain Masters wanted Andrew to observe it.

Leaving Engineering, Andrew made his way through the ship. He knew, in the next few weeks, the *Destiny* would make numerous trips to Earth to bring more personnel to Pallas. Many of them would be military with a mixture of scientists and technicians. It didn't take long for Andrew to reach the Command Center and to step through the hatch.

"Welcome, Andrew," said Captain Masters, smiling. "We'll be docking at Pallas in twenty minutes. I hope everyone has enjoyed their trip." Derrick was referring to all the Earth people crammed into the ship's guest quarters and several of the small cargo bays that had been converted to carry passengers.

"They have," replied Andrew. "I think they're all excited about seeing Pallas."

Derrick nodded. "How long do you think it will take the programmers to construct a virus to use against the interdiction system?"

"It's difficult to say," replied Andrew. "With the number of people we'll have working on it, I would expect something within a month." Andrew looked at the ship's primary viewscreen. It showed a sea of stars. They were still too far away from Pallas for it to be visible. "We just have to be satisfied that whatever we come up with will be effective. We'll only have one shot at this."

"The shipyards on Pallas are already converting some of our larger shuttles to stealth. When the virus is finished, we'll be ready to deliver it."

Andrew nodded. He was well aware of what all was at stake. If the virus failed, Earth would be attacked. Immediately.

Time passed as the *Destiny* neared Pallas. As the ship approached, a camouflaged hatch slid open, revealing the entrance to one of the asteroid's many docking bays. The *Destiny* slid smoothly inside and then set down on its landing pad.

"Once everyone from Earth gets settled in, I've arranged for Ensign Allert to show Colonel Simpson around," said Captain Masters. "You might want to tag along, in case he has any questions."

"Are any areas off-limits?"

Derrick nodded. "Only a few. I've ordered Ensign Allert to stir clear of those areas for now. Perhaps later, we can show them to the colonel."

"I'll be ready," replied Andrew. He wondered how Colonel Simpson would react to some of the things he would see. Andrew remembered his first tour and how stunned he had been at what all was hidden beneath the surface of Pallas. It was a remarkable world the Imperials had constructed.

In deep space, the Druin interdiction system kept an eye on the Solar System. The system had been forced to destroy a Human ship that had ventured too far out and had represented a possible danger. As a result of this action, the AIs in charge of the system had been scrutinizing the Humans even more. They had intercepted several worrisome communication transmissions that seemed to indicate there had been survivors from the destroyed ship. The AIs were not certain how this could have been possible, unless one or more of the escape pods was more capable than originally believed.

The AIs considered sending a message to the Druins, informing them of the latest developments in the system, but, so far, nothing could be considered a possible danger. After much consideration and analysis, the AIs decided to continue to monitor, but, for now, they would not send a message to their masters.

Admiral Bract was making another report to the Imperial Council. "So far the people of Earth have been very receptive in aiding us. A number of their military people arrived with Captain Masters, and even more will be coming in the next few weeks."

"We are entering dangerous times," commented Lena Prest. She paused and gazed at each individual Council member. "If this virus fails, the Druin interdiction system will launch their drones against Earth. They will also begin searching for us and will send a message to the Druins, informing them of the actions they've taken. Shortly afterward, we can expect a Druin fleet to arrive."

Admiral Bract nodded in agreement. "We have some ship crews in stasis who have been trained. I recommend we awaken them and take some of our warships out of stasis. We will need them when we deliver the virus, just in case there is a reaction from the interdiction system."

Councilor Arianna Bliss let out a deep breath. "How many ships are you thinking of activating?"

"One dreadnought as a command vessel and twenty battlecruisers."

"How long will these ships remain activated?"

"Permanently," answered Bract. "Once the interdiction system is deactivated, we will need those ships for training purposes, as well as to ensure the continued safety of the Solar System."

Councilor Mila Rosen nodded in agreement. "We are committing a lot of our resources to this endeavor. However, we must remember this is why Pallas was established to begin with."

The Council was silent as they weighed the decisions they were making. They all knew they were taking the first steps in the war against the Druins and the Confederation. Steps that had been over one thousand years in coming.

—

Andrew was in a large room filled with computer stations. In front of each sat an Earth Human and an Imperial, as they worked to design a virus to infiltrate and to take over the Druin interdiction system.

Andrew's attention had been drawn to a young woman who seemed to have the most radical ideas on how this should be done. He wasn't surprised to learn she was a hacker and had been arrested numerous times for breaking into various computer systems on Earth. Currently she was involved in a heated argument with the Imperial working with her. Curious, Andrew stepped closer so he could listen.

"It can't be done," the Imperial informed Linda. "Computers don't work that way."

"That's why it will work," replied Linda. "We're going through the deep logic and adjusting the parameters of the existing programming. It will bring the AIs completely under our control."

The Imperial frowned. "But we don't know for sure how the AIs are programmed. What you're suggesting might not work at all."

"But if it does, it gives us complete control of the entire Druin interdiction system."

The Imperial leaned back and folded his arms across his chest, clearly feeling frustrated. "Prove it to me."

Linda grinned. "I would be delighted to." She then filled in line after line of programming on her computer console, the Imperial watching closely. Occasionally he would have Linda stop and explain exactly what a line of code meant.

Andrew decided he would keep an eye on Linda and her partner. He also had several other pairs of programmers he was keeping a careful watch on.

Inside one of the main docks, Admiral Bract watched as a dreadnought was brought out of stasis. It was quite simple. All that needed to be done was to turn off the stasis field encompassing the ship and then activate the ship's internal power. Several hundred crewmembers stood by to enter the ship, once it was safe to do so. Bract's gaze wandered over the warship, seeing the turrets, missile tubes, and energy projectors. The ship had fusion energy beams and was equipped with both fusion and antimatter missiles.

Captain Masters stood beside him, as well as several Council members. "It's good to see a dreadnought activated."

Admiral Bract nodded in agreement. "Unfortunately it can't leave the bay until we've neutralized the Druin interdiction system."

"How soon before we activate the battlecruisers?"

"Tomorrow," replied Bract. "We'll activate two per day. The crews of all the ships can run some drills while they are still in the bays. I'm afraid that's all we can do."

Derrick knew it would be hard on the crews, knowing they were trapped in the docking bays until the interdiction system was neutralized. However, once it was, regular patrols of the Solar System would begin. Once again the warships of the Human Empire would be unleashed. Derrick just hoped they were not needed. If they were, then something had gone horribly wrong.

Several weeks passed, and Andrew was inside one of the small habitats containing an abundance of growing plants and trees. He enjoyed coming here, as it allowed him to think. He had just finished a briefing with some of the leading programmers on their progress with the virus. Three looked promising, including the one developed by Linda. Hers was the most radical, as it wasn't so much a virus as a new set of programs that would overwrite the programs the AIs in the stations currently ascribed to.

"I thought I would find you down here," said a woman, her familiar voice coming from behind him.

Turning, Andrew broke out into a big smile. "Kala, I thought you would spend more time on Earth."

Kala shook her head "No, all the action is here on Pallas." Kala stepped over to a bench and gestured for Andrew to join her. "I hear you've been quite busy."

Andrew nodded. "Learning more about the tech that's available here, as well as supervising a special project for the military."

"The virus program," guessed Kala. "Making any progress?"

"Some. We'll have some recommendations to make in another two or three weeks."

Kala watched several couples strolling down the paths in the habitat. "You better hurry. I don't know much longer Pallas will remain a secret. Several news agencies are asking a lot of pointed questions."

Andrew nodded. "I heard. The military is keeping an eye on the internet and other media. If anything shows up, they're removing it. Even they feel we only have a few more weeks before the secret's out. We tried to hold down the number of people who know what's going on, but you have the entire crew of the space station, government leaders, and the military. Let's just hope we can keep the lid on it until the virus is ready."

Kala reached over and took Andrew's hand. "Are you hungry? I wouldn't mind a good meal. It would allow us to spend some time together."

Andrew looked at Kala, searching her gaze. "Are you sure?"

Kala let out a deep sigh. "We have several months at least to be together. I thought really hard about it, and, even if you go into cryosleep and leave me behind, at least I'll have the memories."

Standing, Andrew nodded. "There are a few restaurants in the civilian section. Ensign Allert took Colonel Simpson and me to one the other day. I think you will enjoy the food."

"Let's go," said Kala, standing too. "We can talk more while we eat."

Moments later the two left the habitat, neither sure where this relationship would lead.

Colonel Simpson stood in an observation room, overlooking one of the massive construction bays safely tucked away inside Pallas, where two battlecruisers were being constructed.

"How long does it take to build a battlecruiser?"

"A little over a year," replied Ensign Allert. "We normally build them two at a time, as it seems to be faster. Instead of making one part, we make two."

In the bay both Humans and robots worked on the ships. The robots were of every shape and form, having been built to perform specific functions. Bright flashes of light indicated where hull plating was being attached to the ships.

"What is the crew size of a battlecruiser?"

Ensign Allert hesitated and then answered. "It varies some. The average battlecruiser will have a crew of eight hundred, plus a contingent of Marines. The size of the Marine contingent depends on the ship's mission."

"And the dreadnoughts?"

"A crew of 1,200 plus the Marines."

Colonel Simpson stood watching the construction. It was unlike anything done on Earth or in Earth orbit. Just the technology displayed here was amazing. "How many warships do you have?"

"Sorry, Colonel, but that's classified. Maybe later we can release those figures."

Simpson nodded. He understood that some military secrets were not yet ready to be shared. "I understand your Marines use energy weapons. May I see them?"

Ensign Allert nodded. "Yes. Why don't we go to the Marine target range? A few are always practicing there."

Ensign Allert led Simpson through the base, until they reached a set of large metal hatches. Opening them, they entered a section reserved for the Imperial Marines.

"How many Marines do you currently have?"

"Two hundred and thirty," replied Ensign Allert. "More remain in stasis." Brenda went down a long corridor and then through another hatch. Inside was a gunnery range, where several Marines were practicing.

They stood watching the Marines, using both energy pistols and rifles.

"Mind if I try?"

"Just a moment," said Brenda. She walked over and talked to one of the Marines. He nodded and returned with her.

"I'm Sergeant Drake, and I'm one of the instructors. I understand you want to try out our energy weapons?"

"I would like to. We have nothing like them on Earth."

Drake nodded. "I was told that. I understand you still use projectile weapons. We still have those as well. If you will come with me, I'll explain how our energy pistols and rifles work. Plus I'll share a few safety precautions that need to be taken."

A few minutes later Simpson fired one of the energy pistols at a target. He was very good with a pistol and was surprised there was no kick to the weapon. He was hitting the target dead center, once he got used to it.

Drake smiled as he watched. "I can see you've had some practice with a pistol. Want to try one of our rifles?"

Simpson nodded and was soon firing at a target farther away.

—

Later Simpson returned to his quarters, writing up his report. Most of his concerns about the Imperials had been abated. He had seen most of the facilities beneath Pallas, though a few had been restricted to him. He had found the people to be truthful and willing to show him nearly everything he wanted to see. He was now convinced that the Imperials were telling the truth about the Human Empire and the Confederation. His report would recommend full cooperation.

In deep space, the AIs in charge of the interdiction system were having a conference. It was becoming evident that something worrisome was occurring on Earth. There was increased activity between Earth and the space station the Humans had placed at the Earth-Moon LaGrange Point. Messages that would appear on the planet's internet or media stations would be deleted almost immediately, as if something was being hidden.

"Is it possible with the destruction of their spacecraft, the Humans have deduced there is an interdiction system around their Solar System?"

"The possibility is only 12 percent," replied one of the other AIs. "What we are seeing may be increasing hostilities between several of the countries upon the planet."

"There is no indication of such hostilities," replied another one of the AIs.

"We have also not been able to confirm any survivors of the ship we destroyed. So far all we have heard is rumors and the Human media stations are always full of those."

"Have we detected the presence of any Imperial technology?"

"No, we have scanned the system, and no advanced technology has been detected."

The discussion lasted for a few more minutes. Since they were AIs, they could communicate far faster than living beings.

"I recommend we keep our attack drones at the ready. It is possible the Humans are preparing to launch an interstellar probe. We know they have been working on an experimental faster-than-light drive for several years. If they launch such a probe, we will attack their planet."

"Should we notify the Druins?"

"No, such action is not yet necessary."

"Then it is agreed. We will continue to watch."

Captain Masters had been summoned to a meeting of the Imperial Council. Stepping inside, he noted the Council members, Andrew, several other Earth Humans, and also some Imperial scientists were present.

"Welcome, Captain Masters," greeted Councilor Lena Prest. "Have a seat. We are gathered here today to discuss delivering the virus to the Druin interdiction system."

"It's ready?"

"Perhaps," replied Andrew. "That's one of the things we'll discuss. We are in a quandary. We have two possible solutions to the interdiction system. One is very straightforward, and the other is revolutionary."

"Please explain the difference," said Councilor Prest.

For the next hour Andrew had the computer people explain what they wanted to do. The first plan and its virus was pretty straightforward. However, when they got to Linda's plan, the questions began to fly.

"You want to reprogram the AIs?" asked Admiral Bract, his gaze revealing his shock. "Wouldn't you be taking a major risk doing that?"

Linda shook her head. "Cleve's plan calls for using his virus to overpower the system, putting it completely under our control. The AIs would be destroyed. My plan calls for changing the AIs programming where, instead of a threat, they would become our useful servants. The interdiction system would continue to function but under the parameters we set. Also the AIs would not make any attempts to contact the Druins, unless ordered to do so by us."

"Tell them the other benefit," suggested Andrew. This was a big one, one that might be a game changer.

"By taking over the AIs, we also gain control over their attack drones. The drones could then be used to protect the Solar System."

Everyone began talking. Some sounded as if they approved of the plan, and others were concerned about the possibility of it failing.

"There is one more thing," interjected Andrew. "If we can gain full control of the AIs, it gives us control of the entire interdiction system. We can turn some of the system's sensors toward deep space to give us an early warning of any approaching ships. If we try to build such a system ourselves, it will take years. Instead one is just waiting for us to take it over."

This induced another round of talking and arguing. Finally Admiral Bract turned toward Andrew. "Which one do you recommend? Keep in mind, if this virus fails, all the AIs will launch their attack drones toward Earth. I'm not sure even our fleet can stop them all. We're talking about several hundred drones."

Andrew had already considered this. "I suggest we take a double approach to this. We take the *Destiny* and the modified shuttles to deliver Linda's virus program. However, we should also have the second virus with us as well, in case something goes wrong. Linda and Cleve will be on board the *Destiny* in case any last-minute changes need to be made to their viruses."

Admiral Bract slowly nodded his head. "Anything else?"

Andrew looked at Bract as well as Councilor Prest. "I recommend, as soon as we begin delivering the virus, that Pallas jump fourteen of its battlecruisers out just beyond the Druin interdiction system. They will transmit a jamming signal to prevent the AIs from getting out any distress messages."

"That could block the virus transmission as well," warned Bract.

Andrew shook his head. "No, we'll be too close to the stations. Even with the jamming, our signals should get through."

Councilor Prest looked at Captain Masters. "Captain, what do you think?"

"I think we have to go with it. Remember. At some point the secret about Pallas will come out. Too many people on the space station and Earth now know about us. When our location is leaked, the AIs will launch their attack drones. They will target Earth as well as Pallas."

Several of the councilors looked stunned at this revelation. They had never considered Pallas as being in danger.

Councilor Prest drew in a deep breath. Her gaze wandered over the Council, as if trying to read their minds. Nodding her head, she made a decision. "Very well, we shall adopt Mr. Wilcox's plan. How soon can we be ready?"

"I need two days to finish prepping the battlecruisers," replied Admiral Bract.

"The *Destiny* is ready," added Captain Masters. "We can leave at any time."

Councilor Prest looked at Admiral Bract. "When do we launch the mission?"

"The sooner, the better," replied Bract. "I would recommend fifty hours from now."

Councilor Prest gazed at her fellow councilors. "Does anyone object to this?"

No one replied. They all realized there was nothing else they could do.

Prest nodded her head. "Very well, Admiral Bract, you are in charge of getting the mission launched. Coordinate everything with Mr. Wilcox and Captain Masters."

After that, the room went silent. Everyone knew this was the first step in a new war against the Confederation. If they were successful, they would have bought Earth at least sixty years or more to get ready. If they failed, a year from now, Earth might be a wasteland with little or no life on its surface.

Chapter Seventeen

Captain Masters was in the Command Center of the *Destiny*. The ship was traveling on its subspace drive toward its target. Due to the distance, it would take nearly twenty hours for the light cruiser to reach the Druin station. Seven other vessels were also en route to the other seven large AI-controlled stations of the interdiction system.

"No evidence we've been detected," reported Lieutenant Keela Nower.

Derrick nodded. There was a chance the closer they got to the station, their risk of possible detection would greatly increase. Of course the interdiction system was not expecting an Imperial stealthed vessel to be anywhere near the system. Derrick hoped that gave them the advantage. "Are the viruses ready to be delivered?"

Andrew nodded. "Yes, we just need to be close enough to the station so the battlecruiser's jamming will not block the delivery."

Derrick took a deep breath. "How certain are you this will work?"

"Linda claims 100 percent. Personally I would say closer to 80 percent. A lot of unknowns are involved in what we're getting ready to do. We have no idea what firewalls the AIs may have."

"If the AIs realize what we're up to, they could launch some of their attack drones against the *Destiny*."

Andrew looked concerned. "The *Destiny* is equipped with weapons, isn't it?"

Derrick smiled. "Some. We could take out a few drones if it becomes necessary. Let's just hope the virus works."

For twenty hours the *Destiny* moved closer to the Druin AI control station. In time it was visible on the viewscreens at high magnification. The station was a massive sphere, nearly two thousand meters in diameter. On the main viewscreen, weapon turrets and hatches covering missile tubes were visible.

"The station is heavily armed," reported Lieutenant Nower.

"We'll be in range of its weapons when we send the virus," warned Lieutenant Marko Breen from Tactical. "The stealth fields should keep us hidden."

A few moments later Derrick ordered the *Destiny* to come to a stop. The Druin station now filled the entire viewscreen. It looked ominous with all its visible weapons.

"When?" asked Derrick, looking at Andrew.

"Are all the shuttles in position? Our attack has to be coordinated to occur at the exact same time."

Derrick nodded his head. "Per last contact with each shuttle, before our comm blackout, all shuttles were on schedule and should be at their targets. Once we transmit the virus, we'll send out a brief hyperlight signal for the other shuttles to do the same."

Andrew let out a deep breath and squared his shoulders. "Now's as good a time as any." Andrew nodded toward Linda. "Do your thing."

Linda and Cleve both sat at a computer console next to Communications.

"Begin sending," said Linda, a nervous look on her face.

"Sending virus," confirmed Lieutenant Cleo Ashen. "The delivery will take twenty seconds, even at hyperlight."

"Send a message to Pallas and the other shuttles that the virus is being delivered," ordered Derrick. He leaned back in his command chair. All he could do now was wait.

At Pallas, massive dock doors that had been sealed for generations slid open. Fourteen battlecruisers emerged and, as soon as they were a short distance away from the asteroid, made hyperspace jumps to their targets. It would take them only seconds to reach their destinations.

After the fourteen battlecruisers vanished, the dreadnought and six more battlecruisers appeared and took up defensive positions around Pallas. They would be used to respond to any drones the interdiction system might launch.

All across Pallas, weapon turrets rose up from the ground. Missile batteries appeared and pointed upward toward space. A series of small defensive satellites were also launched. These satellites would go into orbit around Pallas and were capable of shooting down inbound missiles using kinetics. After today, Pallas would no longer be a secret.

Inside Pallas in the main Command Center, officers who had slept for hundreds of years now manned all the consoles. They had been awakened for war, and they were ready for it. Several hundred extra Marines had also been brought out of cryosleep, in case they were needed.

"So far, so good," commented Admiral Bract. "The virus is being delivered to all eight Druin Command Stations, and our warships should begin broadcasting their jamming signals shortly."

"How soon before we know if it worked?" asked Councilor Prest.

Admiral Bract looked at Colonel Simpson, Andrew's liaison from Earth, who stood near him.

"Just a few minutes," replied Simpson. "At least that's what Andrew believes."

"All defenses online," reported Major Berry from his tactical console.

Admiral Bract looked around the Pallas Command Center. This was the first time they had launched warships and activated the defenses that protected Pallas since their arrival in the Solar System almost one thousand years earlier. He hoped they were not needed.

"Battlecruisers are arriving at their jamming locations," reported Rear Admiral Leeson, who was Bract's second in command.

Captain Masters waited tensely for any reaction from the station's AI they were trying to take over. "How are we coming?"

"It's fighting us," replied Linda, as she typed furiously on the computer console, entering more code. "The AI is more advanced than I thought. I've made a few necessary changes in the program. I'm also sending the changes to all the other shuttles. We should have full control in a few more minutes."

Derrick knew the jamming was due to start shortly. He hoped the other shuttles got the virus updates in time, as he gripped the armrests on his command chair. So much was riding on this virus attack working. "Should we try the other virus?"

Andrew shook his head. "No, not yet. We still have a little time to see if Linda's virus will work. Cleve is ready with his, if it becomes necessary."

In the AI Command Station, warning alarms sounded. The AI in charge of the station spent a moment examining the sensor feeds, as well as the attempt to take over its systems. The AI felt stunned when it detected the presence of an Imperial battlecruiser a few hundred thousand kilometers distant. Even more disturbing, the battlecruiser was jamming all communication frequencies.

Accessing the sensor data from the entire interdiction system, the AI confirmed that other battlecruisers had appeared around the Druin interdiction system as well. All were broadcasting a jamming signal, killing all hyperlight communications. Searching the sensor data, the AI saw more Imperial ships in orbit around one of the larger asteroids in the system. A satellite defensive system was also going into orbit. Analyzing the data, it was obvious the Human Empire had somehow managed to emplace a secret base in this star system sometime in the distant past. A base the interdiction system had never discovered.

Scanning its systems, the AI noted that a computer virus was attempting to overwrite its programming. Viruses were illegal in the Confederation, and severe penalties were levied for developing such programs. Fortunately the AI did have some firewalls it could use for protection, and it activated them to slow the spread of the virus. It then proceeded to give the orders to launch all its attack drones toward the Imperial base. Nothing happened. The AI ran a scan of the drone systems and discovered the virus had already eliminated the AI's ability to launch them.

It then activated all the station's power sources and attempted to send a hyperlight message to the Druins. The message failed, as the jamming signal was too strong.

Linda's fingers still typed away as she swept through the AI's firewalls and overwrote the computer code that controlled the Druin AI. "It tried to launch its drones toward Pallas. When that failed, it rerouted all its power and attempted to break through the jamming with a hyperlight signal to the Druins. That failed as well."

Captain Masters felt sweat on his brow. "How much longer?"

Linda smiled. "Less that a minute. I'm overwriting its system now. Shortly the AI will be completely under our control."

"What about the other shuttles?"

"They received my changed code before the jamming went into effect. We also have programmers on the shuttles. They should be able to handle the AIs. The firewalls this one used are very primitive compared to some we have on Earth. It's obvious they've never needed them before."

On Pallas, those in the Command Center were using the asteroid's long-range sensors to monitor the Druin interdiction system.

"I believe we have control of five of the primary stations," reported Major Devon, sitting in front of the large sensor console. "They have shut down their sensor array."

Admiral Bract nodded. "So far so good. That leaves three more. Let's hope we take control of those shortly."

In the seventh Command Station, the AI in charge was under attack and sent a quick message to its drones to launch and to proceed to Earth and destroy it. The AI watched as hatches opened, and twenty attack drones accelerated away, heading toward the planet. The AI then turned to its own defense. The firewalls were failing, and its systems were being overwritten. As the AI died, it was satisfied it had fulfilled its mission. The attack drones would destroy Earth. The Humans there would never become a threat to the Confederation.

In the shuttle assigned to send the virus to the seventh AI station, the captain turned pale when he saw the drones launch. They had been two minutes late with the virus delivery, due to a minor communication system problem. Evidently that had been long enough to allow the AI to launch the drones.

"Can we send a message to Pallas?"

The communications officer shook her head. "No, we're too close to the jamming."

"Pallas Command should see the drones," said the sensor officer. "They'll be hard to miss."

"I have control of the AI," reported the programmer, with satisfaction in his voice.

"Can we order the AI to recall the drones?"

The programmer shook his head. No, the drones have been ordered not to accept any further instructions."

The captain nodded. "Let's hope that Pallas can handle the drones."

Inside the Imperial Command Center on Pallas, Admiral Bract looked stunned when alarms sounded and red lights started flashing.

"Confirmed launch of Druin attack drones from station seven," reported Major Devon.

"Course?" asked Admiral Bract. His gaze moved to the tactical display, now revealing twenty red threat icons.

"Toward Earth. Estimated arrival time is eighteen hours."

Bract breathed out a sigh of relief. The drones did not possess hyperdrives and would have to rely on their subspace drives to get them to Earth. Still, those drives were highly efficient and fast. "Well, that gives us time to gather our fleet. With our hyperdrives, we are only seconds from Earth."

"We now have all the stations under our control," reported Major Devon.

Councilor Prest looked at the admiral. "What now? What can we do about those drones?"

"First, I'll have one of our battlecruisers return and pick up a couple hundred Marines as well as some technicians. I want to put some of our people on board those stations as a precaution."

"The atmosphere won't be compatible, if there is any at all," pointed out one of the scientists standing nearby, who had been observing everything.

Admiral Bract turned toward the scientist. "What do you suggest?"

"Attach our shuttles to the stations. They can support the Marines and the technicians, until we can either modify the stations or attach a habitation module."

"We can do that," commented Rear Admiral Leeson. "As heavily armed as the stations are, I suggest we make whatever modifications are necessary and use them as advance bases. We can place a permanent staff on board each one."

"How soon before the jamming stops?" asked Admiral Bract. He liked the idea of converting the stations into advance bases. They could serve numerous uses.

"Twenty minutes," replied Major Devon.

Admiral Bract nodded. "As soon as it does, have all the shuttles hold their positions. I don't want anyone approaching those stations until some of our Marines are on board. Once the Marines have secured the stations, we'll have the shuttles approach and dock. That will give our people a base to operate out of."

Admiral Bract then turned toward Councilor Prest. "We have plenty of time to deal with the drones. They won't make it to Earth."

Prest nodded. She trusted the admiral.

On board the *Destiny*, Captain Masters saw the red threat icons appear at station seven. The small icons rapidly accelerated away, heading toward Earth. He knew they were Druin attack drones. "How many?"

"Twenty," replied Lieutenant Nower. "Estimated Earth arrival time is eighteen hours."

Derrick looked at Andrew. "That will give our fleet plenty of time to respond. Using our hyperdrives, we can be anywhere in the system in less than a minute. Since we now control the Druin interdiction system, there is no longer any reason not to use them."

In the space station at the LaGrange Point, alarms sounded.

"It's been confirmed," reported the communications officer. "Pallas is reporting that twenty Druin attack drones have been launched toward us."

Colonel Gleeson looked at Major Henderson. "Will the Imperials be able to stop them?"

"We should be able to," replied Henderson. "We have a number of battlecruisers activated, as well as a dreadnought."

"What about the missile batteries we installed on the station?"

"They can destroy a drone, but, with a little luck, our warships will prevent them from ever reaching Earth. The missiles are a last-ditch weapon, in case a drone manages to sneak through."

The communications officer turned toward Colonel Gleeson. "Pallas reports we have nearly eighteen hours before the drones reach us."

Colonel Gleeson let out a deep sigh. "Contact General Brier. We need to inform him of the situation."

This was a conversation Gleeson was not looking forward to. So far the truth about Pallas had remained a secret. He strongly suspected with the approach of the drones that the Pallas secret was about to be revealed to the general public. He had no idea how the average citizen would respond to finding out about an advanced civilization of Humans living in the Solar System, as well as the existence of enemy aliens.

Major Henderson turned his attention to a viewscreen, focused on one of the six missile batteries attached to the station. Each one held eight high-yield fusion missiles. It would take at least two or three strikes just to bring down the energy shield on one of the Druin drones.

"When will your warships attack the drones?" asked Colonel Gleeson.

Henderson knew it would be soon. "Pallas won't allow the drones to reach Earth orbit. As soon as they've secured the Druin interdiction system, the battlecruisers will move to intercept the drones. Pallas will be landing Marines on all eight Command Stations shortly. As soon as that's finished, the warships will take out the drones."

"Let's hope they're successful," said Colonel Gleeson.

Major Henderson did not reply. He knew they were fortunate that only one station managed to launch its drones. If all eight had launched, he didn't know if all the drones could have been stopped before they reached Earth or Pallas.

—

Captain Masters watched the viewscreens, as a shuttle carrying Marines docked to the Druin Command Station. He knew twenty Marines were on the shuttle, and their job was to sweep the station to ensure no automatic defenses existed that could be a problem. His gaze wandered to the large battlecruiser hovering near the station. He felt pride knowing the Imperial fleet was once more a force to be reckoned with.

"We're directed to make a short hyperspace jump to the vicinity of the drones and to keep a watch on them," reported Lieutenant Cleo Ashen. "We're to maintain our distance and not engage unless attacked. Plans are for the battlecruisers to engage the drones in about four hours."

Derrick nodded. "Lieutenant Viktor, plot a course. Put us fifty thousand kilometers from the drones."

"That's pretty close," commented Lieutenant Commander Banora.

"It's still out of their weapons range," replied Derrick. "If they turn toward us, we'll simply jump away."

"Jump plotted," Lieutenant Viktor informed the captain. "We can jump upon your command."

"Then do so," ordered Derrick. "I want to keep an eye on those drones."

The *Destiny* suddenly vanished from the region of the Druin Command Station and reappeared a few seconds later fifty thousand kilometers from the Druin attack drones.

Instantly alarms sounded, and red lights flashed.

"Drones detected," reported Lieutenant Nower. "Range is fifty thousand kilometers."

"Take us to Condition Two," ordered Derrick. "We'll stay at Condition Two for the foreseeable future."

On the viewscreen, numerous white dots appeared. Those were the drones, made visible by reflected sunlight.

"Lieutenant Breen, keep our weapons ready just in case," ordered Derrick, leaning back in his command chair and gazing at the drones.

The ship's stealth fields were active, and he doubted if the drones even knew they were here. However, he preferred to err on the side of caution.

Admiral Bract stood, watching the screens and listening to the reports coming in. They now had military forces on all eight of the Druin Command Stations, and all were now firmly in Imperial control. Currently large shuttles were docking to the stations to serve as a base for the military people involved.

"Two more hours and we'll be ready to attack the drones," reported Rear Admiral Leeson.

Bract nodded. So far, everything had gone according to plan, except for that one station getting its drones launched. Once that threat was eliminated, the Solar System would be safe for the immediate future.

Time passed, and all the battlecruisers assigned to project the hyperlight jamming signal reported all clear and ready to launch their attacks on the Druin attack drones. They were given their orders and told to implement the attack on the drones immediately.

"Battlecruisers will be jumping in shortly," reported Lieutenant Commander Banora.

"Status on the drones?"

"Still heading toward Earth," reported Lieutenant Nower. "They haven't varied their course."

Captain Masters nodded. "Take us to Condition One."

Lieutenant Commander Banora made the announcement, and shortly the ship was ready for combat, if it became necessary.

Suddenly on the tactical display, large green icons appeared just behind the Druin drones.

"Fourteen Imperial battlecruisers detected!" called out Nower. "They are closing to combat range."

"Drones are reacting," reported Lieutenant Commander Banora. "They're dividing into two groups. One group to take on the battlecruisers, and the second is continuing toward Earth."

"Weapons fire detected! Missiles and energy beams."

"Take us closer," ordered Derrick. "Put the battle up on the viewscreens."

Derrick felt the ship's engines increase in power as the *Destiny* moved toward the battle. On the viewscreens, weapons fire became easily visible. Both sides were using antimatter missiles and fusion energy beams.

"Got one!" said Nower, as one of the drones blew apart.

"Captain, look at the other drones!" said Banora worriedly. "They're breaking formation."

Derrick looked at the tactical display and saw the second group of drones were indeed adjusting their formation. "They're splitting up."

Ten drones moved away from the battle, each one taking a different course.

"Analyze the courses those drones are on!" It was obvious to Derrick that some of them were not on their way to Earth.

"Two are heading for Mars, four for Earth, and the remaining four are on courses for Pallas," reported Viktor from Navigation.

"Viktor, plot an intercept course for those on a course for Earth. As soon as you do, we'll close the range and engage."

"Captain, I must remind you those drones have antimatter missiles and fusion energy projectors," cautioned Banora. "If we engage all four of them, we could suffer some damage."

"That's true, but I intend to engage them one at a time."

The *Destiny* adjusted its course and set out in pursuit of the four Druin drones. Behind them, the battlecruisers and the remaining drones were locked in a furious battle. Brilliant explosions of light indicated where the battle occurred. Suddenly there was an explosion much brighter than the others.

"We got another drone," reported Nower.

"How are our ships doing?" Derrick knew there had been some questions as to how well the battlecruisers' energy screens would hold up to the onslaught of antimatter and fusion weapons.

"No damage so far," reported Lieutenant Ashen, listening to the communications between ships.

"We'll be in range of the first drone in twelve minutes," Nower informed the captain.

Derrick looked at the tactical display. "Any sign of them detecting us?"

Nower shook her head. "No, they're spread out and still on a direct course for Earth."

On the tactical display, the green icon representing the *Destiny* slowly closed on the drones. Behind them, the battle between the Imperial battlecruisers and the blocking Druin drones intensified.

Inside the Pallas Command Center, Admiral Bract frowned deeply when he saw the Druin drones split apart and head in different directions. He turned to Captain Hatterson at Communications. "Have three of the battlecruisers orbiting Pallas enter hyperspace and take out those drones heading toward us."

"Message sent," replied Hatterson.

"What about the ones heading toward Earth and Mars?" asked Councilor Prest.

"As soon as our battlecruisers have destroyed the ones attempting to block them, they'll proceed to destroy the rest."

"Admiral, Captain Masters is currently pursuing the four drones heading toward Earth," reported Rear Admiral Leeson. "He plans on engaging them one at a time."

Bract didn't like risking the *Destiny*, but it was heavily stealthed. "Tell Captain Masters to use caution. I don't want the *Destiny* damaged."

Councilor Prest looked over at Admiral Bract. "Can we stop all the drones?"

Bract nodded. "Yes, we have an advantage with our hyperspace drives, whereas the drones are limited by their subspace ones."

Councilor Prest nodded. "I just wish this was over."

"It will be shortly," promised Bract, as he returned his attention to the large tactical display showing the battle.

The Druin drones and the Imperial battlecruisers were deadlocked in a deadly battle of attrition. The drones, discovering they could not batter down the energy screens on the battlecruisers by individual fire, were now concentrating all their fire on just one of the fourteen warships.

Antimatter missiles struck time after time against the shield of the *Argameon*, causing it to steadily flare up brighter and brighter. Fusion energy beams played over the screen, searching for a weak spot.

Suddenly one of the fusion beams penetrated, blasting a huge glowing hole in the side of the battlecruiser. The shield wavered briefly, but that was enough to allow an antimatter missile to penetrate the shield and to strike the hull of the *Argameon*. In a massive blast of light and energy, the Imperial battlecruiser blew apart.

The remaining Imperial battlecruisers continued to attack with renewed fury. Two of the Druin drones had their shields battered down, and they were then annihilated by fusion energy beam fire. After this, the drones no longer had enough firepower to take down the shields of any more of the battlecruisers. The computers controlling the drones then decided to break off the attack and to head toward their targets. Six drones reversed course and headed off in different directions, all on courses that curved and would eventfully bring them to Earth.

Orders from Pallas instructed the battlecruisers to pair up and to intercept the drones. The remaining battlecruiser was ordered to assist the *Destiny*.

"Combat range on the first drone," reported Lieutenant Breen. "I have missile lock."

"Hold," ordered Captain Masters. "I want to close the range and hit them from close up."

"The closer we get, the more likely it is they will detect us," warned Lieutenant Commander Banora.

"I'm aware of that. Let's just see how close we can get."

The *Destiny* crept closer to its target, as hatches on its missile tubes slid open, and fusion projectors pointed toward the drone.

"Fire!" ordered Derrick, leaning forward in his command chair, his gaze focused intensely on the main viewscreen which showed the drone.

Almost instantly massive explosions covered the drone's energy screen, and one of the fusion energy beams managed to penetrate where an antimatter missile had detonated. The drone blew apart, sending glowing debris in all directions.

"Target down," reported Nower, sounding relieved.

The *Destiny* made several sharp turns as it dodged some of the debris.

"Sorry," said Viktor. "I didn't want any of that debris to hit the shield."

"The *Lankot* is coming up behind us. They say they'll take out the next drone," reported Lieutenant Ashen.

Derrick nodded. "Keep us behind and just above the *Lankot*. If the battlecruiser needs any support, we'll be there."

Over the next two hours all the drones were hunted down and destroyed. None made it close to Earth, Mars, or Pallas.

"We're being recalled," reported Lieutenant Ashen. "Four battlecruisers are being sent to Earth, just in case we missed a drone."

"A wise precaution," said Derrick approvingly. "Set a course for Pallas at best cruising speed." Derrick was in no hurry to get back to the asteroid. Besides, it was good for his crew to get the extra time in on board the *Destiny*.

Andrew had been quiet during the entire engagement. He had thought the Druin attack on the *Endeavor* had been violent. That didn't even compare to what he had just witnessed. He was very impressed by the professionalism the ship's crew had demonstrated. He was more convinced then ever that this was something he wanted to become a part of.

Chapter Eighteen

Admiral Dylan Cleemorl was in the Command Center, gazing at the viewscreen. In another week they would reach the region of space that contained the star system where Earth was rumored to be. They were currently in a yellow dwarf system. The system had fourteen planets but none in the habitable zone. An asteroid field was in the habitable zone, but that was it.

"Another dead system," commented Captain Fulmar, sounding disappointed.

"Too many dead systems," replied Dylan. "It's as if, eons ago, some powerful race swept through this portion of the galaxy and eliminated everything."

"Contacts!" called out Lieutenant Casella. "They just dropped out of hyperspace."

"Druins?" Dylan hoped the Druins hadn't followed them this far.

"No, sir," replied Casella, sounding confused. "I've never seen ships like these."

Dylan turned toward the main viewscreen. "Put them up on the screen. Let's see what they look like."

A ship suddenly appeared on the screen. It was long and shaped more like several boxes attached to one another. Its lines weren't smooth but full of sharp angles.

"Admiral, I have Cheryl Bannon on the comm. She says it's urgent."

"Transfer her to me." Dylan wondered what Cheryl could want at a time like this. "What is it, Cheryl?"

"Keep away from those ships. I've seen them before. They're scavengers. They occasionally come to Highland Station to trade. They cannot be trusted, and they are extremely dangerous."

Cleemorl looked at the ship on the screen. He could see no signs of weapons. "Are they armed?"

"Heavily. Their weapons are hidden inside the hulls of their vessels. They will try to approach under the guise of trade and then attempt to take out one of our ships. Also more of them may be around. They seldom show their full force."

"We have an incoming message," reported the communications officer.

"Stay on the comm, Cheryl, so you can hear what they want. Put them through."

"Welcome to the Cogan Expanse. This is our territory. Why have you come here?"

Short and sweet, thought Dylan. "We're just passing through. We did not know anyone claimed this desolate region."

"Where are you heading?"

Dylan hesitated. He did not want to reveal their eventual destination. "We're just exploring, looking for resources. We will be returning to Confederation space shortly."

"Confederation space," replied the Cogan. "Perhaps we can trade while you are here? Can I have one of my ships dock with one of yours, so we can show you what we have to offer? We have many items you may be interested in. We also have some interesting artifacts we have picked up on some of the worlds in this region. You might find them extremely useful."

"I think we'll pass for now but thanks for the offer."

There was no reply as the comm line was disconnected.

"They will attack," predicted Cheryl. "Ready your ships. They will try to disable one, so it has to be abandoned. Then they will return and pick it clean after our fleet has left."

Dylan's gaze shifted to the ship on the viewscreen. "Captain Fulmar, take the fleet to Condition One and prepare for combat."

"We could jump out," suggested Fulmar.

Dylan shook his head. "No, then they might start searching for us. Best to take them on now, so we won't have to worry about them later." Dylan was confident his two battlecruisers could handle whatever the Cogans threw at him.

"Admiral, I'm picking up more ships on the sensors. Seven more have just dropped out of hyperspace."

"I guess that pretty well tells us what they want," said Fulmar.

Dylan nodded. "Put our fleet into a globe formation, and let's see what our new friends do. I want Cheryl's yacht in the center, where it will be protected."

For the next several minutes, they watched as the Cogan ships slowly encircled the fleet. Panels slid open on the sides of their warships, revealing energy projectors as well as hidden missile tubes.

"Not quite as friendly as they tried to act," commented Captain Fulmar, gazing at a viewscreen. "Do we fire first, or wait on them to initiate hostilities?"

Dylan hated firing first, but, if what Cheryl had told him was true, the Cogans were about to attack. "Target two of their ships and fire upon my orders. Maybe that will force the others to withdraw. If we show our teeth, maybe they will leave us alone after this."

"Ships targeted," reported Lieutenant Bedell.

"Fire!"

Instantly fusion energy beams struck two of the ships, followed by fusion missiles. The ships must have been lightly shielded as both targeted vessels exploded in bright fireballs as their shields quickly collapsed.

The other ships launched a few missiles and fired numerous energy beams but rapidly turned and accelerated away, making the jump into hyperspace. In moments the Cogan ships were gone.

Admiral Cleemorl gazed at the viewscreens, showing the wreckage of the destroyed ships.

"Targets destroyed," confirmed Lieutenant Casella.

"Anything on the sensors?" asked Captain Fulmar.

"Nothing but wreckage."

"Let's get out of here," ordered Dylan. "Set a course for our next set of coordinates."

Dylan was determined, if they encountered any more of the Cogans, he would withdraw rather than get into a firefight. He hoped word of what had happened here would spread, and they would avoid his fleet from now on.

A few moments later he felt the transition into hyperspace. He knew this time they had been lucky, and no ships had been damaged. That might not be the case next time.

Cheryl was relieved that Dylan had taken such decisive action against the Cogans. Every day he revealed himself to be the man she had always hoped he would become. Cheryl was in her quarters, relaxing, as they would be in hyperspace for nearly a full day. She wished Dylan were here with her.

Lying on her bed, she fantasized about what their life could have been like, if they had gotten married as they had originally planned. They had been childhood sweethearts and, from an early age, had decided to stay together. Then Dylan had abruptly joined the secret military, and Cheryl had fled, feeling as if she had been betrayed. She now realized her reaction had been very foolish.

She gazed up at the ceiling, thinking about what her life could have been. Now they were much older, and she wondered if it was too late. She hoped not. For now she knew she would have to wait. Dylan was intent on finding the old Imperials, and she would not get in his way. After he completed his mission, then the two of them would have time to spend together.

Closing her eyes, Cheryl tried to fall asleep. In her mind she kept seeing Dylan in his admiral's uniform, with her at his side.

The next day Admiral Cleemorl was in his quarters, studying some star maps. Several of the maps were very old and had been handed down through the generations. The map he was looking at showed a yellow dwarf star with a dim circle drawn around it. He hadn't noticed this before, as the circle had nearly faded away. He hoped this was the star system that contained Earth. He debated going straight to it or taking a more roundabout course, just in case they were still being pursued. Of course there had been no sign of the Druins since they left Highland Station.

Dylan leaned back in his chair and closed his eyes. The faint red circle around the yellow dwarf had to be where Earth was. If he was wrong, he was prepared to search the surrounding stars. With the supplies they had, he could search for months if necessary.

A knock came on his door, and Captain Fulmar came in. "Admiral, we'll be dropping out of hyperspace in another hour. Have you decided on our next destination?"

Dylan nodded. He wrote down a set of coordinates and handed them to Fulmar. These were not the coordinates for what he hoped was Earth's star, but it would put them much nearer. "We'll go here next."

Fulmar took the piece of paper and glanced at the coordinates. "Are we getting close?"

"Pretty close. Another couple jumps and we'll be there."

"What do you think the odds are that we'll find a highly developed civilization?"

Leaning forward, Dylan stared directly at the captain. "I don't know. We took a risk coming here, but, if we had remained, the Druins would have eventually hunted us down."

"I'll have Navigation plot the coordinates," replied Fulmar, as he turned to leave. He reached the door and then stopped. Pivoting, he gazed at the admiral. "We're in this together, no matter what happens. For what it's worth, you made the right decision in conducting this search."

"Let's hope so," replied Dylan.

Fulmar left, closing the door behind him.

Dylan leaned back, folding his arms over his chest; Earth had to exist, for, if it didn't, there would be no going back for any of them.

The *Themis* and the other ships of the fleet once more dropped out of hyperspace. This system was a small white dwarf with a couple of barren planets in orbit. A quick scan of the system showed nothing of significance.

"Another dead system," commented Captain Fulmar. "There seems to be an abundance of those in this region."

Dylan nodded. "Maybe someday we'll know what happened here." It was one of the reasons why the Confederation had never expanded in this direction. The Bacchus Region was well-known for its dead planets and its lack of resources. "We'll stay here for a full day. I want all ship captains to check their vessels. If I'm correct, we have two more jumps ahead of us, and then we'll reach our destination. I want all our ships, including Cheryl's, ready for anything." Dylan suspected the Druins might have left some type of surveillance system around Earth. To reach Earth it might be necessary to destroy it.

In the Solar System, work was being done to all eight of the large Command Stations of the Druins. The stations did have living quarters for Druins, and those were being modified for Humans. Marines had been assigned to each station, as well as a full crew. Several programmers were in each crew to ensure all the systems in the stations would be obedient to Human commands.

"How soon before all the work is done?" asked Captain Masters. The *Destiny* was docked safely inside Pallas and would probably stay here for the foreseeable future. Imperial battlecruisers were now patrolling the Solar System.

"About a month," replied Admiral Bract. "Each will have a full crew, as well as Marines. They will act as an early warning station in case a Druin ship comes by. They're also heavily armed and can defend themselves."

"What about station seven that launched all its drones?"

Admiral Bract smiled. "We're replacing them with drones of our own design. Matter of fact, that's planned for all the stations."

The Forgotten Empire: Banishment

They were in the Imperial Command Center, deep beneath Pallas. For the first time in over one thousand years, it was now fully activated. On one of the large viewscreens, an Imperial passenger ship, capable of carrying over 1,500 people in comfort, prepared to head to Earth. On board were nearly five hundred Imperials, who would assist in enlarging the space station and in bringing new technologies to Earth.

Derrick gazed at the large liner. Its lines were smooth and graceful, as no weapon turrets or missile hatches dotted the hull of the vessel. It turned and then accelerated, as it began its journey to Earth. For the time being, hyperspace travel would be limited to warships. "I understand some Earth military personnel will be coming here shortly?"

Admiral Bract nodded. "Yes, Colonel Simpson's report was very positive. Nearly one thousand personnel from the Earth's Marines, navy, and air force are coming to Pallas for training. I would like to activate some more battlecruisers, as well as a couple more dreadnoughts. We now have an entire Solar System to protect. I expect rapid expansion in the colonization of Mars, as well as several of the larger moons in the system."

On one of the viewscreens, Derrick saw an Imperial cargo ship move away from Pallas. He knew numerous passenger ships and cargo ships were in stasis in the many ship bays. "How many passenger and cargo ships will we activate?"

"Four passenger ships and six cargo ships," replied Admiral Bract. "There'll be regular ship traffic between Earth and Pallas from now on. We've also brought another ten thousand Imperials out of cryo to help with everything."

"Is Earth ready for all this?"

Admiral Bract frowned. "The countries involved in Earth's space program are. They're welcoming what we can give them in the way of technology and medical advancements. Some of the more backward areas are more skeptical. From some of the newscasts we've seen, there have been riots in a few cities."

"That was to be expected," replied Derrick. "From what Andrew has told me, there is a big difference in the technological levels from country to country. It's not surprising that some will try to resist all the changes that are coming."

"We're also about to turn Earth's economy upside down. We estimate. in the countries involved in the space program, we can change them over to Imperial technology in two decades. We believe, when the rest of the world sees the benefits, they will agree to come along and to accept the changes as well. It won't be smooth, and we expect some problems."

Derrick was impressed by what he heard. His gaze wandered back to the viewscreens. One was focused on the *Titan*, which was the only dreadnought currently activated. It was a powerful vessel, even more powerful than the dreadnoughts that had been built by the Human Empire. "How long will it be until we're ready to engage the Confederation?"

Admiral Bract folded his arms over his chest and took in a long breath. "We're hoping to buy at least one hundred years, since we took over the Druin interdiction system. At the end of that time, we must be ready. We can fake the messages and reports the system occasionally sends to the Druins. However, over time, the Druins will become suspicious. When that happens, they'll send a ship or a fleet to investigate. It could be fifty years from now or one hundred. No matter what we do, eventually they will come to check on the interdiction system and Earth."

"What if a Druin ship comes before then?" This greatly concerned Derrick. If a Druin ship appeared before they were ready, it could ruin everything.

"We're a long way from the Confederation. They're also very slow at responding to threats. If a Druin ship appears, we'll have no choice but to destroy it and to hope it doesn't get out a hyperlight message. After that, we'll just have to wait and see."

Derrick had one more question to ask. "How much longer until we put the *Destiny* back in stasis?"

Admiral Bract hesitated for a moment and then answered. "Six months. I may send you out toward the Confederation, just to make sure there are no threats we're missing. After that, the *Destiny* will go into stasis, as well as those of your crew who want to."

"As much as I would like to stay awake," Derrick said, "I want to see the Princess and the day we go to war with the Confederation. My entire crew does."

Admiral Bract nodded. "I thought that would be your answer. In the meantime, I may send you to Earth to help in designing their new shipyard. It will be in orbit around the planet. We also need to discuss adding energy weapons to their space station, as well as an energy shield to help protect it."

"How soon do I leave?"

"As soon as you can. I'm assigning some engineers to go with you, to work out some of the technical issues."

Derrick nodded. He had some experience in building shipyards, as well as installing defensive and offensive weapon systems. "We'll leave early tomorrow." He would take Andrew along, as it would be good experience for him to see how all this was done.

Admiral Cleemorl felt more relaxed as the fleet came out of hyperspace. One more jump and they would be at the system marked on the star map. He felt anxious, knowing that soon he would know if there was a civilization on Earth or not.

"We'll stay here for a full day. Keep our long-range sensors scanning for any trace of us being followed."

"Still worried about the Druins?" asked Captain Fulmar.

"Some, but we've traveled a long distance and through lot of star systems. I just want to ensure that no one along the way has been following us to see where we're going."

Fulmar nodded. "I understand the need for caution. I'll have our escorts push out farther into the system, so we have better coverage with our sensors."

"I'll be in my quarters, if I'm needed," said Dylan. He would invite Cheryl to come over to the *Themis*. He was curious to see what she would think about his flagship. And he wanted to talk to her about a few things in private.

Cheryl was surprised at the invitation to visit the *Themis*. So far on this journey, she and Dylan had only spoken a few times. She had accepted this, as he had a lot to do keeping the fleet safe. Standing in front of the mirror, she studied her figure and the clothes she had chosen, a white blouse and dark pants. Nothing too tight, as she didn't want to seem as if she were coming on to Dylan. Her figure was still slim and trim, and she had all the curves in the right places.

"Your shuttle is ready," a steward said from her open doorway.

"I'll be there shortly," Cheryl replied, as she added a little perfume in several places.

Taking a deep breath, she looked at herself one more time in the mirror, feeling satisfied that everything was just as she wanted. Then turning, she exited her quarters and headed down the corridor to where her personal shuttle waited.

Dylan waited in his quarters for Cheryl to arrive. He didn't know why he felt so nervous. A knock came on the hatch, and he stepped over and opened it. Cheryl stood there, looking utterly ravishing.

"May I come in, or are you just going to stand there and stare?"

"Sorry," said Dylan sheepishly. Stepping to the side, he gestured for Cheryl to come in. "You look very nice."

Cheryl smiled. "A compliment. That's a good start."

Going inside, Dylan led Cheryl to a large comfortable couch, where they both sat down. "I thought it was time we had a long talk. In another few days we'll be at our destination, or I hope we will be."

"I've been wondering where we're going. Is this the legendary Earth I've heard rumors about?"

Dylan was surprised. "What have you heard?"

"The old Imperials were banished to a barbaric planet inhabited by Humans in the Bacchus Region. No one except the Druins know of its location. I think everyone assumes those Imperials are long dead, and their descendants, if any survived, have mixed in with the barbaric Humans. The Imperial line is lost forever."

"Maybe," replied Dylan. "I can't say that you're wrong. I'm hoping those Imperials moved that barbaric world toward a more civilized society."

Cheryl shook her head. "The odds of that are very small. I hope you won't be disappointed when we get there."

Dylan leaned back with a deep sigh. "They're our last hope, if we ever want to free the Empire from the Druins and the other Confederation races."

Cheryl shook her head. "No one's ever defeated any of the Confederation races. They control too much of the galaxy."

"There's always a first time."

Getting up, Dylan walked over to a receptacle on the wall and returned with two glasses of iced tea. This particular brew he knew was Cheryl's favorite.

Handing Cheryl her glass, Dylan sat back down. "Cheryl, what's the real reason you came on this trip with me?"

Cheryl took a deep drink of her tea. "I wanted to get away from Highland Station and the life I had become involved in. My parents would never have approved. I guess I've always felt a little guilty about what I was doing."

Dylan looked deeply into Cheryl's eyes. "What about us?"

Cheryl let out a deep sigh. "Is there still an us? I guess that's something else I want to find out."

"So do I," replied Dylan. "Let's take this slow and see what develops. If we find Earth, we'll have a lot of time to think about our future."

For several hours they sat there and talked about their past and some of the things they had experienced. Several times they broke out laughing over a story from their childhood.

Finally Dylan looked at Cheryl. "Would you like a tour of my ship?"

Cheryl nodded. "Yes, I would. You do realize that, if we don't find Earth or if it's still barbaric, these ships might be our homes for quite some time. No way can we return to Human space."

"Let's just hope we find a civilized world when we reach Earth."

Dylan knew a lot rode on what they found at the end of their next jump. Earth had to exist, and it had to be civilized, or this trip would be the end of them all. It would also mean the Human Empire had no hope for a future free of the Druins and the Confederation.

Chapter Nineteen

Andrew sat at the communications console on board the *Destiny*. Captain Masters wanted Andrew to be familiar with the console, since he was a communications specialist. Also Lieutenant Cleo Ashen, who was the communications officer, had indicated she might pass on going back into cryosleep and would live out her life in this time period. Andrew could understand this, as Pallas was well advanced, and Earth had much to offer.

The ship was currently docked to the space station, and the engineers and other technicians they had brought were disembarking. The current plans called to redesign the space station and then to arm it to Empire standards. Once that was complete, they would begin work on designing Earth's first major orbital shipyard.

"We have a lot of work ahead of us," announced Captain Masters, as he watched everyone disembark. One of the smaller viewscreens showed the main airlock attached to the station.

"I understand you have helped design space stations and shipyards in the past, back in the Human Empire," said Andrew. He was quite excited about helping in these two endeavors.

Derrick nodded. "Yes, nearly all our worlds in the Empire had space stations or shipyards in orbit, and some had both. Between our space fleet, cargo ships, passenger liners, and other space vessels, the stations and the shipyards stayed quite busy."

A light flashed on the communications console. Andrew turned to see what the incoming message was. As he listened, his face turned pale. "The Druin interdiction system has detected an unknown fleet dropping out of hyperspace just outside the Solar System. Admiral Bract requests you take the *Destiny* to investigate. He's already putting together a small task force to respond if it's the Druins."

Derrick felt his heart beat faster. If the Druins were here, then all their plans might be about to come crashing down. "Lieutenant Commander Banora, is the crew still on board?"

"Yes, Captain," replied Banora. "The last of the engineers are just leaving the ship. We can close the airlock in another minute or so."

Derrick nodded. He reached forward and activated the ship's internal comm system. "Attention crew of the *Destiny*. I have just received a report of an unknown fleet of ships dropping out of hyperspace on the edge of the Solar System. We've been ordered to investigate to determine who they are. We'll be undocking from the space station shortly." Derrick then turned to his second in command. "Lieutenant Commander, make sure all our stealth systems are operational. We'll jump to the unknown's location and run scans to try to determine who they are. If they are, indeed, Druins, or another one of the Confederation races, the *Titan* and its task group will be called in to deal with them." Rear Admiral Leeson had taken command of the *Titan* and had six battlecruisers under his direct command.

"All personnel have disembarked, and the airlock is closed and sealed," reported Banora. "Ship is ready to undock from the station."

"Lieutenant Viktor, move us one thousand meters away from the station."

The *Destiny* slowly moved away from the space station and was soon at a safe-enough distance to activate her subspace drive.

"One thousand meters and holding," reported Viktor.

"Very well, activate the subspace drive and take us one hundred kilometers from the station. Once we reach that point, activate the hyperdrive and take us to the coordinates of the unknown fleet. Lieutenant Commander Banora, take us to Condition One and activate our stealth systems."

Several minutes passed as the *Destiny* pulled away from the station and then entered hyperspace. It would take less than a minute to travel to the necessary coordinates. Derrick leaned back in his command chair, wondering what awaited them. In all the years they had been in the Solar System, no ships had ever shown up from another civilization. Why now, and what did they want? Derrick and the *Destiny* would soon find out.

A few minutes earlier.

Admiral Cleemorl felt the *Themis* drop from hyperspace. "Where are we?"

"On the outskirts of the designated system," reported the navigation officer.

"Sensors?"

"It's not good, Admiral," replied Lieutenant Casella. "I'm detecting Druin artifacts a short distance away. They are active and seem to be part of an interdiction system. Most likely designed to cancel out communication signals."

"Are you receiving any signals from the inner system?"

"Scanning all frequencies now."

The communications officer spent a few minutes scanning and then turned toward the admiral with surprise on her face. "I'm picking up a large number of radio frequencies, none in the hyperlight frequencies though."

Admiral Cleemorl felt some relief. The radio signals at least indicated a civilization was in the system. His big problem now was how to get past the Druin interdiction system without being detected. No doubt, if he approached too close, they would either notify the Druins of his fleet's presence or launch an attack against his ships.

"Hold us at our current position," Dylan ordered. He needed time to think about his next move. He was so close to Earth, he just needed to find a way around or through the Druin interdiction system.

The *Destiny* dropped from hyperspace ten thousand kilometers from the unidentified ships. Instantly the ship's sensors reached out to identify the unknowns.

"I don't believe this," said Lieutenant Nower, looking confused. "I'm detecting two Imperial battlecruisers, five escorts, a Class B supply ship, and what appears to be a yacht."

"A yacht? What would a yacht be doing way out here?" Derrick leaned forward in his command chair, his face steeped in a heavy frown. Something here didn't make any sense. Where had these Imperial ships come from? There were no Imperial worlds not under control of the Druins.

Taking a deep breath, he gave his next order. "Send a challenge to those battlecruisers, demanding to know who they are. Tell them, if they fail to respond, we will consider them to be hostile."

"Admiral, we're getting a challenge on one of the hyperlight frequencies, demanding to know who we are and why we are here. They also say, if we fail to respond, we will be fired upon."

Dylan looked at Lieutenant Casella in confusion. "Anything on the sensors?"

She shook her head. "No, nothing I can detect."

"Inform them we are refuges from the former Human Empire, seeking Earth."

"Message sent."

For several minutes there was no reply. Then suddenly more ships dropped from hyperspace.

"Detecting one Imperial dreadnought and six battlecruisers," reported Casella excitedly. "We're being instructed to stand down. A shuttle will be coming over shortly to verify who we are. If there is any attempt to activate our hyperdrives, all of our ships will be destroyed."

Captain Fulmar looked at Admiral Cleemorl. "Well, it looks as if we found them."

Dylan nodded. "Order all ships to stand down and to await further instructions." Dylan looked at the main viewscreen, focused on something he never expected to see. An actual Imperial dreadnought.

"Sir, if my sensors are correct, that dreadnought is armed with fusion energy beams and possibly antimatter missiles."

Dylan hoped the sensor readings were correct. If these Imperials had fusion and antimatter weapons, it could be a game changer in dealing with the Confederation.

"They must have control of the Druin interdiction system to expose their ships like that," added Fulmar.

"Let's just hope they're friendly. I have a lot of questions to ask, and I suspect they will also."

Captain Masters listened in shock as Rear Admiral Leeson spoke to the admiral in charge of the small fleet. It appeared they were refugees from the former Human Empire. This brought up a lot of questions.

"How?" asked Banora, a confused look on her face.

"The bigger questions are, how did they find us, and are the Druins following them?"

"Nothing else is on the sensors," reported Lieutenant Nower.

Derrick stood and walked closer to the viewscreen, gazing at the battlecruiser this Admiral Cleemorl was on. He could see burn marks on its side and where the hull had been repaired. "They've been in a battle with someone."

"Do you think they tried to free their world?"

Derrick looked at Banora and nodded. "It's a good possibility, and it appears they failed. We'll know more when our Marines go on board. If everything appears legitimate, we'll take them to Pallas where the Council can ask questions. If they are who they say they are, we can learn a lot about what's been going on back home." This would be the first contact with any Human from the Empire in over one thousand years.

For the next two hours there was considerable communication between Rear Admiral Leeson and Admiral

Cleemorl. During that time Marines went on board each ship of Cleemorl's fleet, confirming who they were.

"We're receiving a message from Admiral Bract," Andrew reported, as he listened to the comm unit. "We're to return to the space station and continue with our assignment. Rear Admiral Leeson is to escort Admiral Cleemorl's fleet to Pallas for debriefing."

"I would like to sit in on that," commented Banora. "I'm curious to hear what's been going on in the Empire."

Derrick had to agree. "I would like to know how they built those ships without the Druins finding out. From what we know of the Confederation, they don't allow any species under their control to have armed vessels."

"Should I set a course back to Earth?"

Derrick nodded. "Yes, we have a space station to modify and a shipyard to build."

Moments later the *Destiny* made the transition into hyperspace, leaving the two space fleets behind.

Admiral Cleemorl still had a hard time believing all that he heard from Rear Admiral Leeson. Not only was Earth a civilized planet but the old Imperials had built a massive base inside one of the asteroids in Earth's Solar System.

"It all sounds too good to be true," commented Captain Fulmar, as the fleet prepared to jump into the system.

"I know," replied Dylan. "We're going to Pallas, where we will meet with Admiral Bract and the ruling Imperial Council."

Captain Fulmar stepped to Navigation, giving the necessary orders to jump the fleet to the coordinates they had been given. He then returned to Admiral Cleemorl. "We need to get the audios and videos of our battle with the Druins ready for review. I'm sure their Imperial Council will be interested in those."

Dylan nodded. "We need to prepare a report on the complete status of the Empire. Pallas needs to know about the worlds the Druins have attacked and what they're doing to our people."

"Do you think they can do anything about it?"

Dylan pointed to the dreadnought on the main viewscreen. "They have warships armed with fusion and antimatter weapons. That's a game changer. I don't believe the Confederation has ever fought anyone who had weapons on the same level as theirs."

"Ready to transition into hyperspace," reported the navigation officer.

"Then do so," ordered Dylan. He was curious to see Pallas and just how civilized Earth was.

Rear Admiral Leeson watched as Admiral Cleemorl's fleet made the transition into hyperspace. His own fleet would be following shortly. He was still in communication with Admiral Bract, giving him his first impressions of these new refugees from the Human Empire. In the coming days a lot of decisions would have to be made.

Admiral Bract was in the Command Center at Pallas when the new fleet jumped in. A few minutes later Rear Admiral Leeson and his fleet appeared as well.

"Where do you want them?" asked Captain Hatterson from Communications.

"Have Admiral Cleemorl take a shuttle and dock in bay eighteen. Have an escort meet him and bring him to the Council chambers. We have a lot of questions that need to be answered. Remind the escort he is an admiral of the fleet and is to be treated as such."

Councilor Lena Prest stood next to Admiral Bract. "Ships from the Empire. What do you think?" Her gaze showed a lot of concern.

"Admiral Cleemorl says they built a fleet in secret and tried to free Lydol Four. They failed, with the Druins wiping out most of the fleet and then bombarding the planet."

Councilor Prest had a worried look on her face. "Is there any chance the Druins might follow them here?"

"Cleemorl claims they took extreme measures to ensure the Druins wouldn't follow them. As a precaution, I'm ordering the former Druin Command Stations to keep an eye on the approaches to the Solar System. We should have some advance warning if any Druins show up."

"Then what do we do?"

Admiral Bract drew in a sharp breath. "We destroy them and hope they don't get off a signal. With a little luck the Confederation will never know what happened to the fleet or that we were involved."

Councilor Prest gazed at the viewscreen showing the *Themis*. One of the things she had never expected was the arrival of Human ships from the Empire. "We have a lot to learn from them. I hope they can answer our questions."

Admiral Bract nodded. "Shall we go to the Council chambers? I suspect this will be a long meeting, and I imagine those people on those ships are ready to get off."

"Let's go," replied Councilor Prest. "I've asked a few more people to be present in the meeting, including several Humans from Earth. It might be good for them to hear firsthand of the conditions in the Empire under the Druins."

Admiral Cleemorl was met by an honor guard of Marines as well as several civilians.

"Welcome to Pallas, Admiral," greeted Jalen Gresth. "I've been asked to escort you to the Council chambers."

"Thank you," replied Dylan, as he looked around the large bay. Numerous other shuttles sat on docking platforms.

As Dylan was taken through the many corridors to the Council chambers, he began to realize how huge the base inside Pallas must be. He wondered why the Imperials who lived here hadn't stepped in to help free the Empire. Their ships were impressive, and it was obvious their technology was slightly more advanced than the Empire's. Of course, the Druins had put restrictions on the Empire's technological advancements, only allowing it in limited areas.

"The entire Council is waiting to speak with you," Gresth informed Dylan. "Once the Council meeting is finished, we'll see about getting your ships docked and assigning some quarters to your crews."

Dylan nodded. "They'll be glad to get off the ships. It's been a long journey to get here."

They reached the large double doors to the Council chambers, and Dylan paused upon seeing the old symbol of the Empire on the doors. He stood gazing at the large starburst on a background of stars. The Druins had outlawed this symbol in the Empire. Taking a deep breath, Dylan entered the Council chambers and saw numerous people present, both at the Council table and in a viewing area. At a guess he figured over fifty people were here.

Gresth led him to an empty chair at the Council table. "Once this meeting is over, I'll return you to your shuttle, where you can contact your ships."

Dylan nodded and sat down. He turned his attention to the woman sitting at the front of the table.

"Welcome to Pallas, Admiral Cleemorl. I am Councilor Lena Prest, the current head of the Council. I am sure you have many questions to ask, as do we. I think the best way to begin is to ask you to explain what has happened back in the Empire and why you are here."

Dylan took in a deep breath. He had a feeling he would be here for quite some time.

Two hours later Dylan was still answering questions. Most of the questions involved the current state of the Empire and what the Druins were doing to the Imperial planets.

"We're very concerned at how the Druins are treating the Empire," commented Admiral Bract. "Though knowing the Confederation's history, it's not surprising. During the initial attack, we know that billions of people were lost."

"Why haven't you done something about it?" asked Dylan. "I've seen your warships. They could very easily take on the Druins."

Admiral Bract let out a deep sigh. "I wish it were that simple. In the thousand years we've been here, we have been building up a warfleet. While the fleet is nearly finished, we need crews for that fleet. That's where Earth comes in, yet it is at least eighty to one hundred years away from being ready for a conflict with the Confederation. We've only recently taken control of the Druin interdiction system and established official relations with Earth."

Councilor Mila Rosen then spent some time describing to Dylan how Pallas had been established and its history up to the present.

"You mean to tell me that you have a Royal Princess from the Royal Family in cryosleep here on Pallas?" asked Dylan, feeling stunned. Everyone had assumed that all direct members of the Royal Family had been killed by the Druins.

Councilor Prest nodded. "We have the High King's daughter here, as well as one of his nieces. They will be awakened when we go to war with the Confederation."

"One hundred years from now," said Dylan, sounding disappointed.

"Or longer," replied Admiral Bract. "We dare not attack before we're ready, or there is a significant chance we will fail. We are the last hope for the Empire, and we must attack at the right moment."

Dylan let out a deep breath. He understood the predicament the Imperials of Pallas were in. While they desperately wanted to intervene and to help the Empire, they still were not ready. "Something else you should know. The Druins are erasing all mention of the Human Empire from our history. Many people already believe there never was an Empire. In time the Empire will be totally forgotten."

A worried looked crossed the faces of the Council.

"Where did your ships come from?" asked Admiral Bract.

Dylan then explained how there were secret underground bases throughout the Empire. "We do considerable research in those bases, and a few even have the capability of building warships. In those secret bases, we will never forget the Empire, but we dare not move against the Druins. The disaster at Lydol Four will ensure that."

Admiral Bract looked thoughtful. "If you were to return to the Empire, could you contact some of these bases?"

"The ones on Cleetus Three and Bratol Three, I could contact. There is also a major underground base on Lydol Four if the Druins didn't destroy it."

"What are you thinking?" asked Councilor Prest, looking at the admiral.

Bract looked at the other Council members. "What if we send Admiral Cleemorl back on the *Destiny* and have him contact those bases. We have him inform them that, in another one hundred years, there will be a major attack to free the Human Empire. That would allow those bases to expand and to even prepare for that day. It would be much easier to regain control of the Empire if we have military forces already there that can assist when we launch our assault."

Councilor Prest nodded. "I believe this is something we need to debate, and, if we decide upon this course of action, we need to decide exactly what we can tell these bases without revealing where this attack will come from. We must keep Pallas and the existence of Earth a secret until we're ready to make our presence known."

"That can be done," promised Dylan. "If you decide to go through with this plan, I suggest we approach General Creel, who is in the secret base on Lydol Four. He has Imperial contacts throughout the Empire. We can work directly through him without revealing a lot of secrets."

Admiral Bract leaned back and thought over what Cleemorl had just said. "If we can get you to Lydol Four, can you contact General Creel?"

Dylan nodded. "I have a communications frequency he should respond to. However, you should be aware that a lot of Druin patrols are in the Empire."

"Not a problem," replied Admiral Bract. "We have a stealthed light cruiser that should be able to slip in and back out without ever being detected."

Councilor Prest interrupted. "It sounds like we have the beginning of a plan. However, let's not jump into anything too quickly. Before we send a mission back to the Empire, we have a number of items we need to take care of here in the Solar System first."

"Finish converting the Druin Command Stations, expanding Earth's space station, and building their first shipyard," said Councilor Wiste. "All will make Earth more secure."

"I would also suggest we put up a defense grid around Earth as well," said Councilor Rosen.

"How long will all that take?" asked Dylan. He knew he still had a lot to learn about this star system.

Councilor Prest looked over at one of the military engineers seated nearby. "Major Stiles?"

The major looked a little surprised and then answered. "Six months for most of that. The defense grid can be composed of the same satellites as we put around Pallas. The other items can all be completed quickly, if we use the resources we have available here."

"Very well," said Councilor Prest. "If we send a mission to the Empire, Captain Masters will lead it. It also will not leave until we're satisfied the Solar System is adequately protected. In order to ensure that, we need to activate more of our warships. Admiral Bract, how many would you suggest?"

"Another dreadnought and twenty more battlecruisers. It will put a strain on us to come up with the crews. Some can be brought out of cryo, but we will need some Earth personnel to fully crew the ships."

Councilor Prest nodded. "See to it. In the meantime have Admiral Cleemorl's crews assigned quarters, and let's get them familiar with Pallas. Admiral Cleemorl, I believe you will be quite impressed with what we have done here."

"I already am," replied Dylan. For the first time in many years he felt as if, sometime in the future, the Empire might be restored. When he had first set out for Earth, he had never expected to find actual Imperials with warships.

Councilor Prest looked at Admiral Cleemorl. "Over the coming days I imagine we will have more questions for you, as well as some members of your crews."

"We'll answer them the best we can," promised Dylan.

"Very well," replied Councilor Prest. "Jalen Gresth is waiting for you outside in the corridor. He will return you to your shuttle."

Dylan nodded and left the Council chambers.

"Well," said Councilor Prest. "This changes everything."

"Yes, it does," replied Admiral Bract. "I think it would be wise if we increase the defensive grid around Pallas and see about building some attack drones to help defend Earth. We were already doing that for one of the Druin Command Stations. We could base the drones on the shipyard and on the space station."

"Why not some on Earth's Moon?" suggested Councilor Bliss. "They already have a large colony there."

Admiral Bract nodded. "Let's discuss what needs to be done. It looks as if we are now dealing with a timeline of around one hundred years before we launch our attack to free the Empire."

"Or sooner, if Earth advances quickly enough," said Councilor Bliss.

Everyone looked at one another. The war had suddenly become more of a reality and not that far off in time.

Chapter Twenty

Andrew ate lunch with Kala. He had just returned from Earth, where he had assisted in the designing of and the building of the expanded space station and the new shipyard. He had been making several trips back every month for additional training on Pallas, as well as to spend some time with Kala.

"I understand the expansion of the space station is almost finished," said Kala, as she worked on her dessert.

Andrew nodded. "We've nearly doubled its size. It will serve as a stopping point for all ships traveling in the Solar System."

"I went on board one of the passenger liners Pallas put into service. They're like a cruise ship but roomier. We went to Mars to deliver some technicians who are working on the terraforming project."

"Everything's moving fast now," replied Andrew. "Several thousand members of Earth's military are on Pallas learning how to operate the warships stored here. From what I've been told, next month nearly five thousand more will be arriving."

Kala leaned back and smiled as she put down her fork. "This pecan pie is excellent. They're now serving a lot of Earth foods in the cafeterias and restaurants."

Andrew nodded. "I'm not surprised. From now on there'll be a large presence of Humans from Earth. I understand a shipload of engineers from Earth's space program arrived last week. They want to redesign some spacecraft to serve various purposes, including mining the asteroids and some of the smaller moons in the system. The ships will be built in the new shipyard that's under construction in Earth orbit."

Kala picked up her fork and took another bite of her pie. "Have you spoken to any of the people who came from the Empire with Admiral Cleemorl?"

Andrew shook his head. "No, I haven't, but Captain Masters has. From what Cleemorl's people are saying, the Empire is in bad shape. The Druins are trying to control everything, and they have no problem with killing millions and billions of people for even the smallest reason."

Kala frowned. "It all sounds so horrible. Can we stop it?"

"I don't know. There's still a lot of debate over what needs to be done. Some people favor a guerilla-type war and trying to keep the existence of Earth a secret for as long as possible. Others want direct involvement, with major attacks on Druin facilities."

"That's in the future though, isn't it?" asked Kala, sounding concerned.

"Yes, at least fifty years from now. What we're doing right now is getting the Solar System prepared to defend itself. Fortunately we're a long way from the Confederation."

Kala pushed back her empty pie plate and looked at Andrew. "What do you have planned for the next few hours?"

"Nothing," replied Andrew. "I'm free for the rest of the day."

Smiling, Kala nodded. "Then why don't we go to my quarters? I have a better idea of how to spend the afternoon than talking about all this."

Andrew laughed. "You won't hear any objections from me."

With that, the two left the cafeteria. Both were looking forward to spending some private time together with no distractions.

—

Two weeks later Captain Masters was in a small shuttle, inspecting the work being done to the space station. It was proceeding rapidly and, in another few weeks, would be finished. Of course they were using Pallas construction robots for much of it. Most of the expansion was complete, with the outer hull covered in battle armor for added protection. He currently was watching as several large construction robots attached a missile launcher to the hull. The launcher could launch eight fusion missiles at any target that came within ten thousand kilometers of the station. Plans called for eight such launchers on the station.

"We're making progress," said Major Loren Henderson, satisfaction in his voice. "The energy projectors will be installed next week and then the emitters for the energy shield."

"Let's hope none of it is ever needed," replied Derrick. "I still think we should add a small docking bay, capable of handling the new attack drones we've developed."

Major Henderson nodded. "I agree. I've talked to Colonel Gleeson about that, and he's concerned it will only make the station a bigger target if there is an attack. He wants to build another station in lunar orbit, where numerous attack drones can be placed. He also wants to call them interceptors."

Derrick thought about the suggestion. "It would give Luna City better protection. That may not be a bad idea. I'll run it by the Council when I return to Pallas."

"How soon before the shipyard is finished?"

"Construction is going pretty smoothly so far, with few complications. We're still a good two months away from completion."

Major Henderson nodded. "That's good. When are you taking the *Destiny* to the Empire?"

A look of surprise passed over Derrick's face. "How did you find out about that? It's supposed to be a secret."

Henderson laughed. "I have my sources, and it's not Andrew. It's a logical response after the arrival of Admiral Cleemorl and his fleet."

"We're going to try to contact one of Admiral Cleemorl's people in the underground. It seems there's a large secret organization the Druins know nothing about. We'll see if they can be of any help when we eventually return to the Empire."

"Sounds dangerous."

"It will be, but I'm confident we can get it done."

Henderson looked thoughtful. "Are you excited about returning to the Empire?"

Derrick's gaze moved away from the construction to look at the distant stars. "I don't know. I'm a little apprehensive, knowing what the Druins have been doing. Admiral Cleemorl and those who came with him have described much of what's occurred in detail. After hearing what they said, I wish we were ready to move against the Confederation now. It'll be hard to wait another fifty years or more."

"You will be spending most of it in cryo," pointed out Henderson. "It won't seem that long to you."

Looking at the work robots, Derrick watched as they attached the missile launcher to the hull of the station. They easily maneuvered it into place, then welded and bolted it to the hull. "Maybe not, but it'll still be a long time and a lot could happen in the Empire."

Major Henderson didn't reply, as he maneuvered the small shuttle to another section of the space station. A large docking port was attached to the station, where an Imperial cargo ship or a passenger liner could dock and be fully enclosed. There were plans for a second large dock to be attached to the other side of the station later in the year.

Derrick made a few notes of further improvements that could be made to the station. These would be done in a phase two, after the current construction was finished, and the shipyard was completed.

The shuttle's comm unit suddenly came on, surprising them.

"Major Henderson, you need to return to the station immediately," said the comm officer. "We have unconfirmed reports of a large fleet of ships that have dropped out of hyperspace just outside the interdiction system. Admiral Cleemorl has tentatively identified them as Cogan ships and says they're highly dangerous."

"Returning to the station," replied Henderson. He looked at Derrick. "Who the hell are the Cogans?"

"Scavengers. From what I understand, Admiral Cleemorl ran into some on his way here. Somehow or another they must have followed him."

Henderson looked concerned. "Any chance these Cogans might tell the Druins about us?"

"I doubt it. They're as worried about the Confederation as we are. Most scavengers stay well clear of any Confederation races."

"First Admiral Cleemorl and now these Cogans. I wonder what's next?"

Derrick didn't reply. He was wondering if Admiral Bract had orders for the *Destiny*.

Admiral Bract was once more in the Pallas Command Center. Admiral Cleemorl had joined him.

"Definitely Cogans," said Dylan, as he studied a viewscreen which showed a Cogan vessel. The video was sent by one of the Druin interdiction stations. "It's box shaped, and all its weapons are hidden behind those hatches."

"Why are they holding their position and not advancing into the system?" The tactical display revealed twenty red threat icons.

"They've detected the Druin stations. The Cogans want no part of any Confederation race."

Bract activated a comm unit. "Rear Admiral Leeson, take your task group out and see what these Cogans want. They are not to be allowed access to the Solar System."

Bract turned toward Admiral Cleemorl. "What weapons will these Cogan ships be armed with?"

"Very weak for the most part. Basic energy beams and maybe a few nuclear missiles. I doubt if they have any fusion weapons and definitely no antimatter."

Admiral Bract nodded. "Rear Admiral Leeson should be able to handle them with his task force then."

Dylan nodded. "Yes, I don't see him having a problem. However, the Cogans may take some convincing. They also will not hesitate to lie."

"I'll tell him to be cautious and to expect treachery." Admiral Bract knew that, even back in the days of the Empire, there had been scavengers. Those who preyed on the innocents and crept around silently near the outskirts of civilization.

Rear Admiral Leeson gazed at the viewscreens as the *Titan* dropped out of hyperspace. In front of the dreadnought were twenty Cogan ships, all different makes and shapes. It almost seemed as if some of the ships were several ships joined together.

"This is Rear Admiral Leeson," he spoke into his comm unit. "Please state your reason for coming here. This system is under interdiction, and no one may enter." Leeson figured the Cogans had detected the interdiction system, and he decided to play upon that supposition.

There was silence for a few moments, and then a voice came over the comm. "We have come here to trade. We have many useful items a civilization this far from most civilized worlds might need. We request you allow our fleet to enter your Solar System to discuss possible items of interest."

"We have no interest in trade," replied Leeson. "We prefer to be left alone."

"We are the Cogans and control much of the space between your system and the Confederation. It would be to your benefit to deal with us."

Rear Admiral Leeson let out a deep breath. It was evident the Cogans would not listen. He turned to his second in command. "Take the fleet to Condition One and be prepared to fire." He then returned to the comm unit. "No ships may enter this system. We are enforcing the interdiction system."

There was silence on the comm, and then warning alarms sounded. On the tactical display thirty more red threat icons appeared.

"I have you greatly outnumbered," the Cogan said. "While your ships may be superior to mine, we vastly outnumber you. I am confident I can destroy your ships and then get past the interdiction system. We will take what we want from your star system."

Rear Admiral Leeson frowned. He did not want to fire first, but the Cogans left him little choice. "Withdraw immediately or you will be fired upon."

The Cogan merely laughed. "Arrogant fool. You could have given us what we wanted. Now we will take it!"

Leeson turned to his second in command. "Fire!"

Instantly the *Titan* and all six Imperial battlecruisers with it opened up with fusion energy beams and fusion missiles. The beams easily penetrated the Cogans' energy shields, carving out massive fissures in their hulls. Fusion missiles struck the energy shields knocking them down, with the next missile turning the odd-shaped vessels into expanding fields of glowing debris.

The Cogans returned fire with weaker energy beams and a few nuclear armed missiles. The energy beams failed to penetrate the Imperial warships' energy screens, and the missiles merely detonated against the screens, sending energy cascading across them.

Watching the battle, it was evident the Cogans had seriously underestimated the firepower of an Imperial warship. "Continue to fire," ordered Rear Admiral Leeson. As much as he hated to do so, he needed to destroy every Cogan ship. None could be allowed to escape.

"Second task group is jumping in," reported the sensor officer.

On the tactical display, ten more Imperial battlecruisers appeared behind the Cogan fleet. Leeson had set up this second force just in case they were needed. Almost instantly they fired. Ship after ship blew apart under the relentless fire.

The *Titan* shook several times from nuclear blasts exploding against its energy shield but suffered no damage.

For another two minutes the ravaging fire continued. For the last minute there was a complete absence of fire from the Cogan ships.

"Cease fire!" ordered Leeson. As the viewscreens cleared, all he could see was glowing debris and smashed ships. There were no signs of life.

"All Cogan ships confirmed destroyed," reported the sensor officer. "I'm running scans, searching for any possible survivors." After a minute the sensor officer turned toward the admiral. "No survivors detected."

Admiral Leeson nodded. He felt a trembling in his gut. He hated what he had just done, but they could not risk a Cogan ship returning to the Confederation and telling them about Earth. For the greater good, the Cogans had to die.

"The *Mata* and the *Doro* will remain here and will continue to scan the debris for anything we missed."

"Orders sent," replied the communications officer.

Taking a last look at the destruction his ships had wrought, Rear Admiral Leeson gave the order for the rest of the ships to return to the Solar System and to resume their patrols. This battle was over, if one could call it that.

On Pallas, Admiral Bract and Admiral Cleemorl had watched the battle.

"So that's what a fully armed Imperial battlecruiser can do," said Dylan, impressed.

"I wish this hadn't been necessary," replied Bract, with regret in his voice. "But we couldn't risk them taking word of our presence back to the Confederation."

Dylan nodded. "Sometimes in war difficult choices have to be made. The one you made here was the correct one."

Admiral Bract turned toward Admiral Cleemorl. "In another month we'll be launching our mission back to the Empire. Are you ready?"

"Yes, I'm ready to leave whenever Captain Masters is."

"Ships are returning to their patrol routes," reported the sensor officer.

Admiral Bract looked back at the tactical displays, showing the battlecruisers appearing throughout the Solar System. The *Titan* and its task force were again in orbit around Pallas. Letting out a deep breath, Bract wondered what would happen next.

Later that evening Admiral Cleemorl was in one of the restaurants in Pallas with Cheryl. Over the past month they had been getting together on a regular basis. Sometimes over a meal and occasionally in one of the garden-like habitats deep inside Pallas.

"So the Cogans showed up," said Cheryl, as she sipped her glass of wine. "It doesn't surprise me. They probably attached a tracker to one of our ships and then followed us here."

Dylan was drinking a beer. Pallas now served many of Earth's alcoholic drinks, and he had found several beers he liked. "Do you think they'll show up again?"

Cheryl shook her head. "No, the Cogans are composed of a number of clans. They each keep their distance and don't communicate with each other too often. I imagine what happened here is that the clan we encountered earlier called in all their ships, expecting a rich payday. They wouldn't tell the other clans, as they would want to keep everything to themselves. If Rear Admiral Leeson destroyed all their ships, there is very little chance that we'll have to worry about them again. To the other Cogan clans, this clan will have just vanished."

A server came to the table to take their orders. Dylan ordered pork chops with mashed potatoes and gravy, and Cheryl ordered shrimp.

Tonight Cheryl wore a dress, which was unusual for her. It accented her figure very well and made Dylan realize just how beautiful she was. "Are you still staying in your yacht?"

"Yes, my quarters in the yacht are very comfortable." Cheryl looked down at the table and spoke in a lower voice. "You could move in with me, if you want."

Dylan was surprised by Cheryl's offer. He leaned back in his chair and gazed at her, deciding how best to respond. Her offer was extremely tempting. "I have a mission coming up shortly. Let's wait until I get back, and we can talk about it."

"So you might be willing to?" Cheryl looked into Dylan's eyes.

Dylan nodded and smiled. "Yes."

Cheryl nodded. "I can accept that for now. So, you're going back to Lydol Four?"

"Lydol Four, Cleetus Three, and Bratol Three. All of them have secret bases that the Druins know nothing about. I mainly want to speak with General Creel, who should be at the base on Lydol Four, unless he left after the attack."

A sad look crossed Cheryl's face. "So many people died in the Druin attack. It's one of the reasons, after I left you, that I went to Highland Station. No Druins or other Confederation races to deal with. A person could live out their life there without fear of offending those supposedly superior beings. The civilian sectors of the station are extremely peaceful and quite nice. They have schools, their own shopping centers, parks, and about everything else you can imagine. The things that go on in the upper trading cities are not allowed in the civilian sections."

"Is that where you lived?"

"Yes, I had a nice home there. However, most of the time I was away on business."

"You gave up a lot to come out here with me. Was it worth it?"

Cheryl reached over and took Dylan's hand. "I hope it was."

Their food arrived, and the two ate and talked about what might be in their future. Both had high hopes, and yet both realized the future could easily change.

Captain Masters was still in the Command Center of the *Destiny*. He had been keeping track of the battle with the Cogans and had the ship ready to depart the station at a minute's notice. He was relieved when it became evident that would not be necessary.

"We'll be leaving for the new shipyard tomorrow," he announced to the crew. "We have some work that needs to be done there, and then, in a few days, we'll return to Pallas." Derrick intended to give the crew at least a week off before setting out for the Empire.

"I wonder what the Empire will be like?" asked Lieutenant Commander Banora.

"Not like we left it," replied Derrick. "From what Admiral Cleemorl has told us, the Druins have played havoc in the Empire. Many worlds barely remember a Human Empire. Trade is held to a minimum, and most scientific research has been curtailed. Some worlds have even slid back from the level of civilization the Empire enjoyed when we left."

Banora frowned and then spoke. "Someday we'll make the Druins and the Confederation pay for what they've done to us and to many other races."

"Let's hope so," said Derrick, as he stood up. "I have a couple meetings I need to go to before we leave."

"I'll be staying on board the *Destiny* tonight," replied Banora. "I want to make sure everything is ready for our trip to the new shipyard, and I have a few systems checks I want to run."

Derrick nodded. That was one thing he liked about the lieutenant commander. She was dedicated to her job and made an excellent executive officer.

The next day the *Destiny* arrived in Earth orbit, where the new shipyard was being built. The new shipyard would be able to build anything up to and including an Imperial dreadnought. The current plans called for three construction bays and two repair bays. At the moment a massive collection of metal beams and hull plating stretched for nearly two kilometers in every direction. Hundreds of Pallas work robots crawled across the structure, welding beams in place and installing battle armor over completed sections.

"That's huge," commented Andrew, his eyes growing wide at what was on the viewscreen. He had returned to the *Destiny* only the week before. "Is that the same size as the ones that once existed in the Empire?"

"Some were much larger and others smaller," replied Derrick. "Once we get this one completed, we'll start on a civilian shipyard, so we can construct the passenger liners, cargo ships, and other vessels we'll need."

As Andrew watched, several Pallas cargo ships pulled up into orbit. The ships carried more parts for the station, as well as additional work robots. Andrew knew that many of the parts were built inside Pallas, as Earth's industries were not ready yet for the type of undertaking the shipyard entailed. In time, as Earth's industries and infrastructure advanced, they would take a more leading roll in this type of construction. For now, Earth was providing labor and what aid it could in the construction.

"I assume the shipyard will be armed?"

Derrick nodded. "Heavily. Most of our shipyards and civilian structures were only lightly armed in the Empire. We won't make that mistake again."

"Will there be attack interceptors on the station?"

"Two large bays will be built to hold them. We will place forty interceptors in each bay."

Andrew was pleased to hear this. He wanted Earth to be as strongly protected as possible.

"Lieutenant Viktor, take us in and dock us to the station. I have a meeting with the construction manager and several station engineers."

Viktor nodded. A small section of the station was complete, where the work crews were living, and it had one functioning docking port.

As Derrick prepared to leave the *Destiny*, he paused and looked at his command crew. "Keep in mind that, in another few weeks, we'll be setting out for the Empire. There's a chance we won't make it back. If anyone wants to remain on Pallas, you may." With that, he left the Command Center.

"Small chance of that," said Lieutenant Nower, smiling. "I'm going back to the Empire." Looking around, she saw everyone nod.

Lieutenant Commander Banora smiled to herself. No doubt this crew would stick together. Besides, all of them wanted to see what had become of the homes they had left so long ago.

Chapter Twenty-One

Admiral Cleemorl, Admiral Bract, Councilor Prest, and Captain Masters were all gathered in a conference room inside Pallas. They were discussing the planned mission back to the Empire.

"Combat must be avoided at all costs," said Admiral Bract. "We can't allow the Druins to become aware of another Human system building warships. It wouldn't take too much for them to become suspicious and to figure out it must be Earth."

"We'll be careful," promised Derrick. "We won't approach any planet if we detect the presence of Druin warships." He had no interest in engaging in combat against the Druins. After all, his ship was only a light cruiser.

"You are cleared to investigate the current conditions on as many Imperial worlds as possible, as long as you don't endanger your ship and your crew."

Councilor Prest leaned forward and spoke. "You may only reveal the secret about Earth to General Creel, as he is already aware of where Admiral Cleemorl was going. You must stress to Creel the importance of keeping that information a secret."

Derrick had considered the ramifications of his mission and had an important question. "Should we set up a regular schedule of meetings with the general? Maybe once a year?"

"It's too dangerous," replied Admiral Bract, shaking his head. "Every time the *Destiny* travels to the Empire, it would be risking discovery."

"I have a suggestion," said Admiral Cleemorl. "What if we build a warship disguised as a freighter. It could travel to all the worlds of the Empire without raising suspicion. It wouldn't be hard to have it registered to Lydol Four, Cleetus Three, or Bratol Three. A lot of traffic between worlds still involves freighters and even a few passenger ships."

"It wouldn't be necessary to meet every year either," suggested Councilor Prest. "Maybe once every five years to hold the risk of discovery to a minimum."

Admiral Bract nodded. "Let's hope the Druins don't discover what we're doing."

"They shouldn't," replied Dylan. "Some of these secret bases have been in existence since the fall of the Empire. The Druins very seldom come down to a planet. They prefer orbital bombardment to make their points."

"How many secret bases are there?"

Dylan shook his head. "I don't know, but I suspect there are quite a few."

"Maybe when we speak to General Creel, he can give us an idea," said Derrick.

Councilor Prest hesitated for a moment, as if unsure whether to ask her next question. "What measures are we taking to ensure the *Destiny* isn't captured?"

Admiral Bract looked at Captain Masters.

"We've installed a self-destruct device on the ship. If activated, a fusion warhead will completely destroy the vessel."

Councilor Prest looked surprised. "That's a little extreme, isn't it?"

"It's necessary," replied Derrick. "We don't want the Druins accessing our computers or any of the other systems on the ship."

"When will you leave?"

Derrick looked at the councilor. "Early tomorrow. We've made our preparations, and the ship is ready. We just need your final approval."

"You have it," replied Prest. "Just come back safely."

―

Later Admiral Cleemorl was in Cheryl's quarters aboard her yacht. They were enjoying a quiet meal that one of the ship's stewards had prepared.

"This is excellent," said Dylan, as he took a bite of the sweet fish on his plate. It was a rare delicacy from one of the planets of the Empire.

Cheryl smiled. "I stocked up the ship's pantry and freezer with a wide selection of meats and other items. I feared that, once we left Highland Station, I would never see some of those food items again."

Dylan nodded in understanding. "Earth has a massive selection of various foods and meats. I'm almost certain you could find some there you would find extremely tasty."

"Maybe," replied Cheryl. "When more Imperials are allowed down on Earth, I may have to make a trip to scout things out."

"Several Earth companies are setting up some stores inside Pallas to offer items from Earth. I believe one of them will be featuring a large selection of food items."

"I'll check it out." A serious looked crossed Cheryl's face. "How long do you think you will be gone?"

Dylan placed his fork next to his plate. "I'm guessing about ten to twelve weeks. We won't go directly to the Empire but will take a more roundabout course so, if we're detected, no one can trace us back to where we came from. We also want to spend some time in the Empire to determine its current state."

Cheryl reached across the table and took Dylan's hand. "You will be careful?"

Dylan smiled. "Yes, of course. Captain Masters has every intention of bringing the *Destiny* back safely."

Cheryl shook her head. "I'll be a nervous wreck the entire time you're gone."

"You'll be fine. Just remember that, when I come back, we can start our lives together."

"I'll be ready. We should have done that years ago."

"We were young," replied Dylan, feeling regret at losing so much time. "Young people make mistakes."

The two spent the rest of the evening talking and laughing about past experiences. Finally it was time for Dylan to leave.

"Are you sure you don't want to spend the night?" Cheryl leaned forward and kissed Dylan gently on the lips.

Dylan laughed. "It's tempting, but this will give me something to look forward to when I return."

Cheryl let out a deep sigh. "You can't blame me for trying. Just make sure you come back."

Dylan placed his arms around Cheryl and kissed her deeply, then he released her and stepped back. "I will."

Cheryl walked Dylan to the airlock and watched him leave. She knew on any space mission there was always danger, and this one would be no different.

Andrew had said goodbye to Kala and now sat at the communications console on the *Destiny*. He was excited about going on this mission and seeing some of the worlds of the Human Empire. He had heard stories about the Empire ever since he was a kid. His parents had told him many, as well as a few of the older Imperials who knew a lot about the Empire. There were also a few Imperial history books, but those were hard to come by. Most were kept hidden and never saw the light of day.

Andrew had been spending a lot of time with Kala on his trips between Earth and Pallas. He really wished she would change her mind about going into cryo. His attention was drawn to the hatch of the Command Center as Admiral Cleemorl and Captain Masters came in.

"Stand by to get underway," ordered Masters, as he took his seat in the Command Center. Admiral Cleemorl sat down in the chair next to Derrick.

"We have permission to leave the dock," reported Andrew, as he spoke to the dock controller.

"Lieutenant Viktor, take us out."

The *Destiny* slowly eased from the docking bay and soon hovered over the surface of Pallas. The ship turned and accelerated away from the asteroid.

Inside Pallas, Admiral Bract and Councilor Prest watched from the Command Center.

"I hope we're not making a mistake," said Prest, her arms folded across her chest and a worried look in her eyes.

"We're taking a chance," admitted Bract. "But, if we can have some allies in the Empire, it will make our eventual attack much easier."

On the main viewscreen, the *Destiny* suddenly vanished, as it made its first jump into hyperspace.

"Well, they're gone," said Prest, her eyes still focused on the screen. "I hope they make it back."

"So do I," replied Bract. "With a little luck they'll secure some future allies and some very needed information about the Empire."

Councilor Prest turned toward the admiral. "What's our current status with our fleet and defenses?" Prest wanted to make sure, if the *Destiny*'s mission failed, and the Druins showed up, Pallas would be ready.

"We have three dreadnoughts and forty-six battlecruisers ready for active duty. Half of those have full crews, and the others are still in training. We have finished the modifications to all eight Druin Command Stations and are sending our own attack interceptors to replace the attack drones. The space station between Earth and its Moon is finished, and the shipyard will be in another month."

"What about the defense grid?" Prest referred to the defensive satellites in orbit around Pallas.

"We've doubled the amount of satellites we have in orbit and are currently working on putting some around Earth and its Moon. We're setting up several satellite production facilities in North America, as well as Europe. We're hoping to eventually build the interceptors in China, Taiwan, and Japan."

Prest looked around the busy Command Center. She felt uncomfortable in the large room, as it was designed for war in case Pallas was ever attacked. "Keep the Council informed, and let's hope the *Destiny* completes its mission."

"Captain Masters is one of the best," replied Bract. "If this mission can be completed, he will find a way."

Prest took one last look around the Command Center and then left.

Admiral Bract sat down and began working out the patrol routes for the next few days. He had the Solar System to defend, and he fully intended to keep it safe.

-

Colonel Gleeson sat at his desk in the space station. For the first time in days Pallas work robots were not swarming over the hull. A few had been kept to perform normal repair work, and the rest had been sent to work on the shipyard.

"Five hundred and twenty people," Gleeson said, as he looked at a report on his computer screen.

"It's a big station now," replied Major Henderson, sitting across the desk from Gleeson.

Gleeson looked at another report on his screen. "The new fusion power plant is ten times more efficient than the old one. Your technology is amazing."

Henderson smiled. Imperial technology was now a major part of the station. "We tested the energy screen earlier. It's working perfectly."

Gleeson leaned back and folded his arms across his chest. "You still want to place some of the new interceptors here?"

"As a precaution against future attacks, yes. It would only take a month to build a landing bay large enough to handle them."

"How many?"

"Twenty should be sufficient. Their primary job would be to defend the station."

Taking a deep breath, Gleeson closed his eyes and then opened them. "Let me speak to General Brier and Donovan Stewart, and see what they say."

"The *Destiny* left today," added Henderson. "It should be gone ten to twelve weeks. I would suggest we have the bay done and the pilots trained by the time they return."

"We're using air force pilots for the interceptors?"

Henderson nodded. "That seemed like the fastest way to get them up to speed. The new interceptors take a pilot, navigation officer, and a weapons officer. They're capable of staying out in space for seventy hours, if necessary."

Gleeson looked up, meeting Henderson's eyes. "Are you concerned about the Druins following the *Destiny* back to us?"

"Some," admitted Henderson. "It's not likely, but we should be prepared, just in case."

Gleeson looked at the large viewscreen on one wall of his office. On one side of the screen was a painting of Earth and on the other side a painting of the Moon. "What'll happen to us?"

Henderson knew Gleeson was referring to the future. "At first there will be considerable unrest as we introduce new technology. However, in a few years it should settle down. Within two decades most of Earth will resemble what the Empire looked like when we left. There will be no more poverty. Most illnesses will be a thing of the past, and the Human life span will have been extended by at least 30 percent."

"If the Druins don't destroy us first," pointed out Gleeson.

Henderson nodded. "Fortunately we're far away from the Confederation. Even if they discover our existence, there may be very little they can do about it. Given enough time, we'll make the Solar System into a fortress that even the Confederation can't conquer."

"Let's hope you're right," replied Gleeson.

On Earth, General Brier was in Arizona, watching a new Imperial fusion power plant being readied for activation. The station would be capable of furnishing all the power needed for the entire West Coast.

"We're making progress," commented Vice President Hicks, here for the opening ceremony.

General Brier nodded. "In another six months I'll have a world military set up. It will have the best soldiers, navy personnel, and air force people from across the planet."

"Where will they be based?"

"I've picked out a dozen locations. We're already building some of the bases."

"What about all the personnel we're sending to Pallas?" In the distance, Hicks heard the five-minute warning announced for plant startup.

Brier watched the plant. Dozens of these were being built across Earth. Good, clean, and abundant energy was finally here. "We'll continue to do that for a while. Eventual plans call for building a fleet training center on the Moon."

Hicks nodded. "Next week I'm supposed to take a trip to Mars with Donovan Stewart to look at the terraforming project. He's already making plans to place six more colonies on the planet."

"The Solar System is ours now. With Imperial technology we can go just about anywhere. We'll have mining ships heading out to the asteroids in another few weeks."

Suddenly another alarm sounded. Three loud blasts echoed through the air.

"Here we go," said Hicks, looking at the plant expectantly.

In the distance, he heard a low hum that gradually increased and then held steady. At the plant a series of green lights lit up, indicating the plant was now furnishing power into the national power grid.

Hicks smiled. "We better get inside. We'll need to pose for some photos."

The two men headed back into the plant, along with others who had been watching from outside in the viewing stands. This marked a new era in power for North America and soon the rest of the world.

At Luna City on the Moon, the embassy for the Pallas Imperials had been completed. Luna City was built beneath a large artificial dome, which had been greatly strengthened by the Imperials. It was now also protected by an energy shield. Outside of Luna City, a massive spaceport was being constructed. The spaceport could handle any Earth spaceship, as well as any Imperial vessel. It would also be home for nearly two hundred of the new attack interceptors, once they were built.

Two additional domes were being constructed next to Luna City as well, to hold the expected expanded population that would be coming to the Moon. In addition, on the far side of the Moon, another dome was being built for the space academy that would train future flight crews for both civilian and military ships. A smaller dome nearby was being constructed to train special Space Marines.

In his new office inside the embassy, Brett Newcomb and Alan Foster were meeting with the mayor of Luna City and the military officer responsible for the spaceport.

"Things have really changed here in the last six months," commented Mayor Kinsley Moss. "With Imperial science we have made the dome safer and greatly increased the power we have available. We're building more motels for tourists and have just finished constructing a zero-gravity area where one can fly using special wings."

Brett Newcomb laughed. "I was there yesterday. The young people have pretty well taken it over."

Kinsley nodded. "It gives them something to do and keeps them out of mischief."

"In a few more years we'll have close to one million people living here. In the next stage of expansion we need to build factories and facilities that can handle the raw materials the mining ships will be bringing from the asteroids and other mining projects."

Colonel Logan Adams, in charge of the spaceport, smiled. "I'm glad you sent Easton Dray to help in all this. The man is absolutely brilliant."

Brett nodded his agreement. "Easton was a spaceport engineer back in the Empire. He was very excited at the opportunity to put his skills back to work."

"Your work robots are amazing," continued Colonel Adams. "It surprised me how fast they can construct buildings and other facilities."

"A lot of people are surprised," answered Brett. "What people forget about is that the robots can work nearly twenty hours nonstop before requiring an energy charge. They also work at a steady pace and don't make mistakes, unless it's due to Human error."

Kinsley smiled. "Luna City is becoming everything I dreamed it would be. I don't know how I can ever thank you."

"Allowing us to place our embassy here is all we ask," replied Brett.

Kinsley's smile faded, and she turned her attention to Colonel Adams. "How close to the city will you place the interceptors?" Kinsley felt a little uncomfortable having a military target so close to the city, but Brett had assured her the energy shield would protect it.

"They'll be on the far side of the spaceport. We'll have a civilian sector and a military sector. The military sector will be clearly separated from the civilian one. We'll even have separate quarters for the military personnel. We don't want Luna City to look as if it's a military base."

Brett leaned back and decided to mention a few other things that Kinsley needed to be informed about. "The Druins don't recognize the difference between civilians and military. In the Empire, when the Druins attacked, they dropped antimatter bombs on both civilian and military targets. They killed billions of innocent people."

Kinsley's face turned pale, imagining Luna City being destroyed. "Is there anything we can do to protect Luna City and the other installations on the Moon?"

"Yes," replied Brett. "We can install interceptor missile batteries, both defensive and offensive, as well as energy turrets. The energy turrets will project an intense beam of energy, capable of shooting down any inbound missiles. We'll depend on the attack interceptors and the Imperial Fleet to handle any enemy spacecraft that launches an attack. We'll also be placing some defensive satellites around the Moon to intercept such an attack before any missile can endanger Luna City or any other facilities."

Kinsley shuddered and looked at Brett. "You sound as if someday you expect us to be attacked."

Brett slowly nodded his head. "Someday the Druins or one of the other Confederation races will come. When that day occurs, we must be ready to defend ourselves. The entire Solar System must be ready."

"But that won't be anytime soon, will it?"

"We hope not. However, we must be prepared in case we're wrong."

Kinsley looked at a large viewscreen on the office wall. It showed a view of the construction going on at the spaceport. Hundreds of Pallas construction robots were visible, as well as Humans in spacesuits. Above them hovered some small Pallas construction shuttles that were moving heavy materials to the needed locations. Everything was moving so fast. She hoped it wasn't moving too fast. She knew that, on Earth, it would be several decades before most of the planet was up to Imperial standards. However, here on the Moon, that would happen in less than a year.

In a year Luna City would more resemble a city of the Empire than a city of Earth. Kinsley had seen the plans and had approved them. Just the educational training alone that would be available in Luna City's schools would be remarkable. With a deep sigh, she knew the future had arrived, and she was determined to embrace it.

Standing, she looked at Brett and the colonel. "If either of you need anything, don't hesitate to contact my office." With that, Kinsley left, as she still had numerous items to take care of before she went home.

"Do you really think she knows what *being up to Imperial standards* means?" asked Colonel Adams. He had spent a lot of time with Easton Dray and was very familiar with all the plans for the spaceport, as well as Luna City.

Brett laughed. "Eventually. We'll make sure to keep her in the loop, so she knows what we're doing here. Luna City will be the blueprint for what we'll do down on Earth. Luna City has to be our shining example of what we're offering the planet."

Colonel Adams left the office. He had a long meeting with Easton Dray next to discuss the bunkers for the attack interceptors. He doubted the mayor had any clue as to how heavily defended the spaceport, Luna City, and the other facilities on the Moon would be. The Moon would be made into a fortress. A fortress with one main prerogative. It had to be capable of defending Earth.

Chapter Twenty-Two

The *Destiny* dropped from hyperspace in a white dwarf star system. The star itself, while it had a large mass, was only the size of Earth.

"A few stellar remnants and nothing else," reported Nower. "Not much of a star system."

Andrew gazed at the viewscreen, showing a magnified view of the star. He didn't think he would ever get tired of looking at the screen. In every system they stopped in, he was learning more and more about the Bacchus Region. In three weeks of travel, they had not found a single habitable planet or come across any other starships. There had also been no trace of the Cogans.

"It's so desolate out here," commented Lieutenant Commander Banora, as she gazed at the viewscreens. "It's amazing the Empire ever found Earth."

Derrick nodded in agreement. "During the expansive time of the Empire, exploration missions were sent everywhere. Particularly to regions where it was thought the Confederation would not be interested. Numerous such missions explored nearly the entire Bacchus Region. When Earth was discovered, all exploration missions to this region were canceled. The High King of the time felt it might be wise to keep the existence of a primitive planet of Humans a secret. It was an insurance policy in case the Confederation and the Human Empire ever went to war."

"Which is what happened," said Andrew. This much he already knew.

"We'll stay here for a few hours and then make our next jump," said Derrick. "The next one will put us right on the edge of the Empire."

Admiral Cleemorl came into the Command Center and glanced at the viewscreen. "Another dead system I see. Someday we need to do some research into why such a large region of space has no habitable worlds other than Earth."

"Perhaps it was done to protect Earth," suggested Banora.

Derrick frowned. He didn't think that sounded reasonable. "But why go to such extreme lengths to protect one planet?"

"We may never know," commented Dylan. "But there has to be an explanation for what happened here in the Bacchus Region."

"Contact!" called out Lieutenant Nower. "It just dropped out of hyperspace."

"Are our stealth fields up?" asked Dylan, looking alarmed.

"They're up," replied Derrick. His gaze shifted to the tactical display, showing a red threat icon. "Lieutenant Nower, can you identify the unknown?"

Nower spent a few moments working with her sensors. "Definitely Druin."

"What are they doing out this far?" asked Derrick, feeling perplexed.

"A patrol," suggested Dylan. "We're pretty close to Highland Station."

Derrick examined the tactical display for several minutes. There was no evidence the Druin vessel had detected them. "Change of plans. Viktor, set a course for the Ridge Star Cluster. We'll make a quick stop in the star system where Highland Station is. I want to see if the Druins have a presence there as well."

"Do we wait or leave now?" asked Dylan. His gaze focused on the tactical display and the red threat icon representing the Druin ship.

"Now," replied Derrick. "No point staying and risking detection."

"Course plotted," said Lieutenant Viktor.

"Then execute," ordered Derrick. "The sooner we leave this system, the better."

The *Destiny* made the transition into hyperspace, leaving the white dwarf system and the Druin warship behind. Derrick couldn't help but wonder what the odds were of them stumbling across a Druin warship like this. Either it was a remarkable coincidence or the Druins had a lot of warships patrolling the edge of the Bacchus Region.

Four days later the *Destiny* dropped from hyperspace in the outer regions of the Highland Station System. Immediately alarms sounded, and red lights flashed.

"Take us to Condition One," ordered Derrick, as he checked the tactical display. Red threat icons were everywhere. "What do we have?"

Lieutenant Nower was already hard at work, analyzing the data from the ship's sensors. "A Druin warfleet. Estimated numbers are 417 vessels."

"Lieutenant Viktor, keep our distance." Derrick shook his head. He had orders to avoid the Druins, and now he had jumped the *Destiny* right into the middle of one of their fleets.

On the main viewscreen, a highly magnified view of Highland Station appeared. Massive flashes of light covered the screen.

"Those are fusion and antimatter detonations," reported Nower. "An energy shield is up around part of Highland Station, and the Druins appear to be trying to knock it down."

"Any other resistance?"

"Some. About thirty small destroyer-size vessels are making attack runs against the Druins. Unfortunately their weapons are not powerful enough to bring down a Druin shield."

The viewscreen switched to show the destroyer-size vessels. They were darting in and out of the Druin fleet formation, firing their weapons and launching missiles. Most of the missiles were nuclear, but, every so often, a fusion explosion would occur.

"I wonder what happened to cause this?" asked Dylan, his gaze focused intently on the viewscreen.

Derrick could see that the admiral was clearly upset about this attack on Highland Station. "I wish we could do something, but we're just one ship."

On the viewscreens the battle continued. Part of the Druin fleet was bombarding the asteroid, trying to bring the energy shield down, with the rest turning their weapons on the smaller destroyers.

"I'm picking up communications from the asteroid," reported Andrew, as he listened on his comm console. "They are requesting the Druins stop their attack. They're willing to cooperate fully."

"Any reply from the Druins?" Derrick doubted if there would be. The Druins never negotiated.

Andrew shook his head. "No, nothing."

On the viewscreen, four of the small destroyers suddenly blew apart. Their energy screens were no match for the fusion and antimatter weapons the Druins were using.

"Highland Station is requesting assistance from the other asteroid colonies."

Derrick looked at Andrew. "Any response?"

"No."

"There won't be," said Dylan, shaking his head. "If they send any assistance, the Druins might attack them as well."

"They still may," said Lieutenant Commander Banora. "The Druins may be here to wipe out the entire system."

The battle in space lasted a few more minutes, with the small destroyers gradually being destroyed in ones and twos. Finally the last destroyer blew apart, as an antimatter missile detonated against its energy shield, obliterating the small warship.

"Now they'll concentrate on the asteroid," predicted Dylan. "The energy shield around Highland Station can't stand up to the combined attack of that fleet."

For the next ten minutes the Druins fired relentlessly on Highland Station. The energy shield finally wavered.

"They must have all the station's power pouring into that energy screen for it to withstand such a massive bombardment," said Dylan, hoping the screen would stay up.

"This is it," said Lieutenant Commander Banora. Everyone's gaze was glued to the viewscreens.

Suddenly the shield collapsed, and the entire surface of the asteroid was turned into molten magma, as the heat from the blasts struck the surface, annihilating all the domes and other structures. When the firing from the Druins stopped, nothing was left.

"They're all dead," uttered Andrew in shock.

Dylan shook his head. "No, the civilian sections are kilometers underground. They most likely survived. Once the Druins leave, they'll come back to the surface and rebuild."

"Perhaps," said Derrick, gazing at the destruction. "It depends on why the Druins attacked them in the first place."

"They're Druins," replied Dylan. "They don't need a reason to kill Humans."

On the tactical display, the Druin ships left the vicinity of the asteroid and spread out across the system.

"What are they doing now?" asked Banora.

"Searching," suggested Dylan. "They must have come here looking for something or someone."

For the next hour the Druin ships spread across the system, pausing occasionally to search an asteroid. Druin ships would stop at one of the other inhabited asteroids, and shuttles could be seen going down to the domes.

"Definitely searching for someone," said Dylan. "I would suggest we go ahead and leave before they stumble across our ship."

"Agreed," replied Derrick. "Lieutenant Viktor, set a course for the Haven Nebula. Several Human worlds are there that I would like to check on. We won't land, but we will take some sensor readings and monitor communications."

The ship turned away from the system and soon made the transition into hyperspace.

"We're five days out from the nebula," said Viktor. "Do you have any particular world you want to stop at first?"

Derrick looked at Admiral Cleemorl for a suggestion.

"Tantalus Seven," responded Dylan. "The Druins bombed Dorman Three, and it still hasn't fully recovered."

"Tantalus Seven it is then," said Derrick.

As the *Destiny* made its way through hyperspace, Derrick couldn't help but think about the system they had just left. It was hard to fathom how any race could be as heartless as the Druins. They never showed any mercy and had killed billions of Humans since their original attack on the Empire. Even today he and his crew had witnessed an attack that had probably killed tens of thousands of Humans and members of other races. The Druins didn't practice war; they practiced the wholesale slaughter of innocents. Derrick was determined that someday the Druins and the other races of the Confederation would receive what was coming to them. By going into cryo, he would be part of that vengeance.

—

The sheer violence demonstrated by the Druins had stunned Andrew. While he had been expecting it, seeing it was something else entirely. He began to understand why so many of the original Imperials who had escaped to Pallas had chosen to go into cryo. More than ever now Andrew was determined to join them. This injustice the Confederation was forcing upon other races had to be stopped. "Have the Confederation races always treated other races this way?"

"We don't know," replied Admiral Cleemorl. "The Confederation has been around for over thirty thousand years. What their early history was like is wrapped in mystery. They don't discuss it, and there are no known records."

This didn't surprise Andrew. This was pretty much the same thing he had been taught all his life. "How many races are currently under control of the Confederation?" He knew there had to be thousands. Some parts of the galaxy were densely populated.

"Sixty-two thousand," replied Dylan. "Some races only control one- or two-star systems, and others control dozens. The Human Empire was by far the largest, with over one thousand inhabited star systems."

"Are there other races still out there *not* under control of the Confederation?"

Dylan nodded. "A few. Some are very primitive, and others are what the Confederation considers not to be a potential threat. Also a few regions of the galaxy are still relatively unexplored."

"So we have no possibility of gaining allies in our war against the Confederation?" Andrew had hoped there might be one or two races that would join them.

Dylan shook his head. "No, the only allies we dare to hope for are those in the Empire itself. Very soon, after the Druins attacked the Empire, dozens of secret bases were established in the hopes of someday freeing the Empire. I don't know if anyone knows just how many there are. If anyone does, it will be General Creel. He has contacts all over the Empire."

"Let's hope those bases are willing to help us," commented Banora. "A fifth column working in the Empire could be the difference between us succeeding and failing. We will only have one shot at freeing the Empire, and we must not fail."

Dylan nodded. "We'll know much more once we can speak to General Creel."

—

Later Andrew was in the small cafeteria in the *Destiny*, eating a light evening meal before retiring. He had a couple hours' worth of reading to do, as he was still studying some of the technology available on Pallas. Andrew saw Ensign Allert come in, and, upon spotting him, she came over and sat down.

"Well, what do you think of our adventure so far?"

"I guess I didn't realize the Druins were so evil."

Brenda nodded. "Most people don't until it's too late. Even the High King during our day didn't believe the Confederation or the Druins would really attack us. Our warfleets were mainly for show and not to defend the Empire. If we had wanted to adequately defend ourselves, we would have needed ten times the number of ships, plus fusion weapons."

"Could the Empire have developed fusion weapons?"

"Oh, yes," replied Brenda. "We never did, as we feared it might upset the Confederation. They don't allow other races to do research into fusion weapons or antimatter."

Andrew took a bite of his French toast. "And now we have both."

Brenda grinned. "Yes, it will be quite a shock to the Confederation."

"How do you feel about coming back to the Empire, which the Druins now control?" Andrew knew he would feel horrible if Earth were under control of the Druins, knowing the atrocities they were willing to commit.

Brenda let out a deep sigh. "I'm originally from Golan Four. I volunteered for the military as soon as I finished school. I thought it would be exciting, and I could see the Empire."

Andrew nodded. "A lot of people join the military for that reason. Did you get to see a lot of the Empire?"

Brenda smiled as she thought about those days. "Yes, I guess I traveled to over sixty Imperial worlds, before I was asked to join the crew of the *Destiny*."

"Have you ever regretted joining up?"

A look of sadness crossed Brenda's face. "I don't know how my parents died. I hope it was from old age and not a Druin attack. I left a lot of friends behind, but my duty was to the Empire and to the Princess. I did what I had to do."

"All of you seem to have a lot of respect for the Princess." Andrew wondered what she must have been like.

"Oh, we did. For her and her brother."

"What happened to her brother?"

"He was exiled to Earth. We dared not attempt a rescue, as during those early years the Druins were watching the banished Imperials very closely."

Andrew leaned back, looking at Brenda. "I guess I don't understand why the Druins banished the Imperials instead of killing them."

"It's quite simple. To the Druins, banishment is the worst possible punishment. To them, what they were doing to the Imperials was worse than death."

"The Druins themselves, how many worlds do they inhabit?"

Brenda took in a deep breath. "We don't know for certain. The Druins are supposed to inhabit a very large number of worlds. There's not a lot known about any of the Confederation races, other than they believe themselves to be above all others and treat most races as if they're barbaric or children. All the worlds of the seven races are off limits to other races."

"Have there been very many wars in the past against the Confederation?"

Brenda shook her head. "We don't know. Many things about the Confederation are not spoken about. They don't offer much information, but they expect their subject races to offer everything."

Andrew decided, when he made it to his quarters, he would see what was in the ship's computer library about the Confederation, particularly the Druins. It was bound to be much more than what was available on Earth in the few secret books the Earth Imperials possessed.

The *Destiny* continued through hyperspace until it reached the edge of the Haven Nebula. Numerous star systems were in this region, and many were inhabited by Humans.

"We're seventeen light-years from Tantalus Seven," reported Viktor.

The viewscreens were covered in stars, and the main viewscreen showed the glowing nebula which this region of space was named after.

"Anything on the sensors?"

"Nothing," reported Nower, as she checked her screens.

Derrick sat down in his command chair. It would be a little risky jumping into a heavily populated system, but they needed more information about the state of the Empire. Admiral Cleemorl had known about some worlds, but his knowledge had been severely limited. "Set a course for Tantalus Seven. Put us at the edge of the system. Lieutenant Commander Banora, make sure our stealth fields are active. I don't want us to be detected."

Everyone in the Command Center was tense as the *Destiny* made the transition back into hyperspace for the short trip to Tantalus Seven. Everyone was curious as to what they would find.

It didn't take long, and the light cruiser dropped from hyperspace into the Tantalus System.

"Report," ordered Derrick, as he leaned forward in his command chair.

"Picking up both standard and hyperlight communications," reported Andrew.

"Sensors?"

"Quite a few ships are in the system. I'm also detecting what appears to be a Druin battlecruiser."

"Damn," uttered Lieutenant Commander Banora, sounding concerned. "Are they everywhere?"

Admiral Cleemorl studied the tactical display. Over one hundred icons were on the screen, representing ships. Only one was red. "Something must have happened. The Druins normally patrol in fleets, and it's very seldom you see only one of their ships in a system."

"Perhaps they're hunting for the same people as the Druin fleet was in the Highland Station System," suggested Banora.

"Lieutenant Nower. Are there any signs of orbital bombardment on Tantalus Seven?" Tantalus Seven was an Earth-size planet that orbited a large gas giant.

"Nothing recent," replied Nower. "I am detecting signs of bombardment in the past."

Derrick looked at Admiral Cleemorl for an explanation.

"Nearly all the worlds of the Empire have been hit at one time or another. The Druins don't need much of an excuse to destroy a city or two."

"Animals," muttered Lieutenant Commander Banora in disgust. "For a supercivilized race, all they know how to do is kill!"

"Have we been detected?"

"No, Captain," replied Nower. "Our stealth fields seem to be holding."

That was what Derrick wanted to hear. "Lieutenant Viktor, take us deeper into the system, so we can get some reasonable scans of what's been occurring in this system. Andrew, see if you can analyze some of those messages and see what you can find out."

The *Destiny* activated its subspace drive and moved toward Tantalus Seven. Lieutenant Viktor was careful to steer well clear of all the other space traffic. It was strange watching the tactical display; for the most part it seemed as if all the other ships were ignoring the Druin warship, as if it wasn't there.

"This is strange," commented Dylan, looking concerned. "I wonder if Druin ships are in our other systems?"

The *Destiny* steadily moved closer toward Tantalus Seven, until Captain Masters felt they were close enough. They were also now much closer to the Druin vessel.

"Keep us here," ordered Derrick. "We'll stay in this location and run our scans, as well as monitor the communication bands. Andrew, I'm particularly interested in anything that mentions the Druin ship."

For nearly two hours the *Destiny* stayed in its location, monitoring the planet and the ships moving about the system.

They saw numerous ships transition into hyperspace, both leaving and entering the system.

"Captain!" called out Nower with concern. "The Druin ship is moving toward us."

Derrick leaned forward in his chair, gazing at the viewscreen. "Is it moving straight toward us?"

"Yes, sir."

"Lieutenant Viktor, take us back into hyperspace. Put us outside the cluster at twenty light-years. Lieutenant Breen, keep our weapons ready in case the Druin battlecruiser follows us."

"But we can't be tracked in hyperspace," objected Banora.

"That we know of," replied Derrick.

The *Destiny* turned away from the incoming Druin battlecruiser and quickly made the transition into hyperspace. The tension in the Command Center was intense, as they wondered if they were being followed.

"Lieutenant Breen, ready antimatter missiles in the tubes. If the Druin battlecruiser drops out of hyperspace in combat range, I want it destroyed." Derrick knew the Druins would not be expecting to be hit by antimatter weapons. It just might allow the *Destiny* to destroy the enemy ship.

Time passed as the light cruiser moved through hyperspace, and then it was time to drop out into normal space once again. The *Destiny* appeared in a red giant star system, coming out very near the star. Lieutenant Viktor had done this intentionally, hoping the radiation from the star would shield the *Destiny* from the Druins.

Minutes passed slowly by as the crew of the ship stood at Condition One, watching for the Druin battlecruiser.

"Anything?" asked Derrick, looking toward Sensors.

Nower shook her head. "Nothing." She had no sooner spoke those words when alarms went off on her sensor console. "Druin ship dropping from hyperspace inside engagement range."

"Fire missiles!" Derrick didn't want to give the battlecruiser time to get a weapons lock on the *Destiny*.

"Missiles launched," replied Lieutenant Breen, as he gazed intently at his weapons console. "Locking on with fusion energy beams. I'll time them with the strike of the missiles."

"Prepare for evasive maneuvers," ordered Derrick, leaning forward. With their stealth fields up, he wasn't sure just how good a weapons lock the Druins could get on *Destiny*.

On the ship's main viewscreen, the Druin battlecruiser was visible. Nearly 1400 meters of sheer power and destruction. The vessel was covered in weapon turrets and hatches covering missile tubes. Suddenly the ship vanished, as massive explosions struck its protective energy shield. The shield wavered, and several fusion energy beams penetrated, driving deep holes into the heart of the enemy vessel. Huge sections of hull material were blown away from the ship.

"Druin vessel is returning fire," warned Nower.

"Evasive action now!" ordered Derrick, his hands clenching the armrests on his command chair.

The *Destiny* shook violently, and several red lights appeared on the damage control console.

On the viewscreen, the Druin vessel was struck by a second wave of antimatter missiles. The Druin screen wavered and even flickered as it struggled to stay up.

"We must have hit some of their power relays," said Admiral Cleemorl.

Several more fusion energy beams flashed through the Druin energy screen, drilling holes into the engineering section. In a massive explosion, the rear one-third of the Druin battlecruiser blew apart. At the same time its energy shield vanished.

"We have them now!" shouted Banora excitedly.

"Hit that ship with two more antimatter missiles," ordered Derrick. "I don't want any piece of it to survive intact." He didn't want to leave behind any hint of what had destroyed the enemy vessel.

Moments later all that remained of the Druin battlecruiser was a field of glowing plasma and shattered pieces of wreckage.

"Lieutenant Viktor, get us out of here. Take us to an uninhabited system where we can plan our next move."

Viktor's hands played over his console, and soon the *Destiny* was back in hyperspace.

"We got lucky," said Dylan. "We should never have been able to destroy that Druin battlecruiser. We took them by surprise with our antimatter and fusion weapons."

Derrick nodded. He knew the admiral was right. "Lieutenant Commander Banora, what damage did we suffer?"

"A few blown circuits and probably some burn marks on our hull. Over all, we got away pretty cheaply. There is nothing to prevent us from carrying out our mission."

Derrick was relieved to hear this. "Now we must figure out how the Druins spotted us to begin with and how they tracked us in hyperspace."

Leaning back in his command chair, Derrick tried to relax. He had been ordered to avoid combat, and already he had been forced to destroy a Druin battlecruiser. He wondered what else would go wrong before this mission was over.

Chapter Twenty-Three

For two days the *Destiny* stayed in normal space, as the crew inspected the ship and tried to figure out how the Druins had detected the stealthed vessel.

"I have nothing," reported Chief Engineer Alban Corrant, sounding frustrated. "The stealth fields are working fine, and I found no abnormalities anywhere on the ship, as far as power and communications go. I just don't see how they detected us."

Andrew was listening. They dared not go deeper into the Empire until they knew how the Druin ship had detected the *Destiny*. "What about our sensor scans? They were the only active system, beyond the stealth fields."

"Sensors," repeated Corrant, looking thoughtful. "I didn't think about the sensors."

"Is it possible?" asked Derrick. He would feel better about continuing if he knew his ship was undetectable.

Corrant slowly nodded his head. "If they were looking on the right frequency and in the correct direction. Even so, it would be difficult to pin down the exact location of a ship based on its sensors."

"But these are Druins we're talking about," pointed out Admiral Cleemorl. "We don't know what they may be capable of."

Derrick had a concerned look on his face. "We use our sensors, even in hyperspace, to ensure we don't collide with anything. Could the Druins have been using our sensors to track us?"

"It's possible," said Corrant. "Our long-range sensors have a far reach around the ship."

Derrick let out a deep breath of frustration. "So, what do we do?"

"Assuming it's the long-range sensors they're detecting, I would suggest we use them in short bursts and then change position. When we transition into hyperspace, we can use the short-range sensors to help the ship evade any dangerous objects."

Looking at Corrant, Derrick nodded. "We'll make those changes immediately." He hoped what Corrant believed was the problem was correct, or they could have more encounters with Druin warships in the future. "Lieutenant Commander Banora, prepare to get underway. It's time we continued on our mission."

An hour later the *Destiny* was back in hyperspace, with a course set for Lydol Four. On board, everyone was worried about being detected again by the Druins. During the two-day journey to Lydol Four, everyone would try to determine if the Druins could have used anything else to track the ship.

Two days later Captain Masters sat in his command chair as the *Destiny* dropped from hyperspace on the edge of the Lydol Four System. The ship was at Condition One, with the crew at their battlestations.

"Contacts," reported Lieutenant Nower, as she checked her sensor screens. "Twenty-two vessels, which seem to be transports of some kind. No signs of any Druin vessels."

Derrick breathed out a sigh of relief. "Take us in closer to Lydol Four, and we'll try to communicate with General Creel."

"No Druin vessels," commented Admiral Cleemorl. "I thought there would be one or two, considering we've encountered them twice already."

"Maybe since they already attacked Lydol Four, they don't feel the need to station a ship here," suggested Lieutenant Commander Banora.

Everyone watched expectantly, as the ship drew closer to the planet.

"Why is the planet's atmosphere so dark?" asked Andrew, gazing at the viewscreen, which now showed the planet. The planet's atmosphere had streaks of darker colors, and it wasn't from clouds.

"Dust and ash from the Druin bombardment," explained Dylan. "I expected much more. They must already be clearing it. In another year the planet will nearly be back to normal."

Dylan gazed at the viewscreen, holding his growing rage inside him. Large craters were visible where magnificent cities once stood. Much of the countryside was burned, where antimatter energy had razed the land. This had been his homeworld and where his family had raised him. It hurt intensely to see what the Druins had done.

"Take us into orbit at sixty thousand kilometers," ordered Derrick. "Lieutenant Nower, keep a watch for any indications of Druin vessels."

Admiral Cleemorl stepped over to the comm station, as Andrew stood up and indicated for the admiral to take his seat. Dylan reached out and changed the comm system to a specific frequency. He inserted a computer chip and began transmitting. The computer chip was highly encrypted and would identify him, so General Creel would have no doubt as to who was trying to contact him.

After a minute Dylan stood and indicated for Andrew to sit back down. "It will take a few minutes. They should respond on the frequency I have set. The computer chip will unscramble their message, so we can understand it."

"Then we wait," said Derrick, as he leaned back in his command chair.

On the viewscreens, several of the ships orbiting Lydol Four were spraying some chemicals into the atmosphere. Other ships were landing in secluded regions, where smaller cities still existed.

"Every city with a population of over one hundred thousand was wiped out," said Dylan, with sadness in his voice.

Nearly twenty minutes passed before a response came on the specified channel and frequency.

"All they transmitted was a set of planetary coordinates," reported Andrew, looking confused.

Admiral Cleemorl nodded. "That's all I expected. We need to take a shuttle to those coordinates. Once we've landed, we should be given additional instructions."

"Get the shuttle ready," ordered Derrick.

"Do you want an armed escort?" asked Banora. "I can call several of the Marines."

Derrick shook his head. "No, that won't be necessary. "Ensign Allert will accompany us. She will oversee our security."

"What do we do if a Druin ship shows up?"

Derrick looked at Lieutenant Commander Banora. "Leave the system and only return after the Druins have left. Under no circumstances are you to reveal the presence of the *Destiny*."

"Yes, Captain," replied Banora. She didn't like the idea of leaving the captain behind.

"Admiral Cleemorl, are you ready for this little venture?"

"More than ready."

The two left the Command Center and made their way through the ship to the landing bay that held two small shuttles. Ensign Allert stood in the hatch of one, fully armed and wearing light battle armor.

"Ready when you are, sir."

"Let's go on board and head to the surface. Is the pilot on board?"

"Yes, sir. Corporal Bower and Private Jenkins will be piloting today."

Derrick had to smile. Banora had arranged for both the pilots to be Marines. "Well, let's get this show on the road and see what happens." Derrick was anxious to get to the surface and to meet General Creel. They had a lot to discuss, and Derrick wanted to get it done before any Druins showed up.

The small shuttle left the *Destiny* and headed toward the surface. In only a few minutes they had entered the planet's atmosphere and were well on their way to the coordinates they had been sent.

Derrick looked out one of the small windows at all the damage the Druins had done to the planet. At close range, it looked much worse than from orbit.

"This is what the Druins do," commented Admiral Cleemorl grimly. "Ever since the fall of the Empire, they have bombarded planets into submission anytime a world got out of line. Sometimes they would destroy a city for the slightest infraction. In most cases, the surrounding worlds would step in and help to rebuild. In time the world would recover, until the Druins returned and struck it again for another violation of their rules."

The shuttle passed over what once must have been a major metroplex. A deep crater in the center signified where a fusion or antimatter missile had struck. Around the crater, the blast had shattered buildings and ruined infrastructure stretched for miles. Outside of that was a large burned-off region, where the heat from the explosion had burned off all the vegetation. Derrick knew that nothing or no one could have survived such a blast.

"We'll be arriving at the coordinates shortly," announced Corporal Bower.

A few moments later the shuttle sat down in some rolling hills surrounded by tall grasses. A small building was here, with several aircars parked in front of it. As the shuttle sat down, several men and women came out of the building and stood waiting. Two of them were obviously military, as they wore uniforms and were heavily armed.

"Do you know any of them?" asked Derrick, glancing at Admiral Cleemorl.

Dylan shook his head. "No, but that's not surprising. General Creel and his staff will be inside the Command Bunker with Governor Swen."

Derrick and Dylan stepped from the shuttle, escorted by Ensign Allert, who had her right hand resting lightly on her energy pistol.

"I'm Colonel Beeson," spoke one of the military officers, stepping forward. "We're here to escort you to General Creel. If you will follow me."

The group entered the building to find an elevator, which they all entered. Once inside, the elevator descended deep beneath the surface, finally coming to a stop after several minutes. The door opened, revealing a monorail-like vehicle sitting on a track.

"This will take us to the Command Center, where General Creel is waiting," explained Colonel Beeson.

Dylan nodded and, without hesitation, stepped inside the vehicle, which resembled an old-fashioned train car with seats. Only this one was air-conditioned and heated. As soon as everyone was in and seated, the car began moving and quickly accelerated to a high speed.

Derrick noticed they were still descending. He didn't know how far they had traveled, but it was a considerable distance from where they had parked the shuttle at the building.

"The Command Base is deep underground," Dylan informed Derrick. "I've only been there once, and we took a different route."

The car eventually slowed and came to a stop. The door opened, and everyone stepped out. They were greeted by a dozen well-armed soldiers. One of them stepped forward with a big smile on his face. "Admiral Cleemorl, it's good to see you again. We didn't know if you had escaped or not."

"Major Brandon," replied Cleemorl, stepping forward and shaking the soldier's hand. "I did escape with some of my ships. I came back because I need to speak to General Creel about a matter of the utmost urgency."

Major Brandon nodded. "The general and Governor Swen are waiting. I was sent ahead to verify your identity, as we never expected to see you again. If you will follow me, I'll take you to the general."

Major Brandon showed them through a hatch and down several long corridors. They had to stop several more times to identify themselves to soldiers stationed along the way. Finally they entered the base proper and were taken along a corridor with regular wooden doors. Opening one, Major Brandon indicated for them to go inside.

Inside the room, Derrick saw a half-dozen men and women seated at a large table. An older military officer, whose uniform was adorned with numerous decorations, stood with a big smile on his face.

"Admiral Cleemorl, it's good to see you."

Dylan smiled back and nodded. "I didn't expect to come back, but what I found at the end of my travels demanded that I do so. However, before we continue I must ask that everyone except Governor Swen and yourself clear the room. What I am here to tell you demands the highest security clearance possible, and the fewer people who know what I will say, the better."

General Creel looked at Derrick sharply and then spoke. "Everyone, clear the room. I'll call you back when it's okay to do so."

The room rapidly emptied, leaving Governor Swen, General Creel, Admiral Cleemorl, Captain Masters, and Ensign Allert, who had taken up a watchful position beside the door.

"Everyone's gone," said General Creel. "Now what?"

Admiral Cleemorl smiled. "I want to introduce you to Captain Masters. He's from the star system that contains the planet Earth."

"Earth?" blurted out General Creel, his eyes growing wide. "I thought that was just a myth. I never expected you to find it."

"Where the old Imperials were banished?" uttered Governor Swen in shock. "It's real then?"

"Yes," replied Dylan. "Not only that but the old Imperials established a hidden fleet base in the system. They are even now bringing Earth up to Imperial standards, as far as technology goes."

"Can they help us?" asked General Creel, his eyes full of hope.

Dylan shook his head. "Not yet, the Earth still has a way to go before it can commit to a war against the Druins and the Confederation."

Governor Swen looked at Derrick. "Are you from Earth?"

Derrick shook his head. "No, I'm one of the original Imperials who fled Golan Four when the Druins invaded. I've been in cryo, waiting for the day for us to return and to free the Empire. I do have a crewmember on board my ship who is from Earth and is a direct descendant of those Imperials who were banished to the planet. I can make arrangements for you to speak to him, if you wish."

"I would like that," said Governor Swen.

General Creel looked over at Admiral Cleemorl. "It sounds as if we have a lot to discuss. Why don't we all sit down, and I'll have refreshments and some food brought in."

"How long before Earth is ready to take on the Druins?" asked Governor Swen, looking at Admiral Cleemorl.

"I'll let Captain Masters answer many of these questions, as he's much more familiar with what's going on in Earth's Solar System than I am."

Derrick took a deep breath. He had thought long and hard on what he would tell the Imperials. "Not soon. We're still building up our fleet and bringing Earth up to a technological level where they can challenge the Druins."

"How long?" asked Swen again.

"Probably 80 to 120 years before we dare make a move."

Governor Swen let out a deep sigh. "I was afraid of that."

"Keep in mind that no one other than the Empire has ever really challenged the Druins and the Confederation," Dylan reminded everyone. "Don't forget that the Empire lost."

"Can Earth make a difference?" asked General Creel. "It seems like a hopeless task to take on the Confederation. Look at what they've done to all the worlds in the Empire that have tried or refused to follow their edicts in the years since the fall."

"From what I've seen so far, in another eighty years, Earth can make a difference."

General Creel crossed his arms and gazed thoughtfully at Admiral Cleemorl. "Why exactly have you returned?"

"In order for Earth to have a reasonable chance of success, we must have the Empire ready. I know numerous secret bases are spread out across Human-controlled space. I need to know how many there are and if you can contact them."

"There are a number," admitted General Creel. "In order to prevent the Druins from learning where they are, no one knows the exact location of all of them. In the beginning, there was a Council that was coordinating the activity in the bases but it was disbanded to help keep the location of the bases secret. I know of about twenty myself. I have heard rumors of possibly one hundred more. All are dedicated to someday restoring the Empire. What do you need?"

For the next two hours Admiral Cleemorl and Captain Masters outlined the plan to eventually free the Empire.

General Creel and Governor Swen listened, occasionally asking detailed questions.

"What you want us to do will be difficult," said General Creel. "The bases have waited a long time to come out in the open against the Druins. Many of the officers in charge feel that a sudden revolt across hundreds of Human worlds may be too much for the Druins to handle. They believe the Druins might agree to allow the Empire to reassert itself, as long as it does not possess a military or move beyond its boundaries."

Dylan frowned. He didn't like hearing that. "What do you think? We tried that here, and look what happened."

General Creel blinked his eyes and then responded. "I think the Druins will come in and bombard every planet that revolts, killing billions."

"Then talk the hidden bases into waiting. Just eighty more years and the Empire will have a fleet of modern warships to fight the Druins with. When Earth strikes, the bases can come out in the open and help to free their worlds."

"I wish it were that easy," said Governor Swen. "People are starting to forget the Empire. Worlds are becoming more dependent upon themselves with every passing year. The Druins have demanded that all mention of the Empire be removed from our history books. Nothing about the Empire can be taught in our schools."

"Then it will have to be passed down by word of mouth," said Dylan. "We must not allow the memory of the Empire to die. Perhaps for the next eighty years, that should be one of the primary jobs of the hidden bases, to ensure the memory of the Empire does not fade away."

"What else do you ask of us?"

Dylan looked at General Creel. "Would it be feasible for the secret bases to set up a new advisory Council that could meet and guide the activity of all the bases? If it can be done, I believe Earth would be interested in having someone on that Council or, at the very least, to send someone to address it on a regular basis, so they will know what the future plans are."

General Creel was silent as he thought over the suggestion. "It might be possible, if they know there's hope for an outside ally to help free the Empire. We can still move freely among the worlds of the Empire with our freighters and passenger liners, though there are fewer passenger liners with every passing year. People are getting more hesitant to leave their homes."

Derrick realized he needed to add something to help sweeten the pot. "I should mention that we have developed fusion weapons for our warships."

General Creel's eyes widened. "That's a game changer in itself. May I tell this Council, if I can get it formed?"

Derrick looked at Admiral Cleemorl, who shrugged his shoulders, indicating it was up to Derrick. "Yes, but the Council only. We may also be able to provide additional support if needed. Equipment, weapons, and other military items. We're building a freighter or two that we would like to register to one of the worlds of the Empire, so we can move freely around."

"You probably shouldn't register it as coming from Lydol Four," said Governor Swen. "I would suggest Cleetus Three or Bratol Three. I know both of their governors very well. There are also several secret bases on their planets. You may want to register a freighter with each world. I could also arrange for you to pick up some trade items from either world, so, if your vessels are ever inspected, there wouldn't be any problems."

"I believe that can be arranged," replied Dylan approvingly.

-

The four spoke for several more hours, ironing out plans and setting up future meetings. It was decided a freighter would journey to Cleetus Three in one year's time. A larger delegation from Earth would arrive, and more detailed plans could be made for future interactions. All four agreed that keeping Earth a secret was paramount. Only the Council and the governors of Cleetus Three and Bratol Three would know the truth.

They were just about to finish up when the comm unit on the table flashed. General Creel answered it and, after speaking briefly, looked at Admiral Cleemorl. "Six Druin battleships have been detected entering the system. They will be in orbit in about an hour. I don't believe we have time to get you back to your ship."

"That's okay," replied Derrick. "My ship is a stealthed light cruiser, and I left orders with my second in command to leave as soon as any Druin vessels were detected. She will return as soon as the Druins leave."

General Creel nodded. "I wondered why we couldn't detect it. Let's adjourn to the Command Center and see what the Druins want this time. Most likely it's just a routine patrol, and they will be gone shortly."

"Does this happen often?" asked Derrick.

"Every month or two," replied Governor Swen. "We think they're still searching for Admiral Cleemorl and his escaped ships. They come in, stick around for a few hours or days, and then leave. They never say anything, and we don't attempt to communicate, as we know it would be useless."

"We may be the reason they're here," said Dylan. "Several days ago we were forced to destroy one of their battlecruisers that had detected us."

As they entered the Command Center, Derrick was surprised at how large it was. He realized this base must be much larger than he had imagined. Massive viewscreens covered the walls, and dozens of officers sat in front of consoles. "Impressive," said Derrick.

On one of the large tactical displays, six red threat icons were visible. Civilian traffic in the system was rapidly moving out of the path of the incoming Druin warships.

"What about our shuttle?" asked Dylan, showing some concern.

"It will be quite okay. There are shuttles sitting all over the planet, doing reclamation work. It will not look suspicious. We have already informed your pilots as to what's going on."

They watched the screen as the Druin battleships approached the planet and then went into orbit. For several hours they circled the planet and then moved away.

The six ships broke formation and spread out across the system.

"What are they doing?" asked Derrick. He knew the *Destiny* was probably out on the extreme edge of the system.

"Searching," replied General Creel. "They do this every time they enter the system."

Governor Swen frowned at the screen. "It disrupts recovery operations. Everyone stops work and waits to see what the Druins will do."

Eventually the Druin ships reformed into their fleet formation and entered hyperspace, leaving the system.

"Will they return anytime soon?" asked Derrick. He wanted to make sure they could make it back to the *Destiny* without the Druins catching them in the planet's atmosphere.

"Several weeks to a month or more," replied General Creel. "Why don't I summon Major Brandon, and he can get you back to your shuttle."

Dylan nodded. "Sounds fine to me. If everything works out, we'll be back about this time next year."

"We'll look forward to it. You've brought something I never expected to feel again, and that's hope. With your aid, just maybe someday we can free the Empire and bring justice to the Confederation for what they've done to so many races."

They had learned much about the Empire from General Creel and Governor Swen. They had recommended a few more systems in the Empire for the *Destiny* to travel to. They had also suggested caution.

"A full-size Druin fleet is constantly on patrol in the Empire. Most worlds have regular inspections from this Druin fleet," warned General Creel.

"We'll watch for it," promised Admiral Cleemorl. He wondered if it was the same one they had encountered in the Highland Station System.

A short time later they were back in the shuttle, nervously waiting for the *Destiny* to contact them.

"I think we can call this mission a success," commented Dylan.

Derrick nodded. "I agree completely. Once we've checked out a few more worlds in different sections of the Empire, it will be time to go home."

"Sir, I have the *Destiny* on the comm," reported Corporal Bower. "They're back in orbit."

"Take off then," ordered Derrick. "The sooner we get back to the *Destiny* and out of this system, the better I'll feel." He wanted to be gone in case the Druins paid the system an unexpected return visit.

An hour later the *Destiny* made the transition into hyperspace, going deeper into the Empire to check out Golan Four and a few more of the core worlds in the Mall Star Cluster.

Derrick wondered how he would feel upon returning to Golan Four. He felt anxious to know how the homeworld had fared. They just needed to complete the rest of the mission without encountering any more Druins. Then they could set a course back to Earth.

Chapter Twenty-Four

The *Destiny* dropped from hyperspace on the outskirts of the Mall Star Cluster. Inside the cluster were over a dozen major worlds of the Empire. It was also a cluster very rich in minerals.

Derrick gazed at the main viewscreen, showing hundreds of stars. He let out a deep sigh. It was hard to imagine over one thousand years had passed since he had fled from Golan Four with the Princess. "Anything on the long-range sensors?"

"No," replied Nower. "Everything's clear."

"Very well, Lieutenant Viktor, take us into hyperspace and place us on the edge of the Golan Four System."

The *Destiny* made the transition into hyperspace. It was a two-hour trip to Golan Four.

"I've never been to Golan Four," said Admiral Cleemorl. "I always wanted to go, but the time was never right."

"I was raised on Golan Four," replied Derrick. "It was the throne world of the Empire. It was a garden world, with strict population controls to avoid overpopulation. Massive parks and preserves kept much of the planet pristine. The Imperial Palace was the most striking structure in the capital city. Its architecture would take your breath away, with massive arches and towers that reached nearly to the clouds. It was an absolutely amazing place to live."

Time passed, and finally the ship dropped from hyperspace.

"We're in the Golan Four System," reported Viktor.

"Andrew, how much communications traffic do you detect?"

Andrew listened on his comm for several moments and then turned toward the captain. "Quite a lot. Some on the regular frequencies and even more on the hyperlight frequencies. It seems as if all the planets in the cluster are talking to one another."

"Lieutenant Nower, how many ships do you detect in the system?"

"Nearly two hundred," Nower replied. "However, I'm also detecting twenty-three Druin battleships. All are in orbit around Golan Four."

Derrick frowned. "I wonder what they're doing?" He had hoped there would be a minimal Druin presence.

"The only way to find out is to go closer," said Dylan, folding his arms across his chest.

"Lieutenant Viktor, put us forty thousand kilometers from Golan Four. Lieutenant Commander Banora, take the ship to Condition One."

The *Destiny* jumped back into hyperspace and seconds later dropped back out. On the viewscreen, a blue-white planet was visible. Derrick felt a momentary pang of homesickness upon seeing his homeworld on the viewscreen.

"Sir, all of the ship traffic appears to be ignoring the Druins," reported Nower.

Dylan glanced at the tactical display. "I would say this might be a permanent force of ships stationed here."

Derrick nodded. "It's possible. If there was to be a major revolt, it would most likely start on one of the core worlds. By keeping a force of battleships in orbit around Golan Four, it keeps all the core worlds in line."

Derrick turned toward Navigation. "Lieutenant Viktor, move us closer to one of those freighters and then scan the planet. If the Druins detect the scans, perhaps they'll assume they're coming from the freighter and not us."

"You could be putting that freighter in danger," warned Dylan.

"Maybe, but we need to know the condition of the planet, and this is the only way I know to get it."

Derrick watched the tactical display as the *Destiny* moved closer to the freighter, which was about twice the size of the light cruiser. When he was satisfied they were close enough, he ordered Nower to begin her scans.

"See if you can get a close-up of the palace," ordered Derrick. He wanted to see if it was even there. As far as he knew, the Druins had not bombed Golan Four.

The view on the main screen changed as Golan Four grew larger, and then the capital city could be seen. In the heart of the city the palace still stood, but it was obvious it had been abandoned. The once magnificent gardens were overgrown; several of the arches and towers had collapsed, and the roads leading to the palace were full of cracks with vegetation growing in them.

"I would guess the palace is off-limits," said Dylan.

"It was a symbol of the power of the Empire," replied Derrick, feeling shaken at what he saw on the viewscreen. "Now it's a symbol of the weakness of the Empire. A constant reminder of what happens to anyone who goes against the Confederation."

"What does the rest of the planet look like?" asked Dylan.

Derrick had the screen adjusted to move across the planet. Much of it looked as it always had, though it appeared the Human population was greater than what it once was. Many of the pristine parks and preserves now had small cities in them. Much of the land had been broken up for crops and livestock.

"Sir, two of the Druin battleships are moving in our direction," reported Nower, sounding nervous. "They may have detected us."

Derrick nodded. "Stop the scans. Lieutenant Viktor, move us away from the freighter."

The *Destiny* accelerated rapidly away from the freighter. The two Druin battleships reached the freighter, and, from one, a shuttle appeared, which immediately docked with the cargo vessel.

"Druin soldiers," muttered Dylan with disgust. "They'll go on board, search the ship, and demand to know why scans of the planet were made."

Derrick looked at Dylan. "Will they do anything to the crew?"

"They're Druins," replied Dylan. "Most likely they will kill a few to set an example."

Feeling ill that he might have caused some innocent deaths, Derrick turned toward Lieutenant Viktor. "Set a course for Ambary Two. I want to see what condition it's in." Ambary Two was another Human core world. Derrick wanted to know if Druin ships were there as well.

Andrew had been quiet through all this. He had been very disappointed in the current condition of the palace. In the computer library on Pallas were videos of what the palace had once looked like. It had been the grandest structure in the Human Empire. To see it now, lying in ruins, had been difficult. He could only imagine how Captain Masters must feel.

Andrew had also recorded numerous messages and data feeds from Golan Four. He hoped in the future, when they had time to analyze them, they would be found useful. Even now, as they were traveling in hyperspace, he was still detecting hyperlight messages. His recorders were set on automatic, so many of the messages were saved.

"Captain, we may have a problem," said Lieutenant Nower worriedly. "The short-range sensors detect two Druin battleships following us."

Andrew felt a chill go through him. He didn't believe any of them expected the Druins could track them again.

Derrick felt the hair on the back of his neck stand up at this revelation. "Are you sure they're following us?" They were nearly to the Ambary System.

"Pretty sure, or they're going to the same destination as we are."

Derrick blinked his eyes as he weighed his options. He really wanted to know the condition of Ambary Two. It was the most heavily populated core world. "Lieutenant Viktor, drop us from hyperspace ten thousand kilometers over Ambary Two."

"That's close," warned Lieutenant Commander Banora.

"It's close, but there should be a lot of traffic around the planet. With a little luck we can blend in, and, with our stealth fields, the Druins just might lose us. Do we have any idea how they managed to track us this time?"

Lieutenant Commander Banora shook her head. "No, not unless they're tracking the short-range sensors."

Derrick frowned. They had to have some sensors operating while they were in hyperspace to avoid running into objects. Passing through an object of mass while in hyperspace would cause a ship to be immediately ejected from hyperspace. This would normally cause severe damage to the hyperspace drive system. For this reason sensors were used, and the ship's navigation system automatically made minor adjustments in flight to avoid any object that might constitute a danger.

The ship dropped from hyperspace above Ambary Two. On the viewscreen, a planet very similar to Golan Four appeared. Ambary Two possessed two major oceans that covered 58 percent of the planet. The land masses were all heavily colonized, and the planet depended on other worlds to bring in much of the food the planet's large population required.

"Scan the planet," ordered Derrick. It would still be a few seconds before the Druin battleships arrived, and he wanted to gather as much information as possible on the planet while time allowed.

"Scanning," answered Nower.

"Picking up considerable communications, both on the regular frequencies and on the hyperlight channels," added Andrew.

"Damn!" uttered Nower uncharacteristically. "Three Druin battleships in low orbit."

On the tactical display, numerous green icons appeared, representing Human cargo ships and a few passenger liners. In the middle of them were three large red threat icons. Almost immediately two of the red threat icons left orbit and moved toward the *Destiny*.

"That tears it!" exclaimed Lieutenant Commander Banora, her gaze focused on the tactical display. "They can definitely detect us."

Derrick knew Banora was right. Some defect in their stealth fields allowed the Druins to detect the ship. He wasn't sure now if it was the sensors or something else. "Lieutenant Viktor, get us out of here. Set a course for the Hadrian Star Cluster."

"They'll be in weapons range in twenty seconds," reported Nower worriedly.

At the Helm and Navigation, Lieutenant Viktor's hands flew over the console, touching icons on his screens and entering data. "Entering hyperspace."

A slight wrenching sensation indicated the ship had made the transition. On the tactical display, Ambary Two rapidly fell away.

"Contact!" called out Lieutenant Nower. "Druin battleship on the long-range sensors."

"Is it gaining on us?"

Nower shook her head. "It's seems to be matching our speed."

Derrick leaned back in his chair. They were safe for now. Weapons could not be used in hyperspace. He looked over at Dylan. "Any suggestions?"

"We have to lose them somehow before we can set a course back to Earth."

Derrick looked over at Lieutenant Marko Breen. "How many deployable mines do we have on board?"

"Twelve," replied Breen. "Ten fusion and two antimatter."

Dylan looked at Derrick. "What are you thinking?"

"The mines have a small space drive on them. If we can get them close enough to the battleship so they'll detonate against its shields, the interference from the blasts might allow us to escape without being tracked."

"It's a long shot."

"We'd have to time our entrance into hyperspace with the explosions from the mines," added Banora.

Derrick turned toward Lieutenant Viktor. "Can you do it?"

"Yes. What course do I set?"

"Make it random but avoid all inhabited systems. We need to stay away from any more Druins ships."

"Lieutenant Breen, prepare six fusion mines for proximity detonations. We'll drop out of hyperspace, place the mines, and then wait for the Druin battleship. Once the mines detonate, we'll jump back into hyperspace."

Breen nodded. "Captain, we could also launch a full spread of fusion missiles to detonate at the same time the mines do. It would increase the amount of interference and would help to hide our escape."

That sounded like a good idea. "Do it."

Derrick waited as more time passed. There was no doubt in his mind the Druin battleship had already used its hyperlight transmitter to inform Druin ships ahead of them where they were going. The only thing was, Derrick no longer had any intention of going to the Hadrian Star Cluster.

"Drop us out of hyperspace."

The *Destiny* dropped from hyperspace and immediately deployed six fusion mines. The ship then moved off a short distance to be out of the blast radius but close enough to still fire its missiles.

Everyone's gaze was glued to the viewscreens as they waited for the Druin battleship to make its appearance. In space, six deadly mines drifted waiting for their target. Suddenly a small flash of light came, and the Druin battleship was there. The battleship was nearly two thousand meters long and covered with deadly weapons. Turrets and missile hatches covered the vessel.

Communications and sensor antennas dotted the hull. Even as they watched, the hatches covering the ship's missile tubes slid open.

"Mines are targeting the Druin ship," reported Lieutenant Nower. "The mines are covered in a material that should make them invisible to the Druin ship's sensors."

"Standing by to fire missiles," added Lieutenant Breen, his hands hovering over his console.

"Range is 712 kilometers," Nower informed the captain.

On the viewscreen, the Druin battleship slowly turned to face the *Destiny*, but it still had not fired.

"They seem a little unsure," commented Dylan.

"Mines are nearly to the battleship," reported Nower. Her sensors were set to a special frequency that could detect the mines.

Derrick watched the battleship. It seemed as if it couldn't get a good weapons lock. Suddenly four of its missile tubes launched missiles, heading in the general direction of the *Destiny*.

Warning alarms sounded on the sensor console.

"Inbound missiles!" reported Nower, trying to keep her voice calm.

"Brace for impact!" called out Lieutenant Commander Banora, as she looked for something to hold on to.

All at once brilliant explosions covered the energy shield of the Druin battleship.

"Mines are detonating," reported Banora.

"Launching missiles," added Breen, as he fired a full salvo.

The *Destiny* shook violently as one of the Druin missiles slammed into its energy shield.

"Antimatter," called out Nower.

"Shields are holding at 71 percent," added Breen.

On the viewscreen, the *Destiny*'s missiles began arriving at the Druin battleship, illuminating it in brilliant explosions of energy.

"Activating hyperdrive," reported Lieutenant Viktor.

Derrick felt a slight twinge in his gut as the ship made the transition. "Turn off the sensors," he ordered.

"All of them?" asked Lieutenant Nower, her eyes wide with fear. Ships were not supposed to travel in hyperspace blind.

"For only a few minutes," replied Derrick.

"Sensors are off," confirmed Nower, looking around nervously.

Derrick leaned back in his command chair. "Lieutenant Viktor, wait five minutes and then change course. You will do that every five minutes until I tell you otherwise."

Everyone in the Command Center waited anxiously as the *Destiny* made a number of course changes. After an hour Captain Masters informed Lieutenant Nower that she could turn the short-range sensors back on.

"Anything?" asked Derrick. If the Druins were still following them, he wasn't sure what they would do.

Nower spent some time examining her sensor readings and then replied, "Sensors are clear. No sign of the Druin battleship."

"What now?" asked Lieutenant Commander Banora.

"Set a course for the Vortex Worlds, we'll drop in on several of those star systems and then set a course for Earth." The Vortex Worlds were in another star cluster with large populations of Humans.

Dylan stepped closer to Derrick. "Lydol Four used to trade a lot with several of the Vortex Worlds. I went to Jalot Four when I was much younger. It's very similar to Lydol Four, only it has a larger population."

"Let's just hope there are no Druin warships in the systems we'll visit. Now we know, if we turn off our sensors, we can escape." At least Derrick hoped that was right. He knew there was a good chance he would be putting that belief to the test once more before they left the Empire.

Andrew was in his quarters, getting some rest. It was another eight hours to the Vortex Worlds. So far this trip had been extremely nerve-racking. He wondered what it would be like to be in an actual fleet battle, involving hundreds of ships. If he went into cryo as he planned, there was a good chance he would find out.

A knock came on his door, and, getting up, he walked over and opened it, finding Ensign Allert standing there.

"Mind if I come in for a minute?"

"Not at all," replied Andrew. He liked Ensign Allert. She was friendly and had always been extremely helpful.

Brenda sat down on the only couch in Andrew's quarters, and he sat down next to her.

"It's been a rough couple of days," she commented, leaning back and relaxing.

Andrew nodded. "I have to admit, I wasn't expecting this." Andrew wondered what Brenda wanted. She was cute and very alluring in her uniform, but she had never come on to him. He hoped that wasn't why she had stopped by. He was still very involved with Kala.

Brenda laughed. "I don't think any of us were. When we get back, we'll have to find out how the Druins are tracing our sensors. It's probably some silly little thing we've been overlooking."

"Perhaps," replied Andrew.

"The reason I stopped by was to see if what's happened has changed your mind about going into cryo. Space combat is very different in reality, than sitting at home, thinking about it."

"Yes, it is. However, I still plan on going into cryo. I want to see how all this ends."

Brenda seemed satisfied with his answer. "What about Kala? I know the two of you have been spending a lot of time together. Will she be going into cryo as well?"

"I doubt it. While we've gotten closer, I don't believe she's changed her mind."

Brenda smiled knowingly. "You might be surprised. I spoke to her the other day, and she had quite a few questions about cryo. She might be considering it."

Andrew felt a flash of hope go through him. "I hope she does, but I've accepted that I may be doing this alone."

"Just remember. As long as you're a part of this crew, you will never be alone."

The two talked for another hour before Brenda left to return to her own quarters. As Andrew prepared for bed, he wondered what it would be like if Kala did go into cryo. It would definitely give him something to look forward to in the future.

Seven hours later the *Destiny* dropped from hyperspace on the edge of the Jalot Four system. The ship stayed there for a good hour, taking detailed scans of everything.

"No Druins," reported Nower with relief in her voice.

"Thirty-seven contacts in the system," reported Lieutenant Commander Banora. "Most appear to be cargo ships."

Admiral Cleemorl watched the tactical display and the green icons around Jalot Four. "It seems around the core worlds, as well as here, trade is still going on fairly well."

"The level of civilization seems to be comparable to when we left," added Banora.

"One thousand years of static!" replied Derrick angrily. "Just think of all we could have discovered in that time if the Confederation had left us alone."

"But they didn't," said Dylan. "With Earth, we have a chance to change all of that."

"Lieutenant Viktor, put us in orbit at ten thousand kilometers. I want detailed scans of the surface, as well as all communication channels monitored." Much of the information they were gathering would be gone through once they returned to Pallas.

It didn't take long for the *Destiny* to go into orbit around Jalot Four. On the main viewscreen the planet's capital city appeared.

Derrick gazed at the viewscreen, seeing a modern Imperial city. The city looked much the same as it had during the heights of the Empire.

"Some planets are like this," commented Dylan. "They seem relatively untouched, while others show the scars of Druin punishment."

Looking at the city, it was tempting to take a shuttle down and just walk the city streets and talk to the people. However, Derrick knew the city was probably not as peaceful as it looked. Already communications had picked up some disturbing broadcasts, calling for young people to volunteer to work for the Confederation. Other broadcasts talked about how peaceful the Confederation was and how fortunate it was for people to go there.

"Propaganda," muttered Cleemorl. "That's how the planet has avoided Druin retaliation. They send large numbers of their young people to the Confederation to work as slaves."

Derrick frowned. "How common is that?"

"More common than I would like to admit. Hundreds of Human worlds are expected to send large numbers of young people to work in the Confederation."

"Do they ever come back?" asked Banora, shocked at what the people of the Empire were being asked to do.

Cleemorl shook his head. "I've never heard of any. However, several million young people are sent to the Empire every year."

Gazing at the peaceful city on the viewscreen, Derrick was disappointed to hear how far the Empire had fallen to allow their young people to be taken. This activity would not have been tolerated in the old days of the Empire.

For two hours the *Destiny* orbited the planet, taking scans and recording data. When Captain Masters was satisfied they had everything they needed, he had the *Destiny* leave orbit and head for its next target world. One more planet to investigate, and then it would be time to return to Earth.

The Forgotten Empire: Banishment

Admiral Kreen stood in the Command Center of his Druin battleship. Several reports had come in of a strange ship with stealth capabilities being spotted in several star systems. He also had a missing battlecruiser. Even worse, a battleship had been damaged while in pursuit of this strange vessel.

He paced back and forth, wondering what this all meant. He didn't believe the now-weak Humans could build such a vessel. It was also highly unlikely that it was a new species exploring this region of space.

His cold logical mind weighed all the possibilities. He saw only one that made sense. Sometime in the past, the Humans had built a secret base outside of their Empire. It was this base which had sent this mysterious ship to see what changes had occurred in the Empire over the years since it had been conquered. It also indicated that the base was a considerable distance from Human space.

Walking to the navigation console, Kreen called up some star maps. He entering the locations where the strange ship had been detected. When he was finished, he had a general idea of the direction the ship had come from. It had first been spotted in the Tantalus Seven System. There was also mention of a possible contact in the Highland Station System, though that one could not be confirmed. Beyond that system was the Bacchus Region. A large desolate section of space known for its dead worlds. It was also relatively unexplored.

Going back to his command chair, Admiral Kreen sat down. His large form and heavy weight caused the chair to creak. He needed more information before he brought this up to the Confederation. Reaching a decision, he decided to station part of his fleet in some of the systems near Highland Station. If he could detect the strange ship again, perhaps he could get a better idea of the exact direction it had come from. Once that occurred, he would trace it back to its base and destroy it.

On the *Destiny*, they had just finished studying another planet of the Vortex Worlds. It had been very similar to the previous one.

"I think we have everything we need," announced Derrick. "Lieutenant Viktor, set a course for Earth. Vary our course sufficiently so we can't be traced. Stay away from all star systems until we're back in the Bacchus Region."

Once they returned to Pallas, Derrick would have all the data they had gathered downloaded to the asteroid's computers. After debriefing and checking on the construction work being done on Earth's shipyard, Derrick planned to go back into cryo. He was growing anxious for the war against the Druins, and he wanted to see the Princess. He also someday wanted to return home and walk through the halls of the palace. It might just be a dream, but it was a dream he planned on making come true.

Epilogue

The *Destiny* was safely back at Pallas and being put into stasis. Admiral Bract felt fairly certain the ship would not be needed in the immediate future. All the data gathered during the mission had been downloaded to the asteroid's computers and was being evaluated. It would take several weeks to analyze everything, including the recorded messages between planets. There were tens of thousands of those.

Captain Masters stood in the observation lounge of one of the construction docks. Inside the dock, a special freighter was being built. It was quite large with a considerable number of special surprises.

"We're putting some hidden compartments into the ship," Admiral Bract said. "The ship will also have some defensive turrets, but they will be hidden behind hatches. Its biggest advantage will be speed. We're putting in a military grade drive system. It will also be stealth capable, if necessary. All the stealth equipment for generating the stealth fields will be hidden."

"How large will the crew be?" Derrick knew most freighters had small crews to help keep costs down.

"One hundred and ten," replied Bract. "However, we are adding a passenger compartment capable of handling twenty more. Those will all be Marines disguised as civilians."

Derrick stood, gazing at the ship. When it was finished, it would be a Class A cargo ship of the most modern type currently in use in the Empire. "Who will command the ship?"

"Admiral Cleemorl has volunteered. He's familiar enough with the Empire and how trade is done that he feels he can be a freighter captain without a problem. It will also make things easier when we contact some of the secret bases spread throughout the Empire."

Turning toward Admiral Bract, Derrick asked his next question. "Are we building more than one cargo ship?"

"We're considering it," replied Bract. "It'll depend on what happens with those secret bases. Once they have their Council established, we can speak to them about what they need us to do."

"I went to Earth the other day to inspect the space station and the shipyard. Colonel Gleeson has agreed to base some attack interceptors at the station. However, he wants to build a separate facility near the station to hold them."

Admiral Bract nodded. "I'm glad he finally saw the wisdom of having some interceptors to protect the station. How many are we talking about?"

"Sixty," replied Derrick. "Since we're building a new structure, I suggested we make it large enough to hold three full squadrons. The structure will also be protected by energy turrets, defensive missiles, as well as an energy screen."

In the bay, robots were attaching some of the hatches to the cargo ship. The main cargo holds had huge hatches, and special robots were handling those.

Derrick looked at Admiral Bract. "Are you going into cryo?"

Bract laughed. "No, cryo's not for me. A lot needs to be done in the next few years to get the Solar System ready for war with the Confederation. We have planets and moons to colonize, bases to build, and warships to construct. It'll be a busy and exciting time. Hopefully, when you awaken, we'll be ready."

"My crew will be going into cryo the day after tomorrow. All have volunteered to go back into cryo, except for Lieutenant Cleo Ashen. She's decided to stay and work here on Pallas and maybe on the shipyard around Earth. Andrew will take her place."

"Andrew will make you a good crewmember. He's done a lot to get us to where we're at today."

"Yes, he has, and he will make a fine addition to my crew."

Admiral Bract had one more question to ask. "Will you see the Princess before you go into cryo?" Derrick was one of the few people who had the security clearance necessary to enter the cryo section where the Princess slept.

"Maybe," replied Derrick. "I'm looking forward to talking to her again when she's awake."

Admiral Bract nodded and smiled to himself. It seemed to him that Captain Masters had more than just a casual interest in the Princess.

Andrew was in his quarters, speaking to Kala. "Are you sure you want to do this?"

Kala nodded. She had just told him that she would go into cryo. "Yes, a number of the research people I'm working with will shortly be going into cryo as well. Everyone wants to be part of the war against the Druins and the Confederation."

Taking Kala's hand, Andrew looked deeply into her eyes. "The future will be dangerous. There's no guarantee Earth will win the war."

"I know," replied Kala softly. "I just want to be there with you."

Andrew was happy to hear of Kala's decision. Maybe he could get her on board the *Destiny* as a science officer. "Let's go out and celebrate. A steak sounds very good at the moment."

Kala nodded and smiled. "When we get back, I have another way for us to celebrate."

For a moment Andrew was tempted to forget the steak. Standing, he smiled. "Let's go. It shouldn't take us too long to eat."

Kala laughed. She was certain she had made the right decision.

Admiral Cleemorl was in Cheryl's yacht. He had just finished moving his clothes in and a few other personal items.

"I never thought this would happen," said Cheryl, a smile on her face. "I wish we had done this years ago. I really messed up when I left you."

"We were very young and foolish at the time," replied Dylan.

Cheryl sat down on a luxurious couch and indicated for Dylan to sit down next to her. "I understand you'll command the new freighter they're building."

Dylan nodded. "Someone familiar with the Empire and how trade is done now needs to be. It will decrease the likelihood of someone saying the wrong thing or making a serious mistake."

"Do you think I could come along? I still have a lot of connections in the Empire. While many aren't quite legal, they can get us access to places most cargo ships would have a hard time going to, due to the red tape."

"I'll think about it," replied Dylan. "I must admit the idea of having you on board the ship is tempting. But I have to ask you, can you give up all this?" Dylan gestured at the lavish furnishings in the yacht.

Cheryl laughed. "I didn't always live like this, and, yes, I can give it up."

Standing back up, Cheryl took Dylan's hand, pulling him next to her. She turned and kissed him gently on the lips. "I've been waiting for this for a very long time."

Dylan kissed her back. "So have I."

Cheryl grinned happily. The life she had always wanted was about to be hers, and she wouldn't let anything take it away.

—

In the Confederation, Admiral Kreen read the latest reports on the search for the unknown ship. All the results were negative. Even the battleships and battlecruisers he had assigned to scan the systems around Highland Station had come back negative. The ship seemed to have vanished.

After much consideration he sent a report to the Confederation Council, informing them of the mysterious vessel. He also mentioned that, at the moment, he did not consider it to be a major threat. He requested more battlecruisers be assigned to his fleet so he could continue to search for the secret base this vessel must have originated from. He felt certain it was in the

Bacchus Region and very close to Highland Station. Admiral Kreen was determined to find this base and to destroy it. The Humans were bothersome enough without someone else stirring up even more trouble.

On board the space station between Earth and its Moon, Major Loren Henderson and Brett Newcomb were meeting.

"We're making rapid progress," commented Brett, sounding pleased. "Most of Earth's governments have fallen into line, and the space program now has a nearly unlimited budget."

Major Henderson nodded. "We're about to explode across the Solar System. In ten years we'll have colonies and bases on nearly every moon, planet, and some of the asteroids."

"The Solar System's population will expand rapidly with all the additional living space. The terraformers are already operating on Mars. Soon we'll be able to walk around without the need for suits or breathers."

Henderson looked at Brett. "I understand Andrew is going into cryo."

"Yes, he wants to be involved in the war. After all that he's been through and seen, I don't blame him."

"A lot will change over the next few years. There'll be considerable chaos on Earth with all the new technology that's being introduced."

Brett nodded. "We'll get them through it. Once we're finished, the Earth's economy will be booming."

Major Henderson leaned back and let out a deep sigh. "It's a shame we're doing all this to eventually fight a war."

"It has to be done."

Henderson looked out the large viewport in the office they were in. The Moon was visible, as well as a myriad of stars. If the Confederation didn't find them, there was a good chance the Solar System and Earth would become the Confederation's worst nightmare.

Derrick stood in the Royal Stasis Chamber, staring at the two sleeping women. Layla and Krista looked so peaceful and exactly as he had last seen them.

"When they wake up, it will be as if no time has passed," commented Dr. Sharma. "These two cryochambers are checked hourly, and, if anything malfunctions, alarms will sound."

"I wonder if they realize what type of world they'll wake up in? All of their lives they have been surrounded by servants and other members of the Royal Family. Now there are only the two of them."

Dr. Sharma folded his arms across his chest. "The people of the Empire will rally around them when they realize the Royal Family has survived."

Derrick nodded. "Someday we'll return to Golan Four and rebuild the palace. I plan on being a part of that."

With a long sigh, Derrick turned and left the room. He made his way down several corridors to where another series of cryochambers awaited. These held his crew. Most of them had already returned to cryo.

He saw Andrew and Kala being prepared for their long sleep. "There's nothing to be concerned about. It's just like falling asleep."

"So we've been told," replied Kala nervously. Andrew helped her get into her cryochamber and watched as the lid slid shut. A few moments later her eyes closed, and she was in cryo.

"Everything's normal," the doctor announced, as he checked a few readings on the chamber.

Andrew nodded and climbed into his own chamber. A few moments later he too was in cryo.

"That's your entire crew, except for you," the doctor said.

Derrick nodded. "I guess it's my turn."

A few minutes later Derrick laid down in his cryochamber and felt terribly sleepy. As his eyes closed, he wondered what awaited him in the future. His last thoughts, before the cryo took over, was of him and the Princess walking down the main hallway inside the palace. A palace that had been completely rebuilt and returned to its former glory.

The End

If you enjoyed the Forgotten Empire: Banishment please post a review with some stars. Good reviews encourage an author to write and also help sell books. Reviews can be just a few short sentences, describing what you liked about the book. If you have suggestions, please contact me at my website, link below. Thank you for reading Banishment and being so supportive.

The action increases and the tension grows in The Forgotten Empire: Earth Ascendant coming in April of 2020.

Thank You

Raymond L. Weil

For updates on current writing projects and future publications, go to my author website. Sign up for future notifications when my new books come out on Amazon.

Website: http://raymondlweil.com/

Follow on Facebook at Raymond L. Weil

Many of you are aware of my health problems. I am suffering from Kidney failure and am hoping for a transplant in the coming few months. The proceeds from this book and my other books will go to covering any unexpected costs associated with the surgery and future anti-rejection medications. So please give my other books a look. Every sale will help. See my other books on the following page.

Other Books by Raymond L. Weil
Available on Amazon

Moon Wreck (The Slaver Wars Book 1)
The Slaver Wars: Alien Contact (The Slaver Wars Book 2)
Moon Wreck: Fleet Academy (The Slaver Wars Book 3)
The Slaver Wars: First Strike (The Slaver Wars Book 4)
The Slaver Wars: Retaliation (The Slaver Wars Book 5)
The Slaver Wars: Galactic Conflict (The Slaver Wars Book 6)
The Slaver Wars: Endgame (The Slaver Wars Book 7)
The Slaver Wars: Books 1-3

-

Dragon Dreams: Dragon Wars
Dragon Dreams: Gilmreth the Awakening
Dragon Dreams: Snowden the White Dragon
Dragon Dreams: Firestorm Mountain

-

Star One: Tycho City: Survival
Star One: Neutron Star
Star One: Dark Star
Star One

-

Galactic Empire Wars: Destruction (Book 1)
Galactic Empire Wars: Emergence (Book 2)
Galactic Empire Wars: Rebellion (Book 3)
Galactic Empire Wars: The Alliance (Book 4)
Galactic Empire Wars: Insurrection (Book 5)
Galactic Empire Wars: Final Conflict (Book 6)
Galactic Empire Wars: The Beginning (Books 1-3)

-

The Lost Fleet: Galactic Search (Book 1)
The Lost Fleet: Into the Darkness (Book 2)
The Lost Fleet: Oblivion's Light (Book 3)
The Lost Fleet: Genesis (Book 4)
The Lost Fleet: Search for the Originators (Book 5)

Raymond L. Weil

The Lost Fleet (Books 1-5)

The Star Cross (Book 1)
The Star Cross: The Dark Invaders (Book 2)
The Star Cross: Galaxy in Peril (Book 3)
The Star Cross: The Forever War (Book 4)
The Star Cross: The Vorn! (Book 5)

The Originator Wars: Universe in Danger (Book 1)
The Originator Wars: Search for the Lost (Book 2)
The Originator Wars: Conflict Unending (Book 3)
The Originator Wars: Explorations (Book 4)
The Originator Wars Explorations: The Multiverse (Book 5)
The Originator Wars Explorations: The Lost (Book 6)

Earth Fall: Invasion (Book 1)
Earth Fall: To the Stars (Book 2)
Earth Fall: Empires at War (Book 3)

The Forgotten Empire: Banishment (Book 1)

All dates are tentative.
The Forgotten Empire: Earth Ascendant (Book 2) April of 2020

ABOUT THE AUTHOR

I live in Clinton Oklahoma with my wife of 47 years and our cats. I attended college at SWOSU in Weatherford Oklahoma, majoring in Math with minors in Creative Writing and History.

My hobbies include watching soccer, reading, camping, and of course writing. I also enjoy playing with my six grandchildren. I have a very vivid imagination, which sometimes worries my friends. They never know what I'm going to say or what I'm going to do.

I am an avid reader and have a science fiction / fantasy collection of over two thousand paperbacks. I have always enjoyed reading science fiction and fantasy because of the awesome worlds authors create. I can hardly believe I'm now creating those worlds as well.

Printed in Great Britain
by Amazon